Further praise for

Sweetland

Winner of the CBC Bookie Award for Fiction
Finalist for the BMO Winterset Award
Short-listed for the Governor General's Literary Award
Indie Next Pick
Amazon Best Book of the Month

"Part *Independent People* (for the fierce portrait of its main character's unwavering determination) and part *Absalom, Absalom!* (for the unusual set of characters surrounding him), Crummey's latest novel tells the absorbing story of Moses Sweetland's singular battle to hold on to his home on a tiny island off the coast of Newfoundland. . . . [A]s Crummey's elegant prose and storytelling prowess make abundantly clear, no man is an island." —*New York Times Book Review*

"The novel is atmospheric and episodic. . . . *Sweetland*'s pleasures lie in its depiction of island life and in the absorbing details of Moses's tactics of survival; and lastly, in the excavation of this lonely man's soul. As such, it stays with the reader not so much as a story but as a mood of richly conjured melancholy." —*Barnes & Noble Review*

"An evocative portrait of a disappearing way of life, *Sweetland* is also a powerful rumination on what's lost in letting go of the past—and the sometimes-unbearable cost of trying to hold onto it. Michael Crummey's deceptively spare language perfectly matches the tiny island community at the novel's center: beneath the quiet surface, there's huge emotional depth and heart." —Celeste Ng, author of *Everything I Never Told You*

"The elimination of an entire community, and what it represents, is deeply felt. Through its crusty protagonist, Crummey's shrewd, absorbing novel tells us how rich a life can be, even when experienced in the narrowest of physical confines."

—*Kirkus Reviews*, starred review

"Crummey neither glorifies nor denigrates the realities of small-town life, and presents each character with enormous poignancy and respect. The Newfoundlander-accented dialogue adds a tumbling musicality to the prose, authentic without a shred of condescension. This is a graceful, unexpectedly joyful novel that echoes emotionally far beyond the final pages."

—*Shelf Awareness*

"*Sweetland* is purposeful, and it certainly evokes the rawness and fragility of life in Newfoundland. . . . *Sweetland* is . . . a testament to human resilience."

—*BookPage*

"Wry, touching, and filled with insights into the modern human condition, Michael Crummey's spare and sturdy prose in *Sweetland* delivers a kaleidoscopic portrayal of a quirky island community forced to abandon their vanishing way of life. Ignoring government bribes and threats from his neighbors, the obstinate waterman Moses Sweetland defiantly chooses the isolation of his family home off the Newfoundland coast to become a present-day Robinson Crusoe: resourceful, irascible, wily, and wholly unforgettable."

—John Pipkin, author of *Woodsburner*

"What's most appealing about this subtle, entertaining, and quietly moving novel is the humanity of its characters and the genuine feel of Sweetland itself. Each character is real and truly imagined; it's the kind of book and the kind of place where many readers will just want to linger. Communities like Sweetland, with their specific ways of talking and being, are growing less common. Crummey's book is a testament to those places and the people who live there."

—Amazon.com

"*Sweetland* is perhaps a perfect novel for book group discussions. . . . It's also a powerful character study of an older, scarred but undefeated man, as well as a potent portrait of the land and people he adores. . . . Brutality, humor, and beauty are on display throughout *Sweetland*, all couched in energetic prose that is both authentic and thoughtful, much like its protagonist." —*BookBrowse*

"Impetuous and imperious, Moses Sweetland is an extraordinary, beautifully realized character. . . . *Sweetland*, Crummey's finest novel yet, reaches its mythic and mesmerizing heights only after the others depart, leaving Moses—a Newfoundland Robinson Crusoe who even encounters a Friday-like dog—alone on his eponymous island, bracing for a bitter winter both seasonal and personal." —*Macleans*

"Moses is a memorably strong-willed character. . . . [*Sweetland*] also conveys the way that a sense of place is the product of relationships— among the living, with the dead, and, in Moses's case, arising from intimate connections to land and sea." —*Publishers Weekly*, starred review

"Seductive, supple and haunting. . . . *Sweetland* is a wistful eulogy for a dying way of life." —*Toronto Star*

"This is a familiar story, but it is told precisely and heartwarmingly, realistically and without sentimentality. . . . [W]ith this simple and profound story, [Crummey] may become a newfound author for readers of Jon Hassler, Kent Haruf, and other masters of small-town fiction." —*Booklist*

"Michael Crummey's *Sweetland* is a beautiful prayer for a dying island and an elegy for the titular character, who is both haunted and haunting, besieged by ghosts and yet trying to stop himself from becoming one." —Alexi Zentner, author of *The Lobster Kings*

Sweetland

ALSO BY MICHAEL CRUMMEY

Arguments with Gravity

Hard Light

Salvage

Flesh and Blood: Stories

River Thieves

The Wreckage

Galore

Under the Keel

MICHAEL CRUMMEY

Sweetland

A NOVEL

LIVERIGHT PUBLISHING CORPORATION

A Division of W. W. Norton & Company

New York • London

For information about permission to reproduce selections from this book,
write to Permissions, Liveright Publishing Corporation, a division of
W. W. Norton & Company, Inc., 500 Fith Avenue, New York, NY 10110

For information about special discounts for bulk purchases, please contact
W. W. Norton Special Sales at specialsales@wwnorton.com or 800-233-4830

Manufacturing by RR Donnelley, Harrisonburg, VA
Production manager: Anna Oler

Library of Congress Cataloging-in-Publication Data

Crummey, Michael, 1965–
Sweetland : a novel / Michael Crummey.—First American edition.
pages ; cm
ISBN 978-0-87140-790-0 (hardcover)
1. Rural families—Newfoundland and Labrador—Fiction. 2. Newfoundland
and Labrador—Fiction. 3. Domestic fiction. I. Title.
PR9199.3.C717S94 2015
813'.54—dc23
2014031404

ISBN 978-1-63149-110-8 pbk.

Liveright Publishing Corporation
500 Fifth Avenue, New York, N.Y. 10110
www.wwnorton.com

W. W. Norton & Company Ltd.
Castle House, 75/76 Wells Street, London W1T 3QT

1 2 3 4 5 6 7 8 9 0

for Stan Dragland

THE KING'S SEAT

Even unto them will I give in mine house and within my walls a place and a name....
—ISAIAH

HE HEARD THEM BEFORE HE SAW THEM. Voices in the fog, so indistinct he thought they might be imaginary. An auditory hallucination, the mind trying to compensate for a sensory lack. The way a solitary man will start talking to furniture, left alone long enough.

Anyway, voices out there.

He'd gone across to the mainland after a load of wood on Saturday morning and was stranded overnight by the fog. Slept in the wheelhouse under an old blanket with a pair of coveralls rolled up as a pillow. The mauze lifted a little at first light and he thought he might be able to pick his way home. Had the island in sight when the mist muffled in, so thick he couldn't see ten feet past the bow. Cut the engine to drift awhile, listening blind for other boats. Just the lap of waves against the hull for the longest time. The wail of the foghorn on Burnt Head. And in the lull between, a murmur that seemed vaguely human. Then a single wordless syllable shouted, like a dog's bark.

Spooked him. Miles out on the water and that voice seeming to rise from the ocean itself. He had to work up the nerve to respond, hoping there was nothing in that blankness to answer him. Hello, he called. Half a dozen voices shouting wildly in response and he leaned away as if he'd been pushed by a hand reaching out of the fog. Jesus fuck, he said.

He started up the engine and the voices rose, wanting to be heard above it. Put-putted in the direction he guessed they came from, his head cocked to follow the racket being sent up like a flare. A shape slowly taking shape in front of him, a darkening bruise in the fog, the lifeboat's red burning through.

He slipped the engine into reverse to avoid running broadside into the open boat. Figures standing along the length, waving frantically. A dozen or more it looked to be and no one local. Dark skin and black heads of hair. Some foreign trawler gone down on the Banks, he thought, a container ship on its way to the States. All of them in street clothes and not a one wearing a lifejacket.

A man leaned out over the bow as he came around, cantilevered at such an angle Sweetland didn't know what stopped the fellow pitching head first into the water. He looked Indian, Sweetland thought, or some variation of Indian, he never could tell that crowd one from the other. There were more people huddled below the gunwale, none dressed for the weather and half-frozen by the look of them. Sweetland passed a tow rope that the man tied to the bow of the lifeboat and then he made a motion to his mouth, tipping his head back. Sweetland rummaged around for the two Javex bottles of fresh water he carried, grabbed the blanket and a folded canvas tarp, handed them along.

Those faces staring across at him with looks of deranged relief. He was riding low with the load of wood and it occurred to him they might try to come over the gunwale onto his boat and swamp him, much as drowning swimmers were reported to drag their rescuers under. He made what he intended to be calming gestures with his arms and started up the engine to pull ahead to the full length of the tow rope, then headed slow slow slow toward the cove.

Glancing back now and again, startled each time to see what was following in his wake.

I

HE SAW THE GOVERNMENT MAN WALKING up from the water. The tan pants, the tweed jacket and tie. The same fellow who came out for the last town meeting, or one exactly like him—there seemed to be an endless supply on hand at the Confederation Building in St. John's. The briefcase looking for all the world like something that was in his hand when he left his mother's womb. Sweetland turned away from the window, as if he could hide from the man by not looking his way. Glimpsed a flash of him as he went to the front door of the house, heard the knock.

No one in the cove ever knocked at a door. He thought to ignore it, but the knock came a second and then a third time and he pushed away from the table, went out through the hallway. No one in the cove used their front doors, either. Sweetland's hadn't been opened in years and he had to jimmy it loose of the frame. The man standing there lost in the sun's glare, a voice from the nothing where his mouth should be. "Mr. Sweetland?"

He waited until the figure resolved out of the light, until he could see the eyes. "Just come off the ferry, did you?"

"Just this second, yes."

Sweetland nodded. "I must be some fucken important."

The government man smiled up at him. "You're at the top of my list."

Sweetland stood to one side to let the man by. "Cup of tea?"

"You don't have coffee by any chance?"

"I got instant."

"Tea is fine," the government man said.

Sweetland moved the kettle onto the stove while the young one took a seat at the table. He tried to think of when a stranger sat there last, seeing the kitchen for the first time. Low ceilings, the beams an inch or two clear of Sweetland's crown. Painted wood floor, a daybed under one window, a Formica table with chrome legs pushed up to the other. His mother's china teacups on hooks below the cupboards. All so familiar to him he hadn't noticed it in years.

The man's briefcase was lying on the table in front of him like a placemat and Sweetland set a spoon and the sugar bowl on the flat surface of it.

"No sugar for me," the youngster said, setting the bowl to one side. "A drop of milk if you have some." He put the case on the floor beside his chair.

"No fresh," Sweetland said. "Just tin."

"Tin is fine," the government man said. He took a BlackBerry from his coat pocket and held it to the window a moment.

"You're not the fellow was out last time around."

"I just took over the file."

"You won't get a cell phone signal out here," Sweetland told him.

He shrugged. "The edge of the civilized world."

"They was talking about putting up a tower years back. Never got around to it."

The government man gestured past him to the counter. "You have a laptop there."

Sweetland glanced over his shoulder, to confirm the fact. "We got the internet for long ago. Does my banking on that," he said. "Bit of online poker. Passes the time." Sweetland poured the tea and took a seat directly across the table.

"You're not on Facebook, are you?"

"Look at this face," he said and the government man glanced down at the table. "Now Arsebook," Sweetland said. "That's something I'd sign up for."

"I'm sure it's coming."

"I wouldn't doubt it. Given the state of things."

It was an easy road into the subject at hand and he was surprised the government man didn't take it, smiling out the window instead. Perfect teeth. They all had perfect teeth these days. Careful haircuts, accents Sweetland couldn't place. This one might be from the mainland somewhere, for all he could tell.

"So," the younger man said abruptly. "Are you coming to the meeting this afternoon?"

Sweetland almost laughed. "Not planning on it, no."

"I couldn't talk you into it?"

"Listen," Sweetland said, "I'm not the only one who voted against this thing."

"That's true. Forty-five in favour, three against, by the most recent ballot. But as of yesterday, yours is one of only two households who have not agreed to take the package we're offering."

"Two?" Sweetland said.

The government man paused there, to let the information sink in. He stirred his tea slowly, the clink of the spoon like a broken lever inside a mechanical doll.

"It's just me and Loveless?"

"That's where things stand," he said.

Sweetland rubbed absently at the tabletop a moment and then excused himself. He went out through the hall and up the narrow stairs to the bathroom. He put the toilet seat down and sat there a few minutes, leaning an elbow on the windowsill. He could see the back of Loveless's property from there, the ancient barn, the single gaunt cow with its head to the grass. Loveless famously drank a pint of kerosene when he was a toddler, which to Sweetland's mind told you everything you needed to know about the man. He'd suffered a twenty-four-hour attack of hiccups while he passed the fuel, his diapers reeking of oil and shit. No one was allowed to light a match near the youngster for a week.

And it was all down now to him and fucken Loveless.

"Sorry," Sweetland said when he came back into the kitchen.

The government man waved the interruption away. He said, "I have to admit I'm curious, Mr. Sweetland."

"About what?"

"I don't mean to pry," he said, which Sweetland took to mean he was about to pry. "But you're turning down a substantial cash payout. Practically the whole town is against you."

"And?"

"I'm just wondering what your story is exactly."

He didn't like the little fucker, Sweetland decided. Not one bit. He gestured toward the briefcase with his mug. "I imagine you got everything you needs to know about me in that bag of yours."

The government man watched him a second, then pulled a folder from the case. "Moses Louis Sweetland," he read. "Born November fourteenth, 1942. Which makes you—" He glanced up.

"Sixty-nine this fall."

"Math isn't my strong suit," he said. "Next of kin: none."

"Christ," Sweetland said. "I'm related to half the people in Chance Cove."

"No immediate next of kin, I think is what that means. Parents deceased. Brother and sister?"

"Both dead."

"Marital status: single." He looked up again. "Never married, is that right?"

Sweetland shrugged and said, "Look at this face," which made the younger man turn back to his papers.

"Occupation," he said. "Lightkeeper, retired."

"I was let go when they automated the light ten years back."

"You were a fisherman before that?"

"Right up until the moratorium in '92."

"So you've never lived anywhere else?"

"A couple of trips to Toronto for work," he said, "when I was about your age."

The government man made a motion toward his own face, afraid of pointing directly at Sweetland's scars. "Is that where?"

"What else is it you got in there?"

He closed the folder and sat back. "That's everything," he said.

"Not much when you lays it out like that."

"Not enough to tell me why you're so set against this move."

"Just contrary, I guess."

"You'd rather stay here with the dead, is that it?"

"A body could do worse for company."

The government man brushed his fingers lightly back and forth across the edge of the table, as if he were at a piano and not wanting to strike a note. "How long is it your people have lived out here, Mr. Sweetland?"

"Time before time," Sweetland said and then smiled at himself. "People been fishing here two hundred years or more. I expect my crowd was the first ones on the island."

"Because it's eponymous, you mean?"

Sweetland stared blankly.

"It's named after them. Your family and the island have the same name."

"Yes," Sweetland said. "That's what I mean."

They stared at one another then and Sweetland could see the youngster was casting about in his mind for some other tack to take. He put his chin in one hand and tapped his nose with the index finger. Then he leaned to one side to put the folder back into his briefcase. "As you are aware," he said, "the government is offering a package to the residents of Sweetland to move anywhere in the province they like. A minimum of one hundred thousand dollars per household, up to one hundred and fifty thousand, depending on the size of the family and other considerations. Plus adjustment assistance and help looking for work or retraining or returning to school."

"Jesus," Sweetland said, "I thought the government was broke."

The younger man ignored him. "But we will not move a soul out of here unless we have a commitment from everyone to the package."

Sweetland nodded. "Same old bullshit."

"This is not the 1960s, Mr. Sweetland. This move isn't being forced on the town. We will pay to resettle the residents, as we've been asked to do. But we will not be responsible for some lunatic alone in the middle of the Atlantic once everyone else is gone."

"Me being the lunatic."

"There won't be any ferry service after the move. Which means no supplies coming in. There will be no phone service. No online banking, no poker. No electricity. By definition, I'd think anyone out here on their own would have to be certifiable." The government man glanced at his watch. "You've been made aware of the September deadline."

"I been made aware."

"There are people hoping to make the move across as early as this fall, which means everyone would have to sign by the first."

"I am aware," Sweetland said again.

The government man reached into an inside pocket of his coat. "My email address is on there, my cell number, you can contact me anytime."

Sweetland set the card on a shelf above the counter and followed his guest along the hall, to let him out the door he came in. Placing a hand to the back of a chair and then the wall as he went, the room tilting under his feet.

The light blared in through the open door and Sweetland came out as far as the doorstep. He shaded his eyes to gaze down toward the water.

Folks in their yards or on the paths or at the wharf, all busy not looking his way.

The government man was staring down to the harbour as well, and Sweetland couldn't help taking the place in through the stranger's eyes. A straggle of vinyl-sided bungalows, half of them sitting empty. Saddle-roofed sheds and propane tanks and ATVs and old lumber in untidy piles, like trash dumped on the slope by some natural disaster. The white church on the point, the Fisherman's Hall with Rita Verge's hand-lettered MUSEUM sign at the side entrance. A handful of geriatric boats moored off in the cove.

"That's a beautiful view," the government man said. "I can see why you don't want to leave it."

"You didn't strike me," Sweetland said, "as an ass-kisser."

"I work for the government," the youngster said and he shrugged good-naturedly. "It's just part of the job."

He didn't like the fucker, it was true. Not one bit.

He levered the door into the frame and leaned back against the wall. Stared across at an oval black-and-white portrait of his grandfather hung by the door. A young man from another age—a high starched collar, a waistcoat, the chain of a pocket watch, an elaborate waxed moustache.

"Now Uncle Clar," he said. "It's just me and Loveless."

The eyes of the man in the picture looking off to one side, as if to avoid the issue altogether.

Sweetland went out to his root cellar for the last of his seed potatoes, spent an hour setting spuds in the garden. He hosed the rake and spade clean when he was done and set them away in the shed. He washed his hands in the kitchen and through the tiny window over the sink he caught sight of Queenie Coffin next door, scattering a packet of seeds through her window onto the patch of ground below it. Which meant the summer—what passed for summer—was well and truly started.

Practically everyone else in the cove was gathered at the Fisherman's Hall for the meeting with the government man and there was an eerie stillness about the place, as if the island was already abandoned. He expected Reet Verge would be sent across to badger him when the meeting was done and he packed a few things into his knapsack, drove his quad up out of the cove to avoid her. He climbed past the trail to the new cemetery and beyond it to the peak of the hills.

At the top of the climb he stopped beside the King's Seat to take in the view of Chance Cove and the island north and south, even though Jesse wasn't with him. Jesse had asked a thousand times if those stones had been assembled into the vague shape of a throne or if it was an accidental configuration, but no one alive knew the answer. Probably no one else had ever thought to wonder about it.

Sweetland went as far as the lighthouse, to put out a few rabbit snares that he and Jesse could check on in the morning. A surprise to welcome the youngster back, to scour the week's worth of city grit from his mouth.

It was almost four o'clock by the time he made it back to Chance Cove. The government man away on the ferry and the town's emissary come and gone from Sweetland's house for now. He backed the quad into the shed and covered the machine with a tarp, went into the house through the back porch. Ran cold water from the tap while he reached for a glass.

Sweetland drew his hand back when he caught sight of the folded sheet of paper propped inside the cupboard. Stood still while the water ran, trying to think when he'd last opened that door. He used the same glass out of the drain rack for days on end, which meant it could have been planted there any time during the past week. He turned off the tap and took the sheet down, held it at arm's length. YOU GET OUT, the message read, OR YOULL BE SOME SORRY.

He refolded the paper and opened the drawer below the forks and knives, set it in beside the other notes he'd found tucked around the house over the last six months. They were all the same, comically sinister, offering vague threats against his person and his property, all written with words and letters cut from print headlines and glued to the paper like a ransom demand out of the movies. It was a ploy so amateurish that Sweetland would have thought Loveless was behind it, but for the fact the spelling was more or less correct. And Loveless was the only hold-out left besides himself.

Sweetland shut the drawer and took down a glass, drank the water in slow mouthfuls. He couldn't bring himself to take the threats seriously and he'd never mentioned the notes to anyone. He wasn't sure why he was holding onto them. *In case*, was how he thought of it. Though he couldn't say in case of what exactly.

He was up early the next morning with the radio on. Made himself a sandwich and an extra for Jesse, packed them with two tins of peaches. He put on his boots in the porch, carried his coat and knapsack outside. Paused there a moment, listening, then slammed the door as hard as he could. Pilgrim's dog started barking mad where she was leashed in the yard, the sound of it echoing up off the hill behind the cove.

"Shut up, Diesel!" Sweetland shouted, louder than he needed to. "Shut the hell up!"

He puttered around the ATV underneath the purple glow of the street light attached to the shed, strapping his .22 to the handlebars, tying the canvas pack onto the carryall at the back. Heard Pilgrim's door open and close and the sound of the boy running. Glanced up to see him motor along the side of the house. He was within two feet of Sweetland before he came to an abrupt stop and he stood there at attention, staring up into the old man's face.

Lank and pale, the boy was, like something soaked too long in water. The purple light making his face look sallow, cadaverous. "Jesse," Sweetland said. He had never made peace with the youngster's name. It sounded fey, feminine, like something off one of those soap operas

Sweetland's mother used to watch. He'd tried to rechristen the boy with half a dozen nicknames—Bucko, Mister Man, Hunter—but Jesse would only answer to his proper name.

"You going up on the mash?" the boy asked.

"Got a few slips out," Sweetland said. "Thought I might see if I had any luck. Clara know you're up here?"

"Mom's still asleep. I told Pop."

"And what did your pop say?"

"He told me not to be a nuisance."

Sweetland nodded. "Get your helmet out of the shed," he said.

Sweetland drove out the back of his property and when they reached the King's Seat at the top of the path Jesse slapped at his shoulder, shouting for him to stop. He jumped off the quad and ran across to the stones, pulling the helmet from his head. The sun just coming up full, the ocean deepening blue in the new light. Jesse skipped up onto the seat and stood with his arms spread wide. "I'm the King of the World!" he shouted, his voice rolling down the hill toward the cove, picking up speed as it went. "I'm the King of the World!"

Sweetland allowed he was the only person in Christendom who hadn't seen that goddamn *Titanic* movie. Jesse knew the film so intimately he could quote every word of dialogue and sometimes did. He insisted on stopping whenever they passed the Seat and Sweetland waited on the quad while the boy had his moment.

"Come on, Your Highness," he said finally, "the day idn't getting any younger."

Beyond the King's Seat, the trail went east to Vatcher's Meadow where Glad Vatcher summered his animals—half a dozen cows and the bull, twenty head of sheep fenced on forty acres of marsh grass and gorse. There was a gate on both sides so people could cross the meadow when the animals were moved into the barn for the winter, but the summer path circled the field. They drove inland about half a mile, following the barbed wire fence, until they picked up the trail on the opposite side, ravelling east over the headlands to Burnt Head. The plateau was dotted with massive granite boulders that Jesse claimed were called erratics, dropped there by retreating glaciers at the end of the last ice age.

Is that what they're teaching you in school these days, he'd asked.

Saw it on television, Jesse said.

It was a wonder to Sweetland what stuck in the youngster's head. He still insisted on taking off every stitch of clothes just to take a piss and couldn't be counted on to flush the toilet, but he could lecture a body on a hundred different topics—aircraft, the digestive system, moon landings, Mount Everest, ping-pong, whales. Sweetland dreaded getting the boy started on whales. Their Latin names, their numbers and size, their diets, their migration routes, the sound and meaning of their songs. It was as if there was a tape in the youngster's head just waiting for someone to press Play.

Beyond the mash, the trail veered out toward the ocean. Ancient rock cairns placed every twenty feet along the path, to keep walkers from going over the cliff edge in the dark or in stormy weather. Three hundred feet to the surf below. The top of the old light tower was just visible beyond the rise, out on Burnt Head.

Sweetland pulled in behind the abandoned lightkeeper's house which had been sitting unoccupied the ten years since the light was automated. Jesse ran up the rotting steps, holding his hands to the windows and reporting the latest damage. Storm winds had stripped the ocean-side shingles and the relentless wet had rotted through the ceilings, the floors a mess of ceiling plaster and soaked insulation. Mouse shit on every surface. Sweetland hated even to look at the place. "Don't you go inside there," he called.

He took his .22 and backpack off the quad and they headed inland again, the new light flashing on their right shoulder as they walked clear of the ruined building. Just a beacon on a metal tripod drilled into the farthest point of rock these days. A hundred feet north of the beacon there was a helicopter pad built overtop of the Fever Rocks, used by the Coast Guard when they brought supplies to the keeper, or came out for light maintenance. A helipad, Jesse told him it was called.

You're making that up, Sweetland had said.

Am not.

There's no such word as *hellish pad*.

Helipad, Jesse had repeated. Nothing insulted the youngster more than inaccuracy or invention. With the one notable exception, he was literal to a fault. He spelled *helipad* for Sweetland, to underline the word's veracity. He'd always been a champion speller. Near-photographic memory, according to the Reverend. A generation ago, the Reverend said, they'd have called the boy an idiot savant.

I'd say that's about half right, Sweetland said.

Sweetland still called it the hellish pad, over the boy's objections. He never missed a chance to lampoon Jesse's childish seriousness. He had hoped to goad the youngster off the beaten track of his thoughts, to make him look at the world from a slightly crooked angle, though it made no appreciable difference and he kept at it now mostly out of habit. For his part, Jesse seemed to accept Sweetland's mockery as a fact of life, granting him special dispensation to behave like a fool, a kind of court jester in the youngster's kingdom of the exact.

Beyond the pad was a decommissioned winchhouse, and leading down from the winch to the water was a higgledy series of ladders screwed into the cliffs, two hundred feet in length, angled awkwardly to follow the contours of the rock face. The Fever Rocks were the access point for the lightkeeper long before choppers were an option, supplies and materials hauled up by winch from boats below. The ladders were still maintained for emergency access to the light when the weather was too foggy for a helicopter to fly. They looked like something designed and built by Dr. Seuss. Generations of island youngsters had rowed out here to climb it on a dare. Sweetland had managed it once, he and Duke and Pilgrim drunk and in the dark. The sight of it still made him feel slightly nauseous, almost sixty years on.

The path led into a section of scrub forest and passed above a ravine scored into the island's back, and from there on to its southern tip. It was how the keeper used to travel to the south-end light above the Mackerel Cliffs, a five-hour trip by horse and cart back in the day. Sweetland managed it in just over an hour on the quad. The path was rarely used anymore and was nearly overgrown, the spruce crowding in. They had to walk single file, Jesse out in front, the wet branches soaking their sleeves as they went.

Clara had gotten the boy a haircut while they were in St. John's, cropped close at the nape and sides. Sweetland could see the seashell whorls of the double crown at the back of Jesse's head. A lick of hair sticking up between them, a rogue pook that had gone its own way since he'd had enough hair to comb. Before Jesse learned to walk, Sweetland used to twirl it around his finger to make it stand straight, like a headdress feather in the cowboy movies he'd watched with Duke in the old Toronto theatres. Mommy's little Indian, he called him.

The youngster couldn't stand anyone touching his head now and Sweetland thought he might be to blame for that. He could just resist the urge to reach out and smooth the lick down.

The slips were tailed at the base of spruce trees where the runs crossed the trail. They were tied to an alder standard he'd pushed firm into the ground, the silver noose snugged around with brush. A rabbit lying in the first snare and Sweetland knelt to help Jesse work the wire free of the neck, tying a length of string around the paws so the boy could carry the animal across his shoulder.

They walked nearly two hours before they stopped for lunch, settling in a clearing beyond the valley. The peak of the Priddles' cabin half-hidden among the spruce and birch below. The racket of gannets nesting on the Music House headlands drifting up to them where they sat. They had two brace for their efforts and Sweetland laid the rabbits in the grass at their feet, the animals fat and sleek and bug-eyed. He dug out the sandwiches and they ate in silence a few minutes. When Jesse finished his lunch he sang for a while, belting out the details of some bygone disaster, though it wasn't a performance. The audience was irrelevant, Sweetland knew. The song part of a private landscape that surfaced now and then into the wider world.

Sweetland rooted in the bag after a tin of peaches, which was the only fruit the boy would eat. Only from a can, only Del Monte. Sweetland had a cupboardful at the house. He opened the top, passing it across when the song was done.

"Pop says it's just you and Loveless wants to stay now," Jesse said.

Sweetland stared across at the boy, who was focused on the tin, shovelling the fruit into his mouth with a plastic spoon. He hadn't once mentioned that whole business before now. From what Sweetland could tell, the issue of resettlement had never registered in the peculiar peaks and valleys of the youngster's mind, though it had been the main topic of conversation in the cove for years now. "Will I have to go?" Jesse asked. He was still staring into the tin as he ate.

"Not as long as I'm around," Sweetland said.

The boy scooped the last of the fruit into his mouth, tipped up the tin to drink the juice. It was impossible to say what he thought of it all, one way or the other.

"So," Sweetland said. "You just come back on the ferry yesterday, was it?"

"Mom took me to see the doctor into St. John's," he said. Like this was news to Sweetland.

"And what did the doctor have to say to you? You're retarded, is it? Antisocial? Codependent? Mentally unstable? Psychopathic?"

"No," the boy said.

"Well what are you going all the way into St. John's to see him for then?"

He shrugged. "Don't know."

"Your mother's the one should be seeing the doctor."

"She sees him too," Jesse said. "She goes in after me."

Sweetland smiled. "Fat lot of fucken good it's doing her, hey?"

"I don't know," the youngster said.

He'd gone too far, Sweetland thought and he said, "Never mind me." By way of apology.

"I don't mind."

He let out a breath of air, stared away down the valley. Even Sweetland thought it was a lonely life for the youngster sometimes, stuck in that head of his. Surrounded by geriatrics and imaginary friends. And as if on cue, Jesse said, "Hollis went into St. John's to see a doctor one time."

"Where'd you hear the like of that?"

"Hollis told me."

Sweetland's brother, the boy was talking about. Dead fifty years or more. "Is that a fact," Sweetland said.

"He was into St. John's most of the winter one year."

Sweetland got to his feet and busied himself picking up their bit of material, packing it away. "Finish up now," he said. A feeling like bugs crawling on his skin he could only get clear of by moving. "We got better things to do than sit around here jawing."

They cleaned the rabbits at Sweetland's kitchen sink. Jesse on a chair to hold them aloft by the hind paws as Sweetland flicked a blade through the fur above the ankles, peeled the coats down the length of the carcasses an inch at a time. Flesh the colour of mahogany and grained like wood. The mottled guts slopping into the stainless steel bowl of the sink.

The phone rang and Jesse jumped off the chair to answer but Sweetland stopped him, afraid it might be Clara. "You wash up," he said. "It's time you got home to your supper."

The boy rinsed his hands under the tap as the phone jangled on awhile. He said, "Are you going out after wood tomorrow?"

"Might be."

"I could help."

"Take one of these down to your pop," Sweetland said, and he slipped a naked carcass into a clear plastic bag. Jesse waiting with his freshly washed hands held out, as if he was about to receive a ceremonial sword.

After he'd scoured the sink, Sweetland went out the back porch door and walked around to the front of the house. Looked east and west like someone deciding on a route before he ambled down through the cove. He went by Pilgrim's house, but he didn't so much as glance in the windows, scurried past with his eyes averted.

Sweetland carried on to Duke Fewer's barbershop, a one-room shed next to Duke's house. There was a barber's chair as old as Buckley's goat screwed into the bare plywood floor. One wall mostly mirror, the other pasted with faded photos and newspaper clippings yellowed with age. A buzzing neon light fixture, a coat stand, a sink in one corner, a wood stove opposite to heat the room through the winters. Two wooden chairs along the wall below the photos, and, on a low table between them, a chessboard beside a stack of magazines—*National Geographic* and *Time*, *Sports Illustrated* and *Maclean's*—that dated from thirty years before and hadn't been touched in nearly that long.

Duke was sitting in the barber's chair with the three-day-old paper arrived on yesterday's ferry. His praying mantis legs crossed in a fashion that seemed barely human. Didn't glance up when Sweetland came in and looked to have dozed off with his heavy-lidded eyes half-open, but for the habitual tremor in his hands that made the paper shake. "Be done in a minute," he said finally, and Sweetland took a seat, stared down at the game in progress on the chessboard.

Duke bought the barber's chair from a second-hand building supply in St. John's when the cod stocks collapsed and the government ended the inshore fishery in '92. Sweetland had tried to talk him out of it. To begin with, there were only ninety-odd people living in Chance Cove in those days and every one of them got their hair cut in Reet Verge's kitchen, but for Ned Priddle who was bald as a cue ball. And Duke had never cut hair in his life, regardless. Man nor woman was willing to sit in that chair and let Duke at them with the clippers.

Duke rustled the paper. "Pilgrim was by earlier. Said you and Jesse was out checking slips."

"Got a couple brace on the backside, above the Priddles' cabin."

"Pilgrim says Clara wouldn't very happy about it."

"I don't imagine," Sweetland said quietly.

Duke had a straight razor and a shaving cup and offered shaves for a dollar fifty. As far as Sweetland knew, he had no takers on that offer either. A tax write-off, Duke called it when he put out his shingle. Though it was anyone's guess what exactly he was writing off. Twenty-odd years he'd been spending six afternoons a week out here, sweeping the floor and reading the paper, watching passersby through the tiny window beside the door. His ex-wife had abandoned the island twenty-five years ago, his children all shifted off to one part of the mainland or other. He gossiped with the men who dropped in for a cup of tea, a gander at the chessboard, moving a piece here or there. Duke played the white and never lost.

"Who've been at this board?" Sweetland asked.

Duke craned to look over his shoulder. "There's been seven or eight had a go since you was here last."

"You didn't let Loveless touch anything."

"You're in check there," he said and he shook out the paper. "If you hadn't noticed."

"Loveless still thinks it's a goddamn checkerboard."

"He means well."

Sweetland grunted. "So does the fucken government."

Duke nodded, which was as close as he came to laughter. "Didn't see you at the meeting yesterday."

"You was taking attendance, was you?"

"Just Loveless and yourself and Queenie missing. Hard not to notice. Hayward thinks you and Queenie must be having a little something on the side."

"He's not worried about Loveless?"

"Hayward's paranoid," Duke said. "He's not an idiot."

"Well," Sweetland said, as if there was some doubt about the fact.

"You heard he signed up for the package after all," Duke said.

"I heard."

"Just you and Loveless, then."

He glanced over at the man in the chair. Sweetland knew where he stood on the matter, but Duke Fewer was the only person on the island who'd never once tried to sway him, one way or the other. The barbershop felt like the only safe place he had left. "Don't start," he said.

"Makes no odds to me. I'm leaving, government package or no. Laura's crowd have got a room waiting for me."

"Jesus," Sweetland said. "Who's going to take over the barbershop once you goes?"

"You can kiss my arse," Duke said.

"A rake like you got neither arse to kiss."

Sweetland moved his king out of check and Duke folded the paper, climbed down from the chair. An elaborate process, uncrossing those long limbs, setting them upright on the floor. He walked across to the board and lifted his rook, setting it down shakily. "Check," he said.

Sweetland sat back in disgust. "Fucken Loveless," he said.

Duke eased into the empty chair across from Sweetland. Both men stared at the board, like they expected one of those wooden figures to move of its own accord and were determined not to miss it. Duke cleared his throat. "There's some saying they'll burn you out if you don't take that package."

"Some who?"

"It was just talk."

"You heard someone saying they was going to burn me out?"

"Not direct, like," Duke said. "There's people have heard it spoke of."

"Well, they can all kiss my arse."

"People are getting worked up, Mose. A hundred grand is a lot of money."

Sweetland stared at Duke, trying to read what he was saying exactly. If there was a message from someone being passed on second-hand. He said, "You think I should take the package?"

Duke raised his eyes. "You remember what come of the last bit of advice I offered you." He let out a breath of air and gestured toward the board. "You got a move or you just going to stare?"

Sweetland stood up. "Needs to have a think on it," he said.

"I got plenty of newspaper to get through yet."

Sweetland turned back at the door. "Don't you let Loveless touch that board," he said.

ONCE HE'D TIED ON TO THE LIFEBOAT, it occurred to Sweetland he had about a fifty-fifty chance of finding his way in through the fog. He stayed clear of the horn on Burnt Head and jogged west by the compass once he guessed he was well beyond the Fever Rocks. The engine echoing faintly back to him now and then from the invisible cliffs to starboard.

He was crawling, staring through the murk for any sign of land. Even the lifeboat was barely visible when he looked behind.

He carried on, keeping to deep water, trying to estimate how far along the island he'd travelled. He passed a depression in the steep face of the cliffs, a hollow space in the engine's echo coming back to him that he hoped was Lunin Cove. He cut the engine and put out a jigger, letting the line run until it touched bottom eighteen fathom down. He was over the Offer Ledge which meant three miles to the breakwater. He travelled blind another half an hour, the fog thickening as he stared. He stopped the engine and dropped the jigger and it came up on the Tom Cod Rocks less than a fathom underneath him.

The first hint of it came through the white mist as he was bringing up the line—a low droning that seemed as placeless and dispersed as the fog. The men in the lifeboat standing when they heard it, looking around aimlessly. Sweetland sailed west a ways, stopped again. A voice this time, ahead and well off his port side. He made three or four more stops before he recognized it, Tennessee Ernie Ford singing "The Old Rugged Cross" from the church steeple. There was never a bell up there, just a PA system that played hymns out over Chance Cove for an hour before Sunday-morning services. You could hear it miles away on the water on a clear day, and even now Ford's industrial-strength baritone managed to carry through the heavy drapes of fog to where they inched along the shore. "Softly and Tenderly." "What a Friend We Have in Jesus." "Whispering Hope." Sweetland humming along even when the engine drowned out the sound of the recording.

Tennessee Ernie Ford's voice drifted by to starboard until it was imploring sinners to come home from somewhere off the stern, which meant Sweetland had sailed by the entrance. He came about slowly then, making way for the hidden mouth of the cove, and the island loomed out of the grey suddenly, the alien line of the breakwater straight as a ruler above the surface. He fired three shots with his .22 to try and raise someone's attention, to let them know he was coming.

He looked back to the lifeboat, waved to the shadowy figures, all staring in his direction. They did not look altogether comforted to be in tow with him, he thought.

He fired three more shots and then eased into the cove's calm. The white church wavering on the point, still blaring its Protestant entreaties. The wharf slowly becoming solid as he approached it. People who had been on their way to church already standing on the dock in their Sunday clothes, dozens more coming out of their houses up the hill, men and women and children with their dogs alongside, all running to meet the ghostly arrivals.

2

CLARA CAME TO THE HOUSE while Sweetland was in the middle of a Texas Hold 'em table. He'd been expecting her all evening and hadn't been able to pay proper attention to the game. He was playing the short stack, sitting with two pair, jacks over nines. Going heads-up with a reckless newbie who'd signed in as Flush, almost two hundred thousand in the pot.

"You aren't watching porn over there, are you?" she asked.

"Gave it up for Lent," he said and waved her into the kitchen without looking away from the laptop. Clara placed the plastic bag with the rabbit carcass on the table as she sat down.

He checked on the river card and Flush bet all-in. "Ah fuck," he said.

"It's not real money," Clara told him.

"Thank Christ for that." He folded his hand and let out a long sigh, closed the laptop carefully, reluctant.

Clara reached to lift the bag holding the rabbit a foot closer to him. "That's out of season."

"They're peaked out this year," he said. "They'll be starving in the woods come the winter."

"I don't want it in the house," she said.

He looked down at the plastic bag on the table. Watery streaks of blood in the folds. "I only set a dozen slips," he said. "The youngster loves to be out at it."

"Jesse lost a week of school with me in St. John's," she said. "He don't need to miss more."

"It was your dog kicking up a racket that woke him this morning."

"You couldn't send him home out of it?"

Sweetland shrugged. "He asked his grandfather if he could go."

Clara laid a hand across her eyes and there was her mother, Sweetland thought. Clara had almost nothing else of Ruth in her, but that subtle gesture of exhaustion or anxiety or annoyance was Sweetland's sister to a T. He took the meat across the kitchen to the freezer, to put a little more space between himself and that eerie transformation.

Jesse was still an infant when Clara came back to Sweetland and no word of who the father was or what became of him. Clara might have stumbled on the child under a rock somewhere and brought the foundling to Chance Cove to raise as her own for all he knew. Almost ten years she'd been away, first to university in St. John's and then itinerant work on the mainland. Her first months home she walked out to the lighthouse on Sundays with Jesse bundled in a backpack. He could see her coming if he was in the tower, the smudge of her red Gore-Tex jacket moving over the mash. He watched her inch toward him until she was close enough to make out her features, then he'd go down the spiral stairs to put on the kettle.

Sweetland never said a word about her decision to leave for school though he was against it from the start, with Ruthie dead and Pilgrim about to be left alone to fend for himself in the house. And he turned his back on Clara in small, spiteful ways. Let her have what she wants, he thought, without ever thinking it. A barely discernible coldness toward her that he would have denied if she accused him. He sat at his kitchen window as she boarded the ferry on the government wharf. The white of her face turning to look up the hill where she knew he'd be watching. Didn't hear a word from her all the time she was elsewhere, but for what came to him second-hand through Pilgrim or Queenie.

Clara walked all the way to the light on Sundays just to avoid the expectation of going to church, he guessed. She drank tea on the chesterfield while Sweetland crawled across the floor with Jesse, lifted him by the ankles, blowing farts on his belly to make the boy laugh. He'd never encountered a child less inclined to laughter and he took it as a personal challenge to cure him of the affliction. He couldn't say now if he'd sensed something wrong with Jesse even then, or if it was only in retrospect there seemed an unnatural distance in the infant's eyes. The boy seeming to look out on the world from the far end of a tunnel.

Clara barely spoke a word during those visits, watching Sweetland clowning on the floor with Jesse. A pregnant silence between them, as if she was waiting to be forgiven for some offence. Or offering him the chance to ask forgiveness himself. And his failure to do one or the other was one more thing she held against him now. He dreaded talking to the woman, was the plain fact of the matter.

"Jesse is saying he's going to stay with you here after everyone else leaves," Clara said. She'd raised her voice and Sweetland could tell this was the real issue she'd come to talk about. That it took some effort on her part to broach the subject.

"Is that right?"

"You haven't said anything to set the thought in his head, I hope."

"He knows his own mind."

"He's not good with change, if that's what you means."

Sweetland turned back to her from the fridge. "Have you been telling him about Hollis spending a winter in hospital? Into St. John's?"

"Uncle Hollis?"

"Jesse's claiming he heard it straight from Hollis himself."

"What was he in for, tuberculosis?"

"Jesse was talking like Hollis was sitting with us in the woods."

Clara shrugged. "The doctor says its normal enough."

"Normal *enough*?"

"He says Jesse might grow out of it."

"Have they got a name for it yet?" he asked.

"For what?"

"Whatever it is wrong with the youngster."

"There's a spectrum," she said. She was looking down at the table, as if she was embarrassed by the word, by how lame it sounded as an explanation. "And he isn't typical, is what they're telling me."

"I could've told you as much for free," he said. "Saved you the trip."

"The doctor haven't seen enough of Jesse to be able to say more than that. If we lived in St. John's we could get him assessed. We could get him into a school program."

"Jesse won't be happy nowhere else than here," Sweetland said, "I knows that for a fact." He moved the kettle over the heat of the stove. "He wants to come over with me when I goes for a load of wood tomorrow."

"Oh Jesus," Clara muttered.

"It's Saturday anyway," Sweetland said quietly. "You want a cup of tea?" But she was already halfway out the door.

He went for his evening walk before dark. A nip in the air, though they were into the first week of June. The wind just beginning to drop with the sun. He went as far as his room and stage on the waterline, then past it all the way to the metal bell of the old garbage incinerator on the point. Miles out he could see a container ship on its way seaward, the lights just coming visible in the dusk. It looked like a mid-sized city on the horizon, drifting east.

He turned back to the cove, to the white church on the opposite arm, the fenced square of the graveyard on the hillside above the houses. There were a handful of youngsters playing road hockey on the government wharf on Church Side, which was the only bit of flat ground they had access to. Pilgrim's dog bounding back and forth with the players, sent into the harbour after the ball when a wayward shot put it over the side. Sweetland counted seven or eight kids, just about the entire school-age population, save Jesse who had no aptitude for sports. Sweetland glanced back out to sea, the sun low on the horizon, and he waited until it touched down on the ocean before starting in.

He caught a blur of movement up off the path that he stopped to watch through the bushes. Loveless's dog on the loose again. Some kind of miniature poodle cross Loveless found listed in the *Buy & Sell* after Sara died. He'd nagged Sweetland into making the trip across to Hermitage, carried the dog back in the pocket of his coat. Full size now and seven pounds soaking wet. Nothing but skin and grief.

Sweetland called up to the dog in the bushes and he whistled softly, but the animal ignored him, disappearing in the darkening evening. Loveless christened the dog Smut, for the coal black coat on it, though it didn't answer to its name or to anything else, went its own wild way when it wasn't tied to Loveless by a string. Out in the woods all night sometimes, following its nose through the tuckamore after partridge and grouse and rabbit. Showing up at Loveless's door in the morning, filthy and bedraggled and famished. Sweetland expected the dog to disappear altogether someday, taken off by a fox or an eagle, or by coyotes if they ever made it out as far as the island.

He passed Queenie Coffin at her window on his way along, blowing smoke into the open air. She called him over and he leaned against the window frame as she finished her cigarette. She was in her quilted dressing gown, her hair done up in curlers, the old ones he remembered from his mother, held in place with bobby pins. Lipstick on the filter of her cigarette, a book sitting open in her lap. It was rare to see Queenie without a book in arm's reach. She was a voracious reader of paint-by-number romances, of murder mysteries so predictable she could have written the endings herself fifty pages in. It was just a way to kill time, she said, to pass the afternoons, the television on with the sound on mute.

"Cool night," she said.

"She's brisk all right. See you planted your garden the week."

"Yes, don't be trampling them all," she said.

"They'll likely die of the cold if they comes up anyway, maid."

Queenie laughed and coughed wetly into her fist. A voice called from upstairs and she lifted her head to answer it. "I'm just talking to my boyfriend," she shouted.

Sweetland could hear the muffled sound of the television up there.

"Hayward says you wasn't at the town meeting."

"I was putting in the spuds. I'll set aside a barrel for you the fall."

She waved the hand holding her cigarette. "I won't be here the fall."

"You been saying that twenty year or more, Queenie."

She was about to answer him but started coughing in a long, vicious round. It sounded to Sweetland like all her insides were sodden. "Time to give these up," she said when she caught her breath. She took a drag and leaned toward the open air to exhale.

Sweetland tried to remember the last time he'd seen Queenie outside that house. When her oldest children were still youngsters, he thought, before they had the indoor plumbing installed—1969 or '70 that was, sometime after the moon landing. Queenie flipping through the grainy pictures in a *Life* magazine, waving it at her husband. They can put a man on the moon, she told him, we can bloody well have a flush toilet. Hayward argued it was all a put-on, that the images were fakes taken in some Hollywood backlot. Half the people in Chance Cove thought as much. But Queenie got her toilet.

She hadn't crossed the threshold of the house in all the years since. She stood just inside the open door or sat at the window, calling people over for a chat while she smoked. She'd taken in one of the lifeboat survivors when Sweetland towed them in, washed and fed the man and gave him a bed the night they stayed in the cove, but she wouldn't walk down to see him ferried out to the Coast Guard vessel when they left. Three of her children married at the church on the point and she had waited in the kitchen in her best dress, the wedding party walking up to have their photos taken with her in the parlour. A public health nurse came out on the ferry twice a year to have a listen to her heart, to warn her off the cigarettes. Everyone who went off the island for business or to visit family brought back two or three Harlequins to add to her library.

"How's your book?" Sweetland asked her.

She lifted her chin like she was pointing to something across the room and sighed. "I wish she'd stop sending these things to me, it's nothing only an aggravation."

Her daughter was trying to rehabilitate her lowbrow taste in reading material with what Queenie called "serious" books—literary novels, prize-winners, Oprah's picks. Sandra sent them down from Edmonton with encouraging notes scribbled inside the covers. Queenie never cracked a spine, but for the few written by Newfoundlanders or about Newfoundland. She took those on as a kind of patriotic duty, though it was a torture to get through them. They were every one depressing, she said. Or nothing happened. Or there was no point to the story. Half the books supposedly set in Newfoundland were nowhere Queenie recognized and she felt insulted by their claim on her life. They all sounds like they was written by townies, she liked to say.

She turned the open book face down on her lap. "You heard Hayward signed on to the package."

"I been informed."

"Leaves you in a hard spot, I imagine."

"I still got Loveless," Sweetland said, and they both had a laugh over that. He leaned his shoulder on the window ledge. "Never thought you'd allow Hayward to sign on, just the same."

"It's Sandra talked him into it," she said. "Going to put an apartment in her downstairs for us. Can't wait to have us up there, she says." Queenie made the noise in her throat again, to say it was just as likely she'd set foot on the moon as in Alberta.

Sweetland didn't give much for the possibility either. Jesse came to visit Queenie now and then and they sat through a showing of *Titanic* on his laptop. Or the boy would ask after her favourite book or movie or song, about when the toilet was put in or where her children were living now and what they did for work. Queenie had answered the same questions ten thousand times but she had endless patience for the boy. His monotonous interrogation one more tiny room she'd chosen to close herself inside.

"I was born upstairs here," she said. "Five youngsters I had, in the same room I was born in. Hayward can sign whatever he likes," she said and she stubbed her cigarette in an ashtray beside the chair. "I'll be leaving this house in a box."

He was up before light, at his table with tea and the laptop, checking the marine forecast. CBC radio nattering in the background, a plant closing in Burin, the fisheries minister pledging retraining and make-work projects for the people affected.

He should just leave the goddamn radio off, Sweetland thought, enjoy the peace awhile. He headed out into the chill, walked down toward the dock through the stillness, until Pilgrim's dog sent up a racket to mark his passing.

"Shut up, Diesel," he said. The dog strained at her chain and carried on barking until Sweetland reached the waterline. There was a single street light on the government wharf, half a dozen boats moored alongside. Sweetland turned left, away from the wharf, and walked out the arm toward his fishing stage. It was a tidy two-storey building, the second floor a twine loft where they'd knit their cod traps once upon a time. No one knew how old the building was, but Sweetland had seen it standing over the landwash in a picture of the cove from a hundred years ago. It hadn't been used to clean or store salt cod in a generation, but he kept the building in pristine condition, the roof patched and tarred spring and fall, the outside walls ochred red. Even when he worked at the lighthouse he kept it up, scraped and puttied the windows, replaced the shores. Your little museum, Clara called it.

He set the chainsaw and gas can and axe and lunch bag on the stagehead and climbed down into his boat, checked over the motor, the VHF.

Jesse was out of breath when he clomped onto the longers. Shirt out of his pants, his face bruised with sleep. A jacket hanging limp in his hand.

Sweetland nodded up to him. "Hand me down the chainsaw," he said, and a thought struck him. "You're not planning on bringing anyone along, are you?"

"Just Hollis," the boy said.

"I'm not taking Hollis."

"He won't say nothing."

"He never liked being on the water when he was alive. I'm not having the fucker in the boat now. Are you coming or not?"

The boy turned away to carry on a hushed conversation with the dead man. Sweetland couldn't say which way it would go until Jesse picked up the axe and stepped down onto the gunwale.

It was nearly light by the time they turned to the mouth of the cove, pushing out into the whitecaps on the open ocean. A three-hour steam to the bay where he cut his wood and Jesse fell asleep halfway across. Sweetland stood with his face in the wind, watching the shoreline come at him, rising out of the ocean like a slow-moving tidal wave of rock and spruce.

He woke Jesse before he eased into the bay, letting the youngster take the wheel. Steep hills above them, a mix of birch and var among the spruce. "Bring her around over by Nancy's Rocks," Sweetland said, and he walked out along the bow, tying up at a rusted iron ring drilled into the granite several lifetimes ago. They stepped off onto the shoreline together, the boy bounding up into the trees, eager as a dog.

_____

The wind came up through the day and the ocean chopped at them as soon as they cleared the bay on the return trip, the boat riding sluggish with a full load of wood. They swung into the lee of Little Sweetland as they passed, to get out of the worst of it a few minutes. The island humpbacked and barren and solitary. Two single-room cabins on the south side of Tilt Cove, satellite dishes screwed to the walls. Sweetland had never seen anyone use those cabins, though they'd been there for years.

"This is where they put the buffaloes," Jesse said.

Every time they passed Tilt Cove he wanted this fact confirmed and then insisted on hearing the story behind it, the narrative like a toll required to make the passage.

"This is the place."

"How many people was it lived here?" Jesse asked, which was a surprise to Sweetland. The boy had never shown the slightest interest in the detail before.

"There was almost a hundred lived in there when I was your age," Sweetland said.

"What happened to them?"

"They was all shifted out by the Smallwood government in the sixties."

"Where did they go?"

"Here and there," he said. "Placentia Bay. Burgeo, Hermitage. St. John's."

"They're all dead now."

Sweetland nodded over that. He didn't know anymore where the boy's head was going to take things. "Most of them, I expect."

"You helped get them ashore," Jesse said.

"Who's that?"

"The buffaloes."

"It was as good as a concert," he said.

Just home from his first stint in Toronto and working as a deckhand on a schooner shipping dry goods and salt fish along the south coast. The *Ceciliene Marie*. They sailed across the strait to Cape Breton to pick up the bison, the animals harried into individual containers and a crane lifting them off the dock, setting them into an improvised pen in the hold. Two dozen altogether, most of them yearling females. Two bulls. Unlikely-looking things, a thousand pounds each and most of the weight in the massive head and shoulders, top-heavy on those stick legs. The opposite of icebergs, Sweetland thought, nine-tenths above the water. The animals were walleyed, drugged-up and stinking of shit and fear. Five had died in the railcar on the trip from Manitoba, and Sweetland thought it would be a miracle if any survived the ocean crossing.

It was the wildlife department wanting to add another large game animal to the few in the province landed them there. They planned to set the bison out on Little Sweetland to determine there was no disease risk to local animals, after which the herd was meant to be introduced to the larger island of Newfoundland. Though that step was never taken.

The *Ceciliene Marie* sailed past Sweetland to overnight in Miquelon. They got drunk there, the wildlife officers and Sweetland, anchored off the last crumb of New France that was still a French territory. It was the only time he'd ever visited the place. The wildlife officers were all Newfoundlanders but for the fellow in charge, an American from Nevada who requested the stop in Miquelon. He took every chance he could get, he said, to spend a night in France.

Wet and mauzy when they arrived at Tilt Cove the following morning. Dozens of people had sailed out from Fortune Bay and the Burin to watch the event, the harbour packed with boats and spectators on the roofs of the houses still standing in the cove.

There was nowhere for the freighter to dock and they anchored off in deeper water, the buffalo loaded into their individual crates to be ferried ashore on a raft built by the wildlife officers. They'd hired Duke Fewer to tow the raft back and forth with his longliner. Sweetland was on the crane for the first dozen transfers, lowering the boxes onto the flat beside the schooner. The bison sedated and more or less quiet as they were hauled onto dry land. Staggering into the open with a stunned air about them, shaking those big rig shoulders and prancing drunkenly up away from the water. The people on the roofs hooting and shouting in disbelief as the mythological creatures wandered about in a forlorn herd, travelling and turning in a huddle, pawing at the sedge moss, sniffing the salt air.

"They aren't really buffaloes," Jesse announced.

"Is that right?" Sweetland said.

"Bison aren't related to water buffaloes or African buffaloes."

"What is it they're related to, then?"

"Cows," Jesse said. "And goats."

It was some Google search the boy was quoting, a universe of facts at his fingertips. As if, Sweetland thought, he wasn't tiresome enough on his own. "Be that as it may," he said, "does Your Highness mind if, for the purposes of this story, I calls them buffalo?"

"I don't mind," Jesse said.

Sweetland took a turn on the raft after lunch and he stood with a wildlife officer as each crate was floated in, holding the top of the box to keep his place on the narrow flat. Ashore, he stood at the rear as the officer opened the door. If it needed encouragement to step into the open, Sweetland prodded the animal's backside with a stick through a custom-made hole.

They'll come right through the wall if they minds to kick, the officer warned him, so watch yourself.

The animals had all been sedated in the morning but they seemed to be crawling out of that fog as the afternoon wore on. The next-to-last cow was bawling before she was lifted off the schooner, rocking the crate in the air. They cinched the container to the flat, the buffalo's hooves making the walls shake as they spidered around the outside. The smell and motion of the water seemed to unhinge her altogether and she slammed against the box as they started toward the landing site. All the wooden joints coming loose as the animal panicked inside, the container coming apart before they'd travelled thirty yards toward shore. The wildlife officer pitched into the water as the buffalo pushed for the clear and he grabbed a corner of the raft to hold himself afloat. Sweetland made a wild, stupid lunge for the animal's tail.

"As if I could have picked her up like a rat," he said to Jesse.

There wasn't room enough on the raft for the creature to turn around. She tried to catch herself at the edge but bowled over, top-heavy as she was. A splintered wall of the crate was floating beside the raft and the buffalo fell onto it, the wooden sheet tipping beneath her weight. Sweetland standing over her as she thrashed, trying to right herself. She went down slowly at first, submerging like a boat taking on water. But once she was under she sank like a stone, as though she was on a line and being dragged down from below. That dark face staring up at Sweetland on the surface, eyes wide, bubbles streaming from the massive nostrils. He could see her descending through the clear water for a long, long time.

"Could you see her on the bottom?" Jesse asked.

"Too deep out there near the schooner," he said. "Lost sight of her after awhile."

The rest of the animals survived the trip, but for one of the bulls who died within two days of the landing. Calves were born every spring and the remnants of the herd hung on for almost thirty years, though the buffalo never managed to take hold on the island. Sweetland would watch for them on the headlands as he passed by Little Sweetland, those shaggy outlines adrift in the mist like something called up from the underworld.

"What happened to them all?" Jesse asked.

"No one really knows. They used to walk out on the cliffs to lick the salt off the rocks. There's a good many got killed that way. Could be poachers took some of them."

The boy considered that possibility a moment. "You ever tasted buffalo?"

"Now, Jesse," he said. "That would be telling, wouldn't it."

He docked at the government wharf, for the flat expanse of it. Sent Jesse up to the house for his ATV and trailer, unloading the wood from the boat while he waited, throwing the ten-foot lengths up on the cement surface. Loveless stood across the way, leaning against a building about the size of an outhouse where the island's bank machine was located. He had his lapdog at his feet, a bit of string tied around its neck as a leash. He had an unlit pipe in his mouth that he chewed from one corner to the other, running it back and forth like a gear shift.

"More wood," Loveless said finally.

"You've got a real gift for observation, Mr. Loveless."

"Duke says you got enough split and stacked to keep hell in flames half of eternity."

"I'm planning on sticking around a good while."

Loveless looked up toward the ring of houses. "I heard Hayward signed on to the package," he said. And when Sweetland didn't respond he said, "Just the two of us now."

"Two is as much as we needs," Sweetland said.

Loveless said nothing then, his pipe repeating and repeating its mechanical journey.

"Your little dog was running loose out the arm last night," Sweetland said.

"Can't keep 'en barred in, Mose. I swear the little fucker knows how to turn a doorknob."

Sweetland had a look at the animal. There was some other P dog in the mix, Pekinese or Pomeranian, Loveless couldn't remember which. Paid a fortune for it, Sweetland guessed, although Loveless refused to confess how much. Sara would never have allowed such a sentimental purchase where animals were concerned. Lotsa dog on the island, she'd have said. No good for working, that one. He's hypoallergenic, Loveless liked to say, quoting the breeder's advertisement, as if that excused the expense.

"You got to get the dog fixed," Sweetland said. "Won't wander half so much after that."

Loveless reached down and the animal stretched on its back to have its belly scratched, the legs spread wide. "That's a darlin set of balls he got," Loveless said, and he gave the testicles an affectionate little rub. "Be a sin to cut them off."

Sweetland shook his head. He tossed the logs with a steady rhythm, every movement unhurried and deliberate. The wood cast up on the dock like it was coming off a conveyor belt. "Your cow ready to have her calf yet?" he asked.

"Any day."

"Going to look after it yourself, are you?"

"Sara's no use to me dead and gone."

"You were no use to her, alive and well."

"I learned a thing or two off her," Loveless said. "Never you mind."

"She didn't teach you a goddamn thing about playing chess."

Loveless stared blankly, thrown by the sudden turn in the conversation.

"You fucked up the chess game with Duke," Sweetland said.

Loveless took the pipe from his mouth, pointed the wet end down at Sweetland. "Duke told me it was a smart move I made," he said.

Sweetland straightened up from the work, put his hands on his hips. "How many times have Duke lost a game of chess in the shop?"

Loveless raised the pipe to answer but realized there was nothing he could say to that point. He clamped the end back in his teeth and turned to watch Jesse creeping down the hill with the quad. The boy swung the machine around so it sat next to the growing pile of wood.

Jesse took off his helmet and walked over to crouch an arm's length away from the dog, wanting to know how old it was and where it was born and what it liked to eat and if it could be trained to use a toilet. Cut from the same cloth, man and boy, Sweetland thought. And regretted thinking it straight away. There was something wrong with the young one, but he was a different creature than Loveless altogether.

They loaded the trailer with Loveless as an audience and Sweetland dropped Jesse at his door on the way up the hill.

"You going out to check the snares tomorrow?"

"Tomorrow's Sunday."

"What about Monday?"

"If the weather's half decent."

"I could go with you."

"You got school," Sweetland said.

He drove along the side of his house to the shed. Stood the green wood against the fence at the end of his property. It would be next spring before he could cut and junk it up. He had longers in various stages of drying around the property, all waiting for the chainsaw. He was soon going to have to find somewhere else to pack it away. The back porch was full, one side of the shed stacked floor to ceiling with junks in rows, and more along the lee side wall. The twine shed and the old outhouse long ago converted to hold firewood. He'd stolen a section of metal culvert left over from road construction on the Burin, towed it across on Hayward Coffin's punt. Packed it front to back, forty or fifty cords of wood, he figured. People said he would never live long enough to burn it all and he couldn't stay out of the woods after more. It was like having money in the bank.

Sweetland came around at the government wharf with his boat-load of survivors in tow and he threw a line up to Duke Fewer. Call out to the lighthouse, he said. See if Bob-Sam can raise the Coast Guard.

We haven't heard nothing about a ship gone down, Duke said.

Well maybe they was out for a row and got lost. Give Bob-Sam a call.

They were small, slight men, wide-eyed and unsteady on their feet. Sweetland climbed in to lend a hand as they were lifted up onto the dock. From there they were helped along to the Fisherman's Hall where the women swaddled them in blankets and set about spooning soup into their mouths.

There were two still sitting aft when the boat was emptied out, younger than the rest, Sweetland thought. The larger of the two with an arm around the other's shoulders, a blue windbreaker spread over top of them. They looked like they had no intention of moving from where they were sitting.

Sweetland called out to Duke without looking away from them. Go get the Reverend, he said.

The younger of the two was dead and had been for some time. The one still living tried to fend them off with his free hand when they came toward him.

Leave them be a minute, the Reverend said.

That young one won't be any less dead a minute from now, Duke said.

Hand me a blanket, would you, Moses?

The Reverend covered the two where they sat in the boat and settled beside them. I'll call when I need you, he said. He held a bottle of water to the lips of the man still alive and wiped his face with a handkerchief and spoke to him in a low voice. Praying, Sweetland supposed, though it likely wasn't the kind of prayer they were accustomed to. The man didn't take his eyes from the Reverend's face. After a while the Reverend stood and called up to Sweetland on the dock.

They had to shift the dead boy out of the way and it was awkward work. There was almost no weight to him, but rigour had set in, the body like an elaborate piece of furniture. The living man almost as stiff and ungainly, hunched and stepping gingerly, like he was walking over broken glass.

Bring the other one up to the church, the Reverend said to Sweetland. I'll be along in a minute.

He and Duke waited until they were out of sight before lifting the corpse onto the dock. They carted it to the church, still in its sitting pose, the knees bent almost to the chest. Sweetland had the corpse under the arms, its head craned to one side so it almost seemed the face was lifted to look up at him and he kept his eyes straight ahead to avoid the sight of it. Without discussing it, they went past the main entrance of the church to the side door near the back, into the room where the Reverend kept a desk and hung his vestments alongside the purple choir gowns on a piece of pipe. They couldn't see setting the dead boy on the Reverend's desk and placed him on the floor instead. But they both felt it was an indignity to leave him there and Sweetland went to get the table in the vestibule used for laying out the Sunday bulletins.

The Reverend came in the door with Ruthie right behind him then, and they all trooped up the centre aisle to the back where they lifted the corpse onto the tabletop. The Reverend turned to Ruth. Have we got a sheet or anything? he asked.

She was one of the church women who came in early on Sundays and stayed after the service to tidy and spent two evenings a week in the sanctuary to sweep the floor and wash the windows and polish the candle holders on the altar. She went to a cupboard crowded with Christmas wreaths and blank bulletins and mimeograph fluid and dug around at the back until she found a yellowed altar cloth. Pregnant with Clara then, though no one in the cove knew it yet. She helped the Reverend cover the dead boy with the sheet and they stood around him with their hands crossed in front of themselves.

Don't seem right to leave him back here on he's own, Ruth said.

We'll bring him out into the sanctuary once we've found beds for the rest of them. Have someone sit with him.

Ruth turned to the minister, placed a hand on his arm. Could we say the Lord's Prayer?

He hesitated a moment, as if there was something in the notion that made him uncomfortable. I don't see the harm in it, he said finally.

3

THE FERRY SAILED BY THE BREAKWATER through a blear of rain. The ocean beyond in an uproar. The deckhands hunched in neon-yellow slickers as they threw down the hawsers and winched the gangplank to the government wharf.

All of it slightly out of focus from where Sweetland sat watching at his kitchen table, edges and colours blurred by the drifting rain. Two passengers disembarked, men in jean jackets and ball caps, carting duffle bags. They paused halfway down the steps, craning their necks toward the deckhands leaning over the rail above them. They seemed oblivious to the weather, their gestures expansive, unhurried. The man standing behind pushed the other forward finally and they skittered down to the dock.

Sweetland glanced up at the calendar thumbtacked to the wall near the phone, trying to guess how long it had been since the Priddle brothers had come home from Alberta. Before Christmas sometime. The two men hefted their duffle bags and started toward their father's house, over on Church Side. Heads bent against the angle of the climb and the pelting rain.

Batten down the hatches, Sweetland thought.

He opened the laptop to play some poker, hoping the rain might let up before he went out to the shed. Heard the door three hands in, looked up to see Reet Verge come through the porch. She was sausaged into a pink Bench sweater, the sleeves down over her hands against the chill, the hoodie high on her head. The pink material was blood red where it had gotten wet across the crown and shoulders and the expanse of her massive breasts. She looked like a parody of the Grim Reaper, making her rounds.

She leaned against the door frame. "You aren't watching porn over there, are you, Moses?"

"Girl on girl," he said. "How's Your Worship this morning?"

"When are you going to let me clean up that head of yours?"

He hadn't spoken to Reet since his last haircut, eight months ago. She'd used the opportunity to lobby for the package and berate him for being so goddamn stubborn. It was unfair practice, he thought, waylaying him there under the silver cape with his hair only half cut. Waving those scissors at his face. He swore never to go back to her and he was in desperate shape by now. He was tempted to let Duke have a go at his hair, just to avoid the woman.

"I'm growing it out," he said. "Willie Nelson braids, I was thinking."

They watched each other awkwardly a moment. Sweetland trying to guess her age. Fifty? Fifty-five, more like. Old enough to be partying with the smatter of reporters and photographers who showed up on the island when the Sri Lankan boat people passed through. Doing shots of peach schnapps at the Fisherman's Hall with the last straggler from *Saturday Night*, who'd come out to do a follow-up that October, its effect on the people in the community, what they made of it all. He got stranded in an early rage of snow and wind that kept the ferry docked in Hermitage three days. The power went out the first night of the storm and they fell back on kerosene lamps, on arias of static drifting from battery-powered radios. The reporter drinking all day to deal with the boredom, the creeping claustrophobia.

Good God, he said, it can't keep going like this, can it?

Out here, Reet said, a snowstorm is like getting your skin. You never knows how many inches you're going to get. Or how long it's going to last.

She was a hard ticket, Rita. Raised two boys on her own after her man moved out west for work and hooked up with a missus from Catalina. Both of her children through school and long gone to the Canadian mainland. She made half a living in her kitchen, cutting hair. Started up the museum with a make-work grant from the feds. She'd been the town's mayor for three years, a position she didn't want and held by acclamation since Glad Vatcher washed his hands of it. All the negotiations on resettling the community went through her. She managed to use Sweetland's recalcitrance as a bargaining chip to double the government's offer, the extra money enough to bring most of the last holdouts onside—an irony Sweetland was aware of though Reet was smart enough not to bring it up in his company.

"You know I'd rather be staying," she said finally. "If it was up to me."

"The will of the masses," he said.

"Oh kiss my arse."

"Careful now, Reet," he said. "I'm all worked up watching the porn over here."

"It would take more than a bit of porn," she said, "to work up an old fucker like you."

He almost asked her to sit down then. He'd never spent more than the length of a haircut alone with her but he'd always enjoyed the razor wire of her company—her epically foul mouth, her gumption, her raw savvy. She walked across to the table and sat before he offered, though she left the soaked hood up.

"I been elected to have a talk with you," she said.

"Who did you beat out for that job?"

"Acclamation," she said with a rueful smile.

"Democracy in action." Sweetland spread his hands on the tabletop.

"You know Loveless is going to give in," she said. "Sooner or later."

He shrugged and looked away. "There's still Queenie," he said.

"She've never showed her face at the Hall to say she's against this. And Hayward have signed the papers. So it's all coming down to you, Moses."

He spread his hands again, to say *So be it.*

"The question I'm supposed to have answered is, What's it going to take to bring you on board?"

"You got nothing I'm interested in."

"No," she said, and she shook a finger at him out of the cuff of her hoodie. "No fucking way. You are not going to hold this up because of your Christly feelings, Moses. Now you name your price and I'll see what I can do to get it paid."

"Not for sale," he said.

She shook her head. "Jesus," she said. "You thinks you're doing God's work, is that it?"

Sweetland half smiled, thinking she was making a joke.

"I can't figure what else is in your mind," she said. "To cause so much grief to the whole goddamn town and be able to sleep at night."

She wasn't about to leave without having a racket, he realized, and he got up to walk by her, took his jacket down off a nail in the porch.

"You thinks this will all go away if you ignores it long enough," she said. "But it won't."

"That's a threat, is it?"

"That's a simple fact. People got too much on the line to just let it drop."

"Now that sounds like a threat."

She shook her head again but didn't turn to him. Her face hidden by the hood. "Someone is going to end up getting hurt in all this," she said. "And you'll have no one but yourself and God to blame for it. You mark my words."

He let himself out the door and pushed it to behind him, hid out in the shed then until he was sure Reet had left. He put in a fire and opened the main doors, the air smelling of wet hay and woodsmoke. He spent the better part of the day working in the bay of the shed, replacing the floor of the trailer he'd built for the quad twenty years before. All the while turning Reet's accusation over in his head. *God's work*, she said, trying to goad him into talking. Everyone but Duke was after Sweetland to explain himself these days, to offer a rationale for his refusal to leave. He'd tried to parse out an argument in his head for awhile, but every attempt to name what he was holding onto made it seem small, almost ridiculous.

Ruthie had always said any woman crazy enough to marry Sweetland would shoot him dead in the end. It was his reticence she was talking about, his bullheaded diffidence. He could admit to hardly knowing why he felt a particular way about anything. The stronger the feeling, the less able he was to break it down into identifiable categories, into cause and effect. But he wasn't accustomed to being called out for the lack and it served only to make him increasingly close-mouthed and obstinate. His conviction more firmly anchored as the holdouts dwindled, as if to offset the loss in numbers with a blind certainty.

He found himself enjoying it almost, to be the one knot they couldn't untangle. Holding on like grim death and halfways invigorated by the effort. Twisted, Ruthie used to say of him, and Sweetland couldn't argue her assessment. Or change his way in the world.

He finished the job by mid-afternoon, washed up at the kitchen sink and walked the path to Duke's shop. The rain coming down in sheets. Wince Pilgrim was sitting beside the chessboard, Duke facing him in the barber's chair, one insect leg hooked over the arm.

"Look what the wind blew in," Duke said.

Pilgrim lifted his face to the ceiling, listening. The blind eyes glaucous, murky as a fog. "That's Moses, is it?"

"The man himself."

"Jesse idn't with you?" Sweetland asked.

"Clara got him doing his homework up to the house," Pilgrim said.

Jesse used to spend an hour at the barbershop every day after school, but Clara seemed to be making an effort to wean him off his island habits.

Or maybe it was meant to punish Sweetland. He'd walked down expecting to see the boy and was almost sorry to have come now. He wrestled out of his wet jacket, shook it twice before hanging it on the coat rack. He walked across to stand by the heat of the stove, Pilgrim's head turning to follow his footsteps. There was a kettle on the floor by the woodbox and Sweetland filled it in the corner sink.

A figure flicked past the window and the door pushed open, the weather scurrying in just ahead of the Reverend. He turned quickly and slammed the door, leaning against it like he was trying to bar a rabid animal outside. "Mercy," he said.

"Is that you, Reverend?" Pilgrim asked.

"That's some day out there now," the Reverend said.

Duke climbed out of the chair in sections, swiped at the worn leather with a towel. "Have a seat," he said. "Moses just got the kettle on."

"I'll sit by the board."

"That's what you won't," Duke said. "Seat of honour."

"The first shall be last," the Reverend said. "The last shall be first. You know how that goes." And he sat in the wooden chair across the board from Pilgrim.

"I thought you was retired of all that business," Sweetland said.

The Reverend laughed. "A man of the cloth," he said. "Practising or no."

He was dressed in black slacks, a black suit coat, and white shirt buttoned to the throat under his jacket. He sat with his hands folded in his lap, clean-shaven and his white hair oiled back from his forehead. He looked like someone keeping a body company at a wake. The man's business like a stain and no way on God's earth to scour it out now it had set.

"You'll have a cup?" Duke asked.

"I wouldn't say no."

The Reverend was Welsh by birth and had moved to Canada as a student. He was assigned a Newfoundland parish in his early twenties and got married there, he and his wife taking on churches in half a dozen Newfoundland communities over the next forty-five years. He'd come to Sweetland in the seventies and extended his appointment two or three times over, though his wife agitated against it more publicly as time passed. The Reverend was heartbroken to leave when he did, everyone remarked on it.

Sweetland said, "What have I got to work with there?"

The Reverend glanced down at the chess board. He never participated in a game, but he liked to watch its progress, offering advice and suggestions.

"Everyone but Moses have washed their hands of it," Duke said. "They're after me to start a new one up."

"I'm still thinking on it," Sweetland said.

"I got half a mind to put you on a clock."

"I could say a prayer for you," the Reverend offered.

"Save it for No Chance Cove," Duke said.

Sweetland was about to say something in response but thought better of it, for the company.

The church on the point was closed up when the Reverend moved back to Sweetland seven years ago, widowed and retired from preaching. He bought an empty house out behind the church and spent most of his time reading and meandering along the island paths. No one knew what to make of his return or quite how to take him. In his first months back, he made a habit of stopping by Sweetland's shed on weekday mornings. He'd sit in one of the ripped vinyl kitchen chairs against the wall and waste hours of Sweetland's time, listening to the open-line show on the portable radio above the workbench, passing a comment on one issue or other.

He expected the man was working up the nerve to ask after Ruthie, how she was at the end, and if she'd said anything at all that ought to be passed on to the Reverend. It made Sweetland feel panicked to see the man stick his head in the door, though his vocation and bearing made it impossible to send him on his way. Sweetland took to putting a fire in the wood stove, opening the vents and stoking it until the shed was stif-ling. The Reverend would strip down to his dress shirt, but couldn't bring himself to undo even the top button, and he'd sit there with beads of sweat popping on his forehead.

You don't mind the heat.

Likes it warm, Sweetland told him. They says it's good for the joints. You want a cup of tea?

Lord, no.

The Reverend was forced to abandon the fiery pit after half an hour and eventually he gave up the visits altogether. Sweetland lost a lot of good wood in those months, but he considered it well worth the price.

That first fall, the Reverend began volunteering at the school, where he took on Jesse as a pet project, developing a remedial program to help the boy do his sums and to curtail his outbursts and his spells of mindless rocking and chanting. It was the Reverend who'd found the doctor the boy was seeing in St. John's and made the arrangements for his appointments. He hired Clara Pilgrim to come to his house two mornings a week to sweep the floor and wash his three changes of identical clothes. He could be prevailed upon to open the old church to officiate at the occasional wedding or christening or funeral but refused to consider regular Sunday services. To all appearances he'd settled in to live out the rest of his days as a semi-private citizen on the island, before the talk of resettlement.

The Reverend turned to Sweetland. "Has Jesse said anything to you about his time with the doctor?"

"Not so much, no."

Sweetland thought he caught the briefest moment of skepticism or annoyance passing over the clergyman's face. But it disappeared so quickly he might have imagined it.

"They're saying the more structure we can give him, the better," the Reverend said. "I was thinking of having him come to the house for sessions during the summer. Three times a week or so."

"That'll sound like more school to Jesse."

"That's what Clara thinks," he said. He raised his free hand and smoothed the silver hair down around his ears, like he was massaging a question free in there. He said, "Do you think you might be able to talk to him about it?"

Sweetland smiled uneasily. "I'd rather stay clear of that business, if it's all the same to you."

"He thinks a lot of your opinion."

"More than his mother does, for damn sure."

"Between us now," the Reverend said, "it was Clara's idea to ask for your help with this."

"Was it her idea to have you do the asking?"

"That was my idea," Pilgrim said. His face turned away from the room, sheepish.

"I volunteered," the Reverend said, "to bring it up with you."

Sweetland shifted where he stood. Exhausted suddenly and wanting to be left alone. It was all he could do to hold off telling them to go fuck themselves, the works of them.

"It would mean a lot to Clara," the Reverend said. "And to me."

"I'll have to sit with it a bit," Sweetland said, and the Reverend raised his mug to say that was as much as he could ask.

The men bantered back and forth awhile longer then about the Priddle brothers arriving on the ferry that morning, about the hockey playoffs and the weather, talking in the polite, stilted fashion of near-strangers. When the Reverend finished his tea, he went on his way.

"I always feels like that cocksucker is spying on us," Duke said after the door pulled to.

"He's just lonely," Pilgrim said.

"If he didn't want to be lonely he should have gone to St. John's somewhere. Moved into a home for retired clergy."

"There's no such place, is there?"

"Jesus Christ, Mose," Duke said. "Would you slap some sense into that one."

"Can't be done. God knows I've tried."

Pilgrim stood up and set his mug on the seat behind him. "I can get this kind of treatment at home," he said. He stopped at the door. "You going to talk to Jesse like he asked?"

"Go on the fuck home out of it," Sweetland said.

Duke stood at the window to watch Pilgrim make his blind way up the hill in the driving rain, waiting until he'd seen him in through his door. Turned back to the room. "He've got an unnatural interest in that youngster," he said.

"Who?" Sweetland asked, though he'd heard Duke make the accusation a hundred times over.

"The Reverend."

"Jesus, Duke."

"It's not normal, is all I'm saying. Trying to get him alone down to the house all summer."

"I imagine he thinks he's doing God's work."

Duke shook his head. "What's-his-name Bin Laden thought he was doing that, for chrissakes."

It was too miserable to go out in the evening and Sweetland tried to pass the time with a hand of poker. He poured himself a glass of rye but didn't touch it, barely looked at the cards as they flashed up and he lost his stake within an hour. He sat turning his drink in circles on the table. The old house creaked in each gust, the wind throwing buckets of rain against the windows. One of the last hockey games of the season grinding on in the living room, the noise of the crowd rising and falling like a weather of its own. He half expected the Priddle boys to show up, barrelling into the house shit-faced and demanding a drink, going on about the cost of housing in Fort Mac, the money they make working overtime, the skin you could get in the bars up there.

The Priddles were Irish twins, the second born ten months after the first, and they had never done a solitary thing in their lives. They swam and fished and set fires, they drank and poached moose and gambled together. They co-owned a boat and took over their father's crab licence a few seasons until they jacked up to work on the mainland. Disappearing for six or eight months during construction season in Nova Scotia or Ontario, spending the winter months at home, collecting their pogey and making a general nuisance of themselves. They were arrested in Burin for possession with intent to traffic, pleading down to simple possession and a four-month sentence at Her Majesty's Penitentiary in St. John's. In their forties now, and neither had married or shown the slightest inclination to settle down. They were hard men, the two of them, and the other's company seemed to push each to be harder and more reckless than he might have been on his own.

Ned Priddle never quite recovered after Effie died giving birth to Keith. Ned didn't say as much, but he acted as if he blamed the infant boys equally for the loss of his wife and resented their subsequent claims on him. They were left to their own devices as they grew older, more so after their father remarried. They spent most of their time on the water or in the woods. They built a ten-by-ten shed in the valley on the far side of Sweetland, the logs chinked with moss, a single tiny window salvaged from an old wheelhouse, and they more or less lived out there, going feral like cats in an abandoned barn. Over the years the boys had built and rebuilt the cabin in stages, dragging building materials over by quad. It was where they went to get away from it all, they said, when life in Chance Cove got too hectic for their liking.

The Priddles were too wild for most people to take, growing up. Sweetland was one of the few who would have them over the threshold and he saw more of them than their own father through their teens. He lived alone and there was nothing he owned that couldn't be pasted together if it was broken. And he felt he was making something up to Effie by watching out to the boys. Though it wasn't in him to settle on or name exactly what that was.

They'd show up after school and sit, incongruously, to episodes of *The Care Bears*, *The Smurfs*. They came over Sunday nights for the television wrestling and he'd give them a glass of homebrew to drink. They had christened themselves with wrestling names—Tidal Wave and Rip Tide—the two brothers beating hell out of each other on the floor during commercials. Sweetland called them Pancake and Over Easy, the Golden Priddles, a reference they didn't get but were insulted by nonetheless. Keith was the bigger of the two and Sweetland had to wade into the fray to save Barry from the worst of it on occasion. They'd trade insults from opposite chairs awhile then, crybaby and cocksucker being the favourites.

The brothers would bring him a brace of rabbit now and then, helped dig his potatoes in the fall. They'd go across with him after wood and they were sluts for the work, they cut and sawed and hauled with the same gleeful abandon he saw in them as they inflicted pile-drivers and sleeper holds on each other in his living room. He'd pay them for the help with a dozen beer and a couple of skin mags, and they considered themselves well compensated.

Six years now they'd been working a see-saw contract in Fort McMurray, three or four weeks on the job, two weeks off to fly home and drink and smoke and snort all the money they'd made. It was a way of life that had done nothing to make them less trouble. They settled on cocaine as their recreational drug of choice, and the manic high added a nasty flavour to their recklessness. Barry lost the tip of his index finger the afternoon they'd taken turns putting out a lit match with a .22, one brother at a time holding the little flame at arm's length, thirty paces off. Barry so high he felt no real pain. Wrapped the finger in a handkerchief and took another shot at his brother's match.

They showed up on Sweetland less often as time went on, preferring somewhere with easier access to drugs and women. But everyone was on edge when they came home. It was like setting a couple of wild dogs loose in a hotel room. The place wasn't half big enough or particularly suited to the life they wanted to live in it, and there was always some damage in their wake. Sweetland tried to keep his distance, though it was impossible to avoid them altogether.

He raised the glass of rye to his mouth but didn't taste it. The weather was too miserable for even the Priddles to venture out, he guessed. When the last of the day's light was well and truly gone he passed into the living room to flick off the television and went out through the hall in the dark.

Sweetland woke before light, turned heavily in his bed. Drifted off another hour or so. It was nearly eight by the time he got up, walking out to the bathroom in his jockeys and undershirt. He ran the tub while he shaved the uninjured side of his face, where the whisker still grew. Soaked in the scalding water then, as long as he could stand the idleness. He took his "good clothes" from the wardrobe in the bedroom, a thirty-year-old pair of dress pants and a white button-down shirt he'd bought to wear to his mother's funeral. Ran a comb through the oily weave of his hair before he went downstairs.

He refrained from all forms of labour on Sunday. He didn't cut wood or go fishing or weed the garden or check his slips. He wouldn't even go out to the shed to putter at the dozen odd jobs that were only halfways done. He sat in the living room to watch the televangelists for an hour or two in the morning, a habit he picked up from his mother in her later years. *What does it profit a man if he gain the whole world?* they thundered, before imploring the sick and the lame to sign over their meagre savings, their disability benefits. His mother wrote a twenty-five-dollar cheque every week that she entrusted to Sweetland for mailing. He burned each one in the stove, knowing she hadn't looked at her bank balance in the years since her old-age pension kicked in.

Sweetland paid no attention to what the preachers were on about, though he enjoyed watching them pace and throw their arms around and froth at the mouth. They looked like professional wrestlers trying to get a rise from a crowd at Maple Leaf Gardens. He watched the shows for the hymns the choirs performed between the readings and sermons. He was never much for singing himself, but he knew the tunes and he hummed along under his breath.

He had an early lunch of tuna fish on white bread and a tin of peaches for dessert, then spent the first half of the afternoon online, playing poker. Even that caused him a twinge of guilt. Games of chance were the devil's tool according to his mother, and she hadn't allowed so much as a hand of 120s on the Lord's Day when they were youngsters. They sat around in their Sunday best, listening to the eight-day clock tick away the endless seconds. Uncle Clar asleep upright in his chair. A body was allowed to cook food and wash dishes, but the remainder of the day was given over to enforced rest and contemplation, which to Sweetland had always seemed a form of torture.

In his years at the lighthouse there were duties that couldn't be left and he polished the mirrors and watched the horizon to note the ships that passed and made entries about the day's weather and wind in the keeper's journal, he checked the back-up generators or repainted the light tower or tended the garden like it was any other day of the week. He thought the job might have cured him of the Sabbath habit, but it settled on him as soon as he moved back into Chance Cove. As if it wasn't his mother but the house itself that imposed the ritual observance.

Before supper he went for a stroll through the cove, the clouds in rags overhead. He went by Loveless's place, taking the path toward the barn, calling out to Loveless as he passed below the living room windows. The cow was standing in the tiny strip of field alongside the leaning barn, gnawing at the grass she'd already cropped down to the dirt. Sweetland placed a hand against the heat of her belly and the cow shook her head without raising her muzzle from the ground. She looked about ready to drop her calf where she stood.

"She's going to burst she don't have that calf soon," Loveless said, coming up behind them.

"You got neither bit of hay to put out for her?" Sweetland asked. "There's not enough grass left here to feed a rabbit."

"She eat up all the hay I set aside over the winter."

"Well can't you get some from Glad?"

Loveless looked away a moment, chewing at the unlit pipe. "He wants to take that cow away from me, Glad Vatcher do."

"Jesus, Loveless. Why would he want to take your cow?"

"Tried to buy her off me when I brought her over to the bull last fall. Wouldn't hardly take no for an answer."

"He was just trying to keep the old girl from starving to death."

"She got plenty there," Loveless said.

"You should have him come look at her."

"Who, Glad?"

"Yes, fucken Glad. Just to give her a once-over. Before the calf comes."

"There's nothing wrong with her," Loveless said and he looked around himself, one hand picking at his pant leg. He walked close enough to put a hand on the cow's flank. "He was after me to take the package, Moses."

"Well, let him talk," Sweetland said. "Don't pay no mind."

"He was hard about it. He said some things."

"What kind of things?"

"He wouldn't say nothing the like of it to Sara."

Sweetland watched the man a moment. He said, "You haven't been getting any notes, have you?"

"Notes?"

"Ransom notes, like. With letters cut out of magazines."

Loveless stared at Sweetland like he was being made fun of somehow.

"Never mind," Sweetland said. "You look out to that cow."

Loveless slapped the animal's flank. "She's fine, this one," he said. "She'll be all right."

Sweetland was back at the virtual tables early that evening when the Skype icon started jumping for his attention. He clicked it open to answer the call, Jesse sitting at a desk in his bedroom down over the hill. His pale face looming white in the screen's illumination.

"What are ya at, Jesse?"

"Homework," he said.

"Good man."

"What are you doing?" The boy's image was jerky, the voice slightly out of sync with his mouth. There was something sinister in the disconnect, Sweetland thought. He'd always hated that about Skype, preferred talking on the telephone. Though he had no time for the phone, besides.

"Not much," Sweetland said. "Playing a bit of poker."

"Winning or losing?"

"What do you think?"

"Losing."

"Ah kiss my arse," he said.

Sweetland had never gone near a computer before Queenie's youngest daughter packed up and moved to Edmonton five years back. He'd trundled down to her house with his wheelbarrow to collect the desktop he'd bought from her, walked out with the hard drive in his arms. Welcome to the twenty-first century, Sandra said to him. He set the plastic tower down in the bed of his wheelbarrow and came back to the door for the monitor. Don't worry, he'd said, I'm only visiting.

Sweetland never expected to touch the thing himself. He bought it for Jesse, thinking to occupy the boy's attention and save himself the endless interrogation he made of his visits. Clara came to the house with Jesse that evening to help set up the machine, the youngster explaining each individual component to Sweetland as they went.

This is your mouse, Jesse said, pointing to the plastic doohickey beside the keyboard. You uses that to move the cursor.

The what?

This thing, Jesse said, pointing to nothing Sweetland could identify on the screen. Go ahead, he said, move the mouse.

And Sweetland had poked at it with his index finger, like he was prodding a sleeping animal.

It won't bite you, Moses, Clara said to him, grab ahold.

Jesus loves the little children, he sighed.

Jesse spent the weeks that followed walking him through the basics, and he surrendered to the boy's insistence, thinking it would be less trouble than resisting. Sweetland had never so much as used a telephone before his first trip to the mainland with Duke in 1962, and no one on the island had phone service before the electricity arrived in the early seventies. It seemed a minor miracle now to find himself in the house where he was born, Skyping with a twelve-year-old. He heard a voice offstage and Jesse leaned in close to the screen. "Check your Facebook account," he said before the square went black.

Sweetland had lied to the government man about not being on Facebook. Jesse had badgered him into joining, but Sweetland had only one friend. He signed in, clicked on the link Jesse had sent. A YouTube video began loading and he opened it full screen. A two-minute clip of Jesse "The Body" Ventura pile-driving a series of hapless opponents in the ring. It was as though the boy knew how Sweetland felt about his name and was working to alter his opinion.

Sweetland had forgotten about the professional wrestler and was surprised to see him in his prime on the internet. The web was like the ocean, Sweetland thought, there was no telling what lived in the murkiest depths. He allowed it might be possible, if a body knew where and how to look, that everything he'd known in his life and since forgotten could be found drifting down there, in grainy two-minute clips.

He clicked to replay the video, turned up the volume. The floor of the ring pulsing with the impact of those massive bodies, the crowd on its feet. People said it wasn't real, the wrestling, that it was just a pageant of sham fighting, shadowboxing. Jesse Ventura flung himself across the chest of his opponent from the height of the corner ropes, slamming the man backwards onto the mat beneath his weight. Any idiot could see it was choreographed, that the outcome was a foregone conclusion. But that fall looked real enough from where Sweetland was sitting.

The sky was still threatening in the morning, low, patchy fog on the hills. Almost too wet to go up on the mash, but he hadn't been out to check the slips in two days. He packed a sandwich, his .22, his rain gear. Jesse was likely watching the house from his bedroom window and Sweetland wouldn't look that way when he went outside. A look would be all the invitation the boy needed. He drove the ATV up behind his property and climbed slowly out of the cove.

He'd crested the rise and started around Vatcher's Meadow when he saw the quads bombing toward him. He pulled off the trail and waited there. The Priddles whistled past in their army camouflage and ball hats and then spun around to come back up to him. Sat their machines to either side so Sweetland had to turn his head shoulder to shoulder to look at one and then the other. Early for them to be about, though there was no telling their hours when they were on a bender. "B'ys," he said.

"How's Mr. Sweetland?" Barry said.

He glanced across to Keith and nodded. "The Golden Priddles," he said. "Haven't seen you in a dog's age."

"Been spending most of our downtime in St. John's."

"What is it going on in St. John's is so goddamned important?"

"Just life," Barry said. "You should look into it sometime."

"Send me the brochure, why don't you."

"Where you off to this time of day?"

"Got a few rabbit slips out past the keeper's house," Sweetland said.

Barry leaned back on his seat. "Correct me if I'm wrong," he said to his brother, "but I believe Mr. Sweetland here is engaged in poaching activity."

"The fucker belongs in Her Majesty's Penitentiary," Keith said.

"Perhaps we should give the wildlife officer a call."

"Oh kiss my arse," Sweetland said, which got a laugh from the brothers.

Keith leaned across and tapped Sweetland's arm with his index finger. He said, "Father tells us you still haven't signed on to the package."

"Can't deny it."

Keith shook his head, solemn. "The old man says he's going to cut off your nuts with a fish knife, you don't sign."

"Is that a fact," Sweetland said.

"I told him I'd be happy to do it for him, if it came to that."

"Jesus, Keith," Barry said. "Don't mind Keith," he said to Sweetland. "He's just being a fucker."

"I'm just being a fucker," Keith agreed. The two men smiling, enjoying the moment. Though they were both considered residents of the island and had voted for the move.

Barry started up his quad. "We'll drop by for a drink some night before we goes."

"Whatever you like," Sweetland said and he kicked into gear, drove off over the field of marsh grass and moss.

At the lighthouse he grabbed the canvas backpack and the .22 from the quad without looking up at the keeper's house. The Coast Guard had just finished refurbishing the place a year before it was decommissioned. Spent a small fortune roofing and painting it, installing a skirt around the foundation to box in the three-hundred-gallon cistern that collected rainwater in the crawl space beneath the floor. The house fitted out with new furniture and appliances, dishes, cutlery. Sweetland was living alone out there at the time and he tried to refuse most of the upgrades. But some budget line was allocated and had to be spent before the end of the fiscal year.

People in Chance Cove waited until the shingles on the ocean side were stripped off by the wind, and weather seeped in through the bare boards, before they touched it. Everything of any use came out then— fridge and stove, beds, toilet and bathtub, countertops, highboys and dressers, cupboards—the building like a wrecked vessel being stripped for salvage. Sweetland kept clear of the pilfering for fear of losing his tiny pension, though he didn't begrudge anyone what they managed to put to use.

He started along the trail heading north. It was half a mile to where he'd tailed his rabbit slips and it looked like he'd wasted the trip early on. Nothing in the first half-dozen, though one had been taken and managed to twist free. He would have taken up the snares altogether without Jesse to keep him company but for Clara's self-righteousness. He reset the wire slip out of bald spite, settled the spruce branches he'd cut snug to either side on the run. The day was lightening and Sweetland shucked his rain jacket, stuffed it away in his pack. Took a mouthful of water from the Mason jar. Headed on to the next snare.

At first glance he thought a fox or weasel had gotten at the creature in the slip, some savage thing eating ugly, making a bloody mess. It crossed his mind it might have been Loveless's little lapdog to blame. That he might be forced to shoot the pup, to keep him clear of the snares.

He pushed his cap high and knelt to clear the ruined thing from the run. Froze there on his knees. The animal decapitated, the guts and entrails pulled out through a knife's incision in the stomach. Hind feet chopped off. He looked away from the mess and the rabbit's dead eyes were staring at him. The head set in the branches of the tree above the snare, one brown ear nailed to the trunk to hold it in place.

He stood the .22 on its stock and hauled himself to his feet. "Jesus fuck," he said. He took up the packsack and walked fifty feet back along the trail to sit against a boulder. It was too early for lunch but he took out the sandwich, chewing on the tasteless bread and washing it down with water. A shower of rain started to fall and he glanced up, trying to guess how long it might last. He put his rain gear on and made his way back along the path to the snare. He took the grocery bag that had held his sandwich and scooped the ruined game into it. The smear of viscera dark through the white plastic. He worked the fabric of the rabbit's ear over the nail's hold and placed the head in the bag as well.

There were two other rabbits in the snares, both of them violated in a similar fashion. He looked for their heads in the nearby trees but there was no sign that he could see. He filled the plastic bag with the bodies and tied it off and carried it with him, taking up each of his snares as he backtracked along the trail to the quad. He tied the .22 on the rack and walked down past the keeper's house, out to the helicopter pad. It was raining steadily and the wind had come up, his slicker cracking in each gust. He walked to the far end of the platform and flung the foul bag into the sea.

The Priddles didn't come by until their last evening on the island. He'd begun to think they wouldn't show their faces at all. It was an awkward fit they'd made at the best of times and, sometime soon, whatever held them in the same orbit was likely going to wear through. There'd always been a current of animosity buried in their connection to him, as if they resented the fact he was all they had to turn to when they were boys. And some small corner of his heart suspected it was the brothers who'd mutilated the animals in his snares, just to fuck with him. It was well within the compass of their twisted sense of entertainment. And it would have been a relief to Sweetland if that were the truth.

He heard them coming along the path, shouting and laughing their fool heads off. The night so still they sounded like a carnival driving through town, a truckload of drunken clowns with megaphones. It struck Sweetland what an unfamiliar racket it was, people out for a good time, raising hell for the fun of it. It almost made him feel nostalgic the minute or two it took them to come barrelling through the door.

They were too loud for the tiny space and low ceilings. They shouted for homebrew, Keith heading into the pantry to help himself. They could be heard halfway out Church Side, Sweetland guessed. Keith reappeared with beers clutched between all his fingers. The bottle caps setting off the words H*O*P*E and F*E*A*R on the knuckles. My prison tats, Keith explained the first time Sweetland noticed them there, after they'd been released from Her Majesty's Pen in St. John's.

Where's yours? Sweetland had asked Barry.

He got a heart with the word MOTHER stamped across his arse, Keith said.

Keith flicked the caps off the bottles with the base of a Bic lighter as Sweetland took down glasses from the cupboard and set about pouring a share to each. Keith took a mouthful and shook his head like a dog climbing out of a pond. "Jesus," he said. "That's still the worst brew ever I tasted. Remember what we used to call this, Barr?"

"Piss & Boots."

"Piss & Boots," Keith repeated and they fell over themselves laughing. They were both stoned out of their heads, eyes glassy as marbles.

"We could make a fortune off this stuff in Alberta," Barry said. "What is it they calls it? Boutique breweries? They're all the rage up there."

"But it tastes like shit."

"They all tastes like shit, Keith. It's just a question of marketing."

"Well no one's going to buy something called Piss & Boots."

"We could call it Scarface. That would sell. Scarface Lager."

"It's an ale," Sweetland said uselessly.

"Whatever the fuck," Barry said. "Scarface Ale. Scarface Pilsner."

"Scarface Dark," Keith said.

"Fuck, yes. Scarface Dark. Skull and crossbones on the label."

"That's money, that is," Keith said. "Hey, tell Moses here about the cove idea."

"What idea is that?" Sweetland asked while Barry waved the suggestion away.

"Come on," Keith said. "Out with it." He turned to Sweetland. "This is real money we're talking about now," he said. "We could make a killing on it."

"I'm all ears."

"Well," Barry said, "the idea is we buys up the cove after everyone shifts out."

"I'm not moving anywhere."

"Hypothetical, Scarface," Keith shouted. "Speculation is all we're doing."

"All right then," Sweetland said.

"So, houses and sheds and wharves and whatnot. I figure we could get the works for ten or fifteen thousand."

"Hypothetically," Sweetland said, "wouldn't this place be reverted to Crown land once people leaves?"

"So we leases it or some such. We'll let the lawyers worry about that. Then we comes in here and rips out all the vinyl siding."

"Get rid of it all," Keith said with an elaborate swing of his arm.

"Paints the whole place up with ochre and whitewash, puts out a couple of dories behind the breakwater. And we sells package tours to a vintage Newfoundland outport. It'll be like one of them Pioneer Villages on the mainland. Only, you know—"

"Authentic," Keith said.

"That's exactly right. The real McCoy. We could have people out here dressed up in oilskins, take the tourists fishing, show them how to split and salt the cod."

"No one knows how to salt cod anymore," Sweetland said.

"Shut up there, Eeyore," Keith said.

"Whatever the fuck," Barry said. "Feed them a bit of Jiggs' dinner. Get someone to play the accordion, put on a dance."

"We could do weekend packages," Keith said. "Week-long, ten days. People would pay a fortune for that kind of time."

They were always chasing after money when they were high. Sweetland had heard them spin a thousand get-rich-quick schemes, each more unlikely than the last. Bootlegging out of St. Pierre, smuggling drugs up from Mexico by sailboat. Shipping seal penises to the Chinese as aphrodisiacs.

"I got the advertising for this thing all figured out," Barry said and he raised both hands like he was displaying a banner. "Experience Life in Sweetland."

"No, no," Keith said. "Experience the *Sweet* Life in Sweetland."

"That's a fucking gold mine," Barry said. He pointed across the table with his truncated index finger. "All we got to do is get rid of this old fucker."

"From what I been hearing," Keith said, "someone else is likely to look after that end of things."

Sweetland straightened in his chair. "What is it you been hearing?"

"Be a shame to lose him, you ask me," Keith said. "We could fit him out in a sou'wester, put him on display for the tourists."

"The last Sweetlander, like?"

"The genuine article."

"Jesus in the Garden," Sweetland whispered.

The rest of the evening carried on in the same coke-addled vein, the brothers riffing back and forth on one topic or other. Sweetland thought several times to ask the brothers what exactly they'd been hearing about him and from who. But he knew it would come out a useless muddle, half of it exaggerated or misremembered, the other half made up, and he let them go their own way. Keith talking about a woman he was screwing in Fort Mac, reaching into the bedside table for the lubricant he kept there, grabbing a tube of muscle cream by mistake. "That A535 shit," he said, his arms across his guts for laughing. "Lathered her up good and the burn kicked in. And she starts yelling, What the fuck did you do to me? What the fuck did you do? Wasted half the night into Emergency with her."

"Only Keith could make a woman that hot," Barry said.

"Jesus, Barr, tell Mose about the sixty-nine thing."

"Fuck off, he don't want to hear about that."

"I don't want to hear about it," Sweetland confirmed.

"He don't even know what sixty-nine means," Barry said.

"He've got the internet, tell the goddamn story."

"Oh fuck," Barry said. He straightened in his seat, hauling his jean jacket tight at the waist, like someone about to give testimony in court. "I was with this girl," he said. "Nice girl, I liked her. And we were, you know, doing the sixty-nine. And it was pretty goddamn slippery down there. Anyway, I'm face and eyes into her—"

"He *really* liked her," Keith said.

"I practically needs a snorkel to breathe is the fact of the matter. And I'm just about to go off when she rams a finger up my ass. And I snorts in, you know, just automatically. And I inhaled her—her—" he said, struggling to hold off the laughter or find the word he was after. "Her *labia*," he said.

"Fuck," Keith said, already pounding the table. "Moses don't know what *labia* means."

"Cunt lips," Barry shouted. "Right up my nostrils. And she got her legs clamped around my ears. And fuck if I don't start laughing. And I'm choking and cumming and laughing like a Jesus idiot."

"Cunt lips up his nose," Keith roared. His face cherry red, his eyes bulging.

"I almost fucken drowned," Barry said.

"Man Asphyxiated by Woman's Labia," Keith said, which set both men off on another helpless round.

"Best fuck I had in years," Barry said when he'd finally settled down.

Sweetland didn't mind the Priddles once upon a time, it was true. But he was too old for their bullshit now, the relentless, senseless surge of it. It was like being out in a storm too rough to make for shelter, all you could do was keep face on to the wind and ride it out. He sipped at a glass of warm homebrew and waited for the barrage to end.

"We're keeping you up," Barry said an hour later, "we should go. Catching the ferry tomorrow."

"Heading back to Alberta?"

"St. John's," Keith said, and he slapped Barry's shoulder. "Got Fucknuts here an appointment with that shrink Jesse's been talking to. See if we can't straighten him out."

Barry turned his backside toward his brother, slapped the cheek of his arse. "Kiss yer mudder good night," he said.

They spent fifteen minutes more yammering at each other before they finally went out the door, and Sweetland stood there after he latched it closed, listening to them head down the path. It wasn't necessarily a bad thing, he thought, that their mother wasn't around to see the lives they were leading as men.

BOB-SAM LAVALLEE MADE THE TREK in from the lighthouse to look the lifeboat survivors over. They were all suffering from exposure and dehydration, though none of them appeared to be in serious danger. No solid food, Bob-Sam said, just soup broth and water and clear tea.

Any word on the Coast Guard? Sweetland asked.

It'll be tomorrow sometime before they can get a vessel out here, Bob-Sam said. They wants to know what ship these fellows come off of.

There was a name on the lifeboat, he said, but someone scraped it away.

The men were divided up among the houses in the cove and taken off to be stripped of their filthy clothes and bathed and put to bed.

Sweetland's mother was only nine months dead at the time and he was still adjusting to the house without her. The tiny rooms echoing like vaulted spaces. He spent most of his free time with his sister and Pilgrim, eating his meals there and occasionally kipping down on the daybed in the kitchen when he'd had too much to drink to face the two-minute walk up the hill.

He hadn't volunteered to take any of the refugees in and no one would have allowed them to suffer a house without a woman to look after them. He went down to Pilgrim's that evening to see how they were making out and to glean whatever gossip might be making the rounds about their ordeal. Pilgrim was in the rocker beside the stove in the kitchen, a cigarette burning in the ashtray on the table.

Where's the missus? Sweetland asked.

Gone down to sit with the dead one at the church.

She left you alone with those two upstairs?

They're sound up there now, Pilgrim said. They won't stir this night, I imagine.

Well that one down to the church idn't about to stir, I guarantee.

You knows what she's like, Moses. You'll have a drink, he said. I got a fresh batch of shine ready.

Pilgrim was no use in a boat and had never worked a steady job, but he was a dab hand at brewing. Sold bottles of his moonshine door to door through the cove and to the deckhands on the ferry. He tended bar at the Fisherman's Hall during bingo games and dances, the younger men getting a laugh passing off ones and twos as tens or twenties.

He was an "exhaustion product" as the women used to call it, his mother with a grown family and thinking she was through the change of life when she found herself unexpectedly pregnant. Pilgrim's two eyes sightless from birth. She kept him on a tether until he was old enough to untie the knots himself and he became a ward of the community then, wandering from house to house. Every sighted person taking it upon themselves to steer him clear of the flakes, the wharves, the water. His blindness made even the smallest accomplishment seem a kind of magic trick—buttering a slice of bread, reciting Bible verses from memory, cutting cod tongues. The women clapped their hands and fed him raisins and sweet tea and kissed the crown of his head after he'd performed his most recent beguiling trick. There was nowhere in the cove he wasn't welcomed like a son. Pilgrim treated Sweetland's house as his own, staying for meals, spending half his nights sleeping head to foot between Sweetland and Hollis.

Music was the only vocation anyone had ever heard of for a blind child, and the church took up a collection of pennies and nickels to buy Pilgrim a fiddle. The toy violin made of pressboard and lacquer, strung with plastic strings. The church's minister offered a handful of ineffectual lessons and Pilgrim spent hours at a time in a chair by the kitchen window, sawing out approximations of "Turkey in the Straw," "The Lark in the Clear Air," a few local jigs. He had so little aptitude for the music, he didn't know how bad he was. Kept at it until his mother broke down in tears of frustration one evening and his father threw the contraption into the stove.

It wasn't the end of his musical career. Pilgrim had a prodigious memory for the old labyrinthine ballads about murder and shipwreck and star-crossed love. He had no voice to speak of, but he was still called on at weddings and wakes and Christmas concerts to make his tuneless, inexorable way through one disaster or other.

Ruthie worked as custodian at the school and Pilgrim added a disability pension to the pot, along with whatever he made peddling his brew. And they muddled along, like everyone else on the island.

He and Sweetland sat at the table with glasses of shine and their smokes and the rumours already circulating about the men asleep in the town's beds. Mongolian, some said. Trinidadian. Tibetan. Sri Lankan, according to the Reverend. Sweetland was shocked to learn the language they were speaking was English. He hadn't understood a word that came out of their mouths.

Where did they think they were going, I wonder.

Somewhere in the States is where they were told, Pilgrim said.

The Promised Land.

The very same.

They sat in silence a few moments then, until they were startled by a commotion above them, a voice through the ceiling.

Sounds like they might be stirring, Sweetland said.

They could hear someone throwing up and Pilgrim rose from his seat, heading for the stairs. You might want to go get Ruthie, he said.

Sweetland went out the door and down the path at a clip. It was only the thought of the strangers asleep in the houses around him, and the dead boy laid out in the church, that kept him from screaming Ruth's name as he pelted along.

The front door of the church was open and he checked himself as he came up to it. There were candles lit at the front near the body, the pale light just enough to add a little gloom to the dark inside. He whispered Ruth's name as he walked up the aisle but there was no sign of her. He stopped well short of the dead boy under his sheet near the altar. He guessed she was in the minister's room at the back but he couldn't bring himself to walk past the corpse to reach the door, or to call loud enough to be heard. "Ruthie," he said, hissing the word.

He backed up the aisle until he was outside. Turned and started toward the side entrance they had used to carry the body inside earlier in the day. The door swung open as he approached it and the Reverend came through. Sweetland was about to call out to him, but something in the man's demeanour wouldn't allow it. A hunch to his gait, his eyes on his feet. A rushed quiet about the man. The Reverend turned away from the path at the foot of the stairs and skulked through the long grass at the back of the church.

Sweetland looked up at the door. Ruthie still inside there, he knew.

4

SWEETLAND WOKE TO THE SOUND of Loveless's cow bawling, a hollow moaning complaint carrying through the mauzy dark. He lifted himself up on an elbow to look out the window, down past Queenie's house, but there was no sign of lights at Loveless's place. He lay back and did his best to ignore it, but the lowing went on endlessly, a sound so full of helpless misery it made his stomach knot.

Fucken Loveless.

He pushed up out of bed, dressed awkwardly in the black. Dug around for a flashlight in the porch, walked down through the cove. Sweetland went along the path beside Loveless's house to the barn where the miserable creature was calling, unhooked the door and stepped in. The building rank with the smell of shit and rotting hay. He played the light along the barn's length to the spot where the cow stood with her head pushed into the corner. Her back legs wide and the haunches quivering as though she were plugged into an electrical outlet. The calf was hanging halfway to the ground, its nose swaying six inches off the ground. One foreleg still caught up inside the mother. The pink tongue hanging lifeless out of the mouth.

Sweetland walked across the dirt floor, placed a hand to the cow's haunch. The animal's head swung toward him and Sweetland glanced up at the motion, caught sight of a shadow darting further along the wall. He flicked the light across it, picked out the little lapdog skulking through the straw. "Hello, Smut," he said and the dog sat down five feet from the cow. Ears cocked high.

Sweetland reached down to cup the calf's muzzle, the nose wet and cold. He straightened stiffly and wiped the hand on the ass of his pants. "I'll be back the once," he said, to the cow or to the dog or the fetid room itself.

He turned on the porch light in the house and called up the hall. "Loveless!" he shouted. "You got a dead calf out there." He waited a minute, heard the sound of bedsprings shifting. "You're going to lose that cow if you don't get your arse down here," he said.

He went back along the path to the barn. Cast the light around a moment, the dog in the same spot though it was lying down and watching, attentive. Sweetland took off his coat and rolled it into a ball on the ground, propping the flashlight there so it shone on the cow's hind end. He rolled the sleeves of his shirt above his elbows and knelt behind her. "Now, missus," he said.

The dead calf was slick with birthing fluid, gelatinous and cold in the chill. No telling how long it had been hanging like that. The cow was fair gone herself. Sweetland pushed a hand into her, reaching to get his fingers around the foreleg caught up back there. It was tucked at an angle so unnatural he couldn't find a decent grip. He wrapped an arm around the calf's neck and leaned his weight against it, hauling at the leg as best he could. The cow lifted her head to bawl and the dog barked along. Nothing budged.

Loveless came into the barn with a storm lamp in his hand. He had a coat on over his bare torso, a pair of striped pyjama bottoms tucked into his boots.

"The fuck have you got done here now," Sweetland said.

Loveless peered in at the scene a moment and turned around in a panicky circle. "That goddamned animal, Sara," he said to the ceiling, as if the dead woman was watching them from the rafters. "She haven't been nothing but trouble to me."

"It's not the bloody cow's fault," Sweetland said. "What were you doing asleep in bed?"

"I was out with her till almost midnight," he said. "I didn't think she was going to go tonight."

Sweetland gave the man a look. "Well everything's locked up in there now. You should go get Glad."

"I don't want nothing to do with Glad Vatcher."

"Don't be a goddamned idiot."

"You got to do something, Moses."

"Well Christ," Sweetland whispered.

"I can't lose Sara's cow."

"Shut up a minute," he said. Sweetland looked into the black of the vaulted roof, considering. He picked up the flashlight and headed for the door.

"Moses?"

"Don't you touch that animal before I gets back," he said.

He went up to his shed, rifled through a tool chest below the workbench. Collected a pair of canvas gloves, wire cutters, electrical tape. Hung near the door there was a length of thin cable once used to secure lobster traps on the stage and Sweetland slipped it across his shoulder on the way outside.

Loveless stared at the cable when Sweetland came back into the barn. "Jesus, Mose," he said.

"You want to lose Sara's cow?"

He took a moment to consider the possibility, shook his head.

"Bring that light in," Sweetland said. He taped one end of the cable, worked it inside the cow, pushing for the calf's shoulder joint. He forced his second hand in below the first and reached for the taped end blindly, his face against a quivering flank, grunting with the effort. The cow had gone eerily silent and was slowly shaking her head back and forth. "Come on now," Sweetland said, "come on." When he'd hooked the cable around the foreleg he sat back, both hands sliding free at once, drawing the taped end out. He shook the mess from his hands, shucked his forearms and fingers clean with straw, and put on the gloves. He cut the wire to leave himself with an even length top and bottom. "You hold her head," he said to Loveless. "Don't let her come back to me." He wrapped the cable around his palms and once Loveless had a grip on the animal's neck he started in pulling left under right, a steady jigging rhythm, the wire singing with the strain.

After fifteen minutes he stopped to shake the blood back into his hands. He took off one glove and reached inside to check on the cable's progress. He looked up at Loveless who hadn't spoken a word since he started. "You want to take a spell at this?" he asked, but Loveless shook his head.

It was half an hour longer before the cable gnawed all the way through the joint. Sweetland wrapped an arm around the calf's neck again and put his weight into it, shouldering toward the dirt floor as it inched loose and then came free in a sluice of blood and afterbirth. The cow stumbled sideways, leaning her full weight against the barn wall, and Sweetland hauled the corpse out from under her. The amputated foreleg hadn't come free with the body and Sweetland reached back inside to find it. Laid it beside the calf near about where it would have been if it was still attached. Knelt there with his hands on his thighs to catch his breath.

"Will she be all right, you think?" Loveless asked.

Sweetland glanced up at the cow. She was shaking along her length, her head bowed almost to the dirt floor. "How does she look to you?"

The dog crept out of the darkness and sniffed at the calf, at the dead eye staring into the rafters. It took one tentative lick at the snout and backed away. Sat there and looked up at Sweetland. A little blaze of white on its black chest. A tuxedo dog, Loveless said it was called. The man probably paid extra for that, Sweetland thought.

"You got to get this mess cleaned up," Sweetland said as he got to his feet. His clothes were soaked through with the filth, the material dank and cold against his skin. "And if that cow needs anything else, you go get Glad Vatcher, you hear me?"

Loveless was staring down at the slick corpse. "What do I do with this?"

Sweetland started for the door. "Dig a hole somewhere and bury it," he said.

It was light when he left the barn and Queenie Coffin was standing just inside her doorway as he walked by, cradling her elbow, her cigarette held high. She shook her head at the sight of him. She said, "You looks like the tail end of a good time, Moses Sweetland."

"Loveless lost his calf," he said. "As like he'll lose the cow along with it."

Queenie took a slow drag. "I heard her bawling," she said.

"I don't know why he bothered bringing her over to Vatcher's bull this year. He knows as much about animals as I knows about Saudi fucken Arabia."

"He was just missing Sara."

"That's a hell of a way to show it, killing her cow."

"Be a mercy if she goes, probably. And one less creature to have to take off the island."

Sweetland stared at her, standing one step above him in her night-dress and housecoat, the curlers still in her hair. The bright red lipstick making her face look strangely lifeless in the early light, as though it was a mask she was wearing over her real face.

When Queenie was just shy of twelve, her older sister came down with typhoid fever. Glad Vatcher's father ferried out a doctor from Burgeo who quarantined the entire family inside the house. They were kept fed by their neighbours, and Sweetland's mother would occasionally send him over with a pot of soup or a meal of salt beef and cabbage that he left on the front bridge. It was the only time he'd ever knocked on a door in the cove, to let them know their dinner was there. He'd back away from the house then, twenty or thirty feet, watching to see Queenie or one of her younger sisters lean out to take it in.

It was Uncle Clar who framed out the girl's coffin in his shop after she died. Sweetland was with him as Queenie's father shouted the child's height and her breadth at the shoulder through a window, Uncle Clar jotting the measurements on a scrap of wood. Queenie was standing against the far wall behind her father, though he couldn't see her face for shadow and she wouldn't lift her head to look his way.

Poor little lamb, Clar repeated a hundred times as he sawed and planed the boards, as he nailed and sanded and varnished. Sweetland helped the old man carry the finished coffin down and they left it on the front bridge, as he did the family's meals. Queenie's father opening the door to drag it inside. The funeral was held later that morning, the coffin sitting on the bridge again with the dead girl inside. Every soul in Chance Cove standing below it to sing a few hymns and bow their heads as the minister said his prayers. The family watching it all from the parlour windows, the sisters bawling behind the glass. Waving goodbye as the coffin was hefted and carried up to the old graveyard.

Sweetland spent the entire service watching Queenie. She had hidden herself away at one corner of the window, almost out of sight altogether, and she never once looked up at the funeral congregation, never caught his eye, and he was relieved in some obscure way not to have to bear it.

For the life of him now he couldn't remember the dead sister's name.

Queenie raised her cigarette to the gaudy red lips, dragged the smoke into her chest. She looked past him, down to the water. "The Priddles is on their way."

He turned toward the dock where the ferry was already in and tied up. He saw the Priddles heading over from Church Side with their duffle bags on their shoulders and he thought to walk down to see them off. But it was too much to take on. He went up to his house instead and stripped out of his filthy clothes in the porch, left them in a heap on the floor. Fell asleep on the daybed in the kitchen.

Jesse was at the table when he woke, the laptop open in front of him.

"Shouldn't you be into the school?" Sweetland asked.

"It's dinnertime."

Sweetland could see the boy had helped himself to two tins of peaches. "You put in a fire."

"It was cold in here," Jesse said. "You looked cold."

"Put the kettle on for me, would you?"

Jesse crossed to the stove, added a junk of wood to the firebox, pushed the kettle full over the heat. "What happened to your clothes?" he asked.

"Forgot to wear a napkin at supper last night."

"Ha," Jesse said.

It was a recent thing, his ability to separate a person's tone into categories, to pick out a joke for what it was and acknowledge it. Sweetland's role as court jester paying off finally. Or the Reverend's work with him. Or just the boy catching up with life.

"Your mother know you're over here?"

"Poppy knows."

"That don't mean your mother is going to be happy about it."

"Loveless's calf was born dead last night."

Sweetland sat up in his underwear and socks, raked his fingers through his hair before he thought better of it. Looked at his hands, crusted black and red. "Where'd you hear that, now."

"Poppy told me."

He walked to the sink and ran the water until it was scalding, scrubbed at his skin with a brush. Scoured at the blood under the nails. "Did your pop say how the cow was doing?"

"She's lying down," Jesse said. "Won't get up out of it."

Sweetland turned off the taps, shook the water from his hands and forearms, wiped them down with a cup towel. He'd have to burn the clothes he was wearing, he figured. "You're not playing poker over there, I hope."

"Angry Birds," Jesse said.

"Well," Sweetland said. "That's all right, I spose."

What was it about the youngster? It was his seriousness, maybe, that made him seem distant. He was doggedly loyal and affectionate in a standoffish way that a body could confuse for the opposite of affection and loyalty. He had a cat's self-centred indifference to the world as others saw it, a cat's inscrutable motivations. He took odd notions, running off now and again for no obvious reason, disappearing up on the mash or hiding out at the lighthouse or as far as the Priddles' cabin in the valley. He never tried to explain himself after the fact or was incapable of it. He couldn't be trusted altogether because you couldn't guess with any certainty what he was thinking.

When Sweetland moved back into the cove from the keeper's house, he spent most of his evenings at Pilgrim's, eating his supper there and watching an hour or two of television with Jesse. *America's Funniest Home Videos. Wipeout. Two and a Half Men.* Then Jesse would begin the first of the many elaborate stages required to get him to bed. Clara and Wince took turns saying their good-nights and bringing the boy a glass of water and adjusting the pillows to his satisfaction, and then he'd call for Sweetland. Lying in the dark with Jesse to answer endless questions about hockey and fishing and wrestling, about the saucy rooster Sweetland killed when it went after Ruthie, about the boatload of Sri Lankans he'd happened on near Burnt Head.

It was impossible to say what Jesse made of these stories, why he returned to them so obsessively, insisting they be told in the same manner each time. He seemed to be constantly checking the world at large against the one in his head, making sure they were one and the same. Though at night, in his bedroom, it seemed just another ploy to delay the inevitable. Jesse clinging to wakefulness like a drowning man, rousing himself out of near sleep to ask one more thing.

Tell me about the coat, he would say.

What coat? Sweetland asked.

The one you and Hollis wore.

I don't know if I remembers much about it.

You had to go out and check the nets in the morning before school.

You want to tell the story?

No, Jesse said. You tell it.

All right, Sweetland said.

Up before light, the two of them. Putting a bit of fire in the stove, the house cold as stone. A cup of tea and fried capelin and they went along to the stagehead, climbed down into the punt and set the oars. They had to sell the skiff with the inboard after their father died and it was an hour's rowing out to the nets, longer if the wind was southerly. Only the one decent coat between them, their father's old jacket kept on a hook in the porch. Neither of them big enough to fill it out on their own, sitting side by side with one arm each in the sleeves, coming back on the oars. Uncle Clar telling them how they looked like a fat little two-headed man on his way to check his herring nets.

Why did you have to share a coat? Jesse asked.

It was hard times after Father died. Just me and Hollis to look after the fish. Hollis wouldn't as old as you when all that was going on.

Jesse was quiet a moment and then he said, You was with Hollis when he drowned.

That's enough of that now.

But Hollis says—

I heard enough of what your imaginary friend says about it all.

He's not imaginary, Jesse said in the same flat tone.

Well I'm not talking to him either way. You want another story or not?

Clara usually had to call an end to the interrogation, her silhouette at the bedroom door. Last one, she'd say and then stand there to make sure Jesse didn't sneak in another. But occasionally Sweetland outlasted the boy and he lay a few minutes longer, letting the spell of sleep settle in before he moved. Jesse's face blank but animate, a living thing. The last of Sweetland's blood beside him. The smell of woodsmoke in his hair. The untainted sweetness of a child's breath.

Uncle Moses, Jesse whispered one evening. He had turned to face the wall, a sure sign he was about to go under, and Sweetland leaned in close to hear him. I have a secret to tell you, Jesse whispered. Sweetland raised his head, listening, and he waited there a good while before he realized the boy was sound asleep.

He doubted Jesse even remembered the announcement of a secret about to be shared, but some childish part of Sweetland's mind was still expectant in his presence. As if a riddle at the heart of things was about to be revealed. He was like the world itself, Sweetland thought, a well you would never see the bottom of, that might swallow you whole if you weren't careful.

He went to the fridge and leaned into the cool. "You want something else to eat," he asked.

"Can we go see the cow?"

"I had enough of cows for one day."

"You don't have any cows."

"I got to eat something," he said. "And then I got some work to do in the shed."

"I'd rather go see the cow."

"Well go see the bloody cow then," Sweetland said.

He was at the table saw ripping a length of two-by-six to replace the sill in the shed's side door when Glad Vatcher came to see him. He shut down the machine, ran his hand along the cut. Waited for the younger man to say something.

"You had a night, I hear," Gladstone said finally.

"Tried to send Loveless over to get you," Sweetland said. "Was your bull caused all the trouble to begin with."

Glad smiled down at his boots. A faint odour of animal coming off him where he stood in the open doorway. "I tried to talk him out of it," he said. "Offered to buy the cow off him, to save him the trouble."

"You might as well talk to his little dog as talk sense to Loveless."

"He come to see me just now. Cow's laid down and he can't get her up out of it."

"You have a look at her?"

"Poked my head in," he said. "You had some job getting that calf clear from the looks of things."

"Like trying to pull a tooth."

"Loveless wants we should try to get the cow on her feet."

"I had enough of that animal for one day."

Glad let a smile prick at the corners of his mouth, but wouldn't look at Sweetland direct. "There's no one over there to help but youngsters and old men," he said.

Sweetland took a broom from the corner and swept up the spray of sawdust. It was their first conversation since Glad decided to take the package, against everything Sweetland had ever heard him say on the matter. Glad had a finger in every enterprise in Chance Cove, a position he inherited from his father. He and his wife ran the cove's only store, shipped in fishing equipment and outboards and building materials, sold fresh lamb in the spring and beef in the fall. The resettlement talk never amounted to more than talk before Glad signed on. It was hard to blame the man, given the state of things on the island, but Sweetland blamed him regardless.

"I spose it's a waste of time trying to get her up," he said.

"Likely it is," Glad said. "Still," he said.

"Loveless got any rope over there?"

"I'd say Sara had just about anything a man could need, we minds to look for it."

Sweetland took his coat off a hook by the door and they walked over together without speaking, stood just inside the barn entrance to let their eyes adjust to the dim. A crowd gathered at the far end near the cow. Every youngster in school had come to the barn during the dinner break and not a one was going back while the animal was down. Most of the men in the cove were there as well, including some who hadn't spoken a civil word to Sweetland in months. Loveless holding court, both his arms going as he talked.

"He haven't had this much attention since Sara died," Glad Vatcher said.

Loveless was pointing at Sweetland as they walked over. "Sawed up the calf," he heard Loveless say, "like a bit of old driftwood."

Sweetland glanced around at the assembly, to see what they had to work with. Duke and Hayward, Reet Verge in her pink hoodie, Ned Priddle, a handful of others. Glad was the only adult under the age of fifty, the rest nursing one chronic infirmity or other. All the young folk off at jobs on the rigs or into St. John's or somewhere on the mainland.

The cow was down against the wall, panting shallowly and staring blind at the barnboards. "She won't have any life in them legs," Glad said. "She's going to be dead weight to get up."

"You think we can lever her?"

"Might be. Get under her front and back. Move her off the wall. Maybe pass a rope underneath."

They puttered around collecting two-by-fours and concrete blocks and rope and setting the materials in place. There was an old dory propped in the stall nearest the entrance, a plank-board pig of a boat that Loveless had built half a lifetime ago, and they dragged that behind the animal to use as a fulcrum. The cow lying there oblivious, like some biblical queen being attended by servants. They leashed a rope around her neck and put three men apiece at the levers shoved under her front and hindquarters. Counted to three and raised the cow a meagre foot off the ground before she canted off the two-by-fours and folded heavily back into place, the men scrabbling to keep their feet as she fell.

They made a dozen other attempts, changing the size and number of levers, their angles and fulcrums and positions, Loveless pacing uselessly on the periphery and calling, "Don't hurt her, b'ys, don't hurt her." They finally managed to sneak a rope under her girth before she dropped back to the ground. Nailed a block and tackle to the rafters and Glad Vatcher and Pilgrim and every youngster in the barn set to the line. Between the levers and the pulley they raised the creature's frame high enough she could scrabble feebly with her front legs, her weight full on the rope. The big head lolling, her breathing so attenuated they had to set her back for fear she might suffocate.

Two hours they'd been at her by then and they were all beat to a snot, their boots and pants fouled with cow shit and the previous night's gore. They stood around the cow, catching their breath, wiping sweat off their faces.

"She don't want to get up," Loveless said.

"We could jimmy up a sling maybe," Glad offered. "Let that hold her, see if she finds her legs."

"A bit of sailcloth or canvas would do it," Sweetland said.

It was another hour of jiggery at that, raising the cow and working the improvised sling under her torso, hanging the works from three ropes slung over the rafters.

"She looks like she's wearing a goddamned diaper," Duke said when they were done.

Glad Vatcher made a helpless motion with his hand. "We're going to have to leave her there awhile," he said to Loveless. "You'll want to massage those legs, see if you can get some life into them."

Loveless nodded uncertainly, terrified of the animal. They left him to the work, the rest of the crowd meandering toward the door.

"I got some homebrew over to the house," Sweetland said when they were out in the fresh air. He turned to Glad Vatcher. "You're welcome for a glass," he said, and Glad tipped his head to one side, considering.

"All right," he said.

Duke followed them over, and Pilgrim with Jesse hanging onto his arm.

Sweetland brought half a dozen bottles out of the pantry, poured them off one at a time into a plastic measuring cup, being careful to leave the gravelly sediment in the bottle. Passed around glasses of the brew. He handed Jesse half a glass and raised a finger to his lips, tipping his head toward Pilgrim. He opened the laptop and pushed it to where Jesse was sitting.

"Haven't had a down cow to deal with," Glad said, "since I was a youngster."

Sweetland laughed. "Not hard to tell we was out of practice."

"We should have looked it up on the Google," Duke said.

"Not *the* Google," Jesse said. "Just Google."

"Well whatever the hell it is. Bet you there's something on there about lifting cows."

"Every Jesus thing is on there," Sweetland admitted.

"I don't give her much of a chance," Glad said. "She's a hell of a mess."

They sat with that a moment before Duke said, "When do you start moving your animals off the island?"

"We was planning to bring them over September month. Winter them in St. Alban's, at the brother-in-law's place."

"Taking them across on the ferry?"

"Going to have to hire a boat somewhere I expect."

"What'll that cost, a hundred grand?"

"Ha," Sweetland said darkly.

Glad looked down at his shoes. "More than we can afford if the financial side haven't been settled up by then. But we're going regardless. The wife's got her heart set on it." He finished his beer in one draft and stood up. "She'll have supper on," he said.

After Glad shut the door behind him, Pilgrim pointed in the general direction of Duke's seat. "It's too bad you can't learn to cut hair with that fucken mouth of yours."

"I was only asking," Duke said.

Sweetland went off to the pantry after more beer.

"I never thought Glad Vatcher would take the package," Pilgrim said.

"Glad Vatcher can kiss my arse," Sweetland called from the next room.

"It was his missus talked him into it," Duke said. "Wanted to be handier to her crowd in St. Alban's."

"His missus can kiss my arse too," he shouted.

He was half-cut by the time he'd finished his fifth beer and still hours of light left to the day. Everyone gone off to their suppers and he sat in the quiet, rolling the empty glass back and forth between the palms of his hands. Feeling sorry for himself, he supposed.

He sat at the laptop, trolled around the handful of sites he knew. Typed in a Google search on *cow lifting*. Five and a half million results. The Upsi-Daisy Cow Lifter. Harnesses, slings, cranes, buckets, hoists. An infinite library of information and none of it any practical use to them. A window they could peer through to watch the modern world unfold in its myriad variations, while only the smallest, strangest fragments washed ashore on the island.

He went through to the porch, took his coat and hat and walked down to Loveless's, let himself into the barn. Loveless at the far end, sitting on one of the concrete blocks they'd used as a fulcrum, rubbing at a foreleg of the doomed cow with a towel. Sweetland crossed over to them, put a hand to the cow's neck, rubbed between her ears awhile. Her breath intermittent and shallow.

"She don't want to be up," Loveless said. He was chewing angrily at the unlit pipe as he sat there.

"Don't look like she do."

"Sara wouldn't be happy to see it."

Sweetland straightened, put his hands in his pockets. Turned to see the little dog back in its place along the wall. "Hello, Smut," he said.

Loveless twisted around on his concrete seat. "I had that one barred in the porch."

"Well, that's a regular Houdini you got there." Sweetland bent at the waist and held a hand toward the dog, kissing the air to encourage it over, but it only stared.

"He won't come near, you don't have a bit of something to give him," Loveless said.

"What do you use?"

"Steak mostly."

"Is that why he's so interested in your cow, I wonder?"

Loveless raised himself awkwardly off his seat and Sweetland had to reach a hand to keep him upright. "I don't know how Sara managed all of this," he said.

"She was a tough woman."

"I can't do nothing here without her."

"Go lie down for a bit, I'll take a spell."

Loveless started away, but turned back to Sweetland before he reached the far end of the barn. He took the pipe from his mouth and stared at it. He said, "I'm going to take the package, Mose."

Sweetland looked him up and down. "You're tired," he said. "Go lie down a while."

"I got my mind made up," Loveless said. "I got nothing here without Sara."

"Go on," Sweetland repeated quietly, and he watched the shabby figure push out the barn door. Then he dragged the concrete block to the cow's hind leg and went at it with the towel, trying to massage blood back into the flesh. After fifteen minutes he moved to the opposite leg. He leaned his head against the cow's flank a moment, a quiver still discernible in the muscle. "Well now, Sara," he said aloud, missing the woman suddenly.

Sara Loveless. As squat and solid as her cow, they used to say. And almost as simple, ha ha. It was a local sport, making fun of Sara. She had no letters and spoke in truncated phrases reduced to bare fundamentals. Every person and creature and thing was a she. *She need oil change. She got bad head. She raining now. She lazy as a cut cat.* Sara was fond of beer and brandy and went to bed half-drunk most nights. Cursed like a sailor. But laziness was the only form of stupidity Sweetland couldn't abide and whatever else might be said about Sara, she was not a lazy woman. Kept the animals and the garden, cut and cured her winter's hay up on the mash. Tramping around in her rubber boots and an old gansey sweater that swayed almost to her knees. She wrecked a shoulder clearing boulders from her bit of pasture, years ago. Sweetland had seen her punch at it savagely with the opposite fist when it acted up, which was the only bit of doctoring she allowed.

She had never married and seemed completely unfit for it. But she was built for the island, unlike her brother, who sailed in the wake of Sara's industry his entire adult life. How she'd suffered living in that house with Loveless all these years, Sweetland didn't know.

He finished a round of the cow's legs and then stood at her head, rubbing between her ears again, before he started for the door. He thought of the dog, unsure if it was still sitting there against the wall and it was too dark inside now to say. "You coming, Smut?" he said to the place he'd last seen the pup, but there was no sound or motion there and he carried on outside.

He opened Loveless's door on his way along. "Your shift," he shouted into the house and he walked down through the cove, his head buzzing with the first jangly notes of a hangover. He went out as far as the incinerator, stood looking over the open ocean, letting the wind scour away at him.

The ground fell steeply toward the water on the far side of the incinerator and the slope was thick with junk that couldn't be burned, strollers and playpens, paint cans, barrels, a freezer, a bathtub, old hockey skates, a Star Choice satellite dish, four or five computer monitors that even Sweetland recognized as archaic. It was the world's job, it seemed, to render every made thing obsolete.

He turned to see the cove glimmer in the last light, houses and windows glowing faintly orange and red, the colours fading and winking out as he watched. There was no stopping it, he knew. Days when the weather was roaring outside his mother would say, Stall as long as you like, sooner or later a body's got to make a run for the outhouse. The whole place was going under, and almost everyone it mattered to was already in the ground.

Definitely. He was definitely feeling sorry for himself.

He passed his stagehead on the way in the arm and barely gave it a glance in the growing dusk, walking on a few steps before the strange detail struck him. He turned back to look at the door, picked out the shadowy U of the horseshoe he'd put there for luck thirty years ago. And something moving below it, a smudge in the gloom, a little bag, he thought, hanging from a strap.

He had to work up the nerve to step toward it. Stopped when he was near enough to make out the rabbit's severed head. The creature's eyes wide and staring, a four-inch nail driven through the silk of one ear to hold it in place. The head swaying soundlessly in the wind.

HE STOOD OUTSIDE after the Reverend disappeared around the back of the church, deciding whether or not to go in after Ruthie. His head floundering, trying to piece together what he'd seen in some way other than how it seemed. There were a dozen scenarios that were completely innocuous and only one that he knew in his gut to be true. He started back up toward Pilgrim's house, thinking he'd stop at Ned Priddle's place to ask Effie to look in on the sick man. He came around the front of the church just as his sister scuttled out the main doors and they startled away from one another.

Jesus, Moses, she said. Her arms wrapped a cardigan tight about herself. You scared the life out of me, she said.

You left Wince alone up there with those two fellows.

They was sound asleep, the both of them.

Well one of them was puking his guts out when I left.

She skipped ahead then, half running on the path. Why did you leave him? she asked.

He told me to come get you.

But you was right there in the house.

They were having a racket to avoid talking about other things, he knew. And that suited Sweetland well enough.

He followed Ruthie inside but stayed in the kitchen as she went up the stairs. Listened to the muffle of voices through the ceiling, the cough-ing and dry heaves of the sick man. Pilgrim called from the landing, ask-ing him to put the kettle over the heat for hot water, to hand up rags from under the sink, the mop and bucket from the back porch. Sweetland went about collecting the materials he'd been asked for, but couldn't even find it in himself to answer.

Sweetland was best man and father-giver at his sister's wedding, handing Ruthie away when the minister asked, and he passed Pilgrim the ring for Ruthie's finger. Pilgrim was besotted with the girl and had been for years, everyone could see that. He spent part of every day in their company, was a fixture at the Sweetland table. Talk-sang a few ballads to try and impress Ruthie as the women cleared up the dishes. And would never have laid a finger on her but for Sweetland insisting she teach him to dance.

His mother is in the ground for long ago, he said when she objected, how else is the poor frigger going to learn?

Sweetland appointed himself chaperone while Ruthie hummed a tune and wrestled Pilgrim around the tiny kitchen space. Pilgrim topped up on shine to overcome his mortal shyness before his lessons, though it did little to help his dancing.

You're about as graceful as a cow in a dory, she told him.

Got no head for it, he said.

It's only a bit of math, she insisted, and she counted the steps aloud, one two three, one two three.

Ruthie thought of him as a kind of hapless uncle, made fun of his awful voice, snuck up behind him to cover his sightless eyes with her hands and shout *Guess who?* Blind to how the older man felt before he proposed to her. She refused him twice, and it was only her mother's intervention that swung things in Pilgrim's favour.

Ruthie's been leading that poor soul on, she said to Sweetland.

He started in his chair, glanced across at her. Sure, she was only showing him how to dance.

His mother was knitting in a rocker by the stove and her hands paused at their work. She looked directly at her son. You know how Pilgrim feels about Ruthie, she said. Dancing is leading enough for a man in his condition.

Sweetland leaned forward on his knees, his eyes on the floor. Pilgrim have got his heart set, that's plain.

You needs to have a word, Moses.

It made sense to him that Ruthie marry the man, to formalize the relationship already cemented between Pilgrim and themselves. The dancing lessons were just a way of setting them in each other's path. He expected the rest to follow as a matter of course, if there was more to come of it. He'd never considered he might be called on to shift things further along that road himself.

She dotes on you, his mother said. She'll mind what you tells her.

I don't know, he said. That's more your place than mine.

His mother dropped her knitting in her lap, threw her head to one side in frustration. It was you started this whole business, she insisted.

He stared at the tiny woman in her horn-rimmed glasses, surprised every time by the flash of ice in her. All right then, he said.

Ruthie thought the sun shone out of Sweetland's arse in those days. She had always looked to his opinion, over even her mother's. They had never spoken a cross word, she had never refused him a request. Pilgrim was practically family already, he told her, and he had to watch out for them both anyway. It was only a bit of math, he said.

The sick man upstairs was still urging helplessly. There seemed no end of foulness to spew from his guts. Sweetland walked up the stairs with the materials Pilgrim had asked for, placed them in his arms at the landing. He could hear Ruthie's voice speaking low in the room where the refugees were lying. Everything all right? he asked.

Ruthie's here, Pilgrim said. She'll look out to him.

I'll go on, then, he said. Sweetland couldn't look at him, even though the man was blind.

Wince, Ruth called, I needs those rags.

We're all right here, Pilgrim said to Sweetland and he headed steadily along the hallway, turning sharply into the sickroom like a man with eyes to see.

5

ON THE FIRST OF JULY, Hayward Coffin came downstairs to find Queenie dead in her chair by the window, a half-smoked cigarette guttered in her hand. Her book face down on her lap.

The funeral was delayed a day to give Queenie's children time to make the trip back from the mainland. Most were travelling from the oil sands in Alberta, her oldest boy coming from Oregon where he ran a deck and fencing company. All of them forced to wait on the ferry schedule after their flights. The coffin had to be shipped over on the ferry as well, from a funeral home in Fortune, and meantime they waked Queenie on a bare table in the parlour. Clara had washed and laid Queenie out in a purple dress she'd found in her wardrobe, but couldn't dig up a pair of shoes to put on her feet.

"She haven't wore shoes since 1977," Hayward told her. "Put on her slippers," he said, "she might as well be comfortable."

The coffin was heavy as a dory and too wide to be carried through the door where Queenie used to stand smoking and talking to passersby. They had to take out the window above her chair to bring it into the house, and again to lift the dead woman out a day later, half a dozen men reaching their hands to catch her as she crossed into the open air for the first time in forty-odd years. Being careful not to trample the straggle of flowers that had come up from the seed she'd tossed outside.

The Reverend opened up the old church and aired it out the day before the funeral. Clara and Reet Verge and Queenie's daughter swept out the vestibule and polished the dark wooden pews and set out vases of fresh-cut wildflowers. The weather hadn't improved much through the month of June and was still wet and cold into the first week of July. Everyone wearing coats over their mourning clothes. They set Queenie on a trailer behind an ATV and the funeral train followed her down to the church. Sweetland bringing up the rear with Duke and Pilgrim and Loveless.

"Queenie Coffin," Loveless said, "in her coffin."

"She told me she wouldn't going to be around the fall," Sweetland said.

"She been saying that this twenty year," Duke said. "She was bound to be right about it sooner or later."

"A sin to take her out of it," Pilgrim whispered. He had his face lifted high, uncertain about his footing on the dirt path, his left hand inside Sweetland's elbow. "Should have buried the poor woman under the kitchen floor."

"She's dead," Duke said. "It don't matter a goddamn to her where she goes now."

At the church Sweetland guided Pilgrim into the pew beside Clara and Jesse, but the boy swung out a hand to hold the blind man off.

"Jesse," Clara whispered, trying to bring his arm down, but he wouldn't relent.

"What's wrong now?" Sweetland asked him.

"That's Hollis' spot," he said, his eyes toward the front of the church.

"I can make room," Pilgrim said, and he sat two feet from Jesse to leave the space free.

"Well Christ," Sweetland sighed. He sat beside Pilgrim and took out a mouldy hymn book, flipping aimlessly through the pages. "I don't know which one of you is worse."

"It's not like we don't have the room to spare," Pilgrim said.

The sparse congregation murdered a handful of Queenie's favourite hymns without accompaniment, the Reverend playing the first note on a soggy-sounding electric organ. They were all out of the habit and subdued by the occasion. Jesse's was the only clear voice in the church. He had perfect pitch, according to the Reverend, and he showed an unlikely capacity for recalling lyrics. He sometimes forced Sweetland to sit through twenty or thirty impeccably rendered verses of the morose ballads he'd learned from Pilgrim. But he had no patience for the musical limitations of others.

Don't sing, he'd say to Pilgrim, waving his hands and jumping foot to foot like someone standing on hot coals. Don't sing, just say the words.

The wounded sound of the congregation was too much for Jesse and halfway through the second hymn he surrendered, sitting and covering his ears. He rocked back and forth and moaned softly while Clara tried to soothe him, running a hand across his shoulders.

Duke turned to Sweetland from the pew ahead. "I'm with Jesse," he whispered.

The coffin was loaded back onto the trailer for the trip to the new cemetery, a fenced square of hillside that had been ordained to its current purpose only fifty years ago. The old cemetery was tucked away in a droke of trees above the incinerator, up a trail so steep coffins were tied on a sledge and dragged to their final resting place with a rope.

Sweetland lined up behind the family to throw his handful of dirt onto the polished lid and then took up a shovel to help fill the grave, alongside Glad Vatcher and young Hayward Coffin. He was afraid Jesse would stay to watch the morbid proceeding but Clara led him away with the mourners, the boy glancing over his shoulder as he went. The other Coffin boys had gone down to Queenie's house as well and Glad tried to send Hayward after them. "You don't have to be at this now," Glad said, but Hayward shook his head. He was nearly the same age as Glad and the two had fished together a few seasons as younger men. The spade rang against the rocks in the soil with every shovelful as young Hayward stooped and threw the clay down onto his mother, his mouth working fiercely. And they finished the job together without speaking another word.

They made their way down to the reception when they were done, warm enough from the work to carry their jackets. Halfway along Glad and young Hayward began talking back and forth about the weather in Oregon and work, about Loveless losing his calf and the job they had getting the cow on her feet.

"Never gave her a snowball's chance," Glad said. "And she seems right as rain there now."

"Just goes to show, I guess," young Hayward told him.

"You planning to stay for a visit at all?"

"High season," young Hayward said. "Can't afford to miss the work." He looked around and shook his head. It was his first trip home since he left, long before the cod fishery was shut down. "To be honest," he said, "my skin's already starting to crawl being stuck out here. No offence," he added quickly.

At Queenie's house, old Hayward sat against the wall with a grandson on his knee. The Reverend and Jesse staring at the tiny screen of an iPod, sharing a set of headphones to watch that goddamn *Titanic* movie. Pilgrim and Duke and a few others nursed drinks or cups of tea in their chairs while the rest of the crowd milled aimlessly around the cramped rooms that had been Queenie's only weather for most of her adult life. A handful of people lined up to shake old Hayward's hand and offer their final condolences when they saw Sweetland come in, making a public point of their departures that Sweetland ignored.

Sandra was sitting beside Clara on the landing to the stairs, both women holding rum and Cokes. They had gone off to university in St. John's together but Sandra came home as soon as she graduated, teaching at the little school before finally following the rest of her crowd up to the mainland five years ago. She came unsteadily across the room when she saw Sweetland.

"How are you holding up?" he asked, which set her to crying, and he looked away as she collected herself.

She said, "I was going through her things yesterday. Found all the books I've been sending her in a box under the bed. I don't think she touched them."

"No," he said, "she read a few."

"She told you that?"

"She always made a point of saying if it was a book from you she was reading," he said and left it at that.

"I hated the thought of her wasting her time on that Harlequin junk."

"You should know better than most," he said, "she wouldn't going to change to satisfy anyone."

"I know, I know," she said, furious suddenly. "I wasted half my life trying to get her off the smokes. And the other half trying to get her out the door of this *fucking* house." She raised her glass to the faces looking her way. "Sorry," she said. "Sorry." She swallowed half her drink in a single mouthful. "*I was born upstairs here*," she said, her voice lowered to imitate her mother's tobacco-mangled whisper. "*And I'll be leaving this house in a box*. If I had to listen to her say that one more time I would have choked her."

She was on the verge of tears again and Sweetland looked down at his shoes. He said, "I think she was reading one of the books you sent, the last going off."

"Really? Which one?"

"I don't know," he said. "One of the Newfoundland books you sent down."

She nodded emphatically and blew a breath through her lips. "Mom always talked about you," she said. "When she called. She always had a bit of news about you."

"Well," he said. "She had to scrounge for news around here, I imagine."

Sandra kept staring, sizing him up. Drunk enough to be reckless. "You know," she said, "I always thought Mom was sweet on you."

Sweetland laughed and turned halfways away from her.

"She told me once," Sandra said and she waved her hand. "I don't know when this was, ages ago. Before I went off to university. She said she always had it in her head you and her would get married."

"She was having you on," he said. Sweetland glanced across at old Hayward, to be sure their conversation was a private one in the room's racket.

"No. No, she wasn't. She was talking about what it was like growing up around here. Before the lights and all of that. Said you two were thick as thieves."

"We was just youngsters," he said.

She could see she'd embarrassed him. "You need a drink," she said, heading for the kitchen counter to refill her own. She handed him a full glass as he came up to her. She reached into her purse which was hanging over the back of a kitchen chair. "I'm going for a smoke," she said.

"When did you start smoking?"

"Mom's last pack," she said. "Thought I'd finish it off for her. Come out with me."

They put on their coats and walked around the side of the house. Sandra turned her back to the wind to light her cigarette.

"How many left in that pack?"

"Half a dozen or so." She blew a plume of smoke that whipped away in the breeze. She paused then, her head cocked as if to listen, and he did the same instinctively. "Everyone says you're set on staying here."

"Might be I am."

"Must be hard."

"What's that?"

"Sitting in the king's seat on this whole business," she said. "Everyone hung up on your yea or nay. Can't imagine a lonelier spot."

He shrugged. "Verily," he said, aping the minister reading from Psalms at the funeral. Trying to make a joke of it.

"Clara isn't very happy with you," Sandra said.

"Clara was never too happy with me."

"You know that's not true. She thought the sun shone out of your arse when she was a girl."

"Well," he said. "She grew out of that notion."

"I don't know. You're half the reason she came home."

He laughed. "Not fucken likely," he said.

"She wanted you to be around for Jesse. Same as you were for her growing up."

"She never told you that."

"She didn't need to tell me," Sandra insisted. "Why do you think she carried him out to the lighthouse every Sunday? So she wouldn't have to go to church?"

"Never give it much thought, I guess."

Sandra looked drunkenly at the cigarette to see how much more there was to get through. "It's a sin you never had youngsters of your own," she said. "You know what Mom used to say about you? She'd say, That's a good man going to waste, that is."

He was only half listening, still trying on the unlikely notion of why Clara had come back to the island, to see if it fit his memory of the facts.

"What was it happened between you and Effie Priddle?" Sandra asked, and Sweetland glanced across, startled. "You two were engaged once," she said.

"We was never engaged."

"You went off to Toronto looking to make enough money to buy her a ring."

"Who's after telling you that?"

"Was it what happened to your face when you were up there?"

"Sandra."

"I don't think it was," she said, answering her own question. "There's plenty of women would have had you, don't think I don't know."

"We should go back inside."

"Are you gay, Moses?"

He shook his head. "Your poor mother is just put in the ground."

Sandra took a sip of her rum. "Don't mind me," she said. "I'm half-cut."

"I'd say you passed half-cut about three miles back."

"Ha," she said and she raised her glass to him. "I just want you to know," she said. "If you were. It wouldn't make any difference to me."

He shook his head again, a strangled little smile on his face, and he started along the side of the house without her.

Sandra was the last of Queenie's children to leave Sweetland after the funeral. And without giving it much apparent thought, old Hayward packed a suitcase the night before the ferry arrived and went off to live with her in Alberta. The house left exactly as it was, the sheets on the bed and all the dishes in the cupboards. Queenie's extensive library of romances and mysteries in the cardboard boxes she used to store them. It was a decision so sudden that it felt like a second death. The storm door nailed shut. Sweetland was constantly surprised to find the place dark when he looked out his windows at night or ambled by on his walks.

He had taken to stopping in at his stagehead every evening, poking around inside, half expecting to find the last rabbit's head nailed up or some other indignity done to the place. It could be any one of half a dozen men to blame, he knew, or some combination of the group in cahoots. Trying to put a fright into him, thinking he could be scared off. Might be it was Hayward Coffin was at it, he thought, in which case there was nothing more to worry about.

He'd been expecting to see more of Jesse with school out for the summer. But the boy had been knocked off kilter by Queenie's funeral and further again after Hayward's disappearance, which made even less sense to him. Sweetland had been taking him to fish for trout up at Lunin Pond, a bribe to muscle the youngster into sitting through sessions at the Reverend's house, but Jesse lost interest in that excursion in the upheaval around him. He'd been torturing every adult in the cove with the same questions about Hayward's departure, why he left and what he was going to do with himself in Edmonton and whether Jesse would ever see the man again. The day after Hayward left Jesse started claiming he saw a light in Queenie's living room window. Even being told that the electricity to the house was shut off wasn't fact enough to sway him. Sweetland set two chairs outside the window one evening and they stared at the blackened pane until Clara came looking to get him to bed.

"Now," Sweetland said, "you just imagined it."

The boy seemed to hold that demonstration against Sweetland, as if it was designed to make a fool of him, and he grew more standoffish and cold than Sweetland could remember. He was regressing on every level, according to the Reverend. Singing nonsense syllables and waving his hands and rocking on his feet. It was only when he was plugged into some electronic device that the boy seemed to calm down, to lose himself briefly.

The Priddles came back to Sweetland shortly after Hayward went west, and the loss in the cove made even the brothers relatively subdued and reflective. They stayed more or less sober and visited at houses they hadn't gone into in years. Sweetland walked up to the cemetery with them when they went to pay their respects and they stood around the fresh grave, handing a flask back and forth between them. The brothers telling stories of stealing cigarettes from Queenie's stash as youngsters, climbing halfway into her window when she went upstairs to use the bathroom, reaching for the pack where she'd left it beside her chair. Tearing off up to the old cemetery, Queenie cursing at them from the window vent beside the toilet.

It struck Sweetland again it could have been the Priddles who nailed the rabbit head to the door of the stage while he was trying to birth the dead calf in Loveless's barn. For a lark, a little *fuck you* remembrance on their way off the island.

Before they left the graveyard Keith stopped at his mother's marker, kneeling at the white marble to trace a finger across the dates scored into the stone. Barry and Sweetland walked on to the gate. "He's going to have a little bawl now," Barry said, his tone dismissive and affectionate both.

"Spose he can't help feeling it's his fault somehow," Sweetland said.

"He's just drunk is all. He cries watching fucken *Marley & Me.* Keith," he called. "Let's fly the Jesus out of this."

Barry held out the flask but Sweetland shook his head. The boys had never asked him about their mother. It was an odd reticence on their part, he thought, though he was relieved not to have to say anything about the woman or what passed between them.

Barry turned his back on the sight of his brother kneeling at their mother's grave. He glanced across at Sweetland and rolled his eyes. "Keith," he called over his shoulder. "Me and Mose are going on ahead." But he didn't move from where he stood. And they waited there until Keith had finished communing with whatever he imagined his mother might have been before he ended her life on his way into the world.

Two weeks after Hayward left on the ferry for Alberta, Pilgrim came to see Sweetland at the house, Jesse leading him up the path by the hand. A changeable day, threatening rain awhile and then brightening, the clouds scoured away for half an hour before they crowded back.

Jesse sat on the daybed with his headphones, listening to his iPod, in another world altogether while the two men settled at the table. Sweetland watching the mercurial weather as it skated across the afternoon's surface. They talked about the funeral service and Hayward's sudden departure and the Priddles' visit to the island, though the conversation was skittish, distracted. As if they expected any moment to light on a topic more serious and consequential.

The phone rang, so loud in the tiny room that both men started. Sweetland stared at the unlikely contraption where it was fixed to the side of the kitchen cupboard.

"You going to answer that?" Pilgrim asked.

"Trying to think who it might be. No one I wants to speak to, I'm guessing."

"I'd say that's Clara, calling us down to our dinner," Pilgrim said, and he rushed up from the table to look for the corner of the cupboard. He waved his hand until he knocked the phone. "Hello," he said with his back to the room. "No," he said. "Yes, hang on. No, sir, no, he's right here." He held out the phone with a hand over the mouthpiece. "It's that one from the government," Pilgrim said. "The fellow was out here for the last town meeting."

"Well, tell him I'm not here."

"I just said you was."

"Tell him you made a mistake, you're blind for chrissakes."

Pilgrim shook the phone in the direction of Sweetland's voice. "Answer the goddamn phone, Moses."

"Jesus," Sweetland whispered, and he got up to grab it from Pilgrim's hand.

"Mr. Sweetland," the government man said.

"This is he," Sweetland said. *This is he.* He must have heard someone on television use that phrase. And it sounded exactly right for the false prick on the other end.

"I hope you're keeping well."

"I imagine you wishes I was dead, like everyone else around here."

There was a pause on the other end and Sweetland looked down at the slack length of cord that hung to the floor and pooled there in a beige spiral. It was the only phone in the house, a rotary dial that had been installed when telephone service first reached the island in the early seventies. His mother used to haul the twelve feet of cord all the way across the hall to the living room so she could talk and watch the afternoon soaps at the same time. Sweetland forced to duck under it on his way in or out of the house. Used so little now he'd never thought to replace it.

"Mr. Sweetland," the government man said, "I've heard the news about Queenie Coffin. I just wanted to say I'm sorry for the loss."

He turned to look at Pilgrim. "So this is a sympathy call, is it?"

"I've also been in touch with Mr. Loveless and he has committed to signing on to the package, you're aware of this I presume."

"News to me."

Sweetland could almost hear the man roll his eyes.

"I thought I should check in with you," the government man said finally, "to see if there have been any developments since we talked last."

Other than someone mutilating the rabbits on his line and nailing a severed head to his stage door. Other than a drawerful of anonymous threats. Other than Queenie Coffin days in the ground and Hayward packed off to the mainland. Other than fucken Loveless.

"No developments," he said, "no." There was a short intake of breath on the line, and Sweetland could feel the man gearing up a prepared speech. "Good of you to call, all the same."

"Mr. Sweetland."

"Bye now." And he set the phone back in its cradle. He glanced across at Pilgrim, who kept his face turned away. "That was Clara, was it?" he said. "Calling you down to your dinner?"

"Now, Moses."

"You knew he was going to call here today, didn't you."

Pilgrim turned his head left and right. "Clara and Reet have been talking to him."

"And the women sent you up here to make sure he got through."

Pilgrim looked naked and adrift in his seat, not able to set his blind eyes anywhere to anchor himself.

"You're a gutless wonder, you are."

"Jesus Christ, Mose," Pilgrim said. He slapped a hand against his thigh. "You got to stop being so goddamn bullheaded about this."

"Why?" Sweetland said. "Tell me why it is I got to stop?"

Pilgrim made a motion with his arms that seemed almost involuntary, a spasm of frustration and spite. He uncrossed his legs and crossed them the other way. He said, "How much longer is it you expects to be around, Moses?"

"Fuck," Sweetland said. "How should I know?"

"You're an old man," Pilgrim said. "We're all old men. And what's Jesse going to have here once we goes?"

"I don't know. He'll have the Reverend."

"The Reverend is older than we are, for Jesus sake."

Sweetland glanced out the window and back.

"Clara's going to be left alone with the youngster is what's going to happen. She've got a chance to go somewhere with a bit of money to see the boy looked after. And you're going to fuck it up."

Sweetland could hear the man breathing, his head turned away in a snit. He looked over at Jesse sitting oblivious, bobbing his head to his music. Sweetland went across the room to lean over him, took the headphones out of the boy's ears. Jesse grabbed at them, automatically agitated, and Sweetland had to hold his wrists to keep him still. "Jesse," he said, "your Poppy thinks we should all leave Sweetland like Hayward Coffin. Pack everything up and go. What do you think about that?"

"Leave the boy alone, Mose."

"You want to go live in St. John's?"

Jesse's face went still, his dark eyes darting.

"Hey? We'll burn the whole place down and leave, will we?"

Pilgrim was on his feet and coming toward them, both hands aloft like a man about to cast a stagey magic spell. "Jesse," he said.

Sweetland let go of his wrists and Jesse pressed them against his ears, rocking and moaning where he sat. Sweetland took a step back, his own hands shaking. Feeling ashamed of himself, and vindicated, and murderous. He said, "We'll get on the ferry tomorrow and you'll never see anyone you knows from here ever again."

Pilgrim bumped into him from behind and he pushed Sweetland away. Crouched over the wailing youngster. "Jesse," he said, "it's all right now, Jesse. Moses is just playing around."

But there was no pulling the boy out of his spiral. Pilgrim phoned down to Clara and by the time she came running Jesse was on the floor, knocking his forehead rhythmically against the boards. She exchanged words with Sweetland, the two shouting back and forth, Jesse yelling louder still to drown out the noise. Eventually they had to send for the Reverend, who cleared everyone out of the kitchen and spent the better part of an hour trying to calm the youngster. A small crowd had gathered outside and they watched Jesse walk down to his house, leaning on the Reverend's arm like a septuagenarian, exhausted and disoriented.

"I hope you're happy," Clara said to Sweetland as she followed her son along the path. Her voice viciously calm.

Sweetland spent the rest of the afternoon splitting wood. Stunned, and sick of himself, and hoping he might disappear awhile in the mechanical strain of work, of occupation. He stood the junks on the chopping block, cleaving the dry birch and spruce with a clipped thock, like the sound of some massive timepiece ticking steadily. He leaned on the axe to catch his breath and it came flooding back, the look on Jesse's face, Sweetland with a head of steam and barrelling down on the youngster. He reared back with the axe suddenly and flung it over the roof of the shed.

He heard footsteps along the side of the house behind him then and he turned to stacking the freshly split junks. Wouldn't look up from the work even after his visitor stopped behind him.

"You want a hand with that," the Reverend asked.

Sweetland set the wood on the pile along the side of the shed. Brushed the bark from his coat. "You idn't dressed for this kind of work," he said. Sweetland carried on as the Reverend stood watching in his black pants and jacket. "How's the young one now?"

"He was asleep when I left him."

"He's all right, then."

"I wouldn't mind hearing what made him act out like that."

Sweetland shook his head. Acting out, the Reverend called it. Like it was all just a show, something put on to entertain. He swore under his breath, walked out past the shed to look for the axe. Trying to settle himself as he searched around. The Reverend followed behind him to the back wall of the shed and Sweetland brushed past the man, walking to the side door with the recovered axe in his hand. Sat inside with the head in his lap, working the stone across the cutting edge. The Reverend came as far as the door and stood waiting there.

"I imagine Pilgrim already give you the play-by-play," Sweetland said.

"He gave me his version of events."

"Well who am I to argue with a blind man?"

The Reverend looked away out the door and Sweetland thought he might leave without saying anything else. But he turned back to the gloom in the shed. "I know how you feel about that boy," he said.

"What you knows about how I feels," Sweetland said, but the Reverend pushed ahead, talking over him.

"And you might think you're watching out for Jesse in all of this. You've got everyone else convinced. But I don't buy it."

"Is that a fact?"

"That's a fact, yes."

"And I imagine you're about to tell me how you sees it different."

"I think you're being a selfish son of a bitch, is what I think."

Sweetland looked up from his lap, surprised by the obscenity, mild as it was. "Well," he said, "you would be an expert on selfish sons a bitches."

"You can muddy the waters if that makes you feel better. But it doesn't change what's going on here. The only card you have left in this game is Jesse. And you just might get what you want if you keep playing him."

"There's the door," Sweetland said.

"I want you to ask yourself," the Reverend said, "if using that youngster is worth the price."

"You make sure you close it behind you when you go."

The Reverend watched him a few moments longer before he left, pulling the door shut. Sweetland leaning back over his lap, repeating the sickle-shaped motion of the sharpening stone against the blade on his knee, the scrape of it like something working at bone.

He flicked on the radio in the kitchen when he went inside, a voice announcing the dates for the summer food fishery. Five cod per person per boat per day, the voice said. He hadn't eaten a morsel since breakfast and he opened a can of tuna, put two slices of bread in the toaster. Staring out the window over the sink as he waited. Flicked off the radio and slapped Miracle Whip on the toast. Sat at the table, looking at the sandwich a few minutes before throwing it in the garbage can under the sink.

He walked down to Duke's barbershop and let himself in, stood awhile studying the stalled chess game, then scanned blankly across the photos and clippings pasted to the wall. Stopped at an old Polaroid from their second stint on the mainland. Duke and himself grinning at the camera, in hard hats and undershirts. Both of them hungover no doubt. The colours had faded over the years, but it was his old face in the picture, without the purple scarring, without the grafted skin as tight and smooth as the skin of an apple. A shock still, to see himself in that other life, unmarked.

It was oppressively hot all that summer, a pulsing furnace heat through July and August. Six days a week they were at it, twelve hours a day, framing in the sprawling suburbs of York and Etobicoke, hammering two-by-fours in the sink of merciless humidity. He had never felt so recklessly lonely, so desperate to lose himself in the mindless drudge of work, in drink. Homesickness felt like the only thing keeping him alive.

He heard the door and turned to see the proprietor ducking his head under the frame.

"You're looking thoughtful," Duke said. "You have a notion for the game finally?"

"Might be I do."

Duke raised his face to the ceiling. "The night is far spent," he said, "the day is at hand." He crossed to the board and stared. "So what's your notion?"

"Throw the fucken thing in the stove."

"You're not giving up on it?"

"I'm done," Sweetland said.

Duke stood with his hands on his hips a moment before he began moving the pieces back to their starting positions, glancing up now and then to see how Sweetland was taking it. "I hear you had a little racket with Jesse," he said.

Sweetland made a dismissive motion with his hand.

Duke turned the board slightly after he had set the pieces, lifted the pawn on the far left ahead two spaces. The same opening, every time. "Your move, Bobby Fischer."

"I think I'll sit this one out," he said.

Duke nodded helplessly. He climbed into the barber's chair and the two men watched each other in the mirror. "I'm sure Jesse'll be fine," he said.

Sweetland went to bed early, not expecting to sleep. He turned his head periodically to check the time, the digital figures changing at such a glacial pace he finally unplugged the clock altogether. Stars through the window, a she-moon's narrow sliver of light.

She's on her back, Uncle Clar said when Sweetland first asked what *she-moon* meant. This was long before he was old enough to understand Clar's cryptic explanation, and he couldn't remember now when it came clear to him. Likely it was Duke got there first and passed the details on to him. A year older, and more reckless, always pushing ahead of what was handed out. It was Duke took Sweetland dogging the young couples when they were boys, chasing them up onto the mash or to the meadow out behind the church where they snuck off to mess around in the grass.

Pure devilment at first, doing their best to be an annoyance, pelting the couples with crabapples or spruce cones. Battering the hell out of it then, the young fellow flinging rocks at their heads. It was like hitting a hornets' nest with a stick. Until it became something more serious and surreptitious. The game about slinking as close as possible, seeing as much as you could. Sweetland trying to describe it to Pilgrim afterwards, dresses pushed above the thigh, the naked skin and busy hands down there. Bare asses silvered in the moonlight. Pilgrim's eyes wide with blind wonder. Lord Jesus, what a world they were living in.

Watching Queenie Coffin undress through her bedroom window, the summer her sister took sick with typhoid. Queenie Buffett, she was then. The tiny bedroom on the ground floor. Standing up close to the panes to take off her clothes for him, bold as brass. Hair cropped as short as a boy's, pale nipples on a board chest. Hairless skin down there, that foreign crease looking oddly chaste. A simple pleasure between them, to see and be seen. Hardly a sexual thing at all, Sweetland thought, but for the hard-on that troubled him for hours afterwards. At some point he considered he should do the same for her, but Queenie showed no interest in a tit-for-tat exchange. And it was a relief to him that she did not.

He'd sat behind Queenie in the one-room schoolhouse for two winters and they seemed a pair of sorts because of it. But they were just two among the battalion of youngsters that knocked around in the cove together, fishing for conners off the stagehead, carting their dippers up on the mash to pick berries in the fall. During the quarantine she was moved out of the bed she shared with the sister and they jerried up a room with a cot and sheets hung from the ceiling on the ground floor. Sweetland would visit with her at that window, talking back and forth with her through the glass. There was a wooden vent at the base of the frame and he would smuggle treats to her, sweet-bread, raisins, a whip of licorice. Caught sight of her changing as he made for the window one evening and stopped dead. Queenie coming straight up to the panes when she saw him there. Bored out of her mind probably, pent up and restless. Half a dozen times after that she had undressed for him, presented herself a few minutes before putting on her nightclothes, her manner serious and unhurried. Her nakedness like a new thing to him each time, as if another layer had been peeled away.

And then her sister died. Which, it turned out, was the end of many things. He carried on visiting with her through the weeks of quarantine that followed, but never saw her naked again. Stopped expecting or even wanting it. Years later, it was Hayward Coffin who took her up onto the mash, and Sweetland thought nothing of the fact. The exchange at her window something he'd never spoken of, to Queenie or anyone else. Dead and buried up on the hill now, that young girl and her strange, unacknowledged gift to him.

Sweetland looked over at the clock's blank face. He couldn't begin to guess what time it was. Late, was all he knew. He sat up, reached for his clothes. Sidestepped the door, went out the hall and downstairs into the dark of the kitchen. He drew off a glass of water at the sink and drained half in one go. The angry, alien glow on the waterfront flaring beyond Queenie's house when he glanced out the window.

The fire was lighting the entire harbour by the time he made his way to the shore path, flames coming through the stage's ceiling, through the door standing open, through the broken panes in the side window. Sweetland could see all the way across to the government wharf and beyond it to the church on the point, clear as day. He could see his boat set loose from the stagehead, drifting away from the fire toward the breakwater. Cinders were dropping through the floorboards, hissing as they hit the water pooled in the landwash underneath, flankers rising lazily on the drafts of heat, floating out across the cove. Sweetland couldn't get within thirty feet of the burning building but he could smell the gasoline used to set the blaze. The place must have been soaked to go up so fast.

People running out of their houses behind him, shouting over the noise of the fire. Youngsters sent up onto the roofs of nearby buildings to sweep burning embers off the shingles. The Priddle brothers and Reet Verge and a dozen others carted buckets of seawater to put out spot fires in yards and the grass along the paths. Garden hoses sprayed down from houses further up the hill and Glad Vatcher brought his boat along the waterline, dousing the closest buildings with the stream of a pressure washer.

The inferno was so intense that the stage collapsed on itself and fell into the landwash within an hour and there was only watching it then, the entire population standing over the slowly dissipating heat, their clothes and skin stained a pulsing red and orange in the dark light. Sweetland looked up and down the line of eerily lit faces, like some biblical image of the apocalypse. The anonymous arsonists standing there among them, taking it in.

THE ISLAND WAS OVERRUN in the wake of the incident with the lifeboat. As if, for the first time ever, someone had placed Sweetland on a map for strangers to find it. RCMP officers and investigators from the Coast Guard and Transport Canada arriving in twos and threes to take statements from Bob-Sam Lavallee and the Reverend and Sweetland himself.

Bob-Sam had the Coast Guard officers stay at the lighthouse during their visit and they told him what they knew. The men in the lifeboat were, in fact, Sri Lankan and they'd all spent a life's savings to be smuggled into the United States. It was anyone's guess how they ended up bobbing around the North Atlantic. There were two that died in the hold during the trip and they thought they were all going to perish down there before they were lowered in the lifeboat and cut loose. Not so much as a drop of water among them.

What about the ship they were on? Sweetland asked.

They was snuck aboard in the dark, Bob-Sam said. And put off in the middle of the night. Never spoke three words to any of the crew. White fellows, they said. But they could've been Russian or Scandinavian or Spanish.

There were reporters and photographers coming off the ferry runs for a while as well. Most of them stayed only as long as the ferry was docked and they charged around Chance Cove in a mad rush, snapping photos and taking quotes from the folks they spotted on the wharf or outside the houses. They were like a crowd of wild goats let loose in town, butting their heads into sheds and kitchens to nose around with their cameras, tearing off without so much as a kiss-my-arse. The women going on about the cinnamon colour of the refugees' skin and the hair on them so black it gleamed like oil. Loveless inviting them in for watery drinks and Jam Jams, making himself out to be a central character in the events. They was a sight, sir, he liked to say, come out of the fog like a boatload of the dead, poor souls.

Sweetland was poisoned with the whole affair and wished they'd all fuck off home out of it, leave him and the island alone. But everyone wanted to hear his version of events and hunted him down to pose the same half-dozen questions. All of them asking him to spell his name, for accuracy's sake. Sweetland, he'd say as they bent their heads over their notebooks, *S-w-i-e-t-l-u-n-d.*

They glanced up and he shrugged. It's an old Swedish name, he said.

A few reporters settled in for days at a time. A fey gentleman with a southern accent and a limp who claimed to be writing for *The New Yorker*, though nothing appeared there that Sweetland ever heard of. An old-time drinker with a Toronto magazine who asked to be shown some local colour and spent a night passed out under Sweetland's kitchen table with his pants around his ankles.

There was a television crew from the CBC who set Sweetland up near the waterside window in his stage. A crowd of youngsters at the open door to watch and they recruited young Hayward Coffin to hold a silver reflector just out of the frame. The interviewer asking Sweetland how he felt, coming upon those lost souls out there in the fog, to find the dead boy in the lifeboat.

How I felt? he said.

Yes, she said. She was Ruthie's age, or thereabouts. She wore pink slacks and a short white jacket and clownish makeup she retouched whenever the cameraman changed positions or swapped out his battery pack. An air of mainland entitlement about her. She'd come at him with a puff pad before they began and he tried to fend her off. It's for the glare, she explained as she lowered his arm and had a go at his face with the powder. He took a dislike to her that seemed unaccountably fierce.

How I felt? he asked again.

Her eyes didn't waver. Were you surprised? she said.

No, he said. No, I had a letter come the week before, asking me to meet them out there.

She smiled and nodded. She turned to the cameraman and he lowered the camera from his shoulder. She leaned toward Sweetland with both elbows on her clipboard. We're just trying to tell the story here, she said to him, her voice almost a whisper. No one's trying to embarrass you or make you look foolish.

You'll want to talk to my sister, he said suddenly, surprising himself. He hadn't spoken three words to Ruthie since the night he'd caught her sneaking out of the Reverend's office.

Your sister?

She looked after the one that died, down to the church, he said.

Sweetland was devoted to Ruthie who had lost her father before she had a chance to know the man. He was often first awake in the house when she was a girl, and she came out of her mother's room to meet him at the top of the stairs, shivering in her nightdress. He carried her down to the kitchen in the dark of winter mornings, sat her on the stove while he laid shavings and kindling into the firebox, feeding the flames for quick heat. Ruthie chatting away to him about the dreams she'd had or some game she'd been playing with the cat or the size of Mrs. Vatcher's drawers on the line. He'd lift her down once the fire had taken hold and send her into the pantry for plates and cutlery to set the table while he fried a panful of capelin.

Sweetland walked her to the outhouse after dark, watching the stars as he waited for her to do her business. Carried her on his back when they climbed up to the mash to pick berries, Ruthie singing into his ear as payment for the ride.

It was Sweetland who killed the rooster when it went after Ruthie. A creature so vicious you couldn't turn your back to it, his mother carrying a stick to slap it away when she went out to collect the eggs. The red comb flopping side to side as it strutted around in a military rage. Ruthie skipping innocently across the yard one afternoon and the cock flying up at her, slashing at her clothes and face. Talons sharp as fish hooks. Tore her dress at the shoulder, ripped one earlobe so it hung by a string of flesh.

Sweetland beat the bird to death with a barrel stave while his mother sewed Ruthie's lobe back on with needle and thread in the kitchen. He was so savage the rooster couldn't be cleaned to make a meal of it.

That's a waste of good meat, Uncle Clar said, scraping the ragged mess up with a shovel.

Sweetland was still in a lather. He could hear Ruthie bawling in the kitchen where Hollis was holding her arms while their mother stitched the girl's lobe in place. He swung at the animal as Uncle Clar walked past him, wanting to kill the dead thing over again. The ring of wood against the shovel making his elbows tingle. He stamped on the ruined corpse where it fell to the ground.

Bist thee done? Uncle Clar asked him.

I'm done, Sweetland said. Though he knew he was not, and likely never would be.

That same murderous commotion at work in him now, though he didn't know who it should be directed toward, the Reverend or Ruthie. That blind fucker, Pilgrim. The fallen world itself.

What's her name? the reporter asked.

Sweetland looked at her dumbly.

Your sister, she said. What did you say her name was?

Ruthie, he said. Ruth Pilgrim.

I will definitely talk to her, the reporter said. As soon as we're done here.

And he answered her questions about his feelings then, making a bloody fool of himself from all he could tell.

6

THE RCMP PATROL BOAT out of Burgeo motored into the cove a week after the fire. The constable came to Sweetland's house and asked about the smell of gas everyone remarked on and his boat untied and if there was anyone who might be holding a grudge against him or might have a reason to target his property.

"Only everybody," Sweetland said.

The constable made a useless note in his black notebook, and Sweetland thought for a moment about digging the threatening letters out of the drawer where he kept them. But there hardly seemed a point to it.

"So you have no idea who might be responsible?"

"Could be half a dozen people. A dozen," he corrected himself.

"Well," the constable said. "Unless someone comes forward with more information, it isn't likely we'll ever know who set the fire."

"Won't no one come forward," Sweetland said. "I wouldn't tell you myself if I knew."

The constable cocked his head. "Why is that?"

If you scald your arse, Sweetland's mother used to say, you got to learn to sit on your blisters. He said, "I got what was coming to me, I expect."

Sweetland went down to Duke's shop in the afternoon to look in on the chess game that was going on without him. Pilgrim already sitting there with Duke. The two men had been interviewed by the constable as well and they couldn't let the topic go, throwing out names of the most likely culprits, speculating on how they might have gone about it, the idiocy of risking every building in Chance Cove.

"It's lucky you still got the boat anyway," Pilgrim said.

"Whoever it was," Duke said, "wanted to make sure you had a way to get the hell out of here, is what I think."

The chess game looked to be halfways done already. A couple dozen moves made on each side, a third of the black pieces removed from the board. As though time was running out and the players were in a race to finish.

"You still planning on going out for the food fishery?" Pilgrim asked.

Sweetland gave him a look that Pilgrim could sense from across the room.

"Jesse's been asking," he said by way of explanation. "I don't know if Clara would be too keen on the notion."

Pilgrim made a motion with his shoulders. "Might be she's feeling a little more kindly toward you," he said. "Account of the fire taking your stage."

"A silver lining to every cloud."

"Come over tonight," Pilgrim said, "after the youngster's gone to bed. We'll see how it goes."

He watched the house from his kitchen window that evening and waited half an hour after Jesse's light went out. Walked around to the back door and let himself in. Pilgrim called from the living room and Sweetland went along the narrow hall, stood there in the doorway.

"How's the house?" he asked.

"Everyone's grand," Pilgrim said.

Clara didn't turn her head from the television and Sweetland thought it was a mistake to have come. "What is it you're watching?"

"*Mad Men*," Pilgrim said. "Clara can't get enough of it."

Sweetland glanced at the screen. An office of impeccably dressed men from another age, all of them smoking like tilts. Pilgrim got up from his seat. "You'll have a drink," he said and went by Sweetland to the kitchen. "Go in and sit down."

He took a chair just inside the doorway, his eyes on the television. Every fifteen seconds someone lit up a fresh cigarette. It made him crave one himself.

"When was it you quit smoking?" Clara asked, as if she could sense that urge rising in him.

"I don't know. Sometime after your mother died."

"She was always after you to give them up, I remember."

"Ruthie was always after me to do one thing or another. Thought I needed mothering, I spose."

"She thought you needed a wife, more like it."

"Well," he said. And he shrugged at the television.

"I remember you used to let me light them for you."

He looked at her. "I never no such thing," he said.

"You did," she insisted. "I'd sit in your lap and strike the match on the side of the box."

"How old were you?"

"I don't know," she said. "Five or six."

"Ruthie must have loved that."

"Mom never knew a thing about it," Clara said. And then she said, "I can't believe you forgot about that."

"More can I," he said. He hated confronting those lost moments, being presented with some detail from his past and having to look on it like a stranger. It made his life feel like a made-up thing. A net full of holes.

"I still expect to see you with a cigarette, for some reason. Even after all this time."

"I could light one up, if that'd make you feel better."

"There's only one thing would make me feel better about you."

He turned back to the television.

"It wouldn't be the end of the world, would it?" she said. "To live somewhere else?"

Pilgrim appeared in the doorway, holding a drink. "Moses," he said, "where are you?"

"In hell, I think," Sweetland whispered.

The drink was rye and water without ice. Pilgrim hadn't brewed shine since Clara came back to Sweetland with Jesse in tow. Couldn't make it cheap enough anymore to compete with the controller's liquor, he said.

They watched the rest of the show in silence but for Clara setting the scene for Pilgrim now and again. They're in a car, she'd say. He's in a motel room with his secretary. Sweetland and Clara talked aimlessly during the commercials while Pilgrim was making fresh drinks in the kitchen and he tried to keep clear of anything that might sour the visit. Before he left, Sweetland said, "Be all right if I looked in on him a minute?"

"Don't wake him," she said. "He'll be up half the night."

Sweetland went up the stairs with a hand to the rail, padded along the hall to Jesse's room. The door was closed and Sweetland turned the knob carefully. Eased it open and listened awhile to be sure he hadn't disturbed the sleeper. The boy was on his back with all the sheets kicked to the foot of the bed. One knee propped against the wall, both arms flung above his head. He was wearing the only pyjamas he would consent to put on, a pair he'd outgrown years before and refused to surrender, though the sleeves came almost to his elbows, the pant legs rising halfway up his shins. Clara had been trying to get him into something new for months, going so far as to ask for Sweetland's help cajoling.

Jesus, Sweetland told him, you looks like a streel in those machines.

Don't care, Jesse said.

You looks like one of them street urchins got no one belonged to them.

Don't care, Jesse repeated.

The pyjamas made him look hopelessly vulnerable in his bed, his limbs like pale shoots growing out of the fabric, the smooth expanse of his belly exposed. The little well of the navel a thimbleful of darkness. Jesse's face was turned toward the door but angled unnaturally up toward the headboard. He looked like he'd fallen from a height, dropped from a roof-top or a headland and come to rest in that mangled posture. Sweetland wanted to ease the boy's arms back down at his sides, to straighten the leg crooked against the wall. He wanted to lie down with the boy awhile and listen to him breathe.

He allowed himself to lift the bedsheets up over Jesse's chest, but wouldn't even chance touching the youngster's hair before he left. Closed the door as carefully as he'd opened it, made his way back downstairs to the living room where he said his good-nights. He mentioned going out after a few cod when the food fishery opened and said that Jesse was welcome to come if he wanted. And he walked drunk-enly home, with no idea if Clara would allow it or not.

She brought Jesse down to the government wharf two days later, the boy carting their lines coiled in plastic tubs, Pilgrim following behind. Sweetland reached a hand up as the boy climbed into the boat and Jesse turned into his belly to hug him briefly. The first time in years.

Clara helped Pilgrim down and handed their gear to Sweetland. "Make sure he keeps his lifejacket on," she said.

"Have you got a lifejacket for Hollis?" Jesse asked.

"Hollis is staying home out of it with your mother," Pilgrim said.

Clara looked down at Sweetland, apologetic.

"Hollis can come if he wants," Sweetland said. "But I got neither lifejacket for him."

Jesse mumbled a few words to the air beside him and then nodded, listening. "Hollis says he don't need one," he announced.

It promised to be a large day, clear skies and hardly a breath of wind. Sweetland let Jesse take the boat around the breakwater and he glanced back into the cove as they made the turn, the remains of his stagehead a dark smudge on the view, the blackened timbers awash at high tide. Jesse asked a stream of questions about the fire, wanting to know how it started and how hot the fire might have been and if Sweetland planned to build another stage. Sweetland was as evasive as he could manage as the boy pressed on about who might have set the fire and why they might have done it. "No telling people's minds" was all he said about it.

Just as they turned into open water, a harbour porpoise kicked up off the bow. Jesse shouted and pointed as the porpoise veered down and away from the boat.

"Puffin pig," Sweetland said, using the name he'd grown up with.

"It's not a pig," Jesse insisted. He offered the proper name and then spelled it, to underline its propriety.

"Pardon me, Your Highness," Sweetland said, and he waited then for Jesse to ask about the pig they'd had when Sweetland was a youngster. But the habitual question never came, lost in the novelty of steaming out to the ledge, Sweetland guessed, the prospect of going after the cod. Though it felt like another crack showing in their lives together. The boy as good as gone already.

They motored on to Saturday Ledge where he cut the engine. They let out their lines until the jiggers touched bottom, brought them up a yard and started into the work of it, hauling and releasing the full length of their arms. It was the first day of the food fishery and there were boats up and down the shore, on the Shag Rocks, on the Offer Ledge, on Pilgrim's Shoal, and away out to the Mackerel Cliffs at the south end. It almost looked like old times on the water, everyone at the cod.

"Tell me about the pig you had," Jesse asked then.

"What pig?" Sweetland said.

"The pig used to chase you and Hollis."

"I don't remember much about it," he said. He spat over the gunwale into the water. Almost angry to feel so relieved.

"Your father bought a piglet."

"Right," he said. "Father bought a piglet from old man Vatcher one spring, kept it in the shed out back."

As pale and inquisitive as an infant child, it was. Old eyes watching them. He and Hollis fought over who would bring it table scraps and fish guts, the pink snout raised above the rail as they approached the pen. Through the summer it foraged free and learned to follow them around the property, sat outside the door while they ate their meals. A year later it weighed as much as a handbar of salt fish, five feet from snout to tail. It had taken to waiting for Sweetland and Hollis to come home from school, chasing them out to the flake used for drying capelin and squid, the boys jumping onto the surface and the pig rooting underneath in a mock fury. They'd make a break for the shed with the snorting pig at their heels, climb the walls of the pen, shouting down at the creature snuffling beneath them. It shouldered the boards so the building shook, waiting for them to head to the flake. They'd go back and forth between the two refuges a dozen times, until their mother or Uncle Clar told them to stop tormenting the animal.

Jesse turned his head to the water suddenly, taking up his line hand over hand, the water spinning off the nylon as it came over the gunwale.

"You got one already?" Pilgrim asked.

Sweetland tied off his line to help gaff the fish aboard, but Jesse flicked his catch expertly over the gunwale onto the deck. Stood back then, staring at the thing, his mouth open.

The bag was tied tight at the mouth but the jigger had ripped a hole in the plastic and Sweetland could see the rabbit carcasses inside when he bent to free the hook. The heads and back paws removed. Most of the flesh gone off the bones after two months in the ocean.

"Well?" Pilgrim said from where he was standing aft. "Did he get one?"

Sweetland glanced up at Jesse. He tried to smile, though all the feeling had gone out of his face. "He got one," Sweetland said, not wanting to explain what the boy had hauled aboard. Not sure he could. "But he's too small to keep." He used the gaff to lift the bag out over the water and dropped it, watched it sink down into the dark.

"Well there's fish about anyway," Pilgrim said.

"Put your line back out," Sweetland told the boy. "Where was I?"

"Stop tormenting the animal," Jesse said uncertainly.

"Put your line out," Sweetland said again and he handed the jigger across. Once Jesse had fallen into his rhythm, he repeated, "Stop tormenting the animal."

They never had a name for the pig, which seemed strange to Sweetland after the fact. The Pig, they called it. Piggy. Porker. It would eat from their hands and lick them clean, thorough, fastidious, he could still remember the feel of that tongue between his fingers, the warm snout pushing against his palm. Its eyes closed as it worked, the lashes pale and fine.

They came home from school one afternoon and there was no sign of the pig. Piggy, they yelled. Hey, Porker! Ran to the flake whistling and shouting. Cold enough to see their breath as they called. They crept out to the shed, thinking the animal might have learned to lie in wait for them, planning a sneak attack. They slapped at the walls before poking their heads inside. But the pig was gone. Rooting through the garbage pile back of Loveless's house in all likelihood, or stuffing itself on the filth thrown into the landwash from the stageheads. And they didn't think more of it until they sat to their supper, when their father stood to carve a shoulder of pork, laying lavish portions on the plates.

Hollis turned toward him, but Sweetland wouldn't look at his brother for fear of bawling. He folded his arms and sat as far from the meal as his chair back allowed. And Hollis did the same. Sweetland chewing on the inside of his mouth as the adults cleaned their plates. They were made to sit at the table until after dark. He could hear their parents arguing in the pantry and their mother came in to clear the cold food away. Eight months pregnant with Ruthie then, though the boys were told nothing about it and didn't realize a child was on the way until the morning the girl was born. They were sent to their room finally and their father was forced to give most of the meat away so it wouldn't spoil, hocks and crackle, bacon and ribs and chops.

"Father never did speak a word to us about it," Sweetland said. "Took sick that November month, just after Ruthie was born, and he lay in his bed all winter. Died the end of February."

"What was wrong with him?"

"What?" Sweetland said. He'd never mentioned his father dying as part of the story before and was surprised to have it come to the surface now.

"Your father," Jesse said. "What made him sick?"

"No one knows," he said.

Uncle Clar wanted to take the man across to Burgeo or Placentia to see a doctor, but his father wouldn't hear of it. I'll be right the once, he'd insisted. He was almost twenty years older than his wife but still a youngish man, just shy of sixty. And seemed to be getting better, as he predicted, just before he died. Ate a full meal of salt beef and cabbage that Sunday, the first time in months, propped against pillows in his sickbed. Asked after dessert and Sweetland carried up a partridgeberry pudding his mother had boiled in an old baking soda can. His father took three mouthfuls of the pudding, chewing slowly, like he was trying to guess the spices hidden within the whole. Slumped over in bed then, never made a sound.

"He was dead?" Jesse asked.

"Gone," Sweetland said. "Just like that."

His father's ravenous appetite is what Sweetland remembered about the event, how incongruous it was. Eating against his end, Uncle

Clar used to say. The body seeming to know ahead of the man himself what was coming.

Pilgrim stood up, leaned a little ways over the gunwale to start hauling in his jigger.

"Have you got one?" Jesse said.

"Feels like a fair size."

The fish loomed as it rose, pulling dead, the white of its belly flickering out of the dark. "Jesus, she's heavy," Pilgrim said. It came to the surface calm, sacrificial, as all cod did, until it broke the surface where it twisted weakly and came clean off the hook.

"Lost her," Pilgrim said, holding his bald jigger aloft.

"She's right there," Jesse said, pointing.

The fish lay stunned and adrift at the surface, as if it didn't realize yet it was free. Sweetland miles away, stunned and drifting in much the same fashion.

"Right there," Jesse said again, and Sweetland shook himself into motion finally, tied off his line, reached out with a gaff to snag and haul it aboard. It slapped on the deck without urgency and then lay still, its mouth working soundlessly, the silver coin of one eye gaping at the sky.

"How big is she?" Pilgrim asked.

"Big," Jesse shouted.

Sweetland put a hand to the gunwale against the ocean's swell, waiting for the spell of vertigo to pass. "She's a beauty, all right," he said.

It was still shy of noon when they made their meagre quota and started back for the cove.

"You want to clean some fish or you want to take the wheel?" Sweetland asked the boy.

"The wheel," Jesse said.

Sweetland reached into a cooler at his feet for two beers and he sat aft beside Pilgrim, the men cleaning the cod as they steamed in. Gulls swirling above and behind them like a foul plume of engine exhaust, the scavengers screaming and fighting over the guts as they were tossed into the sea.

They finished Jesse's five and Pilgrim's, and Sweetland said he'd look after his own when he got back to the house. He leaned out into the spray to rinse his hands and forearms in the water, and he looked forward then, watching Jesse standing to one side of the wheel, his free hand moving like someone conducting an orchestra. The noise of the engine made it impossible to hear, but he knew the boy was carrying on a conversation with Sweetland's long-dead brother.

"You want another beer?" he asked Pilgrim.

"I'm all right."

Sweetland walked up to the wheelhouse and set the two empties at his feet.

"This is where the accident happened," Jesse said to him.

Sweetland glanced out at the water to get his bearings. They were just passing over the Wester Shoals where he and his brother used to trawl for cod in the fall. "I spose it was Hollis told you that, was it?"

"Poppy told me."

Sweetland looked back at Pilgrim sitting aft. "What else did Poppy tell you?"

"He said you was the only one was there, so it's only you can tell the story."

"What about your buddy there at the wheel? He was there, wouldn't he?"

"He says you'll tell the story when you're ready." Jesse didn't take his eyes from the water ahead, talking in the same flat tone.

Sweetland looked away a minute as the vertigo crawled over him again.

"You don't have to," Jesse said.

"Just this once," Sweetland said. "And Hollis can correct me if I gets anything wrong, how's that?"

"Okay."

"Okay, then." He reached into the cooler for a beer. "We come out to do some trawling," he said.

October month. They had the trawl baited with fresh squid and shot it out, let it fish on the bottom a couple of hours. They'd just gotten the boat that spring, a skiff with an ailing Acadia one-cylinder inboard that they'd bought from Glad Vatcher's father. They'd been the only crowd in Chance Cove without a motor for years by then, still sculling out to the fishing grounds every day. Old Mr. Vatcher took a little cash money and a share of the summer's fish as payment, not half what the boat was worth. A calm day but a strong tide running. Sweetland aft at the tiller, keeping the boat steady ahead of the tide, Hollis pulling in the trawl up forward.

"There was lots of fish on her," he said. "Hollis was gaffing them aboard as they come to the surface. And there was this big one, saw him as he come near the surface, he must've been seventy or eighty pound. Hollis leaned out for it as the trawl come in but the thing sheared off the hook and we passed right overtop of it. So I shoved the engine in reverse, turned on the switch before the piston reached top dead centre and that sent it running opposite. A bit of a jolt, you can imagine. I turned to lean out over the water, gaffed the fish as we drove back to it. Biggest cod I ever seen just about. Hauled it in over the aft board," Sweetland said. He took a mouthful of beer, glanced at Pilgrim in the stern. "Anyway," he said. "Hollis fell across the trawl line when the boat shifted into reverse. He wouldn't expecting it, I guess. And the length of trawl he'd already brought aboard started going over the side again as the boat drove aft. Hooks caught up in his clothes. He went into the water with it."

"Hollis couldn't swim."

"Wouldn't have mattered, him tangled up in the line like that. I shut off the motor soon as I saw he was over, but there was still a lot of strain on the trawl. Rushed up ahead to cut it loose."

"You cut the line?"

Sweetland shrugged. He couldn't bring himself to look at the boy. "Wasn't thinking right," he said. "I had to get him free of the strain, was what I had in my mind. Only way I could figure to do it was cut the line. Worse thing I could've done."

Hollis was only a fathom under water by the time he killed the engine and got forward. He could see the white of his brother's face looking back up to the surface. Hundreds of pounds of fish on the trawl and the weight of it pulling Hollis down and down into that black. Eighteen years old, his brother was.

"I'd have done it all different," Sweetland said. "If I had my time back."

Jesse was nodding his head, still staring out at the water. "He's not mad at you," he said.

It was like a hand out of nowhere against his chest, he almost lost his balance. "He said that, did he?"

"He wanted me to tell you," Jesse said.

"Well then," Sweetland said. And he turned to look out at the open ocean awhile.

They hefted the fish coolers onto the government wharf and carried them up the hill. Jesse ran ahead into Pilgrim's house to get his mother and she came to the door, reaching a hand to help. Clara invited him in for a fry-up, but Sweetland shook his head. "Not hungry," he said.

"Are you okay?"

"Best kind."

"You don't seem yourself."

"More I don't," he said and he tried to smile it off, though his face felt crooked and unnatural.

He took his five fish up to the house and stood at the kitchen counter in his rubber boots to fillet them. Ripping the backbone from its trough of flesh. The layer of dark skin peeling off with a sound like lengths of Scotch tape being unspooled. The meat underneath as white as the driven snow. He packed the fillets into clear plastic bags and stowed them in the fridge.

Stood still in the middle of the kitchen then, one hand at his chest opening and closing, mimicking his own heartbeat. "Where was that," he said into the silence. He went across to a drawer beside the sink and picked through it. There was an open shelf above the laptop with a handful of telephone directories from two decades ago, a row of *Canadian Living* recipe books his mother used to collect. Spare change, ancient keys for locks that no longer existed, thumbtacks, chewing gum, antacids. He shuffled his hand back and forth through the bric-a-brac, as if he was stirring up sediment in a shallow pond. Closed his hand finally on the card he was looking for. He held it out at arm's length, turned it a little to the light from the window.

He dialled the number incorrectly three times, which was almost too much to get through. He stood with the receiver in his hand, trying to quiet his breath. Walked himself through the digits one more time on the rotary dial, listened to the ring travel.

"Hello," the government man said.

"Yes," Sweetland said. He tried to bring the man's face to mind, but the features wouldn't coalesce out of the blur of light that masked him when he'd first arrived at Sweetland's door. He grabbed for the back of a chair and pulled it out from the table to sit down. "It's Sweetland calling," he said.

"Who's that?" the voice said. "Moses Sweetland?"

"Yes," he said. "This is he."

Sweetland was up early the next morning and down to the wharf while the stars were still bright. He hadn't slept and couldn't lie still any longer. He took his chainsaw and gas can, though he had no real interest in cutting wood. He just wanted out of the cove before the news made the rounds.

He drove to Burnt Head and around the Fever Rocks, riding slow as the day's light came up on the world, without a notion as to where he was going or why. He went into the lee of Little Sweetland and stared up at the bare hillsides as he passed Tilt Cove. Not a sign to say where the dozens of houses and flakes and outbuildings once stood. He came about, chugged into the abandoned harbour. There was a wooden wharf kept up by the mysterious owners of the two cabins on the hill, and he tied up there.

Sweetland sat on the dock with a cup of tea from the thermos, waiting for the sun to lift the cove out of shadow. Walked up onto the beach then, strolled aimlessly across the hillside. The community's remains might have been a thousand years old for all that was left of them. There were depressions to show where the houses and root cellars had been, the overgrown outline of shale foundations. Not a board or shard of glass or shingle otherwise, all of it scavenged or rotted or blown to hell and gone. He tried to imagine the buildings in their places, tried to unearth the names of the people who'd lived in them. Dominies and Barters and Keepings.

He glanced toward the harbour now and then, trying to tell by its location which outline had been the Dolimounts' house. It was still standing the last occasion he'd come ashore with Duke Fewer—1966 that was, the first Come Home Year sponsored by the Smallwood government, a campaign to encourage the diaspora of economic refugees to spend their summer vacation at home in Newfoundland. Sweetland had given up working on the schooner to stay closer to Chance Cove at the time, fishing on Duke's longliner, and they'd had a poor season at it. Dozens of people coming back to the cove from the mainland as the fishery floundered. They flaunted their store-bought, handed out suitcases full of trinkets to the youngsters, talked hourly wages and hockey games at Maple Leaf Gardens and how much they missed Newfoundland. Most of them hadn't shown their faces home in a decade and Sweetland couldn't wait for the fuckers to leave.

He and Duke did some hook and line in the early fall and trawled through October, with barely enough luck to warrant the money they were spending on gas. They decided to go across to the Burin to try for moose. A cold rain on the barrens and no sign of a living thing to shoot at for three days. Spent their time tramping through sodden gorse and tuckamore, slept nights in a leaky tent not half big enough to accommodate Duke's appendages. They ate potted meat sandwiches on white bread, drank instant coffee laced with rye. Hands and feet numb from the unrelenting chill and every item of clothes they'd packed soaked through.

I've had enough of this bullshit, Duke said. They were crouched under a square of canvas angled over a scraggly fire, their fourth morning out, waiting for the kettle to boil.

Sweetland had his hands stretched to the flame but couldn't feel any heat coming off it at all. Be a long winter, he said, without a bit of moose meat put aside.

The winter won't be half as long as the last three days have been, Duke said.

They had a two-hour tramp back to the bay where they'd moored the boat and they walked it in silence, one behind the other. They piled all their gear in the wheelhouse and huddled there in misery as Sweetland nosed into open ocean. And they travelled most of the way back to Sweetland without speaking a word.

I been thinking about going up to Toronto, Duke said when Little Sweetland was in sight. Next spring sometime.

You talk to Ange about it?

Duke was recently married, just long enough for his wife to have the one child and be two months toward having a second.

Not yet, no.

What do you think she'll think of it?

Probably she'll be happy to be clear of me awhile.

Yes, Sweetland said. I finds women likes nothing better than being left alone to look after two young ones.

Duke stared across at him.

I'm only saying.

Well shut up out of it, for chrissakes, Duke said. And a moment later he said, You should come with me.

Sweetland shook his head. I hates fucken old Toronto, he said.

Fucken old Toronto pays a buck fifty an hour. Never going to make that kind of money at the fish.

They were swinging out around the cliffs of Little Sweetland, a cloud of mist like a shroud over the east end of the island.

It's Effie keeping you home, is it? Duke said.

We idn't married, Sweetland said.

Duke watched him a second. Jesus, he said, I'm gut foundered.

Sweetland looked up to the headlands and, sure enough, there were a handful of figures standing in the fog, their massive shadows motionless on the cliff edge.

Look up there, he said.

Where?

On the headland there.

Can't see a thing.

Just watch, Sweetland said.

And a moment later the shadowy creatures turned and moved off into the grey.

Jesus, what a size they are.

You think they're fit to eat? Duke asked.

They looks to me like they'd be tougher than the hobs of hell, Sweetland said, even if you managed to get them on a plate.

Duke shrugged. I don't mind chewing, he said.

Sweetland eased off the throttle outside the entrance to Tilt Cove, turned into the calmer water.

It's a big frigging island, Duke.

We'll just go for a stroll, he said. See what we can see.

They walked up out of the cove, following the old path to the pond on the high ground above the harbour, their woollen socks squelching in their boots.

Be hard to get a clear shot in this weather, Sweetland said.

They're big as barns. Pilgrim could probably pick one off.

The trail went through a trough of scrub spruce, not a single tree the height of Duke, but the branches crowding the path held tufts of hair pulled from the bison hides as the animals walked past. An hour to reach the headlands and nothing to see there but buffalo pies, some still steaming in the cold air.

They can't be far, Duke whispered.

They could be halfway to Hibb's Hole for all you knows.

They skirted the cliffs to the east end of the island, walking until they risked not getting back to the boat before dark. They hadn't eaten since morning and Sweetland could hear Duke's stomach grumbling as they cut across the island, the rolling echo like a distant thunderstorm. They walked down into the cove, along the side of one of the few houses still standing, the door long gone, the windowpanes beaten out by weather. Gotta take a leak, Sweetland said, and he turned to the wall out of the wind, let loose against the shale foundation while Duke waited two paces ahead.

This was the Dolimounts' place, Duke said idly. He was facing away from Sweetland, watching the cove. Jim Dolimount? he said. Married to Eunice?

Sweetland staring into the gloom as he pissed, nearly dark inside. The kitchen empty of furniture, the wallpaper stained and peeling. The floor littered with what looked to Sweetland to be buffalo patties, the animals using the building as a shelter to get out of the weather. He leaned to look through into the living room and his water went dry.

They had nine youngsters, Duke was saying, before Eunice had the hysterectomy into St. John's.

Duke, Sweetland whispered. He was tucking himself in but never glanced away, afraid the creature would disappear if he did. He reached for the rifle where he'd leaned it against the house, nosed the barrel into the frame to let it rest on the sill. The animal shifted on its feet, the hooves against the wood floor drumming in the hollow space.

What in the Jesus was that? Duke asked just as Sweetland fired. The rifle shot echoed in the empty room like a cannon, knocking the last pane of glass from the window. Duke was shouting but Sweetland couldn't hear anything over the ringing in his ears.

They tried to haul the buffalo out of the house before they dressed it, but there was no way to get the dead animal through the doorway. Duke brought up a storm lamp from the boat and they butchered the buffalo where it lay, the stink mushrooming in the enclosed space. They carried the quarters down to the water, the thigh bones like a stick over their shoulders, the massive parcel of meat lying pelt side down against their backs. Duke wanted to leave the rest of the carcass where it was but Sweetland wouldn't have it.

Those wildlife officers is out here two or three times a season, he said. I don't want anyone coming around Sweetland looking for poachers.

They dragged the head and spine across the threshold and down to the shoreline, throwing it into a fathom of water. They gathered up the shin bones and the mess of the internal organs in the bloody cloak of the pelt and tossed that into the cove as well, but for the heart and liver that they wrapped in a square of cloth and tucked away in Duke's pack. Sluiced the blood and offal out the door of the house with buckets of water. They crouched in the landwash then to clean the blood off their hands and forearms in the bitter cold of the ocean.

Dark now the once, Duke said. Maybe we should overnight here.

Sweetland shook his head. Darker the better, he said, given what we're carting.

I hope it don't taste like bear meat.

Sweetland glanced across at the man beside him. When have you ever tasted bear?

I haven't, he said. Just don't think I'd like it.

Duke stood and dried his arms on the wet sweater under his jacket, the burnished wedding ring glinting in the day's last light.

Maybe I'll come with you, Sweetland said then. Up to the mainland.

Duke watched him a few seconds, still drying his arms. I thought you hated fucken old Toronto?

Buck fifty an hour, like you says.

Sweetland couldn't say what possessed him to make that decision, any more than he could explain why he'd called the government man to take the package when he did. There was no saying how things might have turned out if he'd stayed at home instead of going to Toronto. But it all went sideways there on Little Sweetland, the buffalo's blood still under his nails, his hands numb with the ocean's cold.

A life was no goddamn thing in the end, he thought. Bits and pieces of make-believe cobbled together to look halfways human, like some stick-and-rag doll meant to scare crows out of the garden. No goddamn thing at all.

THREE MONTHS AFTER the Sri Lankans passed through Chance Cove, the Reverend announced he was leaving Sweetland for another parish. Telling the congregation during a Sunday morning service.

This will come as a shock to you, he said, and I apologize for that.

He and his wife were shipping out within the month, moving to a church closer to her parents, who were aged and ailing and had no one else to watch out to them. Half the women were in tears to hear it. Digging crumpled tissues from dress sleeves to dab at their rheumy eyes. Sweetland glancing at Ruthie where she sat with Pilgrim, one row ahead of him. Stone-faced. As though the news was no surprise to her.

Ruthie's pregnancy was just beginning to show by then and it was an endless source of amusement in the cove. It had taken the blind man that long to find his way into his wife's drawers, people said. Pilgrim had finally figured out which lock his key was meant for. Men stood him drinks at the Fisherman's Hall. Thought you was going to be firing blanks your whole life, they said. Must have been one of them dark fellas off the lifeboat, they said, Ruthie must have took special care of them. Those reporters was out here, they said, she charmed the pants off them.

It was too much for Sweetland to sit through. Go fuck yourselves, he told the tormentors.

Never mind now, Pilgrim said.

Christ, Sweetland said. You just sits there and takes it, that's the worst of it. Makes me sick.

Pilgrim picked aimlessly at the label on his bottle. You're not going to stop them having their fun, he said.

I want to talk to you today, the Reverend said from the pulpit, about our recent unexpected visitors to Sweetland. He read a few verses from the Psalms. He wanted the congregation to imagine themselves in the position of those unfortunates in the lifeboat, he said. To be set adrift without warning or explanation, with nothing to say if they would ever be found. Or if anyone was even looking for them. Orphaned on an ocean that seems endless.

Sweetland had to credit the man for gall, standing up there in his robes with a straight face. In front of his own wife and Ruthie.

We could see it as a metaphor, the Reverend said, for our own place in the universe, for the questions we ask about our own lives.

Ruthie got up as he spoke and she crabbed her way past the others in her pew, whispering apologies, walking for the entrance with a hand to her mouth. People watching her go, nodding or shaking their heads. The morning sickness, they were all thinking. How it was about time the couple had a child in the house. How they had all stopped expecting it to happen and how God works in mysterious ways.

The Reverend droning on about hope and faith, like he hadn't noticed her leaving.

7

A WEEK AFTER HE MADE THE CALL to the government man, Sweetland received a slender stack of forms in the mail. Clara came up to witness his signature, to fold the papers into the self-addressed envelope provided.

"That's it, then," she said. "You sending them on the ferry this week?"

"You take them," he told her. "Be sure they gets out."

She ironed the envelope flat on the table with the palm of her hand. "I guess I owe you a thank-you for this," she said.

He jerked his head back, the motion barely perceptible but enough to stop her following through. He said, "You going to tell the boy now?"

Clara had asked Sweetland not to say anything to Jesse until all the papers were signed. Thinking he might back out and not wanting to risk the upheaval for nothing. "Not just yet," she said. "Want to pick the right moment. He's going to hate my guts for awhile, I imagine," she said, and she tried to laugh at the notion.

"I should be the one to break the news," Sweetland said. "He'll likely blame me for it all anyways."

"Why do you say that?"

"I told him I wouldn't going anywhere. He was counting on me sticking it out."

Clara shook her head. "I'll tell him," she said.

She pushed a clutch of loose papers across the table, information on relocation and retraining and various government assistance programs. "Have you decided?" she said. "Where you're going to shift to?"

"Haven't give it much thought."

Clara stared down at her hands. "You know you'd be welcome to come into St. John's with us," she said.

Sweetland made a noise in his throat to say he'd as likely live on the moon as in St. John's. He shifted in his chair to turn halfways away from her.

Clara tapped the papers with an index finger. "You should hang onto these."

"All right," he said, though he didn't so much as glance at them.

"Jesse will come around," she said.

The first week of August there was a town meeting at the Fisherman's Hall, the government man in on the ferry. Sweetland waited at the kitchen window, watching as people made their way over, Ned Priddle, Glad and Alice Vatcher, Rita Verge, Duke Fewer. He saw Clara heading out with Pilgrim on her elbow, Jesse straggling behind, looking despondent. Maybe the news had finally trickled down to the boy, he thought.

Sweetland gave the crowd a few minutes to get settled into the Fisherman's Hall before he gathered up his chainsaw and gas can and walked down to the government wharf. Diesel barking and lunging at the end of her chain as he went by. The ferry was still docked at the wharf, adding an extra hour and a half to its stop in order to take the government man back to the mainland after the meeting. Sweetland waved up at the crewmen on deck as he walked past. He had his own boat out on the collar and was bringing it in hand over hand when Loveless spoke to him. "Going for a bit a wood?" he said.

Sweetland looked behind to where Loveless was sitting on a lobster pot in the shade of the ATM. He had his little dog on its length of string, sitting between his feet.

"You're not going up to the meeting?"

"Don't like meetings," Loveless said. "Sitting still that long."

Sweetland smiled at the objection. "Sure all you does all day long is sit, idn't it?"

"On my own schedule," Loveless said. "I can get up to take a leak whenever the urge strikes."

"Fair enough."

"You going for a bit a wood?" he asked again.

"Thought I might."

"Late to start across. You'll have to spend the night."

"Might do."

Loveless chewed his pipe back and forth awhile. "You'll just have to leave all the wood behind come this time next year, won't you?"

"Kiss my arse," Sweetland said, and he stepped down into the boat, started up the engine. He hated to see Loveless making sense. It made him think the world was coming apart at the seams altogether.

He had no heart for the work and didn't even bother going all the way across to the mainland, stopping in at Little Sweetland again to wander around the abandoned cove, feeling idle and solitary and anxious. He went by the cabins and shaded his eyes to look in the windows. Metal bunks and Formica tables, an incongruous flat-screen television in both. Gas generators stored beside top-of-the-line wood stoves. Someone working out in Fort McMurray or at the nickel mine in Labrador, he'd heard. Money to burn and two weeks a year to get away from it all. Others said it was eccentrics from the Canadian mainland or the States, people who wouldn't show their faces years at a time. Just enjoyed being able to say they owned an exotic bit of property in a corner of the world no one else had heard of. Sweetland had half a mind to set a match to the buildings, out of spite.

He walked up onto the barrens, toward the headlands where he and

Duke had spotted the bison. The path across the swale had all but disappeared and he had to force a trail through the tuckamore. He stood at the edge of the cliffs, the wind up there rifling through his clothes. He could make out Sweetland in the distance, the long hump of it on the horizon. Even in the full light of day, he could see the intermittent flash of the light on Burnt Head, warning away traffic.

Late afternoon by the time he came back down to the wharf and he started for home, travelling slow. There was a low bank of fog sitting on the horizon, the north end of Sweetland already buried, Burnt Head swallowed in the mist. He took the long way around, past the south-end light on the Mackerel Cliffs where the day was still bright and cloudless. He steamed in close to the island, the rocks to starboard so sheer they looked like something CGId in a Hollywood studio. The sky above the boat confettied with wheeling seabirds, turrs and murrs and puffins and tinkers, their endless chatter echoing off the cliff face. The acrid stink of shit like a single fiddle note that held and held and held in the air. Every ledge up there occupied by birds who nested all summer on the bare rock.

A bald eagle drifted out of the lowering sun, making a lazy sweep above the headlands, and Sweetland watched the entire colony leave their ledges in a rush as the predatory shadow passed over. It was like a waterfall coming down the rock face, thousands of birds in a sudden raucous descent that seemed almost enough to swamp the boat as they clattered past. The cliffs above him suddenly bare.

He came around at the government wharf and docked in the space vacated by the ferry. Glanced up the hill as he tied on and hauled the boat back out on the collar. The hills that loomed over the cove muffled in the crawling sheets of fog.

He'd expected to find the place quiet, everyone inside at their supper, but there was an eerie busyness about the harbour. People standing in small clusters outside their houses, men gassing up ATVs. Everyone strangely focused, like passengers preparing for an evacuation order.

Loveless came down the path from the Fisherman's Hall in a slovenly run, trying desperately to keep his feet. "He've gone missing," Loveless shouted. "We can't find him."

"Who?" Sweetland said. "The little dog?"

"No," Loveless said, and then he looked around in a panic, noticing for the first time that the dog wasn't with him.

"Loveless, who the hell is it gone missing?"

"Jesse," he said. "He've run off somewhere. There's no one can find him."

Sweetland went straight to Pilgrim's house with Loveless on his heels. Pilgrim sitting in a rocker at the window. "We told Jesse you was signed up for the package," he said.

"At the meeting?"

"We thought it might be better in a crowd. Everyone going together, you know. Something he could be part of."

"That was Clara's idea, was it?"

"The Reverend's."

"Well fuck," Sweetland said. "Why'd you let him leave the hall in that state?"

"He wanted to hear it from yourself you was signed on. He was only going over to your place."

"You didn't hear my boat going out?"

Pilgrim lifted his face to the ceiling. "I spose so," he said. "Yes, I heard it."

"Well who the hell did you think it was? Loveless?"

"I never put it together."

Sweetland set both hands on his hips.

"He wouldn't upset, Mose, not like he gets. He was calm as could be. Even the Reverend thought he was fine." Pilgrim shook his head. "Clara figured it might be good for him to talk to you on his own."

"Where's Clara and the Reverend now?"

"Up on the mash, looking for him."

Sweetland threw a jar of water and a few tins of peaches and a flashlight into his canvas pack at the house, drove his ATV out the back of his property. He went up as far as the King's Seat, stopped there to look down over the cove. The barrens east and west shrouded in fog. It seemed a big island all of a sudden. He headed for the keeper's house, stopping to chat with the searchers he passed on the way, people walking in twos and threes along the trails.

There was no real panic among them. Everyone in the cove had taken a turn in an afternoon search party when Jesse had gone missing over the years. They'd spent the better part of a day tracking him down one October Sunday. Duke Fewer found him just before dark, singing "The Cliffs of Baccalieu" in the crawl space that held the cistern beneath the keeper's house. Dry and content there. Sweetland reminded himself of that incident as he drove over the mash. But it didn't offer him a moment's comfort.

He pulled up beside two other quads parked below the keeper's house. The Priddles' machines. He touched a hand to the engine covers, but they were cold. Called out a hello that died in the fog and he did a turn around the house. Peeked into the crawl space, listening to the dank stillness that surrounded the cistern. He went up the steps and forced the front door open, pushing it past the debris that had fallen from the ceiling. An air of galloping neglect about the empty shell. Broken glass and sagging plaster and bare studs where the cupboards and sink had been ripped out. He covered his nose and mouth against the chemical stink of sodden insulation, the pestilential hum of rot. No one had been inside that space in a long time but he walked through anyway, to be sure.

He took the pack off the quad on his way past, headed along the trail where he set his snares. Heard someone coming up out of the valley, called hello. The Priddles came into view then and he waited as they walked the fifty yards up to him.

"Any sign down there?"

"Not a thing," Barry said.

Sweetland looked over the trees in the valley. "He could be anywhere out here if he don't want to be found."

"Coming on duckish now," Keith said. "He'll get spooked when dark settles in."

"He'll be looking for us now the once," Barry said. "Don't worry."

"I'll carry on down. He was wanting to talk to me earlier on. Might be he'll show himself if he hears me calling."

"Everyone's meeting back at the hall if there's no news by ten," Keith said. "Just to do a head count. Figure next steps."

"He'll be home before then," Barry said.

Sweetland made his way as far down as the Priddles' cabin in the valley as darkness fell. The brothers had been by there not an hour before, but it was possible Jesse had snuck in between times, with night coming on. Curled up in the loft. Sweetland stood the cabin door open and waited there a second. "Jesse," he said. Nearly pitch inside and he threw the beam of his flashlight across the furniture, the ladder to the loft under the eaves. Out on the water he could hear a boat inching along the shoreline. Glad Vatcher swinging a searchlight up on the hills, the beam edgeless and diffuse in the fog. He stepped into the room and stood in the black quiet. Trying not to think the boy was lying dead somewhere in the woods.

He left the Priddles cabin and walked back up to the keeper's house, then drove overland on the quad. Stopping every few hundred yards to listen and call out. He could hear voices in all directions, calling the same. He took the trail back down into the cove, parked behind the house. Did a quick walk through, turning lights on in all the rooms as he called Jesse's name. He walked out the arm then, past the burnt-out timbers of his stage, as far as the decommissioned incinerator. Let the beam of his flashlight play around the inside of the metal bell, picking out the blackened shards of incombustible refuse. Stopped short on the remains of the dead calf lying inside the incinerator's maw. Bone showing through the dead leather of its skin. The maggots already done with it.

Fucken Loveless.

Shortly before ten he went back to the house, stood listening in the kitchen. He could tell the boy wasn't in the building but he walked through the rooms anyway, upstairs and down, to be able to say he had. He made his way to the Fisherman's Hall, the main lights on and the room crowded with people. A pot of soup on a hot plate, loaves of bread, cheese and crackers. Tea and coffee. Clara was sitting beside Pilgrim with her hand in his. She nodded at Sweetland quickly but didn't hold his eye. For fear of crying, he knew, and he walked to a seat near the back to spare her having to look at him.

There was no news. Rita Verge had called the Coast Guard and they were sending a chopper with a search and rescue team if there was no sign of Jesse come morning. The Priddles had printed up a satellite photo of the island off of Google Earth and they were gridding it with a marker, circling the most likely spots to look.

"There's no sense tramping around out there in the dark," Duke Fewer said. "Someone's going to get themselves killed at that."

"Well I'm not going to sit here with a finger up my ass," Keith said.

"He'll be looking for us up there now," Barry said. "We just wants to make it easier for him to find us."

"We should get a bonfire going up on the mash," Keith said. "Out at the keeper's house. Over on the Mackerel Cliffs."

"Not the cliffs," Clara said. "Not the cliffs," she repeated. "He could walk right off the cliffs trying to make his way to the fire."

"All right," Keith said, "we'll get a fire going somewhere on the trail, half a mile or so shy of the cliffs."

The Reverend said, "We should make sure all the lights are on here, help him find his way down if he's looking."

"He won't see the lights in the cove till he gets to the King's Seat," Sweetland said. "If he's on the mash, they won't help a damn. Does that PA in the steeple work at all?"

"Hasn't been used in twenty years."

"Be worth checking. You could hear that racket halfways to Little Sweetland. It might lead him in."

"I'll see what I can do with it," the Reverend said.

Before they had finished dividing up into parties and filling the gas tanks of their ATVs, they heard the sickly hum of an amplifier, then the click and scratch of a needle touched on vinyl. Ray Price singing "Just a Closer Walk with Thee." Sweetland saw Clara turn away from them at the first words of the chorus, the back of her hand pressed against her mouth, going off into the dark alone.

Sweetland followed the Priddles up to the King's Seat and on out to the keeper's house where they started a fire in the clearing below the building. Keith went down to the cabin then, to start up the generator and keep the lights on there.

The fog had lifted while they were inside the hall, the sky overhead so clear now that the stars felt almost close enough to touch. Barry had a flask of rum that he offered across, but Sweetland shook his head. Settled in the circle of heat, waiting. The two men watched the flames eat away at the wood in silence. Listening to the vague sound of music from the cove and the endless rustle of the surf against the Fever Rocks beyond the keeper's house, a commotion so distant and so insistent that it almost seemed to be the noise of the stars overhead.

Every hour or so Barry wandered off with a flashlight after deadfall and scrap wood to keep the fire burning, eventually hammering the rails and boards from the deck to feed the flames as the night passed. At some point he came back from the quad with a blanket that he draped over Sweetland's shoulders, and Sweetland drifted off where he sat, despite the rat's nest of commotion in his chest. Woke from a dream of Hollis staring up at him through cold fathoms of water, the white of his face fading as he sank down and swiftly down and no way on God's earth to reach him. Sweetland had no idea where he was. Raised his head to see Barry sitting across the fire, hugging his knees.

"The fire's bringing in the lost sheep," Barry said, and he gestured down at Sweetland's feet where Loveless's little dog was curled up in the orange light.

"Hello, Smut," Sweetland said.

Before first light they boiled a kettle on the coals of the fire and they drank instant coffee and shared out a handful of Jam Jams from Barry's pack. The dog had long since disappeared again on its wander. They talked back and forth about what they might do when the sun came up. The recorded hymns from the church steeple still audible, though barely.

"Could be he's home and dry by now," Barry said.

"They'd have turned off that friggin music for long ago if he was home."

"I expect you're right about that."

When it was grey enough to pick out the chopper pad over the Fever Rocks they packed up their materials and kicked the last coals of the fire apart. Barry decided to walk down after Keith who would otherwise sleep until noon, then meet Sweetland back at the Fisherman's Hall. "Gotta take a leak," Barry said, and he walked out around the corner of the keeper's house. Sweetland was tying his pack on the quad when Barry shouted for him. He had wandered down toward the chopper pad, calling back over his shoulder.

"What is it?" Sweetland asked.

"You see anything down there?"

"Where are you looking?"

Barry pointed inside the Fever Rocks, near the Coast Guard ladder. The sea throwing a white spume up the red cliff face. They walked all the way down to the pad, straining against the gloom. A bit of flotsam down there being tossed against the rocks, lifeless in the ocean currents. Sweetland turned and started up toward the keeper's house. Grunting with the strain of the climb.

Barry called after him. "It might not even be the youngster, Moses."

"That's him," Sweetland said. "That's Jesse."

Barry chased Sweetland back up to the quads where the older man was picking through the materials in his carryall. "We'll drive back into the cove," Barry said, "send out a boat."

"Tide's turning," Sweetland said. "He could be halfways to Boston by then. How much line you got on your machine?"

"You can't carry him up that Jesus ladder."

"I'm not leaving him down there."

"All right," Barry said. "I'll see if I can get a rope on him. Hitch him to the ladder until we can get a boat out from the cove."

"I'll go," Sweetland said.

"You won't help nothing getting yourself killed out here this morning."

"I'm going to need something to hook him with."

Barry watched Sweetland a moment, trying to gauge whether talking was any use at all. "I got the grapple on the front of the quad."

"He won't hold still there for long."

The two men went out across the chopper pad and paused a moment in the lee of the winchhouse, adjusting the gear they carried. They went down the ladder one after the other, pausing now and then to check their progress and to keep an eye on the body being slammed against the rocks. Sweetland was below Barry and he went to the foot of the ladder, stepping knee deep into the ocean down the last rung. He turned sideways to the rock face, hooking one arm into the rail to hold himself steady. He reached his free hand above his head. "Pass me the grapple," he shouted.

"We got about thirty feet of slack to work with," Barry said.

"Tie on the end so we don't lose the works."

The surf surge came up as high as Sweetland's chest and the fierce cold of it slapped the breath from his lungs. Jesse's body rolling in the same swell, his hair wet and plastered to his dead face. Sweetland pitched the grapple toward him underhanded as the sea receded and he came up short. He hauled the grapple in and pitched and fell short a second and a third time between the surges.

"I needs both hands," he said.

"Jesus, Mose."

"Grab my jacket," he said, and he slipped his arm free of the ladder.

Barry braced his knees under the metal rails on both sides and twisted the neck of Sweetland's collar in one hand, held fast to a rung with the other. Sweetland leaned out as far as he could against that halter and swung the line two-handed, landing it five or six feet beyond the body. He dragged it back then, hoping to hook the boy's clothing as it passed over him. The sea coming in above his shoulders, sluicing icy down the back of his coat.

The grapple snagged and let go half a dozen times before he caught something that held. He managed to drag Jesse ten feet along the rocks until the hook came loose and the body floated free. The boy's defenceless head knocking against the cliffs as the waves rose and fell.

"I needs a second," Barry shouted and the two men stopped to catch their breath, climbing up a few yards to get Sweetland out of the ocean. He'd lost the feeling in his legs and had trouble lifting his feet to the rungs.

"We'll never get him up this ladder," Barry said, "even if you manages to hook him over."

"I'm not leaving him there."

"Moses fucken Sweetland," he said, "I swear to Christ."

"One more try," Sweetland insisted. "He's halfways over to us."

He gimped back down into the ocean, waited for Barry to get a grip on his collar, and flung the grapple. Finally brought the boy in his ripped and sodden clothing close enough to grab by hand. He turned face on to the ladder, hooking his free arm through a rung. Barry was after him to step up out of the water but he was too exhausted even to answer. The younger man spidered down beside him, reached around his waist to take the weight of the corpse. His face at Sweetland's ear.

"We got to move up out of this," he said, shouting against the surf.

Sweetland nodded, breathing heavy. "You got Jesse?"

"I got him. We're going to take a step up. You ready?"

The ladder was too narrow for them all and it was a slow, awkward climb above the reach of the ocean. Seawater pouring from their clothes as they went. Barry braced the boy's deadweight between them when they stopped to rest and both men kept their eyes averted from the ruined face, the flesh there shredded and torn, the busted nose misshapen. The left ear shorn from the side of the head.

"We're never going to make it up this ladder," Barry said. "We got to tie him on and go for a boat."

"You go on," Sweetland said. "I'll hold him here till you can send someone around."

"There's nothing worse can happen to that youngster, Mose."

Sweetland swung his hand blindly for the rope and grapple where it was dangling below them, lifted it toward Barry. "Tie us on," he said.

"It'll be a couple of hours before a boat gets out here."

Sweetland stared at him over the boy's mutilated head. "I'll never make it up those stairs," he said.

Barry looked away and shook his head. "You miserable cunt," he said. He swore up at the ladder rising above them. A moment later he hooked the grapple to the rung beside Sweetland's head and threaded the rope under his arms. "You get a good grip on him there," he said and he built a cat's cradle around the two figures and the ladder rails, cursing as he worked. He started up the rungs then, leaving Sweetland with the lost boy in his arms.

"Don't be too long," Sweetland called after him.

"I expects you'll be dead before I gets back," Barry said.

Sweetland glanced down at Jesse, at the pale coins of scalp showing through on the double crown of his head. "I don't doubt but I will be," he said.

THE KEEPER'S HOUSE

And the sea gave up the dead which were in it . . .
—REVELATIONS

I

HE BROUGHT THE BOAT AROUND to the lee side of Sweetland, to the alcove below Music House. The noise of the engine coming along the rock face setting the gannets to wing over the headlands, the sky above him like a snow globe after it's shaken—a raucous swirl of white. He coasted alongside a ledge of granite that sloped into the ocean, turned from the wheel to toss his food pack above the waterline, and then stared over the gunwale to see how much draft he had to work with.

He brought her around a second time along the echoing cliffs, reversing the engine to make the sharp U-turn in the bowl of the alcove. It was the only spot outside Chance Cove that a body could get onto the island, but it was never any practical use as a landfall. Sweetland throttled the motor low and set the tiller level, crouched on the gunwale as she crawled by the ledge, so close to the slab that the fibreglass scraped the rock below. He lifted his legs out over the side, letting the gunwale slide under his hand as he found his feet. Leaned into the stern as it passed, shoving the vessel into open ocean, and she putt-putted toward the horizon. She had enough gas to make it as far as St. Pierre or into open ocean somewhere beyond the Burin if the wheel kept steady and no one intercepted her in the meantime. He stood watching until the boat had all but disappeared. Thinking it was a mistake to have let her go.

There was a steep grassy climb up from the water, and he stashed the food pack out of sight among the rocks, planning to come back for it once he'd settled on a site. Above that first rise he walked half an hour across a swale crowded with petrel burrows, toward the valley's climb where the ground turned suddenly marshy and wet. He could hear the brook running down from the top of the island, though it was impossible to see it under the maze of alder and larch and silvery deadfall that clogged the valley's heart. You could drag a trawler into that mess and no one would ever guess it was there.

He turned to look back the way he'd come. The ocean out there flat calm, blue as new denim. Already there was no sign of his boat and he tried to put it from his mind. Looked up the gnarly length of the valley. He could see the peak of the Priddles' cabin three-quarters of the way up the rise, just where the trees began to thin out. The brothers were there, he knew, come to the island for one last blowout before the final ferry, and he wanted to keep well below that height. He tried to fix on a landmark, but there was nothing particular or distinguishable to shoot for. Everything above him disappeared as soon as he started picking his way into the tangle regardless, and he made his way blindly, stepping over deadfall logs, the bog sucking at his boots.

He had a hatchet to hack through the worst of it, his pack and jacket and pants snagging on brittle fingers of bush as he pushed through. He tripped and scraped his neck raw on a claw of tuckamore. Lost his footing and fell backwards onto his pack, his crown clipping hard off a rock.

He was facing down the slope when he came to and he tried desperately to sit up, then to turn over, lay trapped there like a turtle on its shell, winded and panicky, blood pooling in his head. Blue sky beyond the angry criss-cross of branches above him.

He hadn't thought any of this through clearly enough.

Sweetland tried to force his arm free of the pack, felt something pop in there. "Jesus fuck," he said. He considered cutting the shoulder strap before the adjusting buckle finally came to mind. Once his arm was loose he pushed himself awkwardly upright at the waist. He had to scooch his legs downhill, like the hands ticking on a clock, before he could kneel up and climb to his feet. The back of his head pulsing where he'd smacked it. He tried to guess by the sun how long he'd been out, though it hadn't moved perceptibly from where he remembered it. A few seconds maybe, minutes at most. He hefted his pack, readjusted the strap. Feeling like an idiot.

Ten days he'd have to camp out here in the woods, before the final few residents—Loveless and Clara and Pilgrim, the Priddles, Rita Verge—left on the last ferry run and the place was officially erased from the map. Sweetland's ass was soaking wet. The raw patch on his neck stinging, his head and his shoulder throbbing. He supposed he could get himself killed out here in the meantime and no one would ever find the body. And wouldn't that be a funny end to it all.

He'd thought there would be some kind of send-off to end it, a gathering in the final days at the Fisherman's Hall where the residents would wake the cove before they left en masse on the ferry. Speeches and a few songs and maudlin reminiscence. A chance to drink the island under before surrendering it for good.

But the place emptied out in morose dribs and drabs. Most residents were gone before last winter had settled in. Everyone with school-aged children left by the Labour Day weekend, to enrol their kids elsewhere. The ring of houses growing darker and darker on his way back in the arm from his evening walks as the community was abandoned. Once or twice he fancied he saw a light winking in Queenie's window as he came up the path, that phantom glow like an itch in an amputated limb. He remembered Jesse claiming to have seen the light just after Queenie died and he felt like a sentimental fool to be suffering the same delusion.

You needs to give your head a goddamn good shake, Duke told him when he reported the peculiar phenomenon.

Glad and Alice Vatcher and all their animals shipped out by the end of September and they took Sara Loveless's cow with them. Alice ran the only convenience store on the island and there was nowhere to buy milk or flour or salt beef or liquor after that. Once a month Sweetland or Duke or Clara made a trip across to Burgeo while the weather held in the fall, with half a dozen grocery lists and a wad of cash. But there were months before the spring took hold when the crossing was too risky in an open boat and only what came in on the ferry kept them fed. Loveless seemed to persist solely on candy bars and potato chips from the ferry's canteen, emptying the shelves of Big Turks and Milky Ways and Hickory Sticks every time the ship docked at the wharf.

You're not feeding that junk to your little dog, are you? Sweetland asked.

He looks after hisself up in the woods.

Jesus, Loveless. That's a fucken lapdog you got.

He don't go hungry, Loveless said, never you mind.

Sweetland took to setting bits of salt meat gristle or the leavings after he cleaned his rabbits where he thought the dog might find them, though he expected he was only feeding gulls and rats in the end. Which was what the island was about to be left to.

It was a miserable winter and one household after another packed up and stacked their worldly possessions on the government wharf, ATVs and suitcases and boxes of dishes, waiting for the ferry crew to winch it all aboard, motorboats and washing machines and table saws. Shaking hands and hugging the fewer and fewer left behind. It was like watching dirty water drain from a tub. Sweetland never went down to the dock to see them off, though he could see it all from his kitchen window. The leavers invariably stood at the ferry rail to stare back into the cove and he raised his hand to wave an invisible goodbye just before they slipped out of sight.

He fashioned a lean-to on a ledge the size of a double bed, made himself a thickly needled bunk of spruce branches. It was too late in the afternoon to consider going back for the food pack and the headache he'd given himself when he fell was too fierce to face the hike regardless. He allowed himself a small fire before the dark settled in, laying it against the mossy rock face overhanging the ledge to reflect the heat into the shelter. He hung his soaking pants and jacket from the lean-to's frame to dry. Lay out in the warmth, grateful to be off his feet.

The fire went out as he slept and he woke stiff and chilled. He reached to pull the blanket over his shoulders before he realized where he was. It was nearly dark in the valley, though he could still see a strip of blue sky above his lean-to. A single star just coming clear in the deepening evening. The ache in his head reduced to a sullen discomfort, as if he was wearing a helmet two sizes too small. He ate a cake of sweet-bread and a sliver of bottled rabbit out of his pack and washed it down with half a jar of water.

He thought of his boat again, abandoned and still travelling out there in the waning light. Years ago, he'd spotted a fishing boat from the lighthouse on a wet afternoon, an empty thirty-footer, the outboard locked in low gear. Radioed in the call letters to the Coast Guard, then phoned over to Duke Fewer to drive out and retrieve it. He followed its progress with the binoculars as it chugged past the island, two or three miles offshore. Saw Duke's vessel motoring toward it, steadily closing the distance, corralling the empty boat and turning for home with it tied to the stern.

Sweetland had known as soon as he spotted the boat there was no reason to hurry. Duke found a few dozen cod in a plastic fish box and a lifejacket under the thwart. A pair of cotton gloves on the decking near the outboard. It was registered out of Miquelon where the French were still allowed to fish for cod, and they learned after the fact the man had been hand-lining on his own. It was anyone's guess what had happened to send him into the sea and the body was never found. Another absence without fences or edges or boundaries. Just the boat by its eerie lonesome on the ocean's swell.

No one watched from the lighthouses anymore. And even if someone had come across Sweetland's boat by now, there'd be nothing in the way of organized searchers before morning and no urgency to the looking. He'd be given up for lost before the first rescue vessel turned out.

It was difficult to say, looking back, when he'd made up his mind to stay. He didn't announce or discuss it, barely acknowledged the notion in his own head. Simply carried on with his life like it was just another summer, hauling up his seaweed and planting his garden, cutting and stockpiling firewood. People dismissed the activity as simple bloody-mindedness. Sweetland eating against his end.

As well as his own, Sweetland planted the old garden at the keeper's house, driving out to tend it through July and August, weeding and watering and picking the cabbage bugs off by hand. It wasn't a practical spot for a second garden, but it offered an escape from the draining misery in the cove. And saved having to explain himself to everyone and their dog.

Less than a dozen people were still resident on the island at the beginning of July. Pilgrim came up to the house occasionally to sit an hour with the radio, to report on the latest plans to move into St. John's. Their departure date kept being pushed ahead while Clara tried to arrange a spot for Pilgrim in some kind of assisted living facility.

Assisted living? Sweetland said.

That's what they calls it.

Some stranger comes in to wipe your ass, is it?

Don't be a bastard, Pilgrim said.

Sweetland shook his head. I hope to Jesus I'm dead before I comes to that.

Clara was planning to find a place to live nearby, Pilgrim told him, and she was applying to do a master's degree in some field that involved digging up the ancient dead and guessing at how they styled their hair and what they ate and how they came to their unexceptional ends. It seemed a ludicrous thing to devote your life to.

You haven't said nothing about where you might be shifting, Pilgrim said one afternoon.

I'm not going anywhere, Sweetland told him. Even to himself it was a surprise to have his mind stated so plainly.

What do you mean, you're not going?

I still got title to my property.

You took the hundred grand.

I'll give it back.

It don't work like that, Moses.

Look, Sweetland said. What if I leaves on the ferry in September and comes back on my own a week later. Where's the law says I can't do that?

Pilgrim worked his mouth a few moments. There's no law.

Well I'm just skipping that step.

Skipping it?

I'm not getting on the ferry.

I don't know, Pilgrim said. Seems to me there's nothing that simple about it.

And the blind fucker had been right about that.

In the morning he made the walk down to Music House to retrieve the food bag, setting off at first light, wanting to be out of the open as early as possible. When he worked himself clear of the valley he spent a moment watching the ocean, scanning east and west. But it was quiet out there.

The bag was a green duffle with a single strap that he wore across his chest, leaning forward to balance the weight as he carried it up the rise. In the valley he had to slough it off in spots to drag it through brush, heft it over piggledy moss-covered rock. It was like travelling with a corpse for company. The valley falling into afternoon shadow by the time he settled on his bed of branches, too tired for the moment to open the goddamn bag. He wanted a cup of tea but wouldn't chance the fire. Draped an arm across his eyes and slept.

The noise of the Coast Guard chopper woke him before dark, coming in low over the shoreline. Likely they had spent the day searching the waters beyond St. Pierre and worked their way back toward Sweetland. Three people in the open bay doors, all wearing orange floater suits, all focused on the ocean below, and the sight of them made him feel suddenly ridiculous. He'd thought of it as a private decision to come out to the valley and turn his back on the world, something that concerned no one but him. But he felt now like he'd made a public fool of himself somehow.

He watched the vessels on the water all through the following day. A Coast Guard ship travelling slow toward Fortune Bay. Fishing boats out of Burgeo and Francois volunteering for the search. Searchlights swinging against the black into the evening, the beams scissoring along the shore. One more day at most they'd be out there. And that thought was all the comfort he had to offer himself.

In the days after he'd recovered Jesse's body at the Fever Rocks, before he was well enough to get out of bed, he woke to see Clara sitting beside the window, one hand across her eyes as if she was dozing, or fending off a headache.

Ruthie, he said to her.

It's Clara, she said, lifting her head to him.

He nodded slowly. Yes, he said. And the world began pouring in through that single thumb-sized fact.

We buried him yesterday, Clara said.

Who?

Jesse.

Yes, he said again.

We wanted to wait until you was well enough, she said, but.

He was a good boy, Sweetland said.

Clara stood and crossed the room at the foot of the bed, opened the door to leave. She paused there before she closed it, hidden from his view. She said, I wanted to thank you for getting him. Out at the light, she said.

She wasn't able to say more than that for a long time. He thought she'd left and gone down the stairs when she said, Did you want anything, Moses? Something belonged to him?

Sweetland was too addled to decipher what she was suggesting and he let it sit awhile, though the longer he waited the less substantial it seemed, like a lozenge dissolving under his tongue.

You let me know, she said finally, if you thinks of something.

He had a boatload of dry goods set by for the coming winter, materials he'd smuggled in from Miquelon in the middle of August. Every night for a week he'd made a trip down to the shed that housed the ATM and withdrawn his daily limit. Seven thousand dollars in cash all told. He considered going into Fortune or Placentia or Burgeo, but there wasn't a soul on the south coast of Newfoundland who wouldn't hear of it within three days' time. And after his conversation with Pilgrim, he thought it best to keep his intentions to himself. Took the boat across to Miquelon where no one knew him from Adam.

He tied up next to a raft of sailboats in the tiny marina. There was an office at the gate, a man in uniform behind the plate glass, and Sweetland waved a hand as he passed by, walked up through the town. Single-storey bungalows on an expanse of land that seemed to have been graded level, the streets laid out in a careful grid. He wandered half an hour looking for a shop that might carry salt beef and pickling salt. Stopped into the first grocery store he saw. He took a small cart and drove it up and down the aisles, filling it with flour and sugar and tea. He found a rack of batteries and loaded them all into the cart.

The woman at the cash said, You are staying in Miquelon?

Just picking up a few things for home, he said.

For home?

Yes, he said. Have you got any more of these?

What size?

Double As, I spose. Any will do.

She called toward the back of the store, carrying on an indecipherable conversation with a young man stacking shelves. He disappeared through a doorway and came to the front with an armful that he laid on the counter. He had a shaved head and an angry tattoo across the back of his neck.

Any of these? the woman asked.

Sweetland hooked the thick stack of twenties from his ass pocket and gestured toward her. Do you take this stuff?

Her eyes went back and forth between Sweetland and the money several times. Oui, she said quietly. We will take Canadian.

You don't sell kerosene, by any chance.

No, but there is a place. She spoke to the young man in French a moment. He will get you what you need. How much?

Whatever they got. And ammunition, he said. For a .22. They wouldn't have pickling salt, by any chance?

Pick-ling?

For making the fish, he said. Salt fish?

Oui. Give him five hundred dollars, she said, and then spoke in French awhile. He will bring you your change, she said.

After the young man left, she gestured at the material he had piled on the counter. Should I be worried? she asked.

Sweetland stared at her blankly.

Is it the world that is ending?

It took him a moment to follow what she was asking. No, he said and he half laughed at the notion. Not where you lives, anyway, he said.

He walked around the store a second time, picking through the bottles of oil and red wine vinegar, the racks of spices and shelves of oddly shaped bread, looking for anything useful. When he was done, the woman at the counter tallied up the bill. Sweetland counted out the twenties slowly and by the time he'd finished, a derelict blue Peugeot had pulled up outside. The young man got out of the driver's side and came into the store. He handed Sweetland a fistful of euros in change and then began carting the boxes and bags out to the car.

He will drive you, the woman said. But he has no English.

I got little enough myself, Sweetland said.

Sweetland pitched in to help him load the trunk and back seat. Looking to see what the youngster had purchased on his behalf. There was a single five-kilogram bag of salt and Sweetland pointed at it. Any more? he said. More, he repeated and he stretched his hands apart.

The boy shook his head. C'est tout, he said, and shrugged apologetically. They came in for the last of the supplies and the woman behind the counter spoke to the young man awhile and he glanced quickly at Sweetland.

The drive to the harbour took all of two minutes. They coasted through the gate, the young man nodding to the uniform behind the glass. He backed the car onto the wharf and parked near the boat Sweetland pointed out to him. They unloaded the back seat and the trunk together, piling his purchases on the concrete. The young man glancing up now and then toward the town.

Sweetland climbed into the boat and asked him to pass the provisions down. He gestured with his arms but the young man held one hand aloft. Wait, he said. S'il vous plaît. And then he shouted to someone at the far end of the wharf.

The gendarme wore a blue tunic and a short stovepipe hat with gold piping around the base, like someone out of a cartoon. He looked only a few years older than the tattooed boy and they seemed to know each other well, talking back and forth as he walked out the dock. After a few moments the young man went to the car where he sat on the hood and lit a cigarette.

Bonjour, the policeman said, and Sweetland waved up to him.

May I see your identification?

ID?

You are Canadian?

More or less.

This is France. You have a passport or a driver's licence?

I never needed no ID the last time I come through here.

The policeman tilted his head at an angle that made Sweetland worry about him losing the hat. When was this? he asked.

Jesus, Sweetland said. 1964 or '65.

The policeman watched him steadily. Things have changed since 1964, he said. Where are you visiting from?

Sweetland climbed up onto the dock. Fortune Bay, he said. He walked across to the young fellow with the tattooed neck and passed him the handful of euros as a tip, then turned back to the gendarme.

It's just a bit of salt and flour, Sweetland said. Not like I'm smuggling booze.

Yes, very strange, the policeman said. He leaned over the stack of bags and containers, reached to pick out the boxes of ammunition. These you must leave, he said. You will have to declare the rest when you return to Newfoundland.

What, fill out a form or something?

A customs form, certainly. There will be a tariff to pay. May I go aboard?

Sweetland waved him on and the policeman stepped down into the boat, poking idly through the wheelhouse, looking into the compartments where he stored the lifejackets and fishing line and water jugs. When he climbed back onto the dock Sweetland took his place in the boat, dragging boxes off the concrete. The gendarme looked across at the young man sitting on the car hood and nodded permission to help. He watched the two load the boat then, with his hands crossed behind his back.

We can refund the money for the ammunition, the policeman said.

Never mind, Sweetland said.

When they were done loading, the gendarme took a black notebook from his shirt pocket. He said, I will require your name and address.

Jesse, Sweetland said. Jesse Ventura.

V-e-n, the policeman said as he jotted the name. *R-a*. And address?

Brig Harbour, Fortune Bay.

Brig Harbour, he said, his head still bowed to the notebook. I have not heard of it.

Back of beyond, Sweetland said. Half the people lives there never heard of it.

You will have to report to the customs office in Placentia, the policeman said.

First thing, Sweetland said.

You must bring a passport next time, Mr. Ventura.

Won't leave home without it, don't you worry.

The young man had untied the line and was holding the boat tight to the dock. Sweetland reached up to catch the rope when it was thrown aboard and waved a thank you. As he pulled away he could see the policeman writing the identification number painted at the bow into his little book. All the way home he cursed himself for an idiot, though even then he was hard pressed to say how it might come back on him.

An RCMP patrol boat arrived a week later. Sweetland working in the shed out back when the Mountie came knocking at his door, then turned and called for him. He stood at the open bay of the shed with his hands behind his back. Mr. Sweetland, he said.

He's not here, Sweetland said. Moved into St. John's a month ago.

Mr. Sweetland, the cop said. I was the officer out here investigating the burning of your stage last year.

Sweetland looked him up and down. You got any leads on that?

Mr. Sweetland, the officer said. We have a report from French customs that a man by the name of Jesse Ventura, driving a boat registered in your name, sailed into Miquelon recently. He left with a large quantity of food and supplies that were paid for in cash.

Is that right?

August fourteenth. He also attempted to buy a significant quantity of ammunition for a .22. Did this Mr. Ventura borrow your boat from you?

I guess he must have.

Do you have any idea where I might find Mr. Ventura?

Sweetland shrugged. He's on the internet, if you minds to look.

The officer took a step into the shed, out of the daylight. He took off his hat and held it in front of himself. There was a crease ringing his head where the hat had been. He said, Do you know what he intended to do with forty-four hundred dollars' worth of dry goods?

This is about paying the tariffs, is it?

No, sir. That's a customs issue. Our office was contacted by a government official involved in negotiating the resettlement agreement with people here in Sweetland. They're worried some residents might be planning to breach that agreement. And possibly using lethal force in the process.

Sweetland turned from the Mountie to shift through the tools on his workbench.

Sir, could you step away from the workbench for me?

He turned around and folded his arms across his chest.

Mr. Sweetland, we've been asked to assist in the completion of the terms of the resettlement agreement.

They're sending the cops out here?

It's a question of legal liability on the part of the government, as I understand it. And there's the issue of lethal force. We don't want to see anyone get hurt. I've been asked to let people know that I will be on the last ferry to leave Sweetland. That's less than two weeks from now. And all remaining residents are required to be on that ferry when it departs.

He waited then, to give Sweetland a chance to respond. A moment later he said, You are planning on boarding the ferry.

What if I'm not, Sweetland said.

The officer looked down at the hat in his hands. In that case, he said, there will be a warrant issued for your arrest.

Well, Sweetland said. Good to see my tax dollars hard at work.

The officer smiled and replaced his hat. He shimmied it on good and tight. I would hate to be put in that position, Mr. Sweetland. I honestly would.

Sweetland turned back to the workbench and put both hands to the edge. I'll see if I can't spare you the trouble, he said.

He didn't say a formal goodbye to anyone. So pissed off it didn't cross his mind he might be adding a layer of grief to the lives of others. Or not giving a good goddamn if he was.

He'd carried the duffle bag of food down to the government wharf after the lights were out in the cove and tucked it away in the wheelhouse. In the morning he walked through the house as he might have if he were leaving for the last time. Closing doors, hanging a jacket that he'd left lying on the daybed, washing his few breakfast dishes and putting them away in the cupboards. He left the house with his pack, but stopped himself before his hand was off the door. He went back inside and threw the jacket across the daybed, he walked through the house to open the doors he'd closed. All the cash left over from his spree in Miquelon was in the drawer of his bedside table and he stuffed it into an envelope that he folded and pushed into his back pocket. He took a tin of tuna from the cupboard and opened it, draining off the water. He ate half the fish with a fork, then left the can and the fork on the counter, beside the laptop.

Sweetland could see Pilgrim sitting at his own kitchen table as he walked by. He went around to the back door and poked his head inside.

Is herself about? he asked.

She's not up yet, Pilgrim said. I'll get you a cup of tea.

No, no, Sweetland said. He took the envelope from his back pocket and laid it on the table. I'm just heading down to the wharf. Thought I might go poach a few cod.

What's that? Pilgrim asked.

What's what?

Whatever you put on the table there.

That's for Clara, Sweetland said.

You should have supper with us tonight, Pilgrim said. You're spending too much time alone up there.

If I'm back in time, Sweetland said, I'll come down.

He went out the door and stopped to let Diesel nuzzle his crotch and whip her tail against his legs as she squirmed. Leaned down to whisper into her ears. Bye, Diesel, he said.

Loveless was at the wharf when he got there, looking harried and distracted.

You haven't seen my dog, have you?

Not today.

The frigger's been out the whole night.

Sweetland climbed down into the boat, started up the engine.

Loveless walked to the dock's edge to be heard over the motor. What was it the cop wanted with you when he come out?

He's still trying to figure who burnt my stage. Untie that rope for me, would you?

Loveless leaned down to the capstan. Have he got any suspects?

He was asking a lot of questions about you.

Loveless took the pipe from his mouth, stood gaping a minute as the boat drifted off the dock.

I told him I wouldn't trust you as far as I could throw you.

You're a miserable cunt, Moses.

Sweetland laughed. I spose I am, he said.

Where is it you're heading now?

Thought I might go poach a few cod.

What have you got in the bag?

Mind your own goddamn business, Sweetland said. He turned the nose of the boat to open water, sailing out past the breakwater without glancing back.

A MONTH BEFORE HE PLANNED to leave for Toronto with Duke Fewer, Sweetland walked out as far as the north-end lighthouse and borrowed Bob-Sam Lavallee's horse and cart. He drove it back to Vatcher's Meadow where he tied the horse to the fence and walked down into the cove. He had his supper at the house with his mother and Effie and Uncle Clar. It was coming on duckish when they were done and Sweetland walked Effie up past the King's Seat.

What's this? she asked when she saw the horse and cart.

Thought we might take a little drive, he said.

She wasn't from Sweetland, Effie Burden. Come over from Fortune to teach at the school. Seventeen and never out from under her father's roof before she went into St. John's to do her eight-month teaching certificate. All the teachers on Sweetland were the same, young girls mostly, in their first school. Two dozen youngsters in the one room, staring up at the terrified child at the front. The oldest students were the same age as the teacher, all of them boys who had failed grade 9 once or twice, or left before final exams to fish each spring and were sent back each fall by their mothers. Most of them suffered the time in the classroom just to make a play for the new girl who was away from home and family for the first time. It was a sport to get the teacher on her back up on the mash, or out behind the church. Hardly a one lasted beyond their first year, and there were some who went away with unexpected company, wearing loose clothes to hide the fact during the last months of school. A select few married into the island and stayed on, Effie being the last. Though no one managed to get her small things around her ankles out in the meadow between times, Sweetland could tell you that for a fact.

He was long done with school when Effie arrived. Home from his first stint in Toronto, but away from Chance Cove working the schooner, and he knew her mostly by reputation. Tough as nails, was what he heard. The mouth on her like the edge of a ruler across the knuckles. No one gave her any trouble she couldn't take the seams out of, no one left school to fish before exams were done. No one so much as laid a finger on her sleeve.

She sat in the church pew behind his mother and Ruthie and Uncle Clar every Sunday and the women got to talking. Effie invited back to the house for Sunday dinner whenever Sweetland was off the schooner. It was design on his mother's part, he knew, putting the girl in his way. A sensible child with a bit of education, who wasn't afraid of work. She refused to let Effie help clear the table. Me and Ruthie got hands enough to manage this, she said before leaving them alone with their tea. Uncle Clar dozing on the daybed next the stove, the cat settling on the old man's chest to bat at the handlebars of his moustache.

Effie never spoke about herself, asking instead about Toronto, about Maple Leaf Gardens and Lake Ontario and Yonge Street, about his work on the *Ceciliene Marie*. Sitting across from him in her old-lady cardigan and woollen skirt. Tiny set of teeth in her head. They were her baby teeth, she told him, which had never fallen out and the adult set never come in. There was something eerie in the incongruity, and it made her oddly intimidating. Though she sometimes covered her mouth with her hand when she smiled, the only mark of shyness he'd ever seen in her.

It was a surprisingly warm evening for April. They drove out the path to the south-end light, sitting close enough in the seat that their legs touched. There was no moon and the night fell on them so black they couldn't see more than the vague outline of the horse, the animal walking the familiar path by memory or smell or some other animal instinct. Half an hour along, Effie leaned heavy into his shoulder as they tipped through a rut and she made no effort to move away. She placed her hand on the inside of Sweetland's thigh. They had never so much as kissed, had never touched one another in any but the most inadvertent way, and the weight of her hand on his leg was making his head ring.

He didn't speak or glance in her direction, for fear she'd lose her nerve and pull away. They stared into the dark ahead as Effie unbuttoned his fly, Sweetland keeping both hands on the reins. She seemed not to know the first thing about what she was doing, squeezing and tugging like she was trying to milk a goat, and Sweetland came in streams across his knees and the boards at his feet. It was all he could do to sit upright as the spasms coursed through him.

They were both mortified in the aftermath and for a while pretended nothing at all had happened between them. Effie left her hand where it was until Sweetland finally reached down to button his fly. She shifted to one side, taking a handkerchief from her sleeve to wipe at her fingers, and then scrubbed ineffectually at his pant legs.

Sorry, he said.

Shut up, Moses, she said.

2

THERE WERE NO LIGHTS IN CHANCE COVE after the living cleared out, but there was still fresh water in the pipes, pressure-fed from Lunin Pond up on the mash. It came down from such a height that even the upstairs toilet still flushed.

Someone had been through and emptied the fridge and freezer to spare the house the indignity of flowering rot once the power went off, Clara he assumed that was. He'd lost all his fresh craft and all but two buckets of salt beef tucked away in the pantry. But no one had touched his effects, out of respect or because there was nothing obvious to be done with them. The kitchen cupboards were stacked with dishes and canned goods, the last of Jesse's hoard of tinned peaches occupying a shelf to themselves. His good clothes hanging in the wardrobe upstairs. Rows of bottled beets and jam on the pantry shelves. The early harvest of spuds still in their bins in the root cellar. The shed just as he left it, the tools in their rows above the workbench, the quad sitting under a tarp in one corner. Two red plastic containers of gasoline beneath the workbench. He hefted them one at a time, to see how much he had to work with—one half-full, the other less so. He shook his head at the stupidity of it, of how little he'd worked out in his head.

Whoever cleaned out the fridge had put the kitchen to rights, his jacket hung up and the can of tuna gone, the drainboard placed under the sink. The countertops clear but for his laptop and he was surprised to see it there. He'd paid a lot of money for the thing, almost enough for a wood stove or a second-hand outboard. Only Jesse could have talked him into the ridiculous extravagance. A body could probably get seven or eight hundred for it in the *Buy & Sell*. But no one wanted to mess with a dead man's belongings, it seemed.

He opened the lid and held the power button down, waited for the machine to boot up. There was still a fair charge in the battery and the browser automatically tried to open his poker home page. *No network available*, it informed him.

"No shit, Sherlock," he said. And then made a mental note to stop talking aloud to himself.

Sweetland had gone to Jesse's Facebook page months after the boy died. A flutter in his chest when it occurred to him it would still be there, available to anyone who cared to look. He didn't know what he expected to find, some scrap of the youngster clinging among the profile pics and *Titanic* bric-a-brac and pro wrestling video clips. There were plenty of postings on the newsfeed, but there was nothing recent on his wall. The last messages were all from around the time they lost him, youngsters from the school writing in to say how much they were going to miss him. Small remembrances from Sandra Coffin and a handful of others who'd left Chance Cove long ago. It struck Sweetland how they were all addressed directly to the dead boy. As if the world he created on Facebook was eternal, a kind of afterlife where he could read the messages himself. One from Jesse's mother that Sweetland couldn't bring himself to finish. For a while, he came back to the page every few days, as though something might have changed in the meantime. Jesse's status or his profile picture. A message from Jesse himself appearing from the other world. There was something crudely voyeuristic in the practice and Sweetland was mortified to have given in to the impulse. Eventually he forced himself to keep clear of it.

He powered off the laptop and sat a long time at the kitchen table. He stared out at the abandoned buildings, at the empty cove behind the breakwater, thinking not much. He considered putting water on to boil for tea or to scrub the ten days of dirt off himself, but he didn't move from his seat. The afternoon's light dwindling steady and he watched it go, a rattling brook of panic running through him. There was an eeriness to the kitchen's silence that he couldn't dismiss, a subtle absence it took him hours to place—the hum of the fridge that had underlined the quiet in the house for decades. He shook his head when he finally recognized it. "You're a goddamned idiot," he said and his own voice startled him. He was up out of the chair to start a fire then, to light a candle, to find something to eat.

He walked out through the hall on his way to bed. Not even the second-hand glim of the light over the shed coming through the windows to lessen the pitch. The space made strange by that blackness and he kept a hand to the walls to find his way.

It was a doll's house Sweetland lived in, built for the dimensions of people stunted by a diet of salt fish and root vegetables. The upstairs hallway as snug to his shoulders as a coffin. He took a last piss in the bathroom, which had been Uncle Clar's bedroom when he was a youngster, long before the electric lights and the indoor plumbing. Sweetland's mother slept with Ruthie in those days, Sweetland and Hollis across the hall in a room about the size of their bed. On the coldest nights of the winter his mother would send him or Hollis to sleep with the old man, for the extra warmth. Uncle Clar in his long underwear turning toward the wall as Sweetland crawled under the covers, an oven-heated beach rock at their feet. Night now, the old man said, God keep thee.

It never struck him, the strangeness of that archaic word. *Thee.* It was Effie pointed it out to him. A petrified holdout from another age. He'd known a handful of elderly Sweetlanders who made use of it when he was a youngster, as if it was something a person grew into as they aged.

Clar was ninety-three when he died, a wizened leprechaun of a man by then, his toothless face caved in by age, a hump on his back from an accident in Sydney mines when he was in his thirties. He was too crippled to be any use on the water. He had a wood-shop out back where he spent every day but Sunday, building chairs and trunks, boats and window frames. Though Sweetland could only remember him puttering mindlessly in latter days, muttering to himself or snatch-singing under his breath.

The portrait of Clar beside the front door used to hang in the parlour before he died. Who's that good-looking young fellow in that picture? Sweetland's mother would ask the doddering old man.

That's me, Uncle Clar said.

Go on, she told him. You was never that handsome.

That's *me*, he insisted, indignant.

They'd never really gotten along, his mother and Uncle Clar. They bickered as a matter of course and cursed one another on occasion, though it was so ritualized it seemed nearly affectionate. Blood of a bitch of a woman, Uncle Clar would say in the heat of their arguments and he would turn to Sweetland, looking for confirmation.

Sweetland lived in the house alone after his mother passed, and again after he moved back from the keeper's house when the light was automated. He slept in what had been her bedroom, the same floral-patterned wallpaper, the same grey battleship linoleum on the floor. A double bed with a wooden trunk at the foot, a highboy. The door caught on the bed frame before it could swing all the way open and he had to turn inside the room and close the door in order to lie down. It was a delicate dance step he'd watched his mother perform a thousand times before it became his own, and he managed it blind now, without thinking. Stripped out of his clothes, hung them on the wall hooks beside the bed. Crawled under the covers and fell immediately asleep.

He didn't dream or stir through the night. He could tell it was late when he woke by the way the light fell in the room, and he hung his legs over the side of the bed, pushed himself upright. There were a few habitual moments of vertigo and he waited until they passed, then walked down the hall in his socks and undershirt to the bathroom.

He caught a glimpse of himself as he passed the mirror and started. Turned to the glass, his hands braced against the sink. He looked like the psycho in one of the slasher flicks the Priddle boys rented from Vatcher's store in their teens. A grizzle of white beard on the uninjured side of his face. His hair shaved close to the scalp. Sweetland raised a hand from the sink, swiped it across the quarter inch of fierce white bristle. His head like something you'd use to scrub a toilet. "Jesus in the Garden," he whispered.

He'd stopped into the barbershop the day before Duke left for good in July, took a seat in the leather chair. He threw a ten-dollar bill up on the counter. Let's see what you got, he'd said.

What are you talking about now, Duke asked.

Last chance at a paying customer.

Duke held his arm out to show off the extravagant tremor he'd been living with for years. You don't want this hand at your head with scissors, Mose.

Use the clippers.

For Christ's sake.

Is this a barbershop or not?

I got everything packed away.

Sweetland got down from the chair to poke through the cupboard below the counter. It was all stacked there neatly, where it had been since the shop opened. Three nylon capes and a handful of scissors and combs. Two straight razors, a mug holding a pristine shaving brush. The clipper still in its box. Sweetland slid the machine free and plugged it in. He shook out one of the nylon capes and sat back in the chair, securing the Velcro around his neck.

I wants it nice and tight at the back and sides, he said.

Sweetland's face seemed to surface out of a filmy mist as he watched the hair fall away in clumps. The lank earlobes looking almost scrotal, the still-black eyebrows thick as gorse. The skin grafts on the right side of his face, even after all these years, shockingly rabid.

You coming down to the wharf tomorrow? Duke asked.

Going in to pick a few berries first thing.

Awful early for blueberries.

Been a good summer, Sweetland said. Half of them's already ripe. They'll go to rot on the bush someone don't pick them soon.

Duke stepped back when he was done and the two men stared into the mirror.

You're a natural, Sweetland told him.

Fuck you, Duke said quietly.

After he ate breakfast, Sweetland took his canvas backpack down to Duke's shop. A CLOSED sign in the tiny window but the door was unlocked. Duke had left behind the barber's chair and the mirror and the chessboard on its low table. His photos and newspaper clippings taped to the wall, the space above the chessboard almost completely covered.

You don't want to take any of these with you? Sweetland had asked him.

Duke shook his head. That's all is holding up that wall, he said, is Scotch tape.

There was a section of articles about the Sri Lankan boat people in their red lifeboat, most from the St. John's paper, though there were five or six from the mainland. Black-and-white pictures of the cove. One or two insets of himself with captions. *Local fisherman, Moses Swietlund.*

Newfoundland fisherman rescues Sri Lankan boat people. There was an article up there about him receiving the Coast Guard medal out at the keeper's house, a year after the event. A couple of Polaroids of him with Bob-Sam Lavallee and two officers in their white tunics, of him wearing his medal beside Pilgrim and Ruthie and the baby.

Clara was almost three months old by then and Sweetland doted on her, feeding the girl her bottle and changing her shitty diapers and walking the floor, humming little songs to quiet her when she fussed. Holding her by the ankles and blowing farts on her belly to make her laugh. He could see how much Clara meant to Ruthie, that the wonder of the child was almost enough to redeem the road she'd travelled to have her. And Clara was Sweetland's way back into Ruthie's life, a place they could safely set their wounded affection for one another. They never mentioned the night at the church with the dead boy under his altar cloth. It was a sunker awash at low tide, and they rowed a wide berth around it.

Sweetland glanced down at Duke's chessboard. The black and white pieces in their neat opposing rows, but for the one white pawn that Duke had placed ahead two spaces before he left the room for the last time. His habitual opening. For a moment Sweetland considered taking the board back to the house with him. But he was miles away yet from playing a chess match against himself. He reached down, lifted a black pawn up two spaces to meet its opposite.

"Your move," he said.

He went to the cupboard below the mirror, taking the straight razors and the cup and three bars of shaving soap. He unscrewed the razor strop on the side of the barber's chair, and he set all the materials into his pack.

From there he went down to the Fisherman's Hall to pick through Reet Verge's museum. He had to force a window at the back of the building to get inside. Mostly junk she'd collected, old stovetop irons and one of Uncle Clar's handmade highboys, a white nightdress that belonged to Sara Loveless's grandmother. Net-knitting needles, cod jiggers, a killick.

An antique phonograph with a horn-of-plenty amplifier that belonged to old Mr. Vatcher, a slender stack of 78s beside it. Something by Don Messer. Two survivors of an eight-record set of *The Messiah*. Sweetland wound the mechanism and released the stop, the table creaking into motion. He placed the needle on the spinning record, the sound of static giving way to "Turkey in the Straw." Pilgrim's standby on his toy fiddle. The machine pumped out an astonishing level of noise and Sweetland lifted the needle halfway through. Stood listening to the quiet, like someone afraid he'd woken a sleeper in another room. Let the turntable slow to a stop on its own.

He came away from the museum with a storm lamp, with the scythe and sharpening stone he'd donated out of his shed, and three kerosene lamps to light the kitchen and his bedroom. But there was nothing else of any use to him.

He scoured the cove looking for a boat. He went through sheds and fishing rooms, amazed to think every punt and skiff and motorboat had gone with the last residents. He lay awake half a night, trying to think how he might get on the water, when Loveless's dory came to mind.

In the morning he walked to Loveless's barn and hauled the derelict craft into the open air. It was made of rough board and weighed about as much as a small car. The bastard child of a night of tormenting they'd rained on Loveless—Sweetland and Duke and Pilgrim and the Priddles. Useless, they called him. Kerosene Head. Didn't know his ass from a hammer. Too fucken lazy to shiver.

Loveless was suffering through one of his intermittent infatuations at the time. They were all one-sided and hopeless, though none more so than this latest fixation. He got his hair trimmed every Monday morning in Reet's kitchen. Invited himself by to watch *Land and Sea* or reruns of *The Love Boat* in the evenings. He made a goddamn nuisance of himself, keeping tabs on her whereabouts every minute of the day, wanting to know who she spoke with on the phone. Followed her around like a lamb after its mother.

It was a joke in the cove, Loveless in love, and abusing the man was their favourite drunken entertainment. Loverless, they called him. Couldn't nail a woman with her legs tied open. Reet Verge wouldn't let a man like him lick her shoes, they said.

The accusations stung Loveless into an uncharacteristic spell of industry. He squirrelled himself away in the barn for months, hauling lumber from Vatcher's store, boxes of nails and paint and more besides. He refused to say what he was up to back there until he asked Sweetland to bring his quad and trailer to the barn.

Well Christ, Sweetland said when he saw it. Did Sara help you with this?

Not a nail, Loveless said defiantly.

Well Christ, Sweetland said again.

It was meant to be a tribute to Reet, he realized, a declaration to the world, a kind of courting. It looked more or less the way a boat ought to look, which Sweetland counted a major accomplishment. But he doubted the thing would float. They muscled it onto the trailer and brought it down to the harbour where Sweetland backed it out on the slipway. Loveless sitting up on the thwart to row her maiden voyage across the cove.

How does she feel? Sweetland asked as the dory drifted free.

Finest kind, Loveless shouted back, an edge of panic in his voice.

Even from the shoreline Sweetland could see that every seam was seeping water. What did you caulk her with? he asked.

Loveless was trying to turn her head back to the slipway before she went under altogether. Paint, he shouted.

They managed to make it seaworthy enough that youngsters could beat around the harbour in her, but it was never fit for anything more than that. The Love Boat, Sweetland called it. It hadn't been near water in a decade when he dragged it outside. Daylight showing through half the seams. He walked slowly around the vessel, like a man stalking an injured creature, looking for the quickest way to kill it.

He tied the dory onto his ATV trailer and rode it to the government dock where he backed it down the slipway until it was sunk to the gunwales, seawater pouring in through the cracks. He left it there on the trailer for two days and nights to let the old boards plim up. On the third morning he turned it face down on the wharf and set about raking out the seams. He found a ball of caulking cotton tucked away with Uncle Clar's old tools in the shed, the strands on the outside as dry and hard as wood, but he pried away until he reached a layer still waxy enough to be pliable. He chinked it in with a maul and chisel, then puttied the seams tight. He had half a tin of yellow oil paint he'd used on the outhouse before it was relegated to wood storage, and he slapped a layer on the dory's upturned hull.

He gave her a full forty-eight hours to dry before he turned her right side up. Pushed the boat back down the slipway and tied her to the dock. There was an old set of oars tucked in the shed rafters and he took those down and sanded and varnished them. He carved thole-pins by the light of the oil lamp and fashioned a bailer with the top half of a Javex bottle and then he went to bed, thinking the dory was probably at the bottom of the cove already. But she was riding high and more or less dry in the morning. He bailed out the bit of seepage before he untied her and set the oars. He hauled around the little cove two or three times, the dory moving like a cow in the water, low and heavy and awkward, and he was winded with the effort when he tied on twenty minutes later. But he had a boat to knock around in.

For two weeks in the middle of September he left the house in the dark each morning, walking to the north-end light to spare what was left of the two containers of gasoline. He spent the day out there harvesting potatoes and carrots and turnip, cabbage and onions, parsnip, storing the vegetables in the cool beside the cistern. Planning to ship the whole load to the cove on the quad and trailer when it was ready. The Coast Guard had sent a crew out earlier in the summer to sheet up the windows and doors of the house with plywood. Even the low door that led to the cistern was barred shut and marked with a DANGER—KEEP OUT sticker. Eight-inch screws placed every ten inches, Sweetland cursing each one as he torqued them free.

He got caught out there one afternoon in a pelting storm of wind and rain. He had wet gear in his pack but the rain fell in sudden steady waves and he was soaked to the skin before he so much as lifted his face. The keeper's house was barred shut, the door to the old light tower padlocked, and he passed a wet night in the dank crawl space while the weather howled. He laid his slicker on the ground and huddled under one of the burlap sacks he'd brought for the potatoes, shivering awake every few minutes with the chill. Making a list of materials he planned to stash at the keeper's house if he managed to live through the night—blankets, matches, a dry change of clothes. A tent, a barbecue. Homebrew, a side of beef. Duke's barbershop. A duffle bag of sunshine.

He fell asleep as he added to his ludicrous list and he dreamt of Jesse rocking beside him with his arms around his knees, singing "The Cliffs of Baccalieu." He woke in the black and reached for the boy, his hand closing around one bony knee. "Jesse," he said, but the youngster carried on with his interminable ballad like Sweetland wasn't present. He turned and grabbed Jesse by the arms, shaking the boy as he shouted his name, and he woke up in the teeming black alone. Sweetland felt around blindly, kicking his legs as far as they could reach, just to be sure nothing was in there with him. "Jesus fuck," he whispered.

He listened to the marine forecast each morning after the gardens were put away and if the day looked fair he took his jigger and line down to the Love Boat to spend a few hours after his fall fish. He pulled around the breakwater into open ocean and went as far as Wester Shoals, forty-five minutes of rowing if the wind wasn't blowing onshore. He let the boat drift on the shoal ground and ran his line overside until it touched bottom. He was never out of sight of land, and he kept an eye to the west'ard for signs of weather kicking up as he jigged the lead weight. The boat wouldn't fare well in any kind of sea, he knew that. Most days he caught upward of ten to fifteen cod in the space of an hour or two and that was as long as he cared to be on the open Atlantic in Loveless's craft.

He fried himself a meal of fresh cod, or made fish and brewis, or stewed the cod's heads with potatoes. He cleaned and salted what he couldn't eat fresh, stacking the fish in briny piles. It was a process he hadn't been involved in since the advent of flash freezing in the fish plants, sometime before Hollis died, and he'd forgotten how to salt the fish properly. Done right, the kite-shaped slabs of meat would last till the End Times of Revelations. But it was a ticklish business that people spent a lifetime refining. Burnt was better than maggoty, he remembered that much, and he buried the snowy flesh in waves of salt until he started running shy and was forced to skimp.

He had his snares up on the mash, on runs in the bit of alder underbrush near Vatcher's Meadow. He had two dozen laid along a mile or so, and he walked up to check the snares once he'd come in from fishing and had cleaned and put away the cod. If the weather was too dirty or uncertain to chance going out in the dory, he went first thing in the morning. He stripped and gutted the rabbits at the sink, boiled the carcasses until the flesh was falling off the bones. Bottled the meat and boiled the bottles to seal the covers tight. Stacked them in the pantry with his beets and relishes and jams and homebrew.

He went up to the mash early after the first night of frost in October, knowing the chill would have set the rabbits running to keep warm. He headed for an outcrop of bald stone at the south end of Vatcher's Meadow where Glad's sheep used to huddle out of the worst of the wind and rain, and he climbed beyond that to the straggle of alder and gorse where he'd set his snares. He could see the grey glove of a rabbit in the first slip as he approached and he shrugged an arm free of his pack, set it down behind him as he knelt to work the snare free of the furred neck.

The sun had come full into the sky. He had to shade his face beyond the brim of his hat and even so he had trouble picking out the details in front of him. He kept his eyes on the trees, watching for the next slip, and there was something amiss when he saw it, though the glare made it impossible to say what exactly. A rabbit in the snare, but it lay away from the cover of the bush. It looked to have been dragged to the wire's limit, the standard hauled from the ground to put it on display in the open. He slowed as he came closer to it, glancing around as if there might be an audience watching to see his reaction.

Sweetland knelt beside it, leaning on his rifle. The rabbit was on its back with the legs splayed wide and the guts torn out, the stomach cavity empty. But there was nothing human about the mutilation—the animal's head was still attached, the wire slip biting into the neck—and Sweetland let out a breath he didn't know he'd been holding.

The eyes would be gone if it had been a crow or an eagle, Sweetland knew. A fox most likely, after the easy pickings.

"Now, Mr. Fox," he said aloud.

He reached to clear the snare but his hands were shaking and it took a minute before they were steady enough to ignore. He stood holding the rabbit by the ears, trying to decide if it was worth his while bringing it home. "Now, Mr. Fox," he said again. He underhanded the corpse into the bush and reset the slip before moving on.

None of the other snared animals were touched. But it was a regular feature of the line afterwards, to lose one or two rabbits to predation. Sweetland considered trying to trap the fox, or sitting out on the mash near a fresh kill and shooting the thing when it came nosing around. But he found himself feeling oddly disappointed the days there wasn't a mutilated carcass in one of the snares. He'd never laid eyes on the fox he was feeding, but even the sign of the creature's presence cheered him, as if it was a kind of conversation he was having with the animal. And he came to think of the fox as company on the island.

He walked an hour or more each evening, going out as far as the old incinerator to watch the horizon, to look in on the remains of Loveless's calf petrifying in its metal tomb. He tapped the steel toe of his boot against the bell of the incinerator, to hear it ring hollow.

The weather had turned for fall and even the warmest days had an edge to them, the wind cold enough to warrant a jacket. The dark coming earlier each evening, and he was often surprised to turn from the glim of light on the horizon to see the cove already settled into night. The abandoned buildings huddled and lifeless, their windows black. A gaudy rash of stars above them.

He'd expected the place to feel larger with everyone gone, the way the house had after his mother died. Echoing and unfamiliar, caverned with absence. But it seemed smaller and strangely intimate, as though it had shrunken down to fit his solitary presence. Licked clean of all claims but his own. He went freely into houses he hadn't thought to enter in decades, picking through pantries and kitchen cupboards for tinned food, for pickled beets and onion and bottled moose. Combing through closets and drawers for clothes or materials that might be useful, for batteries and tools and utensils.

Toilet paper.

He hadn't thought to purchase any in Miquelon and had only five rolls under the bathroom sink. That scarcity worried him as much as his meagre store of food. In all the houses he'd gone into, there was never more than what had been left on the dispenser beside the toilets. Often not even that. He expected to run out before the snow settled in for the winter and he lay awake nights, walking himself through houses and sheds in the cove, picturing what he might be able to use as an alternative. Cut-up squares of carpet torn from a floor, rags made from clothes left behind in closets, unused rolls of wallpaper. Nothing seemed the least bit practical or likely. He considered Duke's slender stack of magazines at the barbershop but he knew the glossy paper was a lousy substitute. And in the process of dismissing the magazines, Queenie's library of romance and mystery came to mind.

He had rifled through almost every building in Chance Cove, but hadn't stepped foot in Pilgrim's or Queenie's, out of respect for the most recently passed. He had to pry the nails from Queenie's door to get inside, stood still in the kitchen a minute. Cold must, the expectant stillness of objects abandoned in a rush, ages ago. A cup and plate left on the counter. Queenie's ashtrays scattered on every flat surface, though they'd been cleaned of their butts and ash before the funeral. The mouth of the green fridge propped open with a broom handle. Avocado green, Queenie said it was. She'd never seen an avocado in her life and didn't know if it was fit to eat, but it was a nice shade of green. A calendar on the wall beside the fridge showed July of last year. The house like a stopped clock, waiting for someone to wind the spring to start it ticking again.

Sweetland walked through the living room to the stairs. He'd never been up those steps in his life and he went cautiously, as if he might happen on someone coming out of the bath in their small clothes. Had to stop himself calling hello to the empty space. He found the books against one wall, beside the bed. He hefted three boxes from the top of the nearest pile and made his slow way along the hall. Another waist-high row of boxes stacked two deep in the spare room. "Well, maid," he said. "I'm set for a while anyways."

He rationed his use of the radio to save the batteries, listening for the forecast in the morning and allowing himself half an hour before he doused the lamps at night. He missed the comforting chatter when he was about the house or working in the shed during the day, the background voices giving the weather or arguing the import of some political upheaval half a world away. He'd never sat inside without that company. Even when he worked at the lighthouse he carried a radio wherever he went, setting it near a window to lessen the static. Saturday-night blues on the CBC, rogue signals washing ashore from the States. Even French-language stations from Montreal and St. Pierre he could listen to for hours at a time, just for the impenetrable music of their conversation.

Everything around him seemed louder without it, like someone had turned up the amplifier on the world. The steady metronome of the tides, the endless industrial racket of the gulls. The sound of rain approaching out over the ocean, how he could hear it coming miles off before it hammered across the island like a herd of wild animals passing through. A storm door kicked off its latch somewhere in the cove, banging and banging and banging in the wind, until he walked down the path to find it and tie the latch shut with a length of twine.

A couple of times a week he ambled as far as Duke's barbershop. Missing the man's company. He sat in the barber's chair and he used one foot to spin a lazy circle, not looking at himself in the mirror as he passed it. The place managed to smell like a barbershop though it had never operated as one, Barbicide and shaving cream and cheap aftershave, a richly chemical soup that Sweetland found calming. He always gave the chessboard a cursory once-over before he left the shop, shaking his head at the lack of progress, the two pawns locked in their stalemate. "Duke Fewer," he said, "I got half a mind to put you on a clock."

On Sundays he did no work and he made the walk to the light at Burnt Head, just to fill the day. After his night huddled beside the cistern he had cut the padlock on the old light-tower door with a hacksaw and he went out there specifically to revisit it, climbing the ringing metal stairs to stand at the high windows of the glass room, watching weather systems play across the horizon in their massive swaths of cloud and precipitation and wind. He brought binoculars to scan the open ocean, across to the dusky outline of St. Pierre and Miquelon where the Frenchmen carried on their imaginary European pantomime, and back to the cliffs of Little Sweetland.

Most days there was nothing else to see. He felt nearly invisible up there and he didn't mind the feeling as a rule, though now and again he was blindsided by an apocalyptic loneliness he was afraid he might be unequal to. As if he was the only living creature on the face of the earth. He hadn't consciously thought what it would be like to be alone on the island, imagined it vaguely as an extension of his experience working at the lighthouse when he spent most of his days to himself. But he was coming to see that those years of seclusion were diluted by comparison—a temporary appointment, an approximation of solitude.

He stopped at the King's Seat whenever he passed it, looking down over the cove and east and west to either end of the island. *I'm the king of the world* was the phrase that came to his mind, though he never spoke the words aloud.

Beside Pilgrim's house, the only other building in the cove he hadn't gone inside was the church. Knowing already there was nothing in there of any use.

A bishop or deacon or some other church mucky-muck came out from St. John's to hold a deconsecration service in July, and Sweetland was hired to close up the building, shutting off the power and boarding the windows with plywood. The Reverend standing by as he worked, handing him the hammer or the drill, holding the boards as Sweetland fixed them in place.

What is it you're trying to save her for exactly? Sweetland asked.

Just sentimental, I guess.

Sweetland was about to lock and board the main doors when the Reverend decided he wanted to do a final walk-through.

Afraid I might be forgetting something in there, he said.

The only light inside came from the vestibule where the doors stood open and the two men carried flashlights into the artificial gloom. The pews receding in their dark rows like waves strobing onto a beach.

They went through to the back office where the cupboards and closets had been cleared out. The air smelling of old carpet and bleach. The Reverend rummaged through the abandoned desk, holding the flashlight with one hand and rifling with the other. Two drawers whistled shut in quick succession and he cleared his throat, the way Sweetland remembered him doing before starting in on his sermons. *Pardon me*, it sounded like.

I never did thank you, the Reverend said, for sending the note after Ruth died.

Sweetland hadn't been in that room since he happened on the Reverend and Ruthie sneaking out opposite doors of the church, the day he'd towed the Sri Lankan lifeboat into the cove. He'd almost forgotten the event it was that long ago. Or he'd forgotten how it made him feel in the moment. But it struck him fresh, hearing the Reverend speak her name as they stood there—how it didn't seem a time or location crying out for a quick fuck, with a dead boy under a sheet outside the door.

It meant a lot to me, the Reverend went on, not to hear the news second-hand.

Ruthie asked me to let you know, Sweetland said.

She had a rough time of it.

The last few months was bad. It was a blessing when she give it up.

The Reverend turned off his flashlight and stood still in the black across the room.

Sweetland said, You knew about Clara all along.

Ruth told me she was pregnant.

That's the reason you left when you did, I imagine.

That's why I left, he said. And that's the reason I came back. Clara, he said. And Jesse.

Strange you haven't said a word to Clara about it, all this time.

I don't think that's what Ruth would have wanted.

Sweetland threw his head back and laughed. That's very Christian of you.

The Reverend cleared his throat again. I was hoping we might have gotten this conversation out of the way years ago.

How many others were there?

How many what?

All them parishes you moved through, Sweetland said. Ruthie wasn't the only one you dipped your wick into.

Well, the Reverend said. She was better off without me, don't you think?

Sweetland scrubbed at his temples with the knuckles of both hands and sighed. That's a job to say, Reverend.

There was a long pause between them, like they'd lost their way in the woods at night and were afraid to take another step forward.

You remember that young one, Sweetland said. The fellow died on the lifeboat we had in here.

I remember him.

I thinks about those fellows now and then, Sweetland said. How they wound up here, of all places.

Wasn't in their minds when they started out, I'm sure.

What was it you said about it all? In that sermon?

You remember a sermon of mine?

Just the one. It was something about all of us being in the same situation. Lost on the ocean, like.

The Reverend shifted behind the desk. I was always a bit obvious when it came to preaching, he said.

Sweetland scooched his backside up onto the cupboard where the bulletins and mimeograph machine used to be stored, his flashlight trained on the floor between his feet. He flicked it off before he spoke again. I been wanting to ask you, he said. What happened with Jesse last year. You believe he drowned himself?

On purpose, you mean?

Everyone else seems to think as much.

The Reverend flicked his light slowly on and off, on and off. I have no idea, he said.

Hazard a guess for me, then.

Honestly? I don't think Jesse had it in him.

He was all guts, that youngster.

I don't think the idea would have occurred to him, is what I mean. He might have made his mother's life hell for a while with tantrums or going to the bathroom in his clothes or God knows what else. But killing himself? I don't think so.

It was an accident, then.

You know how literal he was. He saw your boat missing down in the cove, I'd say. Might have thought you'd already left for good.

And what? Headed out to the lighthouse to see if he could spot the boat off of Burnt Head?

Seems about right. And then the fog came in.

He missed the cairns on the path, you think. Fell off the headland out there in the fog.

More than likely.

Sweetland looked up into the darkness. He couldn't tell if the man believed what he was saying. Or if it made any real difference to think it was true.

The Reverend flicked his light on and off again, on and off, the face of it pressed against his hand so the flesh lit up like a Chinese lantern.

Did Ruth tell you she used to talk to me about Hollis? he said.

Hollis? Sweetland said vaguely, as though he didn't recognize the name.

Your brother, yes.

No, she never said. Not that I remembers.

She told me Hollis was—what did she call it? He was a bit touched, she said.

He was a strange creature, all right. Moody, like. He'd go weeks at a time and not say a word to a soul. Got right low, sometimes. Spent half the days in bed. Always had his head into his school reader or some other book.

He wanted to leave Sweetland to finish high school, didn't he?

He talked about it. I imagine he'd have gone over to Burgeo or Fortune or somewhere if Father was still with us. But there was just me and Hollis to go after the fish.

Ruth thought he was sick with something. Physically ill, I mean. That's what Mother told her.

She didn't even know he was at the Waterford in St. John's those months he was gone. She thought he was doing some kind of schooling.

Well we couldn't very well tell her that her brother was in the mental, could we? She was just a youngster still.

She knew a lot more than you gave her credit for, the Reverend said. And he stopped there. Waiting to be encouraged, Sweetland knew, but he wouldn't give the man the satisfaction.

That story about Hollis falling across the trawl line, the Reverend said finally, and you cutting it loose to take off the strain. She didn't believe a word of it.

None of this is any of your goddamn business, is it?

Sorry, the Reverend said. Occupational hazard.

They settled back into silence awhile longer, though there was no leaving things where they sat. Each man trying to wait out the other.

Ruthie never said a word to me about any of this, Sweetland said.

She wasn't looking to cause trouble, the Reverend said. We were just talking about Hollis and she mentioned the story about the codfish running under the boat and you throwing the engine into reverse. She spent a long time thinking about that fish.

The fish, Sweetland repeated dumbly.

She said she saw you coming in alone and knew something was wrong. Ran down to the stage to meet you. And there was plenty of cod in the boat. But nothing the size you talked about.

This is what she was paying attention to when she heard her brother was drowned, was it?

It was a long time before it came to her, the Reverend said. And she'd probably never have taken note if there weren't other things about the day that struck her funny. She said Hollis was different that morning. Happy almost. Gave her a hug, told her how much he loved her. Did the same with your mother.

Sweetland was drumming his heels against the wall involuntarily and he made himself stop.

Ruth thought he had it in his mind before he left the house, the Reverend said. To cut the trawl line himself, let the weight take him under.

Jesus fuck, Sweetland whispered.

And you made up some story about a fish because you wanted to spare your mother.

Sweetland nodded in the dark. Set to hammering his heels against the wall again. That would have been the end of the woman, he said, knowing her son killed himself.

It occurred to Sweetland he'd lied to Jesse for the same reason he lied to his mother, to spare the boy knowing the truth about his imaginary friend. He raised his face to the ceiling, fighting the ridiculous sense they were all standing in the darkness beside him, his mother and Ruthie and Hollis. Jesse.

Hollis was suffering, the Reverend said.

I expect he was. I wouldn't very good to him about it all.

It wasn't your fault, the Reverend said.

That's your professional opinion, is it?

If you like.

I'd have done things different, Sweetland said, all the same. And a minute later he said, You misses him something awful, I spose.

Who?

Jesse.

The Reverend flicked the light into his palm again, the pink lamp of his hand aglow across the room. Sweetland could see the dark bones of his fingers under the skin.

Yes, he said. I miss him something awful.

———

He took the scythe up to the new cemetery to cut the grass back around the graves.

He'd been the unofficial custodian of the cemetery for years, mowing and raking the plots and keeping up the fence and straightening headstones tipped by frost heaves. He never named it as a reason for staying behind on the island, though it sat at the back of his mind beside all the other reasons he never articulated. Watching over Jesse's grave. But he hadn't gone near the place in his time alone in the cove. He hadn't even walked up to the graveyard to look in on his way down from the mash, which had been a regular side trip since his mother died.

He avoided the mowing until he risked the season's first snowfalls, dragged his ass up the path wearing a hair shirt of dread. The grass past his knees by then and he had to cut a trail in from the gate toward the family stones. There was a new marker among them, a white wooden cross he didn't notice until he was near enough to read the inscription, hand-lettered in black: *Moses Louis Sweetland 1942—2012.*

It was set beside Jesse's grave, in the same row as Ruth and Uncle Clar and his mother, and he laughed when he saw it, as if he'd managed to pull off an elaborate practical joke. But it was a fright to him all the same. They had never raised a marker in the graveyard for Hollis, lacking a body to mark, and it never occurred to Sweetland that someone might see fit to put one up for him. He left without finishing the mowing and spent the rest of the day anxious, expectant almost. Though he couldn't settle on what was disturbing him exactly.

He woke in the middle of the night and lay still a few moments. Seeing clearly what the visit to the graveyard had lit up for him, what he'd been avoiding all this time—that surreal, impenetrable experience on the Fever Rocks, lashed to the ladder with the dead boy in his arms. Sweetland was shivering uncontrollably before Barry finished making the climb and he shouted after the man, wanting to be untied from the corpse. Bawling for all he was worth. Barry didn't hear him over the ocean's racket or ignored what he heard and Sweetland watched those distant legs disappear at the top of the ladder. He bent his face to Jesse then, rested his forehead against the cold nape of the boy's neck. Counted off seconds and minutes to mark the time passing but lost himself in the run of numbers, which made the wait seem infinite, and he spent what felt a long while in miserable silence. His teeth jackhammering as the fits of trembling ran through him. He pissed into his soaking clothes for the brief warmth of it and was colder again moments later.

Jesse, he said, and then looked up the endless length of the ladder to stop himself talking to the dead boy. He could feel himself drifting despite the ropes at his back, his hold on the visible world slipping, and he started singing to stay awake. "Michael, Row the Boat Ashore" and "Rudolph, the Red-Nosed Reindeer" and "Twinkle, Twinkle, Little Star," as though it was the youngster he was trying to comfort. He sang the three childish songs in an endless round, his arms like a useless tourniquet around the last of his blood.

Sweetland sat up in the bedroom's blackness, feeling for his clothes. He lit the storm lamp in the porch and carried it outside where the flame curtsied in each gust of wind. He walked his quavering bowl of light up the path to the graveyard where the white marker was set in the ground beside Jesse's. The cross couldn't be left there, he knew. It was a false thing, which made the boy's death seem even more inconsequential than it was.

He hadn't brought any tools, thinking the cross had simply been knocked into the dirt with a maul. He set the lamp down in the grass beside Jesse's headstone, crouched behind the wooden marker and levered his arms beneath the cross-tie to pry it loose. Pushed and hauled from the top, trying to rock it free. He brought the lamp in close and parted the grass around the base to see it had been set in concrete.

He caught a blur of movement outside the circumference of light then, a shadowed scurry that made him swing around in the dark. His heartbeat in his ears. "Fucken rabbits," he said. Decided it was a job for daylight after all and walked down the path to his house. Refusing to allow himself a glance left or right as he went.

He went back up to the cemetery in the morning, before he'd so much as started the fire, and sawed the cross off at the base. He carried it down the hill on his shoulder. My cross to bear, he thought, ha ha. He propped it against the back wall of the house while he laid a fire in the stove and boiled the kettle. Briefly considered sawing it up and burning it, though there was something in the notion that seemed sacrilegious. After his breakfast he dragged the cross into the shed, angling it awkwardly among the copper pipe and door trim and two-by-fours and dip nets stored above the rafters. Then he took his scythe up to the graveyard and finished mowing the long grass.

There was a fall of snow the last week of October, a wet slurry that came down through the morning. Sweetland sat at the table longer than usual. Dealt himself a hand of solitaire and drank a bare-legged cup of tea. The snow covered the roofs of buildings and the packed earth along the paths and showed no sign of letting up. It would likely be gone by next morning, he knew, but it made him think about the winter he was about to sail into, how much of it he'd be forced to spend at the kitchen table with little enough to fill the time. No television, no online poker, no visitors. He'd have to find something to occupy himself besides solitaire if he didn't want to lose his mind altogether.

There were two boxes of Queenie's books in the porch and he brought the top one into the kitchen, set it on the table. Newspapers were as much as he'd read in his adult lifetime, the odd "Laughter, the Best Medicine" column in a *Reader's Digest* at the barbershop as he waited for Duke to make a move. All the years at the lighthouse he never wanted for distraction, the job kept him busy most of the daylight hours and through part of the night as well. He'd never cracked the cover of a book.

He opened the flaps and took out a handful of paperbacks. He didn't know what he was looking for. Something not too thick, he was thinking, something without the tiny print that made every page a torture to get through. Something that might have a bit of dirt in it—he wouldn't put it past Queenie to enjoy a bit of dirt in her reading material. He shucked through the box, romances all from what he could tell by the flowery cover art, by the breathless titles. The cheap paper was effective in the bathroom, but he didn't think he could stand to read the goddamn stuff. He went through the second box and was all but ready to abandon the notion when he happened on the book she was reading at her window the last time he spoke to her there. There was a bookmark just past the halfway point, which was as far as Queenie made it, he guessed. And there was something in the notion of finishing it for her that appealed to him. The way Sandra had soldiered through Queenie's final pack of cigarettes.

"Well, maid," he said aloud. He flipped through the first pages, turned it over in his hands, hefted it like he was trying to guess the weight. It was no small thing for Sweetland to sit at the kitchen table in the last light of the afternoon, to open the cover and iron it flat with the broadside of his hand. On the title page there was an encouraging note from Sandra to her mother that Sweetland turned past without reading. He took a breath before he started, as though he was about to jump face and eyes into a cold pool of water.

Half an hour later he was ready to throw the bloody thing in the stove. Three afternoons in a row he sat in the day's last light with the book, feeling like a man sentenced to dragging beach stones up the face of the Mackerel Cliffs. He looked at the cover each time he quit reading, flipped it to inspect the back. A quote from a Toronto paper about "authentic Newfoundland." Whoever wrote the book didn't know his arse from a dory, Sweetland figured, and had never caught or cleaned a fish in his life. "Jesus fuck," he whispered.

Queenie would never have gotten all the way through the thing, he guessed, even if she'd lived. He considered adding it to the paperbacks sitting beside the toilet upstairs, flushing it one soiled page at a time. But the book seemed to require another kind of send-off altogether. He took it with him on his walk the evening of the third day, out past the ruins of his stage and on to the incinerator at the head of the cove. He walked beyond the wooden rail that circled the bell and clambered a little ways down toward the water and he threw the book into the ocean. The pages made a small fluttering explosion as he let it go, like a partridge flushed out of underbrush. It was too dark to see it land, but he heard it strike the water's surface.

He didn't feel anything like the satisfaction he expected and thought maybe he should have done something more practical with it after all. He started back toward the dark ring of houses and was startled by the moon rising over the hills, the pocked face a livid red and nearly full, as clear as an object set under a magnifying glass. Unnaturally close on the horizon and spooky as hell. Sweetland kept his eyes on it as he made his way along the path and was almost among the houses before he saw the light in Queenie Coffin's window. He stopped still, watching the glow of that dull yellow square. He blinked quickly three or four times. He scanned along the Church Side hills, out as far as the point where he saw nothing but the habitual black. And when he turned his eyes back to Queenie's house the window was dark.

THEY DIDN'T SPEAK the rest of the way to the south-end light after Sweetland buttoned his fly. Effie sat with the soiled handkerchief in her fist, not knowing where else to put it. They stopped and tied up at the light, walking on in the darkness to the Mackerel Cliffs. Sweetland reached to hold the back of Effie's dress as they came near the sheer drop and they stood looking out at the ocean. Close to one another, but not touching.

Effie talked for awhile about going home to stay with her parents over the summer, about the worst of her students at the school and how she liked boarding at old Mrs. Priddle's house. Sweetland quiet in the dark. He'd brought Effie out to the light to tell her about his plans to go to Toronto with Duke Fewer in the fall, but he was shy to bring it up after what happened between them in the cart and decided he would do it another time.

Sweetland was almost twenty-six years old and he had nothing against the notion of marriage on principle. It was something he'd always expected to come to, though it never seemed more concrete or more urgent to him than that. And nothing in particular had happened between him and Effie to suggest she was anxious to move things along, before she brought it up after their dinner one Sunday afternoon. He'd just finished describing the buffalo sinking into the black water at Tilt

Cove, the bubbles streaming from those great nostrils. It might have been his third or fourth time telling the story for all he knew, he was new to the art of entertaining female company. She'd been looking into her lap and he thought she'd stopped listening some time ago. She turned her head toward the clatter his mother and sister were making at the dishes in the pantry and stood to go help, touching one finger to his shoulder on her way past.

I might marry you, she told him, if you asked me.

He watched Effie disappear into the pantry then, his ears ringing like she'd struck him with a hammer. Perhaps I will, he said, though he couldn't tell if she caught the words or not. He glanced across at Uncle Clar to see if he'd overheard the exchange, but the old man was sound asleep. The cat on his chest looking in Sweetland's direction, giving him that solemn, witchy stare, seeming to say, *Now, that's done*. Months passed and neither of them had breathed the word *marriage* since, though it followed them around like a dog on a leash.

The lighthouse flashed its beam out beyond them in a slow, steady strobe that gave depth and definition to the height they stood at, the breadth of the ocean below. The wind rolling up the cliff face and gusting above the ledge to push at their shoulders. Effie mentioned getting cold standing out in the open, but she didn't move when he suggested going back to the cart. She knew they'd come all this way for a reason and he could see she wasn't about to leave without hearing what it was. She was quiet after he told her about going up to Toronto to look for work. She stared out across the water and he couldn't tell what she made of the notion.

I'll be back before Christmas, I expect, he said.

That's all right, she said.

She turned toward the light and he followed her back to the cart. They rode all the way to Vatcher's Meadow in silence. The memory of the trip out made Sweetland hard again, though he knew enough about women not to expect her hand on the inside of his leg. He glanced across now and then but she was staring straight ahead, her arms folded over her stomach.

Sweetland tied the horse to the fence at the meadow and Effie was out of her seat before he could offer a hand to help. I'll walk you down, he said.

You got to sluice out that cart before you brings it back to Bob-Sam, she said.

I'll look after it, he said.

They went by the King's Seat and down into the cove, walking on as far as the church and up to old Mrs. Priddle's house without passing another soul out in the night. Before they reached the front door Effie stopped and turned to him. Too dark to tell her features. He reached for her hand but she was still holding the soiled handkerchief and they both pulled away when he touched it. He turned halfways to go, but hesitated there.

You won't be too lonely? he said.

I can look out to myself.

He left her then, walking up on the mash to drive the horse and cart out to Bob-Sam Lavallee at the lighthouse. Trying to interpret her response all the way there and home again.

3

THROUGH THE END OF OCTOBER and the first days of November, Sweetland spent his afternoons gathering brush and deadfall on the mash above the cove. He carted a rubbish pile of lumber that was stacked and going to rot beside Loveless's barn these twenty years or more. He lugged up three worn-out tractor tires left behind by Glad Vatcher, using the quad to haul them one at a time, despite the fact he was nearly through his gasoline. Wanting to make something spectacular of the bonfire for the boy.

He rifled through the closets of the cove's empty houses to find a long-sleeved shirt and a pair of pants he could stuff with hay. Sweetland was a youngster the last time anyone bothered burning an effigy on Bonfire Night. It was decades since anyone even called it Guy Fawkes' Night. He'd never known who Guy Fawkes was before Jesse looked him up on the internet and made his report, spelling the man's last name and offering a thumbnail sketch of his claim to infamy. A radical from another time, a man involved in a plot to blow up the Parliament Buildings in London.

Sweetland had already forgotten what Guy Fawkes's grievance was and how the plot came undone. There was nothing in the story to make him wish ill on the man's memory. It was just a bit of mindless sport when he was a youngster, watching the vague shape of a person lifted over the conflagration. Like seeing the aftermath of suicide bombings on the news, or watching people ruin themselves in biking mishaps on YouTube. A vicarious thrill, to be horrified and somehow comforted at the one time. The crowd gathered close to the fire and shouting as the flames caught hold in the clothes.

He made the head out of a brin bag, also stuffed with straw, and he drew on the eyes and mouth with the last dribs of the yellow oil paint. Hung the figure on a hook in the shed, stepped back to consider it. That's what's left of you, Mr. Fawkes, he thought, for all your scheming. A few rags stuffed with straw.

It was pouring rain and cold on the morning of the fifth and it was only the thought of disappointing Jesse that kept him from skipping the event altogether. The weather cleared some in the late afternoon and he walked up the path at dusk with a yogourt container of kerosene and the straw effigy under his arm. His pockets jangling with half a dozen bottles of homebrew. Four potatoes wrapped in tinfoil stuffed among the beers. His breath white in the chill, the air smelling like snow.

The mound of scrap wood and brush was Sweetland's height, with the tractor tires thrown on top. He made a torch with a rag on a stick of driftwood and soaked the rag in kerosene. Then he walked around the mound, pushing the flame into the wet underbrush until the fire caught in half a dozen spots and took up through the centre. By the time the early dark had fallen, the mash was alight with the blaze, so hot Sweetland had to stand twenty feet clear, and still he could feel his face burning. The bonfire made the blackness beyond its circle seem complete, as if the houses below and the ocean beyond it had disappeared into the void.

He waited until the fire had burned back a little and tied the effigy to a pole he'd cut for the purpose, holding it over the height of flame and the dirty rags of smoke from the tires. It was a full minute before the pants ignited and the figure seemed almost to explode then. Sweetland shouting into the darkness above the bonfire as the clothes shrivelled and fell away in burning strips.

He dropped the pole onto the mound and crouched in close to the fire, shielding his face with one hand as he placed the potatoes into the coals nearest the edge. He stepped back to where he'd left the home-brew and stood there in the heat. Raised a bottle to the flames. "Now, Mr. Fawkes," he said.

There were half a dozen fires this size along the mash when he was a youngster. People gathered in clusters, or wandering back and forth from one to another. The men half-loaded on whiskey or shine, women trying to keep track of the youngest children. The night crackling with voices. Every year someone's outhouse was dragged up the path and thrown onto a burning pyre, the dark erupting with flankers. The crowd cheering. He and Duke would take a run at them after the initial inferno had burned back, coming down in the coals on the far side of the largest fires, sending up a shower of sparks, occasionally setting their pant cuffs alight.

The tradition had all but died out on the island before Jesse arrived. The last few years the boy had helped Sweetland collect scrap wood and spruce branches near the Mackerel Cliffs. They weren't allowed to set the fire anywhere near Vatcher's Meadow or to burn tires or any other "hazardous waste" according to the letter from Rita Verge. Municipal regulations, she said they were. It wasn't much above a glorified camp-fire they put together, but Jesse counted down the days to Bonfire Night the same as he did for Christmases and birthdays. He scorched marsh-mallows and wieners on alder sticks while Sweetland described the fires they had one time, the days and weeks they spent building the pyres, the mash lit up like a carnival midway till the small hours of the night. Promising the boy next year they'd haul his old outhouse up the path and burn it. Or steal a few tires or stuff an old shirt with straw. Next year, he offered every November. Next year.

Sweetland fished the potatoes out of the coals and let them cool a few minutes at his feet. Opened the tinfoil gingerly, using his pocketknife to break the skin, steam snaking into the cold air. The roasted flesh dry and sweet and he ate three of the plain spuds, one after the other. He'd finished four bottles of the homebrew and he stepped away from the heat to piss into the blackness. The silence roaring out there beyond the fire's chatter and he listened awhile after he was done, feeling the chill creep into his clothes. And something moved in the pitch, a scuffle near his feet that raised the hair at the back of his neck. The something slipped past him and Sweetland staggered to one side, turning in time to see the creature disappear around the bonfire. "Jesus fuck," he said.

He crouched down and waited a few moments. Not quite able to credit what he'd seen. "Smut," he said. He pursed his lips and kissed at the air.

The little dog appeared at the opposite side of the fire, peering at Sweetland warily. He called again but the animal lay down where it was, the head held high. He stood up straight and the dog got to its feet, backing away.

"All right," Sweetland said. He retreated to the spot where the last potato lay on the ground, trying not to take his eyes from the tiny animal. He knelt and peeled the tinfoil away, cut a section of potato skin, tossed it toward the dog. He'd never known a dog to eat potato skin, but he guessed the creature was near to starved, wandering up on the mash alone all this time. It must have gotten loose before the last ferry and been left behind. A wonder it was alive at all.

The dog crept up to the food and sniffed a moment before eating it, then looked across at Sweetland. He tossed another section, a little nearer himself, and the dog crept that much closer. Sweetland talking softly all the while, asking the animal questions about how it had managed to miss leaving on the ferry and what it had done to keep itself alive and who was a good dog? Each bit of food he dropped closer to himself and the last morsel of potato he held in his outstretched hand. The dog considered it a long time before sneaking close enough to take it. Retreated a yard and ate the potato and then stared at Sweetland again. It was a ragged-looking thing, burrs and sticks caught in the overgrown black coat. The fur so long it was impossible to see the dog's eyes behind the straggle. Sweetland raised his palms in the firelight. "That's all I got," he said. He wanted, more than anything he'd wanted in a long time, to touch the animal. But it moved away from him, closer to the heat of the fire. "You been living off my rabbit snares, I'm guessing," Sweetland said. "Haven't you, Mr. Fox."

The word struck him then, the odd congruity. "Mr. Fawkes," he said. "Mr. Fox." He wished he'd brought up some sort of meat to offer the dog. But he didn't move an inch for fear of scaring it off, even after it curled up and fell asleep.

The dog stayed close to Sweetland after Bonfire Night, following him at a discreet distance when he checked his rabbit slips up on the mash, coming by the house for food. The animal couldn't be coaxed inside, though Sweetland stood at the open door with morsels of rabbit or salt beef. He dragged Diesel's doghouse up from Pilgrim's yard and set it in the lee of his own place, laying an old bath towel inside, and from the look of things the dog was making use of it. Before he doused the lamps at night he opened the door and called good-night. With no idea if it was within earshot.

There was a stretch of fine weather in the middle of November, mild and clear and calm, and Sweetland went out in the Love Boat to fish each day. The little dog chased him down to the wharf that first morning and stood at the concrete edge barking its fool head off as Sweetland rowed into the cove. He sat the oars a minute and watched the ridiculous creature running back and forth the length of the dock, yapping so fiercely it reared up on its hind legs.

"What in Christ is it you wants?" Sweetland shouted. He turned about, rowing toward the wharf, and when he was within six or eight feet the dog made a suicidal leap for it. Sweetland twisted in his seat to catch it and there were a few seconds of thrashing and cursing before the boat settled. And by then the dog was curled on a folded square of tarp in the stern. It lay there as Sweetland rowed out to Wester Shoals and didn't move until he'd caught his fish and hauled back in and stepped onto the beach. Sweetland dragged the dory above the high-water mark and tied the painter to a chain he'd set around the base of a rock. The dog still hadn't budged when he leaned in for his fish. "You coming?" Sweetland asked, and it jumped over the gunwale, shadowing him up the path.

There were still a few cod around and he came in with three or four fresh fish the first couple of mornings that week. Two days in a row then he caught nothing more than dogfish, which he brought in to feed to the animal. Decided he would row toward the north-end light to try his luck elsewhere.

It was remarkably still for the time of year, the ocean like a mirror beneath him even after he cleared the breakwater. A fact that afterwards he thought should have been a warning to him. He had an easy job pulling toward the nearest bit of shoal ground to the east, though it was twice as far from the cove as Wester Shoals.

He put out his line and struck the fish right away. He couldn't even get the jigger to touch bottom before the weight of a cod took the line and had to be hauled in. They seemed to be in a race to get out of the water and he filled the small pound at his feet in the space of forty-five minutes' work. The last fish he hooked came up heavy, the weight on the line growing as it came closer to the surface, and it was a job getting the creature aboard without swamping the dory. A big fish, near the size of a small goat, he hadn't seen anything the like of it since he was a child. Sweetland stood to manoeuvre the thing aft, where it kicked and flipped a few minutes before lying still. The dog jumping off its bed to avoid the slap of the tail's massive fan, moving cautiously up to the bow.

Sweetland was still winded with the effort of bringing it aboard when he rolled up the line and set the jigger away. Jesus, it was a fish. He sat a few minutes just looking at the thing. Glanced to starboard then to see how far he might have drifted offshore and there was nothing out there but the white muffle of fog that had closed in without his noticing. He turned where he sat, as if he might see something more substantial to the horizon behind him. Fog snug as a blindfold in all directions.

"Well fuck," he said, and the dog lifted its head to look at him. "Never you mind," Sweetland said. He tried to place the sun but the light was so faint and diffuse he couldn't say. The island lay to the starboard side when he first put out his line, but it was anyone's guess whether he'd turned about as he worked. He shouted first to his left and then to his right, hoping to hear some answering echo off the cliffs, but the fog swallowed his voice. They were close enough to the north-end light he expected to hear some hint of the foghorn, which would help with fixing his location, and he sat still a long time, waiting for it to register. But it never did.

He put the line out to see if he might guess the way the current was running by its drift, but it sat plumb from the gunwale. It occurred to him the jigger hadn't touched bottom when he was fishing and he might have drifted off the shoal ground altogether. He let it out to the full of its length without bringing up. Deep water. But he couldn't be more than half an hour off the land and he started rowing in the direction he was pointed until he guessed half an hour had passed. He shouted over his shoulder a few minutes before turning and rowing in the opposite direction. He carried on an hour or so, to allow for the time he'd travelled the other way, then shouted uselessly into the wall of white.

He sat with the oars across his lap awhile, feeling like an idiot. He glanced over his shoulder to see the dog staring at him. He turned away and talked with his back to the animal. "We're going to have to wait it out, Mr. Fox," he said. "Might mean a night on the water, if we're unlucky enough."

He had no sense of time passing as he sat there. The fog settled closer and he sang aloud for the company of his own voice, the same dreadful children's songs he'd sung to Jesse. The massive fish lying aft flickered occasionally. Sweetland drank a mouthful of fresh water from the Javex bottle and poured a drop into the bailer for the dog. He ate one of the cakes of hardtack he'd packed as a lunch, chewing the dry bread to a paste that he washed down with more water. He opened the one tin of peaches he'd carried with him, sharing the slices with the dog before he drank off the juice. He gutted a fish over the side of the boat, flicked the liver into his palm, and held it under the dog's nose. It sniffed warily at the cold lump of flesh. "Go on, Mr. Fox," Sweetland said, "it's good for what ails you." He cleaned three more fish and fed the raw livers to the dog, then rinsed his hands in the ocean. He sat up straight and turned slowly side to side. His arse was numb from sitting hours on the wooden thwart, his back like a strip of leather being twisted from both ends. He shipped the oars to settle into the bow, lifting the dog out of his way and setting it on his chest where it curled up and slept again.

Still light when he came to himself, but dusky enough he could tell it was late afternoon. He raised himself above the gunwale, scanning around, trying to pinpoint the sun before he lost it altogether. A glim over his right shoulder and he rowed in that general direction, toward what he hoped was the west, stopping now and then to call out and listen to the nothing beyond them. He carried on longer than it made any sense, just to have something to do with himself, for the warmth of the work, rowing until the night had settled full on the sea. He set the oars under the gunwales then and stood to piss into the salt water. He looked down at the spot where he knew the dog was lying. "What kind of a fucken bladder have you got?" he said.

He shook out the tarp in the stern to use as a blanket. Then he lay back on the bare wood to wait for daylight.

He woke to the dog growling, the ridiculous toy rumble of it on his chest. Still dark and the fog thick around them.

"What is it now?" he said.

The dog carried on awhile, as though it heard someone creeping outside a closed door, and Sweetland shushed him. He lay still, trying to identify what it might be. Picked out a shapeless sound in the distance, a low murmur so vague he thought he might be imagining it. The dog barked once into the darkness and Sweetland sat up out of the bow, his head cocked to place it. Could be the foghorn at the north-end light wailing out there, though he couldn't explain why he'd missed it before now. A vessel in the shipping lanes maybe, warning others away. It was a fool's game to chase after it, but he couldn't help himself. He set the oars and started pulling in the direction it was whispering from. The dog standing in the bow when he glanced over his shoulder, staring into the fog and the black.

The sound grew steadier as he approached it, a hum underneath the blind night he was travelling through. What in Christ's name was it? There wasn't the distinct rise and fall he'd expect from a foghorn, just a muffled drone that suggested the outline of something solid when it wasn't being listened to carefully.

He came back on the oars in a steady draw and he started singing to match the rhythm, an old-time hymn he was surprised to have called up. His voice clinging to the old rugged cross, like he was belting it out at a revival meeting. He paused now and then to listen, feeling each time on the verge of naming the drone as it grew more distinct, falling back to the hymn as he rowed. Stopped suddenly in the middle of a verse, the oars dripping water.

It was Tennessee Ernie Ford he was hearing, that southern baritone cutting clear through the fog. "The Old Rugged Cross." He'd been singing along even before he could say what it was he'd been hearing. The dog barked behind him, impatient to get moving.

"Shut up, Mr. Fox," Sweetland said. He reached over the gunwale for a handful of the icy water, splashed it across his face. He didn't think he would credit his senses if he was alone, if the dog wasn't hearing the impossible song as well. It barked again while the music rolled over them. "All right," he said. "Fuck. All right."

It was another half-hour of rowing toward that voice before the sound of waves on the breakwater loomed at his back. Sweetland turned to follow the line of stones to the harbour's mouth. Surprised to see they were coming toward Chance Cove from the west, as if they had some-how managed to circle the island. It was still dark, but the fog had lifted enough that he could make out the white of the church on the point as he pulled into the cove. And not a sound to be heard now he was in sight of the place. He looked over his shoulder where the dog was two paws up on the gunwale, the little tail wagging furiously.

He guided the boat toward the beach and the dog was over the side as soon as the keel touched in the shallows, away up the path toward the mash. Sweetland called after him, though he knew it was a useless gesture. He hauled the dory halfways out of the water, which was as much energy as he could muster. He tied the painter to the chain and walked up the path to his house in the black.

It was near noon before Sweetland woke on the daybed in the kitchen. He lit a fire and put on the kettle and a pot of water to shave. He opened the door and called out to the dog but there was no sign of it. The air suddenly seasonal, cold and cutting.

After he'd washed and eaten, he went down to the beach with three longers and a sheet of canvas under his arm. The tide had risen and the dory was floating free, still tied to the chain-rock. Sweetland hauled it in and dragged it up off the landwash. The fish were sitting in the three inches of bilge water at the bottom of the boat, too high now to consider eating. He tipped the dory up on its gunwale to shake them onto the beach, took out the drain plug and sluiced the mess with seawater. He laid the three logs beside the chain-rock and dragged the dory up beside them, turning it face down onto the longers. He tied the canvas over the boat and he took the oars back up the path and tucked them away in the rafters of his shed.

He called to the dog when he came out the door, whistled up the hill toward the mash. Turned back to the cove, looking out as far as the white clapboard church on the point. The boarded windows. The squat finger of the steeple where the music used to play.

Sweetland and the Reverend were almost outside after their final walk-through of the church when the Reverend put a hand to his arm.

One more spot, he'd said.

There was a stairway off the vestibule that led to a trap door and they climbed through that into a darkened room the size of a bathroom. They flashed their lights around the tiny space. The ceiling twenty feet above them.

I should take these, the Reverend said, and he collected an armful of records that were stacked on the floor near the PA apparatus.

You got plans for those? Sweetland asked him.

Just don't like the thought of leaving them behind, I guess.

The Reverend went ahead of him through the trap door and Sweetland made a last sweep with his light to make sure nothing had been overlooked. When they were outside, he closed and locked the doors and handed the keys to the Reverend. Then he set the two-by-fours across the door frame and screwed them into place with the cordless.

Sweetland watched the church a few minutes, talked himself into walking out to the point. He went around to the side door that led into the minister's office, to see that it was still locked and nailed shut. He circled the building, checking the plywood on all the windows. He came around to the main doors finally, looking close at the two-by-fours across the width. Nothing had been touched or tampered with that he could see. Sweetland glanced up at that empty steeple and then he turned away toward the cove. The water flat calm. He looked up the hillside, scanning across the houses. They all seemed to lean down toward him with a hand at their ears, listening intently. He raised his eyes past them, toward the mash, and called out for the dog.

On the way up the hill he stopped into Duke's shop, took a seat on the cold red leather of the barber's chair. Trying to calm his thoughts with the chair's lazy twirl, the room's lingering undertone of aftershave and conversation. He imagined telling his story to Duke as he sat there, imagined the man's skepticism about the details. You're dreaming, he'd have said. You been drinking bad brew. You needs to give your head a goddamn good shake.

"That's what I needs, all right," Sweetland said, as if Duke was sitting across the room. He took a breath as he pushed the chair in its slow orbit about the room. "A goddamn good shake."

He glanced down at the chessboard as he swung by and brought both feet to the floor to brake his movement. Raised himself from the seat.

There was a game in progress on the board. Half a dozen pieces, black and white, set off to the side. The black king in check.

Sweetland stayed in his kitchen the rest of the afternoon, drinking home-brew and playing solitaire. He left the radio on for the comforting babble of the outside world washing up on the shore of his own. Between hands he walked aimlessly to the living room and back again. He lifted the phone and listened awhile to the nothing in the receiver before he set it carefully into its cradle. He went out to the hallway periodically to stand in front of Uncle Clar's portrait, the man's eyes staring endlessly off to one side, like he was listening to someone in the wings. He took the frame off the wall finally, carried it into the kitchen. He looked around the room a moment, set it down on the daybed. He took his seat at the table and raised his glass to the young old man who still refused to meet his eyes, who was still listening to a voice just offstage.

Sweetland dealt himself another hand. He turned the cards slowly, scanning back and forth along the line, talking over the sound of the radio to his grandfather. Telling him about Loveless's boat and fishing with Loveless's dog who had been scavenging off his rabbit slips up on the mash. How he'd come to call him Mr. Fox, or Mr. Fawkes, as you like. About being lost in the fog that crept over them on the water, the odd absence of the foghorn on Burnt Head, and the voice that led them in past the breakwater.

"Queerest Jesus thing," he said. "Ruined a nice load of fish on top of it all," he said, without raising his eyes from the cards. "Had to dump the works of them on the beach today." He tapped an index finger on the tabletop, placed the three of clubs on the four of hearts, the ten of clubs on the jack of diamonds. "There was one," he said, "biggest fish I seen in years. Size of a goat, he was. Had to throw him aft by himself. Could have lived on that one for weeks."

Sweetland tapped his finger again, glanced out the window. He couldn't for the life of him remember seeing that fish when he flipped the dory and shook the load onto the beach. He turned back to the cards, but he'd stopped seeing them. Trying to picture the enormous cod among the slurry of water and blood and fish meat.

He said, "It's just a fucken old fish, Uncle Clar."

It was nearing dusk, the sun already touching the water somewhere out beyond the Mackerel Cliffs. He didn't want to go down there in the dark and he wouldn't sleep without knowing. He went to the porch and pulled on his coat. Leaned back into the kitchen and said, "Keep the fire in, would you, Clar?"

He whistled for the dog on his way down to the water. Half drunk and unsteady on his feet. The windows of the houses he passed darkening with the day's passing, a wind moaning mournful through the dead electrical wires strung from eave to eave overhead.

He stumbled across the loose stone of the beach toward the pile of fish. A congregation of gulls still praying over the offering there and Sweetland waved his arms as he approached, shouting to clear them away. They hopped sullenly to one side, just out of arm's reach. Sweetland stood over the mess they'd made, eyes pecked out, bellies razored open and the guts pulled into the air. But there was no sign of the goat-sized fish.

He used a stick of driftwood to pick through the mound, pushing offal and ruined carcasses left and right. Uncovered the prize beneath the garbage, like something deliberately hidden there, to keep it out of harm's way. Sweetland reached to grab the tail, as thick around as his calf, hauled it onto a clean patch of beach. It was covered in blood and slime, but the body was untouched by the scavengers. Even the eye still in its socket, staring up at him.

He walked over to the dory beneath its canvas shroud, knelt near the bow and fished under the gunwale for the bailer. Untied it and went to the water's edge to dip it full. He sluiced the big fish clean, went for more water and turned the creature over to wash down the opposite side. It had been out of the ocean so long it wouldn't be fit to eat, but he hefted it in both his arms and started up off the beach, stopping now and then to rest along the path to the house. "You fucken cow," he said.

"Uncle Clar!" he shouted when he was within hailing distance. "You should see this thing! Clar!"

He unlatched the door with his shoulder and worked it open with his elbow, kicked in the door to the kitchen.

"Look at this fucker!" he shouted as he crossed the room, and he bent in close to the framed photograph to present it. "Jesus," he said. He turned and dropped the fish on the counter, the tail lolling into the sink. He took off his coat and pushed his shirt sleeves to his elbows, rinsed his hands and forearms with cold water from the tap. He opened a cupboard and took down a bottle of rye, poured himself a tumbler.

It was nearly dark in the kitchen and he lit two lamps, added wood to the fire. He stood at the counter, looking down at the magnificent thing. Leaned closer a moment, looking for the stink of rot. Brought his nose near enough he could feel the cold coming off it on his face. Breathed in the clean smell of salt.

He sat at the table with his drink awhile. His face twinned in the black panes of the kitchen window. When he was good and drunk he went to the porch after his splitting knife. He brought a lamp close for the light, worked the point into the throat under the gills, sawing through cartilage. Turned the blade to slit the belly, the sound of the tight skin letting go like a zipper being undone. He leaned his weight forward to take off the head, throwing it into the sink. Reached inside the opened torso for the intestines and stomach, closed his fingers on something solid in there. About the size of a baseball. He stepped back, his knife and bloody hands in the air like a surgeon over an operating table. He glanced across at the photograph, Uncle Clar's eyes askance, refusing to watch the proceedings. Sweetland reached back into the cavity and closed his hand on the object, pulled it free with the viscera. He picked the stomach clear of the blood and offal. Slit a hole in the membrane and shook the contents into the sink.

"Jesus fuck," he said.

A rabbit's decapitated head gazed up out of the basin. The silky ears limp and bedraggled, the black eyes wide and staring back at Sweetland.

"Now, Uncle Clar," he said. He wiped his filthy forearm across his mouth. "What would thee make of it?"

He went to bed blind drunk, crawling up the last few steps and along the hall to the bedroom, and he dreamt drunkenly of his mother in his arms, of carrying her up the narrow stairs of the house, the steps moving under his feet like an escalator, the landing above them rising further away even as he climbed toward it.

His mother lived to eighty-four and died of congestive heart failure after a long decline. Sweetland had carried her up and down those stairs for weeks before she took to her bed for good. She was almost weightless by then, her head tucked into his shoulder, one hand picking mindlessly at a button on his shirt. She'd baked fresh bread every day while she was able, for the salve and relief of burying her hands in the warm dough. But it had been years since she'd made her last batch. Her fingers so twisted with arthritis they looked like claws of driftwood.

He set her under the sheets at night, sitting beside her as she said her prayers, her hands held childishly over her nose. Before he left her for the night she said, Don't have me die among strangers, Moses.

Go to sleep now, he said.

When his mother couldn't leave the bed any longer, Ruth moved back into the room across the hall and Sweetland slept on the daybed in the kitchen. They took turns sitting with her, staring out the window as she slept. Sweetland had never seen his mother in a state of undress and he left the room when Ruthie bathed the woman in the morning. Pacing the upstairs hallway until his sister called him back in to help change the sheets.

The public health nurse came out on the ferry twice a month and she left a stack of adult diapers and medicated ointment for the bedsores on the old woman's back and buttocks. Are you in any pain? she asked, and his mother shook her head no. The nurse inserted a catheter and gave them instructions on changing the bags and keeping the equipment clean.

Your mother should be in a hospital, she said. You know that.

We can look out to her, Sweetland said.

If the catheter causes an infection, the nurse said, she'll have to be admitted.

How will we know? Ruth asked.

The nurse touched her nose with one finger. You'll know, she said.

The Reverend was a regular visitor to the sickroom in those last months. He read the old woman Bible verses and they prayed together before he left. Ruthie stayed with them, but it was another intimacy that was too much for Sweetland. He paced the hall or sat outside while the Reverend ministered to her, their voices through the door a muffle that rarely surfaced into coherence.

I'm some disappointed in the both of them, he heard his mother say, and the Reverend's voice answered in an indecipherable monotone. Not one grandchild, she said sharply, dismissing whatever platitude he'd offered up. Talking as if Ruth wasn't sitting next to her in the room. Not one youngster between the two of them, she said.

Uncle Clar sat upright in Sweetland's head then. Blood of a bitch of a woman, the old man said.

His mother's mind began leaving her as her body did, a slow fitful decline. She spent more and more of her waking life among the people she'd grown up with, talking to Ruth like she was her own mother or a young Queenie Coffin, taking Sweetland and the Reverend for her father or one of her brothers. Even when she saw her son for who he was, she misplaced most of his history.

Whatever happened to your face? she asked.

Cut myself shaving.

His mother watched him doubtfully. You're not old enough to be shaving, she said.

It was comical at first, a harmless diversion, and the old woman seemed more or less content lost in her youth and her childhood. But in her last weeks alive the confusion turned sour, an undertone of panic settling in. She was tormented by the wet weather ruining a phantom load of fish spread to dry on the long-gone flakes. She asked to see her dead son and couldn't be comforted with lies.

Hollis is down to the stage, Sweetland told her, he'll be up the once.

He's not well enough to be out at the fish, she said. Don't you be torturing him.

Mother, he said.

You'll be the death of that youngster, you keeps torturing him.

Hollis is the best kind, he said, don't you worry about Hollis.

Why won't you tell him I wants to see him? she said. She was angry enough to chew nails.

He'll be along the once, don't you worry.

His mother turned her face toward the wall. You always hated me, she said.

He looked away from her then and saw Ruth watching from the doorway.

She's not well, Ruth told him.

I knows she idn't.

She don't mean what she's saying.

I knows that, he said.

The day she died his mother woke occasionally to look around herself, dropping off again without seeing anything, but for one instance when she caught and held Sweetland's face beside her. Where am I? she asked.

Home, maid, he said. In your bed.

She shook her head and stared up at the ceiling. She turned to him again, the motion so laboured it was hurtful to watch. She nodded toward him gravely. Who are you?

Moses, he said. Your son.

She shook her head again. I don't know you, she said, and she closed her eyes.

He leaned in close, laying a hand over one of her twisted hands. Mother, he said, but she was already asleep. And dying among strangers, for all he tried to save her from it.

Sweetland woke to a disturbance he couldn't place at first, an agitation in the air that he thought was part of the hangover he'd spent the previous night concocting. He climbed out of bed too quickly and had to steady himself with a hand to the headboard and before the dizziness passed he recognized the sound. A chopper in the distance, the wet whup whup whup approaching the island.

Sweetland pulled on his pants and the filthy shirt he'd worn the night before, stumbled out to the window at the end of the hall which faced the island's north end. The Coast Guard helicopter was miles off when he caught sight of it, a speck in the blue, moving toward Burnt Head. A crew coming out for fall maintenance on the light. It disappeared behind the height of land as it descended and Sweetland made for the stairs, hands on the walls to keep his feet.

He pulled on his coat and boots in the porch, stepped back into the kitchen long enough to grab the rabbit's head from the sink where he'd left it. He opened the main doors of the shed, pulled the tarp off the quad. Set the choke and turned the ignition, the motor rolling and falling flat, rolling and falling flat. Weeks since he'd used the machine and he flooded the engine in his panic to start it up, he could smell the fuel wafting up from the motor. He set off on foot instead, not sure there was enough gas to get him there regardless, not wanting to waste time. He went up the steep slope toward the mash, carrying the creature's head by the strap of its ears. He stopped at the King's Seat to catch his breath. A cold morning but he unzipped his coat, already sweating under the layers.

He walked past the remains of his bonfire, the thick coils of wire from the tractor tires orange with rust. He went through the gate to cut across Glad Vatcher's meadow and before he made the other side it came clear to him he'd have been better to take out the ATV's plugs and wipe them dry with a rag, tried the engine again. The Coast Guard had an hour's work on the light at most. Even if there was some maintenance on the helipad or the ladder, he doubted it would keep them out there long enough. He swore up at the sky and then he swore at his boots.

Beyond the moss and tuckamore of the mash the trail moved into a rolling moonscape of granite where it skewed out toward the flat ground on the headlands, and for long stretches it ravelled within an arm's length of that sheer drop. Sweetland was still feeling a slight vertigo hangover and he hugged the inner edge of the path, keeping his eyes on the cairns placed to show the way until he heard the helicopter start up, the static whine of the ignition. The tower of the old lighthouse was in sight when he raised his head, the slow beat of the blades making their first tentative revolutions beyond it.

He came over the rise and went down the path with his arms in the air, shouting uselessly into the racket. The chopper already airborne and over the open ocean when he rounded the corner of the keeper's house, the air around him buffeted by the mechanical storm. He chased after it stupidly, stumbling down to the helipad. He stood at the centre of the platform, like the needle on a sundial, watching the helicopter until it had disappeared in the blue.

The wind faffered around him, picking at his clothes. He was suddenly hungry and cold, his shirt soaked through with sweat. He looked down at the rabbit's head in his hand, curious as to why he'd carried it out here. It was meant to convince the Coast Guard crew of something, he knew, though it seemed a ridiculous prop now. He thought of how he would have looked to them, waving the foul thing, raving on about the mutilation of rabbits on his line, the head he'd found nailed to his stage door. The voice leading him out of the fog and the phantom chess game underway at Duke's abandoned barbershop. He patted at his pockets distractedly, like he was looking for reading glasses or cigarettes. Almost relieved to have missed the crew. He walked to the edge of the pad and threw the rabbit's head back into the ocean that had briefly surrendered it.

He turned to the lighthouse and the island then, started slowly up the rise. Sweetland walked along the front of the building where the plywood near the cistern had been reset with screws. All his materials, the dry clothes and food that he'd stored in the dark beneath the house locked away now, or confiscated. He thought to stop in at the tower to dry himself in the greenhouse warmth of the glass room but the door didn't budge when he tried to open it. There was no lock on the latch and he stood looking at the closed door with his hands at his sides. Saw the fresh welts along the seams where the Coast Guard crew had torched it shut. A dozen spot welds around the frame. Sweetland ran his hand along the edge, the bump of each weld still warm from the acetylene.

The crew would make a report about the broken lock on the tower and the board removed from the skirting when they got back to St. John's. Kids out from Fortune Bay on a weekend drinking spree, they'd put it down to. Vandalism and mischief. Cokeheads home from the Alberta oil fields, looking for trouble.

Not some lunatic geriatric holed up on his own out here. Losing his frigging mind.

He checked his slips on the way back along the mash, out of habit more than intention. There was a single animal in the snares and he carried it home by the feet, the animal's ears brushing the ground as he went.

The dog was waiting near Diesel's house and ran out to meet him as he came through the back of his property. "Now, Mr. Fox," Sweetland said. "Where have you been hiding." It waddled along on its back legs awhile, nosing the rabbit in Sweetland's hand.

He went into the porch and paused there, looking back to see if the dog would follow. It stared at him, its head cocked, but didn't come any closer. He left the door wide behind him, thinking the dog might change its mind eventually. He walked through the porch and stopped two steps into the kitchen. The butchered fish lay in its own gore on the counter, the muck of it running down the cupboard doors to the floor, bloody streaks dried to the wood. The black-and-white picture of his grandfather propped on the daybed.

Sweetland crossed to the stove and lit a fire, waited for the flame to take hold in the splits. Then he filled the woodbox until it was roaring. He set a pot of water on the stove and dug out a bucket from beneath the sink, splashed half a cup of Javex into the bottom. He scooped the remains of the codfish into two plastic bags, carried them out behind the shed. The dog following him and watching as Sweetland dug a hole to bury the mess, and he tamped the dirt down firm. Then he went back inside and sat beside the portrait of Uncle Clar to wait for the water to boil.

He spent what was left of the daylight hours scouring the kitchen. He scrubbed the floor with a brush and then mopped it, standing in the porch while he waited for it to dry. He stood on a chair to empty the shelves and wipe them down, and then he set about cleaning out the cupboard drawers. Lifted out the cutlery tray and stopped still when he saw the folded sheet of paper beneath it.

He could see the line of letters glued to the inside and his hands were shaking when he laid it flat on the counter. YOU GET OUT, it said, OR YOULL BE SOME SORRY. Sweetland leaned on the counter, rubbed his face across his shoulder. A feeling like bugs crawling beneath his clothes. No telling how long it had been sitting there, waiting for him to come across it, but the threat had a biblical air about it now, something irrefutable and final. He balled the sheet and turned to the stove, threw it into the fire. Set the damper back without waiting to see it catch.

He scrubbed his hands clean and then he set the rabbit in the gleaming sink to dress it, the naked carcass inching free of the fur. He scooped the head and feet and the entrails into a silver bowl that he set aside as he quartered the rabbit. He went out to the root cellar for potatoes and carrot and turnip and when he came back to the kitchen the dog was lying near the stove, sniffing at the blood in the air. Sweetland stopped in the porch doorway and they stared at one another.

"I hope you wiped your feet before you come in," he said finally.

He lit the two lamps and made a pastry for his stew and set the crock-pot in the oven. He picked the heart and liver from the silver bowl and he fried them up with a little meat he'd set aside and when it had cooled he put it down for the dog. He watched the animal push the bowl across the floor with its muzzle, licking the dish clean. Sweetland filled the empty bowl with water and when the dog had its fill of that it stretched out in the heat beneath the daybed.

Sweetland changed out of his filthy clothes while his supper was cooking, boiled them in a metal tub, rinsed and wrung them in the sink, hung them on a line above the stove. He sat to the table with the rabbit stew and as he lifted the first spoonful he caught sight of Uncle Clar leaning against the wall across the room, eyes averted, pretending to pay Sweetland no mind.

He went to the daybed and hefted the weight of the picture frame. Considered setting it back in the hallway where it had been. But he carried it into the porch instead, hung it on a nail kitty-corner to the door. So Uncle Clar would have at least that much company when he came and went.

THEY FOUND WORK building split-level bungalows among crews of Italians and Hungarians and Caribbeans. They were so far outside the city that it was only Saturday evenings they could make the trek into Toronto. They drank at the Caribou Club, a new bar catering to the expats who'd left Newfoundland to work in Ontario's packing plants and factories, in the auto sector, on road gangs. Economic refugees mourning the anachronistic little world they'd abandoned, the squat saltboxes that housed three generations, the brawling weather, the root cellars and fish flakes and outhouses, the rabbit warren of bloodlines knitting the tiny outports into impossible tangles. Old Sam and Dominion Ale and cod liver oil, Tibb's Eve and Candlemas Day and Sheila's Brush and Radway's Ready Relief, Jackie tars and colcannon and breakfast fish. A weakness for superstition and singing and tribal politics. An antediluvian vocabulary spoken in accents so inbred and misshapen they felt like foreigners everywhere else in the city.

The club was on College Street in the heart of Little Italy. A yearly membership fee of two-fifty. They drank with familiar strangers from Conception Bay and the Codroy Valley and Placentia, from the French Shore, the Bay of Islands, the Burin. Men who made twice their wages packing meat or watching bottles trundle along conveyor belts or marking time on assembly lines of one description or other. The crowd drunken and good-naturedly nostalgic, arguing the merits of punts and skiffs and dories, talking Joey Smallwood or the Newfie Bullet or Churchill Falls or whether beer mixed with ginger ale was a fit drink for a lady. The Caribou Show Band packing the dance floor, dressed in their red polyester sport jackets.

They stayed until the club closed its doors and then moved on to house parties, sometimes winding up in a city park or a cemetery where they slept under trees or between the graves. Woke on damp grass in the open air, their clothes and hair wet with dew. They took their all-day hangovers to a restaurant on College with a bottomless cup of coffee, then to the movies at the Odeon or to wrestling shows at Maple Leaf Gardens, before hitching a ride back out to the worksite in the evening. Talking all the time about when they might be able to jack up and move home.

There were letters from Effie telling Sweetland the weather and how the fish were running, and she rated the minister's Sunday sermons as though she was grading a student's exam. Ned Priddle came home to Chance Cove from the mines in Buchans, he wasn't twenty-five, she wrote, and almost bald. She took the ferry back to her parents' house in Fortune that July and the letters arrived less frequently as the summer passed. Sweetland felt less obligated to answer in turn, relieved to be free of the chore. He'd never had call to write much down and was surprised by the work of it, by how little he could make of words on a page. There wasn't much to be said besides the drudgery of the job and the relentless heat. Mostly he talked about what was happening in his absence ("The capelin must be all but done by this time." "I imagine you're up after the partridgeberries with Mother these days"). And he closed each letter with the promise he'd be home before Christmas.

4

THE SNOW FELL AND STAYED ON the ground by the beginning of December, as it used to when he was a boy. The days closed in to dusk by mid-afternoon, settling to a coal-black pitch by four thirty with only the lamps to work by. Sweetland hadn't relied on lamps since the first generators came to the island in the late sixties. Glad Vatcher's father bought them second-hand out of the *Family Herald*, from farmers on the prairies who had no need of them after their electrical service came through. Old Mr. Vatcher ran power to two dozen houses from four in the afternoon until he was ready for bed. He'd flash the lights three times before shutting it all down for the night, to give people a chance to find their oil lamps or bank their fires and get to bed themselves.

Sweetland couldn't top up the lamps without thinking about Loveless. Nine-year-old Sara refilling the family's lamps on the front bridge, leaving Loveless alone for all of two minutes when she stepped into the house on some forgotten errand. The pint glass of kerosene empty when she came back outside and no idea what might have happened to it before she smelled the oil on the toddler's breath. She stink bad, Sara said, waving a hand to clear the memory of those fumes.

It was months before a doctor had a look at him and he pronounced Loveless fit and healthy. It was the hiccups that saved the child from the worst of it, he said, keeping him awake a full twenty-four hours. He'd likely have suffered brain damage if he'd slept, the doctor said.

Didn't sleep when she drink the oil, Sara used to say as explanation for her brother's peculiar ways, but she have a lot of catnaps.

Sweetland was burning through the kerosene more quickly than he remembered it going and he allowed himself only a couple hours of light in the evenings as he cooked and ate his supper. He sat in the dark with his tea, listening to the radio for the news and weather, a damper on the stove lifted half off, the fire adding shadow to the blackness.

During the brief hours of daylight he kept himself busy with anything he could turn his hand to. He dug footpaths to the shed and the woodpiles, and down the hill as far as the government wharf. He put on a fresh batch of homebrew that fermented in a carboy near the stove, he drained his empties and boiled the bottles to sterilize them. He removed a vinyl window from Glad Vatcher's house to replace the leaky wooden window at the back of the shed. He fished for brown trout up on the mash, lighting a fire by the pond to cook them in the open air. He stripped and cleaned and rebuilt the quad's starter engine, drained the oil and replaced the air filter. He let the motor run a few minutes when he was done, took a spin down as far as the government wharf, to be sure he'd set everything back where it belonged. He had no more than a quarter tank of gas left and a litre in one of the red containers. He parked the quad under its canvas tarp and expected to leave it there until the spring.

The dog wandered off on its own during the day but came barking to be let in after the lamps were lit. It lay at his feet beneath the table and followed him upstairs when he took himself to bed at eight or nine o'clock. Sweetland heated a beach rock in the oven and carried that with him in a pillowcase, slipping it under the covers to warm the sheets. The dog lay at the foot of the bed beside the rock or nosed its way under the blankets to curl against Sweetland's back. He slept a dead sleep as the house clicked and whined into the deepening winter.

He often woke in the middle of the night, feeling rested and ready to start the day, though he could tell by the stars through the window it was too early to move. It was something he'd come to expect since he started going to bed in the early evening, this lull in his sleep. As if a body required the break before he finished dreaming. A natural intermission. He'd taken to filling the dead time with plans for the following day, with lists and inventories, with family trees, mindless mathematical sums. The number of stairs he'd climbed at the light tower in his time as keeper (268 stairs x [(365 days x 10 years) x 3 trips a day]). The number of strokes he and Hollis put in at the oars going to and from the traps before old Mr. Vatcher sold them the second-hand skiff. The names of everyone in the Loveless family back four generations. Three nights in a row Sweetland drifted to sleep trying to fish up the name of a fierce Salvation Army woman from Heart's Desire who was married to Loveless's great-uncle Baxter.

Occasionally he tried to recreate one of Jesse's lectures on volcanoes or icebergs and it was a surprise to realize how little of the boy's endless yammer he'd taken in. He couldn't recall any of the Latin names of the whales or what exactly defines an ungulate or the name of the rocks dropped by glaciers. The boy claimed Sweetland and St. Pierre and Ramea and most of Newfoundland's south coast were submerged by the weight of the glacial ice sheet and they had all bobbed above the surface like corks as the glaciers retreated. It was a fact Sweetland remembered only because he'd pooh-poohed the fanciful notion for months afterwards. Jumping up and down on the mash, then waving at Jesse to hold still as he cocked his head. She bounced that time, he'd say. Did you feel it? He'd give another little hop while Jesse stared at him with a look of stoic disbelief.

It was Sweetland's job to remain ignorant in those ritual exchanges, to offer inane questions and commentary, to nitpick and quibble while the youngster tried to sink his objections under the weight of pure knowledge. They were like pro wrestlers circling one another in a ring where all the moves were choreographed, the winner predetermined. Sweetland hadn't realized how much he enjoyed the farcical pageant, how much he'd been missing it. But the memory of Jesse's dogged seriousness in the face of his clowning was so raw that it forced him out of bed, and he learned to stay clear of it, moved on to other distractions.

Most nights he pictured a map of the island and set about naming every feature and landmark from the south-end light to Chance Cove and on to the Fever Rocks, before he did the same thing along the lee side. The litany started at the Mackerel Cliffs and went from there to Pinnacle Arch, to Lunin Rock, the Devil's Under-jaw, the Flats, Murdering Hole, Tinker Cliffs, Old Chimney, Gannie Cliff Point, Wester Shoals, Mad Goat Gulch, Upper Brister, the Founder. He took his time, being careful to include as much detail as possible, as though the island was slowly fading from the world and only his ritual naming of each nook and cranny kept it from disappearing altogether. Coffin Pond, Cow Path Head, the Tom Cod Rocks, the Offer Ledge, Gansy Gulch, Lunin Cove, Lower Brister, Watering Gulch, the Well. Each time, he remembered some additional feature, an abandoned grebe's nest, the heart-shaped fissure in the sea-stack rocks near Music House, the radio beacon west of Clay Hole Pond. The map each time becoming more complete.

It was a night in mid-December when Sweetland wandered up into the valley above Music House on that imaginary map, and for the first time he placed the Priddles' cabin in its place, two-thirds of the way to high ground. He'd never thought to name it before and it occurred to him he hadn't made the trip out there since having the island to himself. The brothers had a generator at the cabin which meant there'd be gasoline stored there, a resource so obvious he felt stupid not to have thought of it. Beyond that essential, there might be cans of beans or corned beef or Chef Boyardee pastas; batteries and matches; bottles of rye or dark rum or Scotch; soap and shaving cream; magazines or old newspapers or books of word searches. The thought of the plunder on the opposite side of the island was so diverting, Sweetland was afraid he wouldn't sleep the rest of the night. But eventually he drifted off.

Blue skies when he woke, but the morning looked for weather. An augural bank of cloud away off west and south. The temperature hovering around the freezing mark, a clammy feel to the air. The radio forecast saying snow or rain or some mix of the two, depending on how the system tracked. Wind and a couple of days of December fury coming on, and it wasn't sensible to head out there with that sentence hanging over him. But the thought of the cabin, now that he'd struck on it, was impossible to resist.

He stripped the tarp off the quad. There was enough gas to get him partway to the lighthouse, which would save him lugging a full container all the way back across the island, and give him a ride home into the cove through whatever weather was coming. The Priddles had never locked their place to his memory, but he brought a hammer and a set of screwdrivers and the axe, just in case. The dog chased him as he pulled out of the shed and started up the path toward the mash, Sweetland driving slow and glancing back now and then to see the animal was with him. He cut across Vatcher's Meadow and he was halfway to the lighthouse when the engine sputtered and quit. Sweetland sat on the machine a few minutes after it died, as if all it needed was a rest, as if it might pick itself up after a nap and carry on.

The clouds were a long ways to the south, the day still bright. He glanced up at the sun, ghosted on both sides by blurred reflections of itself. Sun hounds, Uncle Clar called them. A fierce bit of weather approaching, all appearances to the contrary. He had an hour's walk to the light and that far again down to the Priddles' cabin. And he was likely going to find himself holed up there awhile.

He climbed off the quad, took his pack from the carryall. He called for the dog, turned a circle where he was standing. The ground lying flat as far as he could see and no sign of the animal. He put his fingers to his mouth, whistled for all he was worth. He looked up at the sun hounds, watched them shimmer as the moisture being pushed ahead of the storm flexed and bowed. He whistled again and shouted until he was hoarse. A little dwy of snow blew in off the ocean from the distant clouds. "Jesus fuck," he said.

He walked on to the lighthouse as the storm descended, a soft, steady fall of snow settling on his shoulders as the sun disappeared. By the time he crested the rise above the keeper's house the wind had shifted to the east and was blowing hard, catching him broadside. The snow suddenly wet and heavy and driving and Sweetland kept his head down to protect his face, to be able to take a breath without choking on the drift. He carried on past the lighthouse for the shelter of the path through the tuckamore, the trees offering some protection from the weather. The snow blowing overhead in fierce sheets but it was surprisingly warm and quiet out of the wind, and Sweetland opened his coat as he went, making his way toward the valley. He was fifteen minutes into that descent when the dog burst past him on the trail, bounding ahead. The black coat barely visible under the spray of white in the fur.

"And where the fuck were you?" Sweetland shouted. Relieved to see the animal.

He'd caught sight of the cabin's peak at the head of the valley, but it disappeared again as he moved down into the trees. He was at the door before he knew he was close. There was a drift of snow across the front of the building and he kicked it clear, stepped inside behind the dog. The cabin backed right into the eastern ridge and out of the wind. Sweetland shut the door behind him and listened to the silence. Except for the occasional rattle in the chimney, there was nothing to say a storm was on. He looked down at the dog, its breath coming in plumes. It was colder inside than out, a chill the room had been storing up for months.

The brothers spent no time at the cabin over the winter and the woodbox by the stove was nearly empty. A bit of kindling, a pile of sawed-up two-by-four scavenged from the remains of the deck at the keeper's house. A Bic lighter beside the flue. Sweetland set about making a fire, leaving the stove door open an inch to let the draft take up through the dry kindling. Looked around the room as he waited for the heat. The cabin was a storey and a half, with bunks in a loft built under the eaves. A window over the sink against one wall. A square table beneath the loft, a loveseat the brothers had sawed in half to make it easier carrying out from the cove. It was stuck together with nails and duct tape, a predominant slump across the middle. There was a poster-sized outline of Newfoundland tacked on the opposite side of the room. It was a commemorative map produced in 1966, *Come Home Year* in a faux-antique script across the top.

Hardly the cornucopia of delights he'd been dreaming about. Sweetland was familiar enough with the cabin that none of it was a surprise. It was hard to believe he'd made so much of it in his mind, lying alone at three and four in the morning.

When it was warm enough inside to take off his coat, he poked through the cupboards over the sink. Two plates, two bowls, a mismatch of glasses and mugs. A plastic baggie of Tetley, a tin of Maxwell House instant. An unopened kilo of sugar, one of the few things he had plenty of. Half a dozen boxes of Kraft Dinner, three Styrofoam containers of Cup-a-Soup. A half-empty jar of peanuts, a flask of vodka. A pack of rolling papers. One lonely tin of Flakes of Ham. Sweetland dug through the cutlery drawer for a can opener and he set half the gelatinous meat on a plate for the dog. He ate the rest of it from the tin, savouring every salty mouthful. Thinking it was enough on its own to have made the trip worthwhile.

He carried the kettle outside and filled it with fresh snow, set it on the stovetop where it spat and hissed. Then he walked to the lean-to built against the waterside wall of the cabin where they kept the generator. Hoping for more firewood, hoping for several gallons of gasoline. The room was padlocked shut and Sweetland took the screws off the lockset in the door jamb, pushed the door as wide as it would go. The generator sitting in shadows at the back of the narrow space, one gas can beside it. Sweetland reached to touch it with his boot and the container shifted where it sat. Not half full. Enough to get the quad back to the cove, and a trip to the lighthouse from there if he ever needed it. But no more than that.

There was nothing else of any use to him. A couple of paint cans, a stack of roofing shingles. A shovel with a broken handle. A coffee can full of roofing nails, screws, a dozen cigarette butts. Sweetland picked through the can to collect the butts and he took them back inside the cabin. He brought in more snow to add to the meltwater in the kettle and then he sat at the table with the flask of vodka, poured himself a shot in a coffee cup. He'd never cared much for vodka and he let it sit there while he straightened the smashed butts and scraped the tobacco from the paper tubes onto the tabletop. There was enough to roll three cigarettes with the papers in the cupboard. He tore strips of the thin cardboard from the cover and rolled them tight to make a crude filter for each one.

"Now, Mr. Fox," he said. The dog was curled on the loveseat and lifted its head to look at him. "Who's got it better than this?"

There were moments, he had to admit, when he sounded slightly unhinged. He'd had plenty of quiet time since missing his chance to escape with the Coast Guard to consider whether he was losing his grip on reality and he found it hard to argue otherwise. But he couldn't make himself believe it. And he was surprised to find he was more or less content with his predicament now, with his place on the abandoned island with Loveless's little dog and Jesse's grave. He held to what he'd chosen and managed to make a sort of peace with the bizarre incidents that had become a feature of his days, accepted the fact that some of the world he lived in couldn't be found on a map. A crazy person wouldn't be capable of separating the strangeness from the rest of his life, he thought, of settling in the midst of it. But he allowed it was possible that all crazy people thought that way.

He lit one of the hand-rolled and took a slow drag on the butt. His first taste of a cigarette in twenty-five years and he held the stale smoke in his lungs a long time.

Halfway through the flask of vodka he was feeling sick to his stomach. The foul alcohol or the shot of nicotine, or a combination of the two. He was drunk enough to push on, regardless, poured the cup full and lit the second of his three smokes. His head buzzing like a neon light. He'd almost forgotten how much he loved the cigarettes, what a poisonous comfort they were.

The one night the Sri Lankan refugees stayed in Chance Cove he'd spent most of the evening alone in his kitchen, chain-smoking to tamp down the thought of Ruthie and the Reverend in the office behind the altar. He barely slept, waking before light and picking up the Rothmans on the nightstand. He smoked one on the side of the bed, tapping the ash into his palm. Smoked a second in his underwear before he dressed and walked down through the cove, a handful of stars clinging to the darkest edges of the morning.

No sign of life but for the front doors of the church standing open and he gravitated toward them without intending to step inside. The candles were lit at the front and he could see the silhouette of people sitting in the pew next to the boy's body. His first thought was of Ruthie and the Reverend, meeting up again while the rest of the town slept. He turned away and stood outside the doors, facing the cove. He lit up a smoke against the rush in his chest, stared out at the water, considering whether it was his place to go in there and say something. He felt like setting a match to the church, burning the goddamn thing to the ground.

He was almost finished his smoke when he was startled by the sound of a voice behind him, a single indecipherable syllable. Spun around to see one of the Sri Lankans in the open doorway. It was the fellow he'd thrown the line to at the bow of the lifeboat, who had gestured to ask for water. He was dressed in a flannel work shirt three sizes too big, a pair of oversized pants cinched to his hipless frame with a belt, the cuffs turned halfway up his shins. He looked like a youngster wearing a costume of grown-up's clothes for a Sunday School play. He nodded at Sweetland and gestured to his mouth again.

Sweetland shook a cigarette from the pack and passed the man a book of matches, but the Sri Lankan's hands were too shaky to strike one. Sweetland lit the smoke and lit one for himself as well. He waved a hand toward the door. Sorry for your loss, he said, and the Sri Lankan muttered something unintelligible and sorrowful. And then they smoked in silence awhile.

Sweetland kept glancing into the church over the man's shoulder, thinking of Ruthie and Pilgrim exchanging vows up at that altar. Ruth had bawled the whole night before the ceremony, seventeen and set to ruin her life on Sweetland's say-so. The girl's hand trembling as Pilgrim slipped the ring on her finger, her face raw and swollen under the wedding veil. She did not love the man in any fashion, that was plain enough, but she soldiered through it. And Sweetland never saw his sister cry another tear in the years that followed, never heard her utter a word of complaint about her marriage or the husband she'd been tied to. He had taken a false comfort in those facts and was gutted now to see how wrong he'd been about it all.

There was a rustle of movement inside the church and he watched the brother of the dead boy limp out of the shadows, dressed just as strangely, and leaning all his weight on Ruthie's shoulder. She looked steadily at Sweetland as she approached, her face set. Defiant. And Sweetland dropped his cigarette, crushed it out under his shoe so he wouldn't have to hold her eye. The Sri Lankan he'd been smoking with reached for the young man's free arm and Sweetland made a move to take Ruth's place, but she shook her head. We're fine here, she said.

He watched them make their slow way up the path. Sorry for your loss, he said again.

He had no inkling how long he would drag those peculiar men in his wake. He almost resented having found them out there for a time, thinking he'd never have discovered the truth about Ruthie otherwise and would have been happier not knowing.

Impossible to say now when it changed for him, when he started to see himself and his sister's life mirrored darkly in that story—forcing the girl into a marriage she didn't ask for or want, setting her adrift on that ocean without so much as a drop of water to drink. He might have been speaking to Ruthie and not the Sri Lankans as they left the church that morning. And for years he would have to fight the urge to whisper the phrase in every private moment they had before she died: Sorry for your loss.

The wind turned sometime during the night and he woke to the sound of weather against the front of the cabin, sleet slashing across the door and the window beside it. Pitch-black. The frigid cold in the room enough to tell him the temperature had dropped when the wind shifted.

He'd burned through every bit of firewood in the cabin during the day, and after he'd finished the flask of vodka he had taken the axe to the firebox and the ladder to the loft and burned those as well. All that was left for him now was a small pile of green wood he'd cut while there was still daylight. He tried to light a fire with it, but the wind whistling in the chimney wouldn't allow the draft to take, pushing smoke back into the cabin. The flame sputtered anemic and heatless and went out altogether while Sweetland nodded off. He'd been too drunk to think of retrieving blankets from the loft bunks before he burned the ladder and he lay cramped on the loveseat under his coat the whole night. The dog curled in his lap was the only bit of heat in all the wide world. His two feet gone to ice.

The morning was a long time coming, the day's first grey light shrouded by the storm's weight. Sweetland went out to piss on the lee side of the cabin and he took the axe down into the valley, looking for deadfall that would be dry enough to burn. Wind whipping the snow so he couldn't see more than a few feet in any direction. After half an hour of scrabbling blind he had an armful of dry sticks and he managed to light a fire to boil meltwater for tea. He hung his jacket over the heat and he had a breakfast of freeze-dried soup that he shared with the dog. When the dead wood was roaring he put a junk of green spruce in the stove where it spit and burned blue and gave almost no heat. He looked down at the dog where it was still lying on the loveseat.

"What about you?" he said. "You look like you'd burn."

He spent a lot of time staring at the commemorative map of Newfoundland. Even from across the room he could see how badly detailed it was. Only the largest communities and bays and islands were identified. He walked over to look closer. Little Sweetland was there, and Sweetland lying in the open Atlantic beyond it, but neither warranted a name.

He went across to the cupboards and picked through them a second time, moving every item on the shelves, lifting the cutlery tray, looking for a pen of some sort, a marker. His search rewarded with a stub of pencil and a tightly wound baggie of marijuana. "Well now, Mr. Fox," Sweetland said. He still had one hand-rolled cigarette that he was saving for a special occasion and he considered that this qualified. He broke it open and mixed the tobacco with the weed, rolled himself two joints. The marijuana dry as dust, an ancient stash the brothers had probably forgotten. Sweetland wet one of the joints in his mouth to keep it from burning too quickly. He smoked half the reefer, choking on the ragged draw and fighting to keep it down. He pinched out the flame to save the second half for later and then he sharpened the pencil stub with a knife, waiting for the stone to hit him.

Nothing to it, not that he could say. He felt completely straight.

He sat in front of the map of Newfoundland and wrote *Sweetland* across the irregular yellow oblong where he had spent almost his entire existence. Wrote *Little Sweetland* across the smaller island two inches above it. And he spent the better part of an hour then, adding missing names along the coastline, drawing in small islands that had been inexplicably left out. Folded his arms when he'd run through the inventory he carried in his head, considering the place. On a whim he reached up to draw a circle in the centre of Fortune Bay. Wrote *Queenie's Island* across the face of it. He carried on then, dotting the shoreline with islands and communities and features that didn't exist, naming them all after people he knew. *Bob-Sam's Island. Jesse's Head. Priddle's Point. Pilgrim's Arm. Vatcher's Tickle.*

He stepped away when he thought he was done, admiring his handiwork. Reached up to draw a line through the faux-antique *Come Home Year.* Wrote *Stay Home Year* above it. Giggled aloud then and felt immediately self-conscious. Stoned out of his head, he realized.

He glanced across at the dog. "Some clever, hey?"

The animal turned a few circles on the loveseat, then flopped down with a sigh.

"Oh fuck off," Sweetland said. He lit up what was left of the joint and smoked it down to the cardboard filter.

The weather moderated while he was at work on the map. Cold still, the wind blowing strong, but there was nothing falling. It was going to be a bitter night at the Priddles' cabin with no wood to burn and Sweetland decided to make a run for the ATV. He put the lighter he carried with him and the Bic he found at the cabin in the baggie with the second joint and the rolling papers, tucked the package away in the inside pocket of his coat. He packed up his few things with the Kraft Dinner and Cup-a-Soups and then took a look around the room to make sure he hadn't forgotten anything. He went across to the map of Newfoundland, nipped the push-pins from the wall. Folded the paper in four, stuffed it into his backpack.

"Let's go," he said to the dog, and it came as far as the door but balked there. "Come on," Sweetland said. "We got to move we wants to get home out of this." And he pushed the dog out with the toe of his boot. Grabbed the gas can from where it sat beside the generator in the shed.

It was a steep climb out of the valley and he was breathing heavy by the time they reached level ground. He set the gas can at his feet before they left the trees altogether, shook out the numbness in his arms. The dog sitting beside him, waiting. The temperature had somersaulted above freezing again, but the wind was going to be full on in their faces when they turned inland at the lighthouse. "Gird up your loins, Mr. Fox," he said. He was still stoned, he knew, which accounted for the lightness in his tone. He had a mind to turn back for the cabin suddenly, thinking he wasn't in any shape to know sense. But the notion went astray just as quickly. "Hup, two," he said and he hefted the gas can.

It had started to rain by the time the keeper's house was in sight, a steady fall that soaked through the shoulders of his jacket and his pants. The dog's hybrid fur useless in the rain, sopping and pasted to the scrawny frame. Sweetland struck by just how little there was to the creature beneath the wild coat. Before they topped the rise the rain had turned to sleet and he could see the dog was shivering, not enough meat on its bones to keep warm. It kept glancing back at Sweetland mournfully. He called the shaking dog over, setting it inside his coat and bringing up the zipper so it was just the animal's head exposed to the air. A steady quiver vibrating against his chest as he went on, the wet soaking through his shirt.

He was on the stretch of path over bald rock that ravelled out within a few feet of the headlands, the ocean roiling black below. Not hard to imagine Jesse losing his way here in the fog. The wind whipped at the gas can Sweetland carried, wrenching his shoulder with every gust, threatening to take him over the edge. He stopped long enough to tie a length of string to the handle and hauled the red container over the ground behind him like a sledge. He guessed he was half an hour's trudge from the ATV and he carried on with his head down against the driving sleet, stopping now and then to turn his back to the wind. He couldn't feel the skin on the good side of his face and he winced and chewed and yawned, hoping the motion would bring some life back into the flesh.

He was two hundred yards past the ATV before he knew it, his eyes at his feet and nearly closed against the sleet. Turned his back to the wind to catch his breath, spotted the lonely machine behind him. Another fifty yards on he would have missed it altogether.

His hands were numb with the cold and he had trouble fitting the finicky nozzle on the gas container. The dog had disappeared into his coat where it had shivered itself to sleep and he kept an arm across his stomach to support its weight. Spilled a tumbler's worth of gas trying to set the nozzle in the tank's opening one-handed, swearing under his breath. After he filled the tank he tied the rest of the gas onto the carryall and started up the machine.

He turned into the wind and drove slow, leaning behind the handlebars for the little protection they afforded, peeking over the top now and then to be sure of the path. Grateful to be sitting down, to be conveyed. He cut across Vatcher's Meadow, drove by the King's Seat, and inched down the steep path into the cove. He set the quad away in the shed but didn't bother with the tarp. Wet to the skin and ready to lie down beside a fire. He went through the porch into the kitchen and unzipped his jacket halfway, the dog stirring at the cold air, its black muzzle coming into the open.

"Now, Mr. Fox," Sweetland said. "Who's got it better than this?"

It stretched its neck up to sniff at his face. Licking at the mess of snot and spittle frozen to his chin.

THEY WERE LAID OFF CONSTRUCTION in mid-September and almost left for home before they hired on at a steel mill in Hamilton, lucking into the union positions through a connection at the Caribou Club. Sweetland was against taking the job. He'd met men who planned to work in the steel plants a winter and had their twenty-year service watches from the company. But Duke had spent most of what he'd earned over the summer at the Caribou. His wife at home nursing the youngster and the new baby.

I can't go back to her with nothing, Duke said. We won't even have time to go on the trawl if we leaves now.

Sweetland shook his head.

Two-ten an hour, Duke said. Think of the ring you could bring back to Effie.

Promise me, he said, we'll go home out of this.

Back by Christmas, Duke said, on my mother's grave.

The steel mill was a city unto itself. Massive coke ovens, storage tanks and elevators, engine rooms, stock houses the size of city churches, miles of train tracks and gas lines and elevated piping that criss-crossed the blackened acres. Cooling stations, smoke and creosote and slag, the molten glow of the pour-offs at the open hearths like some evangelical's vision of hell. Everything was in motion, cranes and railcars, conveyor belts shifting ore pellets to the blast furnaces, coal cars shuttling from the battery to the ovens, sheets of heated strip steel rolling through rotating cylinders. All of it seemed to be moving at cross purposes and the unremitting noise of the place was a physical thing, hammering against them. The air heated and condensed, packed with dust and steam and a nauseating chemical sweat. Men darting among the machinery like rats, their faces grimed with soot.

They worked seventy hours a week and couldn't drink enough in the off-hours to wash the taste of the mills from their mouths. They went to work hungover and nursed their heads with a thermos of rum and Coke. They met a university dropout in the lunchroom who introduced them to marijuana, rolling and smoking before the shift started. Sweetland didn't feel a thing from the weed that he could point to, but the place seemed almost bearable when he was stoned.

They kept an eye on the foreman through their shifts, taking their chance to sneak into the noisiest, most inhospitable crannies to pass a joint. They lit up somewhere different each time, as if they were trying to throw a tracking dog off the scent. The relentless mechanical whirl moving around them at impossible angles, at breakneck speeds. And as he wormed out of their most recent pot den one October afternoon, a corner of Sweetland's clothing caught in the contraption and he was sucked into that vortex, his pants and underwear ripped clear of his body and he was dragged along a few interminable seconds before the alarm tripped out and everything shuddered to a halt. Sweetland still in the grip of the thing, one shoulder skinned raw and the right side of his face unrecognizable, his free hand cupped around the sear in his butchered lap.

He came to briefly in the ambulance. Duke was tucked into a corner, his appendages in that narrow space folded away like the blades of a Swiss Army knife. Sweetland lifted one hand to gesture in his direction. That's the last fucken advice I ever takes from you, he said.

5

THROUGH THE MONTH OF DECEMBER the radio was slowly strangled by Christmas carols. The CBC morning show counting down the shopping days as they dwindled. Sweetland gave no thought to his own place in the season until the afternoon of the twenty-fourth when he surprised himself by retrieving the tree from the shed.

He didn't bother with decorations at all after his mother died, and he was relieved to be free of the chore. Most houses in the cove had artificial trees, but his mother had always insisted on the real thing. Sweetland would hike to the back of the island, spend a day on snowshoes, picking through the straggle of spruce forest. Hunting for something that didn't look half strangled, or lopsided, or otherwise misshapen by the poor soil, the driving weather.

It wasn't until Clara came back to Sweetland with Jesse in tow that he picked up an artificial tree on a trip across to Burgeo. Just to have something for the boy to look at, a place to lay the gift Clara had picked out and wrapped and signed Jesse's name to. But Sweetland made a shaggery of stringing the lights and garland and hanging the glass bulbs, a job he'd always left to his mother. It was finicky work with no practical mechanical principles to guide him. When he was done the tree looked vaguely terrifying, and Jesse refused to go near it.

Sweetland discovered his current tree while watching a hockey game, in a Canadian Tire ad featuring the four-foot-high ornament, the bulbs and lights built right in. Out of the box and plug it in and your job was done. It had a handful of settings to make the lights flash intermittently or light up in a corkscrew run, or in rotating sections from top to bottom. He had Glad Vatcher order one in for him and he put it up in the living room the day it arrived, the ninth of December.

That fucken thing is *silver*, Duke Fewer said when he laid eyes on it. What kind of a tree do you know is silver?

Everyone in Chance Cove had a laugh over it, but Jesse loved the bizarre confection. He was seven at the time and he sat in the tree's presence for hours, his face blank and blissful, like someone stoned on hash brownies and staring at the stars.

Sweetland laid the box on the kitchen table and cut through the masking tape holding it shut. He set the tree up on the table, the star at the top almost touching the ceiling beam. Stepped back two paces. It was nothing to look at without the lights, gaudy and lifeless, and he immediately regretted hauling it out. Packed the thing back into its box and set it in the porch, planning to throw it onto the pile of refuse below the incinerator in the morning. Something he should have done, he thought, when it came down last year.

Clara and Pilgrim had come over to see him on Tibb's Eve, with a fruitcake and a flask of rum. It was the first time Clara had been in the house since the day after Jesse was buried. She gave Sweetland a hug that felt like something she'd been rehearsing for months. And was glad to have out of the way.

Sweetland had been keeping to himself all fall. Passed his days puttering in the shed, out of view of anyone below. It was Clara he dreaded seeing and he could tell it was the same for her. Impossible to keep clear of Jesse, even when he went unmentioned. That loss reflected back and forth between them like a bell ringing and echoing home off a cliff face.

You haven't got your tree up, she said.

Don't think I'll bother with it.

You got to have a tree, Pilgrim said.

And what difference do it make to you? You can't see it there anyway.

It's the spirit of the thing, Pilgrim said. He had his two hands spread wide, a gesture that dredged the word *beseeching* from the murk of Sweetland's church years.

Would you mind? Clara said.

Sweetland looked at her, surprised. I thought maybe, he said.

No, I'd like it, I think. I think it would be good. Jesse loved that tree.

Get the blind fucker a drink, he said. I'll go dig it out of the shed.

There was hardly a Christmas light to be seen down through the cove as he walked back with the box in his arms. A dozen houses still occupied, scattered outposts of blinking green and blue lights in the dark. A mild year and no sign of snow. An air of desperate pretend about the season's scattered trappings.

They took their drinks into the living room where Sweetland set up the tree on top of the television. He turned off the overhead and they finished the flask and half the fruitcake and Sweetland went to the kitchen to stoke the stove and fetch a bottle of rye. The alcohol seemed hardly to touch them for a long time and they got quietly drunk together in the auroral glow of the tree lights as they pulsed and dimmed.

Jesse used to say it was like the lights were breathing, Sweetland said.

Why is that? Pilgrim asked. He roused himself in his seat where he'd been drifting off.

They're on a timer, Clara told him. They glows brighter a second and then fades out.

We used to have candles in the branches, remember that, Mose? On those little clip-on candleholders. They was only lit ten minutes the whole of the season. And someone standing by with a bucket of water in case the tree caught fire.

Sweetland gave Clara a look. You wouldn't know but he seen it with his own two eyes, he said.

Leave him be, Clara whispered.

Tell us about the orange you used to get in the wool sock you had for a stocking, Pilgrim.

And you was lucky to get that, the blind man said, swinging his glass wide enough the drink lipped over the side. We'd keep the orange peel, he said, and soak it in a glass of water with a bit of sugar. And we'd drink that down, honey-sweet.

How many generations of youngsters have he bored to death with that story, I wonder.

He bored me to death with it, Clara said and she rolled her eyes.

Oh kiss my arse, Pilgrim said, the both of you. He tried to get to his feet and failed, the ice in his glass rattling onto the floor. Jesus, he said.

Clara and Sweetland dragged Pilgrim up off the couch and they shuffled awkwardly into the kitchen.

We'll never get him down the hill like this, Sweetland said. Let him sleep it off on the daybed.

They laid him out there beside the stove. Sweetland sat at the kitchen table as Clara untied Pilgrim's boots and worked them from his feet. There was a quilt folded at one end of the bed that she shook out and tucked around his shoulders, Pilgrim already sound asleep. She leaned in to kiss him and lost her balance, reaching a hand to catch herself. She straightened from the daybed and turned around carefully. Fuck, she said. I'm wasted.

One more for the road?

Why not, hey.

She sat across from Sweetland at the table and he poured them each a generous shot of rye, topping the glasses with Sprite. Pilgrim snoring across the room, a high, strangled sound like wind through a leaky door seal.

He's a fucken piece of work, that one, Sweetland said.

Clara pointed at him with her drink. You don't say a word about him.

Wouldn't dream of it. Loves him like a brother. Sun shines out of his blind arse.

It's not many men would have been as good to me as he've been, I know that for a fact.

Coming home with Jesse to be looked after, you mean?

That, she said. And the rest of it.

The rest of what?

Me not being his youngster.

Sweetland didn't so much as flinch, but he felt suddenly, miserably sober. He glanced at the man asleep on the daybed and then back across the table at Clara.

He's blind, Moses, she said, he's not an idiot.

Sweetland shook his head. How long have he known?

From the beginning. Why do you think him and Mom had no youngsters all those years?

What, they didn't?

Nope.

Never? Sweetland said. Not once?

Jesus, I don't know about never, Clara said. Never for a long time though. Long before I come along, anyway.

He told you all this?

After Mom died. Thought he should come clean with me, I guess.

It struck Sweetland that Clara was assuming he already knew the truth of the matter, that it wasn't a secret she was divulging. Which likely meant Pilgrim assumed as much as well. The heat in the room was stifling. He got up from his chair and opened the door to the hallway, stood in the door frame a few minutes with his back to the kitchen. Breathing in the cool.

How's Uncle Clar doing out there? Clara said.

He's all right.

Sin to leave him alone out in the hall like that, don't you think? You should put him in the porch here, so's he'll have some company when you comes and goes.

Clara, Sweetland said without turning to look at her. Do you know who your father is?

Not a clue, she said. But I got my money on Loveless. And then she started giggling. Fucken Loveless! she shouted and she laughed drunkenly, almost hysterical. She caught her breath long enough to say, Can you imagine? Mom and Loveless?

That's my sister you're talking about, Sweetland said, and Clara doubled over at the table, slapping her hand on the Formica.

Jesus loves the little children, Sweetland said. He made his way to his chair unsteadily, waited there while Clara calmed down and wiped her eyes, ran her hands through her hair.

Sorry, she said. Couldn't help myself. She grimaced across the table and tapped at her front teeth with a fingernail. Can't feel a damn thing, she said. And then she said, I expect you knows his name. My father's. But I don't care, to be honest. She tossed her head toward the man snoring beside the stove. We did all right, she said, not knowing.

Sweetland nodded down at the table. That's grand, he said.

I don't know how Mom managed to keep it a secret in this town, that's what really amazes me.

It don't seem likely, I grant you that.

Clara got up from her seat and steadied herself with a hand to the back of her chair. I should head home out of it, she said, before I makes a fool of myself.

What about Jesse? Sweetland said.

What about him?

What happened to his father?

His father got laid, Clara said. And I got knocked up. Just a one-night thing. Didn't even know the guy's last name.

Jesus, Clara.

You want to know the worst of it? she said. It wasn't even a decent bit of skin.

Jesus, Clara.

She wavered on her feet, fighting to hold herself still. She covered her eyes, her mother's gesture with a drunken weight added to it, the heel of the hand pushing her nose and lips askew. I hates the thought of leaving Jesse up there, she said. With no one even to cut the grass on his grave.

Sweetland had expected Clara to bolt for St. John's as soon as the resettlement money came through and he didn't know what it was kept her from leaving but grief. And he supposed that was enough to hold a body still a long time. He thought of Sandra claiming Clara had come back to the island to have him in Jesse's life. He'd stopped himself asking Clara about that a dozen times and stopped himself again now. For fear it wasn't true.

She staggered past him, through the porch to the outside door. You'll be happy to know, she called, I won't remember a word of this tomorrow. And she sang out merry Christmas as she left.

He took the tree down in the morning and brought it to the shed with Pilgrim still passed out on the daybed. He and Clara never acknowledged the conversation and Sweetland was happy enough pretending it never happened. Though he had a hard time looking at Pilgrim ever after. All the talk the man sat through at the Fisherman's Hall about Ruthie looking after those dark-haired men in her house. About the mainland reporters saying she gave the best "interview" they'd ever had, ha ha.

Pilgrim never breathing a word about what he knew from the beginning.

The weather turned bitter on Boxing Day, with winds out of the north-northwest that made the temperature feel colder still. Sweetland left a trickle running in the sinks upstairs and down to keep the pipes from freezing. It was too frigid to leave the kitchen at night and he bunked down on the daybed, the chill waking him when the fire burned low. He stirred the coals and filled the firebox until it was humming and crawled back under the quilts.

The dog stayed indoors except when Sweetland went to carry in a turn of wood from the shed, which was just time enough for the animal to look after its business and roll in the snow and sniff at the wind with its head high in the air. It didn't show any interest in staying out longer and spent the better part of a week in front of the stove while Sweetland dozed on the daybed or played endless games of patience or polished the soot off the glass bells of the kerosene lamps. He went out to the shed on the third day and took a ratty old herring net out of the rafters. He broke into Reet's museum a second time and came away with a net needle and a ball of nylon and, on a whim, stepped into Duke's barbershop to take the pile of magazines beside the chessboard, his face averted to avoid seeing whether or not the game had progressed since his last visit. He strung the herring net across the length of the kitchen and he spent hours trying to knit the thing into workable shape, walking back and forth to string the cables together. Leafed through a *National Geographic* to rest his back.

Every day the radio weather predicted clear skies and milder than normal temperatures along the south coast. Sweetland glancing out the window each time he heard the forecast and talking back to the announcers. "I don't know where you fuckers is living," he said.

There was drifting snow at the windows, the details of the outside world fading in and out like a television signal from the seventies. Time drifted and bowed in much the same fashion, the wind rattling endlessly in the chimney, the days blurring into one another. It was only the radio that kept them in order in Sweetland's head, and when he turned it off to save the batteries he had trouble recalling the day of the week.

The cold moderated a little on New Year's Eve and Sweetland broke open a fresh batch of homebrew, making his way through half a dozen bottles as he listened to the year wind down on the radio. He called out the ten-second countdown to the dog, standing in the kitchen in his boots and coat with the .22 under his arm. He went to the door as the last seconds ticked away and the dog followed him outside. A clear evening lit by the moon, the wind just brisk enough to add an edge to the frost. Sweetland raised the rifle toward the hills ringing the cove and fired off three rounds to welcome the New Year. It was something people on the island had been doing as long as he could remember, standing at their doors to shoot into the air at the stroke of midnight. Sweetland feeling drunkenly nostalgic and willing to waste a precious handful of shells. His shots echoed off the rock face overhead and the dog cowered by the shed doors, growling at the racket.

"It's all right," Sweetland said. "Just having a bit of fun."

And he froze then, hearing the pop pop pop of a rifle in the distance, up on the mash, he thought. The dog barking madly at the night sky and Sweetland shouted at the creature to shut up. He heard it again, pop pop pop, down over the hill this time, in the cove. More shots following on their heels, and Sweetland ran around the side of the house, standing in the open there. Looking over the dark cove below, the silvered silhouette of empty buildings. He raised the rifle and fired another shot into the air, stood with the cold stock against his face as the echoes died away. Waited there a long time listening, the silence below like a tide rising to lap at his boots, at his frozen knees, at the waist of his coat.

He turned finally and hustled back into the house, rushing to lock the door and put out the lamp, and he sat on the daybed beside the stove with the .22 across his lap.

The cold woke him. The fire in the stove guttered to ash and the air in the kitchen crystalline, an arctic stillness about him. He was on the daybed in his boots and coat and he didn't move for fear of rolling onto the dog. He felt around for the creature, but it wasn't anywhere within reach. And he realized then he'd left the dog outside, when he ran into the house and barred the door. Hours ago, he guessed.

Sweetland was calling for it before he'd even gotten to his feet, yelled its name from the open door. The moon gone down and only the stars for light. He walked around the building, calling into the wind. He crouched at Diesel's doghouse to look inside, the towel on the floor drifted over with snow. He walked a little ways down toward the cove, shouting at the top of his lungs.

He went out to the shed where he'd seen the dog last and he found a blur of tracks beyond it, to the back of his property and heading through drifts to the path leading out of the cove. Sweetland went into the house for a hat and gloves and the rifle, a flashlight. The dog spooked by the flurry of gunshots and could be anywhere up there, he guessed. Running mad on the mash until it holed up somewhere out of the wind. There wasn't enough meat or fur on the creature to keep it alive through a night this cold, that much he knew.

He put in a fire, so the kitchen wouldn't be a complete icebox when he got back. Took an old blanket from the shelf over his boots and went to the shed where he stripped the tarp off the quad. He picked up a red gasoline container from beneath the workbench and shook it. Put the empty down and grabbed the Priddles' container beside it, poured the last of the fuel into the tank. It hadn't been started since the cold snap settled in and Sweetland wasn't even sure it would turn over. The engine rolling sluggishly at first, like something buried in taffy. He didn't want to flood it and he took his time, coaxing the reluctant spark along, leaning over the machine like he was protecting a flame in the bowl of his hands. When it finally took hold it roared in the enclosed space, choppy and discontented. Sweetland kept it alive with the accelerator and he let it idle a long time after it settled into a steady rhythm. He thought long enough on the gunshots he'd heard at midnight to take his last box of ammunition from a cupboard over the workbench and he packed it with the blanket into the carryall. Opened the front doors and kicked the machine into gear, edging out into the night. He couldn't guess how much time the dog had left, if it was still alive at all. He stopped long enough to close the doors behind him and then started up out of the cove.

Sweetland paused at the top of the path, beside the King's Seat. It was buried in drifts of snow, just one cold stone arm visible, but the mash beyond it looked to have been scoured clean by the wind. He stood holding the handlebars as he lurched over the frozen trail around Vatcher's Meadow, driving slow and calling as he went. He couldn't see much beyond the headlight's reach and he stopped occasionally, shutting the engine off to shout the dog's name and listen.

He left the quad on the far side of the meadow and started walking, afraid the noise of the machine might be driving the animal further away. Now and then he stopped, thinking he'd heard some motion ahead or behind him. But it was just the nylon whiff of his own pants as he walked, the toggle on his jacket zipper knocking in the wind. Near noises made strange in the dark.

He was close enough to Burnt Head he could see the light over the rise, an intermittent glim like photographs being taken, away in the distance. The wind had dropped while he wasn't paying attention and a calm that felt otherworldly had settled on the night. He was about to call for the dog again when he saw the first of them moving on the rise. Dark figures outlined in flashes against the horizon, heading toward the lighthouse.

Sweetland stopped still where he was, flicking off the flashlight. Watched without moving, to be sure his eyes weren't deceiving him. Another, and then another, following the same path down toward the keeper's house. He'd left the box of ammunition in the carryall on the quad and he considered going back for it now. But he was afraid to look away, thinking it might all disappear if he did. He watched the silent procession swell above him, dozens more trailing in from the blackness and disappearing down the ridge toward the Fever Rocks.

When the last of the figures passed out of his sight he made his way up toward them, moving slow in the unearthly quiet. He could see the keeper's house over the rise but there was no sign of the walkers. He waited until the building's details came clearer to him in the dark before he went down toward it, stayed close to the side of the house, edging up to the far corner. Allowing one cautious eye beyond it.

There were hundreds of them standing on the headlands. All clustered close to the cliffs of the Fever Rocks, as many people as ever lived in the cove, he guessed, and not a sound among them. All facing the ocean where the intermittent light stirred the blackness. A pale glow about the unlikely congregation though the moon was down, each figure silhouetted against the night sky. An air of waiting about them so palpable that Sweetland held his breath as he watched.

He felt exposed there, as if he was spying on some secret ceremony and bound to be found out. He turned to sneak off the way he'd come when someone brushed past him, a hunchback in a black overcoat, limping toward the rest. Sweetland fell back against the lighthouse to keep his feet, holding out the barrel of the .22 in both hands to fend off the night. They were still walking down from the rise in a steady trickle, he saw, their faces blank and unhurried. They went past without showing the slightest concern to have him there. Strangers every one of them, though he felt they knew him. That he was known to them somehow. A woman in a headscarf turned her head as she went by and smiled blankly. An eerie incongruity to the expression on her face. The teeth in her head too small for her mouth.

The cold woke him. Light outside when he opened his eyes, midmorning already. He could hear the trickle of water running in the sink, though the stove was long dead and the room ticked with frost. A heated beach rock at the small of his back the only hint of warmth in the world. He reached behind himself, touched a hand to a matted tangle of fur.

The dog licking at his bare fingers. He shifted carefully to get a look at the animal, the head coming up to greet him.

"Now, Mr. Fox," he said. He scratched underneath the dog's ears and it leaned its weight into his hand. There was a streak of white fur on its black chin, like a soul patch, and Sweetland stroked it between his fingers. "I hope you had a better night than I did."

The dog jumped to the floor and shook itself and Sweetland pushed himself upright. His head two sizes too small for all it carried. He was still wearing his coat and boots, the .22 leaning against the foot of the daybed. He spent a few minutes trying to separate out the night, to set what was real from what he might have dreamt lying there on the daybed. The dog ran up to nip at his pants and then clattered across the painted wood to the door, scratching to be let out. "Hold your horses," Sweetland said.

He opened the storm door and the dog ran into the cold air, cocked a leg against the clothesline pole. Sweetland keeping a close eye, not wanting to let the creature out of his sight again. He was about to call it in when he looked across at the shed doors and the mad trip up on the mash came back to him, the walkers parading to the light. He went to the side door and listened a moment before he went in, expecting he didn't know what. Found the quad there, trussed underneath the canvas tarp, with no sign the machine had been moved in weeks.

He was oddly crestfallen to see it. A symptom of too much time alone, he guessed, to have felt almost grateful for the company of the nameless dead filing out past the light. To be disappointed seeing he'd dreamt or imagined the entire thing.

The dog had followed him in to nose around the room and Sweetland called it from the side door as he was leaving. "Mr. Fox," he said, and it came out from behind the red gas cans under the workbench, sitting at the door to be let out. Sweetland staring at those three containers. He went across the room and picked them up in turn. All of them empty. He lifted the tarp off the back of the quad and opened the carryall, took out the blanket he'd packed there and the box of ammunition. He put the shells back in the cupboard over the workbench and turned to leave, but had to catch himself against a rising spell of dizziness.

He lifted his head to the rafters once it passed. His eyes coming to rest on the white wooden cross directly above him, his name hand-lettered there in black. And he nodded a simple hello.

THE FIRST WEEKS AFTER the accident Sweetland drifted through porous layers of pain and narcotic relief. Duke quit the job at the steel mill to be closer to the hospital and he spent all of his time there, scavenging meals off trays left in the hallways, finding an empty bed to sleep in at night or kipping down in the abandoned television room.

Sweetland was barely capable of carrying on a conversation those early days and Duke talked up the revolving cast of men in the other beds on the ward instead. Wanting to know where they were from and what they did for a living and how many youngsters they had. Half the people in the hospital were from elsewhere in the world, it seemed, from Italy or Greece or some Balkan country they'd never heard of. He ran errands for patients who needed cigarettes or chewing gum or a letter posted. An elderly man from Spain admitted for bypass surgery spent the long hours of his convalescence teaching Duke to play chess. After the Spaniard was discharged, Duke tried to pass on what he'd learned to Sweetland, using a checkerboard borrowed from the television room, improvising chess pieces out of beer caps, paper clips, pennies, empty syringes. The nurses and custodial staff stopping to check on the progress of the latest game, laying wagers on the outcome.

When Sweetland was too tired or stoned on medication for chess, Duke wandered the hospital aimlessly, flirting with the nurses at the desk. He mopped the floors on the ward if he found a bucket unattended, just to have something to do with his time.

You ought to go back, Sweetland told him finally.

You're here a long while yet.

And you got no work. And a wife home with a youngster you haven't even laid eyes on.

I can wait.

You fly the fuck home out of it.

You kiss my arse.

A rake like you, Sweetland said.

A week they argued it back and forth until Sweetland ratted him out to the nurses, telling them Duke had been living in the hospital more than a month. He heard the racket down the hall the next morning, Duke shouting at the top of his lungs as he was hauled away by Security.

Sweetland woke in the hospital dark that night to see him sitting in a chair by the bed.

You're a lousy cunt, Moses Sweetland, Duke said.

How'd you get in here?

It's not a fucken bank or anything. I walked in.

I'll call Security, Duke, I swear to God.

I'm going, Duke said, don't get a hard-on. He leaned in close to the bed. I just wanted to know if there's a message you wants passed on to Effie when I gets back.

Tell her I won't likely be home for Christmas, Sweetland said.

6

AFTER THE COLD SNAP, THE WEATHER reverted to its regular schizophrenia. Snow, followed by days of rain and sleet, ice pellets. Thaws followed by sudden freeze-ups that made the paths treacherous to walk. None of it matched the forecast he was getting on the radio. There was a storm in February that lasted two full days, a fierce gale of wind and snow drifting halfway up the kitchen windows. The radio announcer calmly calling for scattered flurries and moderate easterly winds and a low of minus one.

It took days to dig out from the storm. A permanent gloom inside from the height of snow over the windows, the paths to the shed and the outhouse shoulder high and no wider than the upstairs hallway. He and the dog suffering a long fit of claustrophobia in the tiny lifeboat of the kitchen, until a thaw set them loose. Four afternoons of sunshine and a south-easterly warm enough to pass for July, waterfalls of melt off the eaves of the buildings. Two nights of steady rain and the snowpack disappearing so quickly Sweetland could watch it go, inch by inch. The radio like a broken record repeating its call for flurries and moderate winds and minus one.

It had been comic at first, to see the forecast so far off the mark day after day. But there was something increasingly disturbing in the disconnect. It seemed a sign of a widening fracture in the world.

He got up with the light each morning and washed and fed himself and he occupied his waking hours with whatever chores the day required. The dog at his heels as he went about the property, or on its wanders up to the mash or down through the cove. From the kitchen window Sweetland would catch sight of it on the government wharf or nosing along the side of Queenie's house and he'd watch until the dog was out of sight. There was a comfort in knowing it was out there on its own trajectory, that his house was one of the many points on the animal's compass.

There were days the dog wandered off as soon as it was let outdoors and there was no sign of the creature again before dark. Sweetland waiting each evening to see it go by the kitchen window, to hear it barking outside or scratching at the door. It went straight for its food bowl and afterwards lay at Sweetland's feet, dozing but watchful, wanting him to settle for the night on the daybed so it could do the same.

In the few minutes between waking and getting up, Sweetland combed leisurely through the dog's fur, working twigs and shards of tree bark and burrs from the tangle as it slept beside him. It was the only time the animal allowed that sort of intimate attention. As a rule it balked at being picked up or coddled or mauled, shying away and growling. Sweetland tried to clip the hair around its eyes before Christmas, thinking the creature must be half-blind behind those bangs. But it refused to let him near with the scissors and kept a wary distance for days afterwards. He wasn't willing to chance losing the dog's trust altogether and gave up the idea, settling for the idle grooming he was allowed. Like a chimp picking nits from the fur of a companion.

Before it was fully awake the dog stretched and rolled on its back, legs splayed while Sweetland scratched its belly. Its testicles were nearly hairless and they made an impression in that posture, two bald fruit in their wild nest of fur. He thought of Loveless talking about the darling set of balls on the dog. Out looking for love half the time it wandered off, Sweetland guessed, trying to scare up a female canine whose rear end was no higher than a beef bucket. "I expect you're shit out of luck on this island, Mr. Fox," he said. And he gave the testicles the affectionate little rub he'd seen Loveless bestow. "Shit out of luck."

For years he'd had the same lonesome feeling about Jesse—that the boy was stranded on the island of his own peculiar self, that he'd never find a soul fit for his eccentric way in the world. Between the ages of five and six, Jesse was a compulsive masturbator. He would have a go at himself anywhere the mood struck, at school, in a church pew, in the living room while they were watching *SpongeBob SquarePants*. His mouth half open, his face blank as a doll's. It seemed a completely asexual activity, an itch he scratched absently, though it was hard to argue the point when parents of other students complained. The Priddles christened the boy Jerk-off, a name that was in common usage around the cove for awhile, and Sweetland badgered Jesse to keep it in his pants. Put that thing away, he'd say. The boy ignoring him until Sweetland reached to tap the back of his head. Put it away, he repeated.

Clara thought it was a phase and seemed willing to wait it out. Leave him be, she said. You'll just make him self-conscious about it.

He could stand a dose of self-conscious if you asks me, Sweetland said.

He'll grow out of it, she said.

Clara had been right about that. Though the memory of it always made Sweetland feel heartsick and embarrassed for the boy. He never believed Jesse had abandoned the practice altogether, or that the urge wouldn't come back to haunt him when he hit his teens. That he wouldn't want more from the world than it had to offer him on that front.

He allowed he might be wrong to think so, God knows it wasn't his particular area of expertise. At the age of seventy, he was still technically a virgin. He wasn't in the habit of thinking of himself as such, but he couldn't argue the fact.

On his first trip to Toronto, Duke arranged a date for him with a woman who worked the weekday lunch counter at a nearby Woolworth's

and occasionally turned tricks in the evenings. A welcome to the mainland, Duke called it. She was ancient, Sweetland thought at the time,
though she couldn't have been older than thirty-five. A mole high on one
cheekbone that made her seem vaguely French. A shrill, mechanical
laugh that could have cut sheet metal.

He did not want to have sex with the woman. He was worried
about making her pregnant, about catching some mortifying French
disease. He'd never used a condom and was afraid of looking like
an idiot trying to put one on in front of a stranger. He made an
effort to back out of the arrangement, which he hadn't gone looking
for to begin with.

Already paid for, Duke said. Ask for a blowjob, it's better than
screwing anyway.

He was so hard when she went down on him that he couldn't feel
a thing other than pressure, an insistent discomfort, as though it was a
medical procedure of some kind being performed on him. He had
both hands on her head, trying to release his cock, and he came in
spite of himself, suffering through a grating convulsion that was completely devoid of pleasure. He rolled onto his side, curling up in a
defensive position.

What the Christ was that? he asked.

I know, she said. Tell your friends. And she winked at him. Marion,
her name was. She was still wearing the mustard-yellow polyester uniform from the lunch counter, a blue name tag pinned above her breast.

Nothing more then before Effie Burden fumbling at his fly in
Bob-Sam's wagon on the way to the light at the Mackerel Cliffs.

And that was the end of such things for him.

He still walked as far as the lighthouse on Sundays if the weather was
anywhere shy of miserable. It was a slow trip out, an hour longer than
walking in summer. He didn't bother trying to break into the light

tower at Burnt Head, built a small fire in the lee of the keeper's house and boiled snow-water for tea, sitting on his coat, feeding the dog stale Purity crackers and salt fish and slivers of bottled beet.

Before starting back he walked down past the house to look out at the Fever Rocks and beyond them to the busy grey-blue of the ocean. He thought he might catch a glimpse of a container ship swinging wide for the eastern seaboard of the States, some evidence of the world rumoured beyond the island's ark. But there was only the endless conveyor belt of the waves ticking toward the shoreline.

He never went down as far as the cliffs, not since the night he'd watched the crowd assemble there in their echoing cathedral silence. A lunatic's vision, he expected, though something about it seemed beyond his capacity for fabrication, even drunk as he was. And he felt it would be a trespass to walk where those strangers had been standing, hushed and oddly expectant. He couldn't recall a single detail of those faces in the light of day but it still niggled at him, the sense that he'd known them in another lifetime, that their names were adrift below the surface and just about to come to him. But he never managed to hook a single one.

Since the first snow of the fall he'd been taking the short detour to the new cemetery on his way back down into the cove. He walked through the rows to spend a few minutes with the dead lying there. His closest blood lined off near the back fence, his mother and Ruthie, Uncle Clar and Jesse.

Jesse had liked to follow Sweetland up to the cemetery when he cut the grass or spent a morning painting the fence. It was the only time Sweetland actively discouraged the boy's company, knowing it would lead to questions about Hollis's absent marker. Clara thought that might be the reason Jesse fixated on him—the lack of definition to the loss, the absence of a clear resting place. The thought that Hollis was somewhere out there still.

It makes Hollis sad, Jesse said one afternoon. Not having a headstone with the others.

Is that right? Sweetland said.

It makes him feel lonely.

Well, boo-fucken-hoo. Tell him when he stops wandering around the cove with you, maybe we'll put one up for him.

And Jesse had carried on a dialogue with Sweetland's dead brother then, walking through the graveyard to discuss the size and colour and style of headstone Hollis might prefer. It made Sweetland nearly mental at the time, listening to that one-sided conversation, and he told Jesse to shut up or bugger off home out of it. But he had less and less room to judge the youngster. He knelt to clear the fresh fall of snow from the names and dates on the stones, Jesse's and Uncle Clar's and Ruthie's and his mother's. Queenie Coffin's and Effie Priddle's. Old Mr. Vatcher and Sara Loveless. Saying hello to each of them aloud and telling them the weather and what he planned to cook for his supper. Like a Jesus idiot.

The flour he'd bought in Miquelon was brown and had no preservatives and he lost most of it to mould and weevils by the new year. He'd known there wasn't enough salt meat to see him through the winter, even rationing it as he did. The rabbit and occasional brown trout and cured cod he lived on was so lean he couldn't keep the flesh on his bones. His clothes began to hang off his frame in unfamiliar ways, sloughing at his shoulders and hips. He added an extra hole in his belt with a hammer and four-inch nail, to keep his pants from slipping around his arse. He ran out of store-bought liquor and salt beef halfway through January month. He had a final meal of rabbit stew the first week of February and he cut the last morsels of meat on his plate into bite-sized chunks, sharing them out with the dog. He put the plate on the floor to be licked clean of gravy and when the dog looked up again he showed his empty hands. "All gone, Mr. Fox," he said.

The snow in the woods on the mash was too deep and rotten to allow for setting snares and, with the exception of a single partridge he'd managed to shoot on a walk to the lighthouse, he subsisted on home-brew and root vegetables and the cod he'd put up in the fall. He had eaten through the fish that was properly cured. All that was left to him was under-salted and slimy, the stacked layers of flesh gone green at the edges. He soaked the brine from the fish overnight and boiled it most of an afternoon, adding fresh water every hour, just to make it palatable. He put down a bowl for the dog, who nosed it awhile and walked away to lie three or four feet distant with its head on its paws. Sometimes the maggoty fish sat there a full day before the dog gave in to its hunger, chewing at the sour meat with an obvious distaste Sweetland wouldn't have thought an animal capable of.

"Go catch your own goddamn dinner, you don't like it," he said.

On occasion the dog did just that, carrying home bones it discovered up on the mash or dug out of someone's backyard garbage pile, and it lay near Diesel's house, grinding at a long-discarded T-bone or the jaw of a sheep or a young cow.

Sweetland saw the animal trotting up from the waterfront one afternoon with its head held high, some flaccid creature in its mouth. He stood at the kitchen window as the dog came closer, watching it stop now and then to drop its cargo and walk around it, until it had found a more manageable way to carry the awkward load. It was a bullbird the dog had gotten hold of, the black and white creature about the same size as the dog's head. Dovekies they were called elsewhere in the world, according to Jesse.

It was an unlikely catch. Sweetland hadn't often seen bullbirds west of Cape Race and they were usually gone out to sea by the first of February. He knelt over the dog, who growled to have him so close to his prize. "All right there, Mr. Fox," he said, and he gave the dog a flick with the back of his hand. He picked up the bird and turned it over. It wasn't oiled that he could tell, and there was no obvious injury to explain the dog's luck. Sweetland ran a thumb along the breastbone and then stood to look out at the harbour, shading his eyes to see the water against the sun's glare.

He went into the shed for a dip net stored in the rafters and walked down the path. Before he was halfway to the shoreline he could see them rolling in on the tidal surge. Dozens of bullbirds dead in the water, the corpses like tiny buoys off their moorings and drifting in past the breakwater. More again already grounded on the beach. Sweetland scooped up eight or ten and he walked back to the house with the loaded dip net on his shoulder, seawater dripping behind him.

He sat them in a row on the counter and leaned there a minute to look them over. He picked one up, turned it one side and the other, admiring the symmetry of the face. Beautiful creatures, he'd always thought. Sleek and delicate looking, plush as a child's toy. Hard to imagine them spending months out on the winter Atlantic without ever coming ashore.

The bird's breastbone jutted against his thumb beneath the down. They were all in the same emaciated condition, which likely meant they had starved. So little flesh on their bones he didn't know if it would be worth the effort of cleaning them. But the thought of a single morsel of fresh meat was making his legs shake. He put on a pot of water to scald the birds, to make them easier to pluck. And while he waited for the pot to boil, he went back to the shoreline to gather more.

He cleaned them outside the porch door and he had to light a lamp to finish the tedious work, the naked bodies stippled and scrawny and unhealthy looking against the snow where he laid them. There wasn't enough meat on the carcasses to roast and he made soup instead, with potatoes and turnip and carrot, a couple of whole onions for flavour. He boiled the pot long enough to kill anything organic and he set down a bowl for the dog before sitting to his own. They ate in the same greedy silence then, Sweetland gnawing every morsel off the bones and sucking out the marrow. The dog licking its bowl the length of the kitchen floor. It was awful food, gamey and scant, but Sweetland finished four of the birds before he pushed away from the table. Already looking forward to the meal he'd make of the others.

In the morning he walked down to the shoreline where the gulls had made a mess of the bullbirds on the beach and were still working over the remains. He walked out as far as the incinerator with the dog running alongside or in the tuck above the path. Stopped short a little ways past the metal bell. Hundreds more of them on the surface beyond the breakwater, floating dead. The birds so delicately calibrated they'd starved within hours of each other, the organs shutting down one at a time.

Sweetland had never seen the like before, though he'd heard rumours of similar things. Gannets at Cape St. Mary's disappearing from Bird Rock by the tens of thousands on the same day last summer, travelling north after food. Tinkers showing up in the Florida Keys over the winter months, foraging hundreds of miles beyond their southern range.

There was a new world being built around him. Sweetland had heard them talking about it for years on the Fisheries Broadcast—apocalyptic weather, rising sea levels, alterations in the seasons, in ocean temperatures. Fish migrating north in search of colder water and the dovekies lost in the landscape they were made for. The generations of instinct they'd relied on to survive here suddenly useless. The birds and their habits were being rendered obsolete, Sweetland thought, like the VHS machines and analog televisions dumped on the slope beyond the incinerator. Relics of another time and on their way out.

It was just days after the dog brought up its bullbird that the light at Queenie Coffin's window reappeared.

Sweetland saw it as he walked back in the arm from the incinerator or through the window over the sink when he washed up the evening's dishes. He did what he could to ignore its intermittent presence, staring into the dishwater while he finished scrubbing the pots, reminding himself to keep his eyes from the windows the rest of the evening. Or walking the long way across to Church Side and up by Duke's barbershop, so he could pass Queenie's house opposite her window. Even during the day he stayed as far from it as his house's proximity allowed.

But the light appeared earlier and for longer stretches of the evening, as if it was being fed by his lack of attention. Eventually he talked himself into walking past the light, keeping himself as far clear as the path would let him and not ever looking directly inside the illuminated room. Even out of the corner of his eye he could see there was someone at the window and he battered the rest of the way to his house in the dark, the dog running after him. Shut the door and stood with his back to it. His rubbery legs quivering and he started to giggle there in the black, like someone stoned out of their mind. The dog jumping at his thighs and barking in its confusion. "Jesus fuck!" he shouted and fell back to giggling hysterically. Caught his breath finally and he went shakily into the kitchen to peek through the window over the sink. But the light was gone.

He made the same walk each of the next three nights, trying to guess who it was he glimpsed as he hurried past. It seemed sometimes to be a pale figure standing behind the glass, at others he thought it was someone in black sitting to one side. Could be there was more than one person in the room. Or no one at all and he was imagining the whole thing, but for the light which was too insistently present not to be real.

He went to the window one morning and stood looking into the room, hoping it might give him some clue. He pressed his face to the glass, shading his eyes with his hands. Half expecting a buffalo to walk into the living room from the kitchen, or something equally unlikely. But it was just the furniture sitting where it had always been, Queenie's chair and the chesterfield near the stairs, the five-thousand-piece jigsaw puzzle shellacked and framed and hung on the far wall as a painting. All of it inert and poker-faced.

He made up his mind then to stop outside the window after dark and settle the question, for better or worse. He ate his supper like it was his last, chewing slowly and deliberately, tasting nothing. He washed the dishes, waiting for the full of night's darkness to fall, and when the light appeared he walked around the front of his house and down toward Queenie's. Stopped well away from the window and he took his time as he stood there, staring at the yellow oblong cast onto the snow by the light, and then the window frame itself, studying each peeling board. There was no one inside the room when he finally worked up the nerve to look. Queenie's empty chair turned out toward him. Sweetland had been holding his breath without knowing it and he let the air out in a rush, lifted his face to the cold stars.

He watched the room awhile then, thinking something might happen in there, but nothing did. It was a bitter night to be standing still and eventually he turned to walk home, throwing one last glance over his shoulder. Saw the child standing near the glass. He let out a whimper with the shock of it, and then covered his mouth to stop himself making another sound.

The girl was naked and stared out at the night with the same brazen look she had sixty years ago, her hair cropped short as a boy's. Her child's body stripling and oddly beautiful and distressing, just as he remembered. It took him a moment to register the fact she wasn't alone in the room, that there was a woman seated in the chair at the window. Her hair in curlers and her head bowed toward a book in her lap. They were holding hands, the girl and the old woman beside her, though they each seemed oblivious to the other's presence. "Queenie," Sweetland said aloud. He raised a hand tentatively, as a greeting. But neither acknowledged him or seemed to know he was there. The woman in the chair turned a page with her free hand, a lit cigarette between the fingers.

He stood watching the two until he heard his teeth chattering with the cold. And he stayed a long while afterwards, not wanting to give them up, thinking they might meet his eyes eventually. When he couldn't stand still a moment longer, he headed toward his place, walking backwards until he lost sight of the girl. Shuffle-ran to his porch to haul another coat overtop of the one he was wearing. By the time he turned the corner on his way back to Queenie's the light was out.

He watched for it every evening afterwards, at the sink and during his walks, and always one last time before he turned in for the night. But he never saw the light or the child or the old woman again.

March came in like a lamb. There was a warm spell in the lead-up to St. Patrick's Day that Sweetland didn't trust for a second. Waiting for the storm that followed the holiday. Sheila's Brush it was called, arriving in the wake of St. Paddy and usually heralding a full-on return to late-winter misery.

He took advantage of the mild temperatures to work outside, though he stuck close to home. He left the stove cold one morning and climbed up on the roof with the chimney brush. He'd improvised a pole by duct-taping broom handles to either end of an old stair rail salvaged from Loveless's house, worked it hand over hand into the chimney, pushing the metal bristle down the flue. Hauled the brush up by its string and repeated the manoeuvre half a dozen times to scrub out the soot. Sweating in the sun's fickle heat. The mythical storm was like a letter he half expected in the mail, and each day it didn't show he was almost disappointed.

He looked up at the hills surrounding the cove, sunlight making them ring with meltwater. He'd always loved that sound, waited for it each spring. Hearing it made him certain of the place he came from. He'd always felt it was more than enough to wake up here, to look out on these hills. As if he'd long ago been measured and made to the island's exact specifications.

The dog appeared to take the beautiful weather at face value, wandering further and further afield during the days, sometimes not coming back to the house until Sweetland was long asleep. It barked outside to be let in and Sweetland shuffled across the kitchen in the dark. He stood the door open and the dog ran straight for the dish by the stove where its food had been sitting all day. Sweetland stood listening to the porcelain scrape of it in the darkness, waiting for the dog to finish. It jumped onto the daybed then, turning circles among the quilts to settle in. Sweetland all the while complaining about being woken up and the mess it was making of his bed with its filthy paws. "You got a perfectly good doghouse out there to use," he said. He drifted off listening to the dog grooming itself, the lap of its tongue as calm and insistent as water dripping from a tap.

He woke with a start, later than he was used to getting up, sunlight in the kitchen. The day already underway and he lay there nursing a centreless sense of dread. He'd forgotten to do something important was the feeling, but he couldn't place the thing. He was up and had lit the fire and was walking to the door to piss into the snow when it struck him the dog hadn't woken him in the night, coming back to the house. That it had been out wandering since the morning before.

The weather was mild enough that the animal might have kipped down in the bush or just meandered up on the mash all night, as it used to do when it was Loveless's dog. Sweetland listened awhile to the run-off rattling down into the cove from the hills, thinking it was almost time to move back into the upstairs bedroom. Thinking he might be able to tail some rabbit slips on the mash before long. The morning still cool but already warming in the sunlight. And he knew it a certainty as he stood there that he would never see the dog alive again.

He didn't leave the cove to go looking, not wanting to admit by his actions what his heart knew to be true. He puttered around the property, to be close by if the dog came back. Mid-morning he took a bucket of tar onto the roof and patched around the chimney flashing. It was a chore that didn't need doing strictly, but he could keep an eye on most of the cove from up there and into the hills. He stayed on the roof until it was time to eat. Before he climbed down the ladder he put his fingers to his mouth and whistled, and he stood listening as the echoes swung across the hills. Watching for any sign of movement in that world of endless stillness.

In the afternoon he walked along the paths with a bit of salt fish in his shirt pocket. Not much to tempt the animal with, but he had nothing better to offer. He felt sure it was nowhere close, but he couldn't stop himself going through the motions regardless. Most of the houses in the cove were built on shores or rock foundations and he kept an eye for cubbyholes the dog might have crawled into, kneeling at the likeliest spots and calling its name. He went out Church Side to the meadow and then backtracked around the harbour, walking all the way to the incinerator. He stopped there, leaned a little ways into the iron darkness, waited for his eyes to adjust. Dirty snow drifted against the far wall. Black lumps of unidentifiable refuse. Loveless's calf just inside the entrance, the bare skeleton collapsed and so jumbled by scavengers it would be almost impossible now to identify the creature for what it was.

After he finished his supper that evening he took up the dog's bowl and threw the two-day-old food into the stove. Washed it along with his own dishes and refilled it with the leftover potato and fish he'd cooked for himself. Set the bowl back beside the stove.

He sat at the kitchen window, looking out at Diesel's doghouse in the failing light, listening for the weather on the radio. He went to the door every half-hour to whistle up to the hills. And again when he woke to take a piss in the middle of the night, standing on the doorsill in his small clothes, the chill licking at his ankles. Decided as he stood there that he would go up on the mash in the morning and set a few snares, see if he couldn't get a bit of fresh craft to eat.

He hadn't slept much before he woke to piss and didn't sleep at all afterwards, staring at the kitchen window for the first sign of light. Getting up now and then to set a junk of wood in the stove. There was no rush, he knew that for a fact. And he was anxious to start out all the same.

He lit a lamp and warmed a panful of salt fish and French-fried

potato for his breakfast. He packed a jar of water and a lunch of cod
slathered in partridgeberry jam, to spare himself one more meal of plain
salt fish. Put two cans of peaches and the last of the box of ammunition
in the pack, half a dozen snares to keep up the charade he was going
after rabbits. Tied a set of snowshoes to the leather fastener. Overcast,
the wind steady out of the south and the morning looked for rain, so he
packed his yellow slicker as well. Drove the quad on the last dregs of
his fuel past the new cemetery and out of the cove. It was barely light
by the time he reached the King's Seat and he turned the machine off
there, balanced himself up on the stone arm of the Seat. Facing inland,
trying to guess which direction to set out in.

He put his fingers to his mouth and whistled, the sound falling
quick and hard. The mash beyond him still black and featureless.
"That's a big fucken island, Sweetland," he said. He sat back on the
quad and waited there until it was light enough to pick out the orange
tire wire and charcoaled wood of his bonfire pushing up through the
snow. Sweetland started up the quad then. He drove around Vatcher's
Meadow, moving slow. Looking and pretending not to look.

He'd almost reached the rise ahead of the north-end light when the
engine began falling off, gurgling along ten feet or so and spinning out
before kicking in another few seconds. Sweetland turned the machine
off and took his pack from the carryall. Walked over the rise, down to
the keeper's house. He went beyond it to the cliffs above the Fever
Rocks for the first time since the night he'd witnessed the gathering out
there, turning a circle to take in the headlands. Felt the first drops of
rain strike his face. He pulled on his slicker and started along the path
toward the Priddles' cabin. Winter a mess in the trees, the snowpack
melting underneath. He went through to his thigh in the rotten snow
and spent ten minutes working his leg free, using the butt of the .22 to
shovel, wrenching his foot back to the surface. Lay there catching his
breath while the rain pocked his jacket. "Break a fucken hip," he said
aloud. "Where will you be then."

The dog was light enough to trot along on the surface of the snow-pack, and Sweetland strapped into his snowshoes, trudged a mile past the cabin turnoff, setting his snares haphazardly as he went. Wasting his time on a fool's errand and angrier with every miserable step he took. So poisoned he felt ready to shoot the dog himself if he found the bastard thing alive.

He walked the length of the island from the Fever Rocks to the south-end light in the rain. Ate his lunch as he walked so as not to waste daylight. His pants and boots soaked through. He made his way along the lip of the Mackerel Cliffs, thinking the dog might have come foraging through the detritus of last year's breeding season. Broken eggshells and the occasional puffin's bill scattered like sand dollars in the bare moss nearest the cliff edge, a tinker's wing snagged in a bit of gorse.

Late afternoon and the light already dimming when he saw it lying twenty yards ahead, black and red against a patch of snow. Stopped where he was, turned toward the cliffs. "Now, Mr. Fox," he said. The ocean roiling a thousand miles below him.

When he was ready, he walked over to the dog. Impossible to say what had gotten into it, though it looked like the creature had been worked over by a parade of scavengers. It lay on its back, the head torqued sharply up and to one side, its milk-white teeth bared. The eye picked from the one socket he could see. The stomach was open and the cavity stripped clean. Sweetland looked beyond it a little ways, saw scattered tufts of its black fur flickering like down in the wind and wet. He shucked out of his pack and knelt beside the creature. Tried to push the lips of its cold muzzle back down around the teeth.

It was too much of a mess to carry uncovered and he hadn't thought to bring something to wrap it up. He took off his slicker and laid it on the ground, set the dead animal on the coat and used the arms to tie the bundle tight. Started back for the cove in the cold, steady downpour with what was left of the dog tucked under his arm. The wind rising and driving across the top of the island, blowing so hard over the exposed ground he had to walk at an angle to stay upright, leaning hard to port into the gale.

He stopped shivering halfway to the King's Seat, which he guessed was a bad sign. Most of the feeling in his legs was gone and he had trouble keeping his feet on the path down into the cove, using the stock of the .22 like a cane. He let himself into the kitchen and stood in the middle of the room, dripping rainwater on the wood floor. Realized in the quiet of the house that he was bawling helplessly and likely had been for some time. His shoulders hitching on the ragged sobs.

He changed out of his soaked clothes, peeling the material away like layers of skin. His head was pulsing and he could feel the first glimmer of a fever stoking its furnace somewhere in the body's basement. He wanted to lie down for five minutes but knew he wouldn't have it in him to get up. He lit the storm lamp, put on the heaviest coat in the porch, and carried the yellow slicker out to the shed for a shovel. The wind had dropped with the sun, but there was no let-up in the rain. Sweetland walked his burden up to the new cemetery and set it down in the lee of Jesse's headstone, placing the storm lamp beside it. Then he pushed the head of the spade into the grass over the boy's grave.

A foot below the surface the earth was still frozen solid, the shovel ringing against the flinty ground as he swung with all his weight. He carved out a shallow bowl and laid the animal there in its slicker shroud. It wasn't deep enough by half but Sweetland was too exhausted to dig further into the frost. He placed the shovel over the open hole and walked back down to the shed for a salt beef bucket, headed on to the landwash in the gathering darkness. He filled the bucket with beach stones, carried them back up the path. He stopped every ten or twelve steps to set the weight down, moving to the opposite side of the bucket to change arms. Hefted the rocks, shuffled another ten steps along. Looking up to the glow of the kerosene lamp where he'd left it in the graveyard, working his way back to that tiny beacon.

He knelt beside the new grave, laid the rocks carefully on top of the dog's body, to spare it any more scavenging. He shovelled the wet earth over the stones, stepping the mound flat with his foot. He sang most of an old hymn under his breath then, humming in the spots where the words escaped him, *The night is dark and I am far from home, hmmm hmm hm hm*. He turned away when he was done and shuffled toward the house, dragging the head of the spade in his wake.

He forgot the lamp where it sat near the headstone and it threw shadows across the boy's name until the small hours of the morning when it dimmed and bowed and flickered and finally went out in the rain.

CLOUDS OF DOCTORS APPEARED at his bedside after each new surgery, talking back and forth in what sounded to him like Latin or some other dead language. A single nurse among the nine or ten young men. She stood beside a bearded, bespectacled chain-smoker to hold his ashtray and his files. The doctor's accent like the Nazis Sweetland had heard in war movies at the Park Theatre or the Odeon. The doctor set his cigarette in the ashtray before he lifted the sheets and folded them down around Sweetland's knees to display the ruined flesh in the patient's lap.

Traumatic degloving lesion of the penile and scrotal tissue, he announced to the assembled group. The skin presenting avulsion was fixed to the penis through a pedicle formed by a flap in the coronal sulcus, and the skin at the scrotal base was preserved. We assumed the skin's viability due to the pedicle with what appeared to be good vascularization. The left testis was covered with the remaining scrotal skin, the right testis was buried in the inguinal region until grafting could be conducted.

Sweetland all the time watching the nurse, the ashtray in the palm of her hand like a waitress's drink tray. Her head turned to one side while the sheet was lowered, out of respect for Sweetland's modesty. The bearded doctor took a pen from his breast pocket to point out a particular feature of the slash and burn in Sweetland's lap and all the young men leaned in closer to see it.

We left a small area at the dorsum penis uncovered—here—as we opted to wait for healing by second intention. It all appears to be progressing satisfactorily. We expect recovery of normal sexual function within three to six months.

Sweetland looked away from the nurse, staring up at the acoustic ceiling tiles.

The extensive damage to the testes and the vas deferens, however, make recovery of fertility unlikely. Now—

Where is it you belongs to? Sweetland interrupted.

Sweetland had never spoken a word to the man or to any of the doctors in his entourage. They might have thought he was deaf and dumb, for all he knew. The doctor leaned away from the bed and glanced across at the nurse. She offered the ashtray and the doctor took up the cigarette. He said, I beg your pardon?

You're not from around here, Sweetland said. Where do you belong?

Austria, the doctor said. I am from Austria.

I don't know it, Sweetland said.

Near Germany.

Sweetland nodded. I knows Germany.

The doctor motioned at the sheets and the nurse set the ashtray and files down to cover Sweetland up to his chest.

Sweetland cleared his throat. Does the nurse need to be here?

The nurse?

I wanted to ask after something, he said.

I'll just be outside, the nurse said, and she held the ashtray out long enough for the doctor to stub the butt of his cigarette. The doctor folded his hands behind his back when she was gone and rose up an inch on his toes. Now then, he said.

What you said just now, Sweetland said. And he glanced toward his waist, pointing with his eyes.

Yes.

I don't know what any of that means.

Well, the doctor said. All indications are, you will be perfectly capable of having sexual intercourse. Once you have healed, of course. We don't recommend it at the moment.

He turned to the young men, to allow them a moment to acknowledge the humour.

We attempted a surgical reconstruction that would allow you to produce and ejaculate sperm in a normal manner, he said. But we have not been as successful as we would have hoped.

Meaning what exactly?

Are you a father, Mr. . . ?

Sweetland, he said.

Mr. Sweetland. Do you have children?

He shook his head. I was thinking, he said, maybe someday.

I'm afraid, the doctor said, this will not be possible. He looked steadily at Sweetland.

How long before I can batter the hell out of here?

There is one more surgery for the face and neck.

No more surgeries, he said.

Mr. Sweetland.

I'm fine the way I am. I feels fine.

The doctor rose up on his toes a second time. He turned to the assembly and said he would meet them outside. He patted his pockets, looking for his cigarettes as he waited for the last of them to file out.

This final surgery I speak of, he said.

No more surgeries.

It is not necessary, the doctor said. Strictly speaking. It is largely for cosmetic purposes. To deal with the scarring and discolouration. It will help make the injury less apparent. Your face, he said and he gestured toward it. Of course, it's up to you, he said.

How long before I can leave?

If everything goes well, if there are no secondary infections or other complications, I would say four to six weeks.

A month, then, Sweetland said.

A month, the doctor said. He opened the cigarette pack, offered it toward the bed. Sweetland took one, leaning forward as the doctor struck a match. You are anxious to get home to someone, he said. Someone is waiting for you?

Sweetland shook his head. Not really, he said, no. He blew smoke up at the ceiling. There's no one waiting, he said.

7

HE WOKE TO A GALE OF WIND and sleet and high winds that brought waves overtop of the breakwater. The house creaking on its foundation, the windowpanes bowing like sails in each gust. The tide turning and on the rise. He felt oddly glassy and disoriented and thought to keep the dog inside out of the weather until he remembered it dead and buried up in the new cemetery.

He had a hard time travelling down to the beach, leaning into the teeth of the gale. His hat torn off his head and sailing away. Salt stinging his eyes as wind whipped the spume up the hill. The tarp over the dory was long gone and the boat swung wildly at the end of its painter, tipping on its side and over onto its belly as the sea muscled in. Sweetland waded up to his knees as the waves receded, trying to get a handle on the line to drag the boat to safety. The suck of water sieving rocks and sand from beneath his boots. Another wave flipped the dory a full rotation in the air and took Sweetland off his feet altogether, both hands on the rope to keep from being hauled body and bones into the wilderness of the cove. He scrambled up, hauling all he was worth to bring the boat close. Dragging it as far off the landwash as the length of rope allowed, the sea rising high enough around him to set it afloat. He worked to untie the painter, his hands almost too numb to manage. He leaned back on the bow when it was free, nudging the boat inches at a time, until he wedged it into a sheltered nook above the beach where he guessed it might be safe. Loaded its belly with beach rocks and rusted lengths of iron scrap and anything else he thought might weigh the dory enough to hold it against the wind.

He stripped out of his soaking clothes when he reached the kitchen, wrapped himself in a quilt. From the kitchen table he watched the breakwater disappear in surge after surge of white, thinking each time the entire thing might disappear. He trawled through the radio dial looking for a forecast, to see how bad things might get, but couldn't make out more than a few words over the storm's static. Moderate winds, he thought he heard. Flurries. Minus one.

The massive stones placed at the mouth of the cove were shifting as he watched, the breakwater settling and coming apart like ice dissolving in a bowl of water. The ocean pouring raw into the cove for the first time in a generation, the waves lipping up over the government wharf, pounding onto the beach. The salt of the water's spray blowing against his windows, riming the glass. If his stage hadn't been burned, he knew, the storm would have taken it down and floated every stick out into the Atlantic.

The feeling slowly came back to his hands as he sat there, a burning sensation in the palms that was almost pleasurable. He looked down to see the red scars of the rope where he'd grabbed and held on while the ocean tried to take him under.

By suppertime he was burning up with a fever, too sick to move much beyond the kitchen. He was on his feet long enough to light a kindling fire to boil the kettle and to drag himself up the stairs to the bathroom so he could sit. Shivering so violently he had trouble staying on the seat. Downstairs he made himself a mug of pap, crumbling stale crackers into sweet tea, and he crawled back into the daybed before he could finish even that. The weather in a rage outside.

The fever broke two days later, but he was still too weak and unsteady to leave the house. He sat at the kitchen window, listening to the forecasts and trying to match them to the conditions outside, though there wasn't a single reliable detail in the announcements. As if the island had drifted into its own latitude, beyond the reach of the CBC's meteorologists.

He leafed aimlessly through Duke's magazines without reading a word or even registering the pictures. It was a mechanical activity that offered some relief from the tedium of fatigue, a sense of forward progress, of time passing. Picking up one after another and blindly turning the pages start to finish, reaching for the next. He'd made his way through to the bottom third of the pile when he began coming across the mutilated articles, squares and rectangles cut from the pages, and even then it took a while to process what he was seeing. He went to the drawer where he'd put away the threatening notes and he spent half an hour matching them to the words and letters scissored from the headlines. The door to the barbershop was never locked and he supposed anyone could have slipped in and borrowed a magazine for the purpose at hand. Though he couldn't guess why they might see the need to return it when they were done.

All those months the man had held his counsel in Sweetland's presence, refusing to offer a word of advice one way or another. Sweetland shook his head. "You're a lousy cunt, Duke Fewer," he said. He didn't know if he should be amused or murderous or heartbroken. But he didn't have it in him to feel much of anything at all.

He burned the notes and the magazines in the stove and he occupied himself then with simply staring out the window. Hours watching the slice of cove visible from the kitchen table. He could see the ruined line of the breakwater, the remaining stones lying low in the ocean, the waves pushing past them into the harbour's calm. It was the end of the government wharf, that loss. Though it would be years, he guessed, before the sea managed to finish the job.

He was days into that vigil before Sweetland noted the extended lull in the world he was observing. That there hadn't been a sign of a living creature in all the time he'd sat there. Even the gulls seemed to have disappeared. He'd grown accustomed to silence and stillness in his months alone. But the absence out there seemed of a different order altogether and it gave a new focus to his sedentary time at the table, watching to prove his observation wrong.

Near the end of March he caught sight of a ring seal inside the remains of the breakwater, the dark head bobbing in the shallows of the cove. It was early in the year to see them this far south and Sweetland waited at the kitchen window a long time. Afraid he might have imagined it, just to address the lack he was seeing out there. He was ready to dismiss the sighting altogether until he spotted the creature near the government wharf. He went in and out of the porch, gathering up his coat and boots, rummaging for ammunition. His limbs felt brittle and insubstantial, every motion shadowed by the fever's aftermath. His heart pounding in his throat.

He started down the path with the .22 and then turned back to the shed, to haul the oars down out of the rafters. Hoofed his awkward load toward the water, his coat hanging open, his head bare to the wind. It was bitterly cold despite the sunshine, but he didn't feel a thing in the rush. Giddy with seeing the animal, taking it as a sign the world was shifting back into an orbit he recognized.

He went to the government dock, which was high enough to give him a shot anywhere across the cove. Spring seals tended to sink and even if he managed to hit the animal he'd likely have nothing to show for the effort. If he was lucky, it would float at the surface long enough to get Loveless's boat in the water. He was too weak to hold the rifle steady and he knelt behind a capstan to rest an elbow on the metal.

A lop on the cove, sunlight strobing across the surface. A dozen times he thought he spotted the seal amid the glimmer and black. Saw it bobbing in the shade of the breakwater rocks finally, its sleek head like something carved out of stone and sanded smooth. Sweetland took a breath, letting it out slowly. A spit of ocean kicked up and the sound of the rifle echoed in the ring of hills behind him. Sweetland scanned back and forth across the area he'd fired at. He might have missed the creature altogether and it wouldn't come up for air again until it was safe in open water. It might be floating there dead or already sinking to the bottom.

Loveless's boat was still weighted with beach rocks and iron junk. Sweetland emptied the bilge as quickly as he could manage, using the butt-end of an oar to hammer the frozen stones free of one another. He set the drain plug with the heel of his hand and he dragged the boat toward the landwash. It seemed to have gained weight in the winter cold, Sweetland grunting it backwards in foot-long increments. He went around to the bow once he reached the water and shoved it out far enough to float, used an oar to pole into deeper water after he climbed aboard.

He pulled across the cove toward what was left of the breakwater, craning over his shoulder as he went. He was almost on top of it before he caught sight of the body, a dark figure just under the dark surface. He hadn't thought to bring a gaff or a hook in the rush and he hauled his sleeves up past the elbow as he drifted toward it. He lifted one oar clear of the thole-pin lock and leaned over the gunwale to bring the water-logged weight of the corpse alongside, trying to lever it closer to the surface. Reached down into the stinging cold with his bare hand.

The animal's coat was slick and surprisingly loose on the body. He wrapped his fist in the hide, leaned the other hand on the gunwale to ratchet the thing out of the water, and a young boy's lank head of hair broke the surface, the scalp glowing a tuberous white beneath it. The sight clapped all the breath from Sweetland's lungs. He fell back against the far side of the dory, his feet kicking against the boards in spasms. He lifted his head over the gunwale and vomited into the ocean, choking on the bile. He drew in a wet, ragged breath and screamed up at the hillside, at the blank houses. He dropped into the bilge, his back against the gunwale, his eyes on the low sky. "Leave off me," he said. "For the love of Jesus, leave off me."

The dory drifted around as he lay there, swinging Sweetland toward the body again. It had turned belly up and he could see the smashed nose and missing ear, the eyes wide and staring at the clouds. He grabbed the oar and flailed savagely at the thing until he was far enough away to set the oars and row back toward the beach. A sickening, guttural grunting in the air, like the sound of someone being electrocuted. He was halfway up the path to the house before he recognized the sound was coming from his own mouth.

When he reached the house he turned the kitchen table on its side, dragging it crabwise into the porch and nailing the Formica across the door. He didn't put in a fire but he kept the radio on low for the intermittent comfort of human voices as the tidal signals drifted in and out. He slept in troubled snatches, coming to himself like someone shaking themselves out of a nightmare. Kept himself awake making a list of what to pack, debating the best time to start out and the likeliest way off the island. It was a bad time of year to chance the crossing, especially in a crate as feckless as Loveless's dory. It was riskier to row out past the north-end light around the Fever Rocks, but twice the distance to round the Mackerel Cliffs. He would have to hopscotch across to Little Sweetland, break into one of the cabins there to spend the night. Then try for the mainland the following morning if the weather held.

He stayed clear of the windows, spying on the cove from behind a curtain's edge. He hadn't hauled Loveless's dory up onto the landwash when he came ashore, jumping over the bow into water past his knees, sloshing up onto the beach, raving like a lunatic. The boat had been drifting unmoored around the harbour ever since. There was just enough of a breakwater left to stop it floating away altogether and Sweetland watched for it to come back into shallow water or close enough to the government wharf to get a line on it somehow. Trying not to think what else might be drifting unmoored inside the breakwater.

He emptied out his packsack to take stock of what he had on hand, shaking the thing upside down on the kitchen table. A dozen shells for the .22. A pair of woollen vamps. The crumpled map he'd stolen from the Priddles' cabin at the height of his glassy stone and forgotten about. He set the map on the counter and went about packing the bag with tins of peaches, with salt fish wrapped in tinfoil, the last of his ammunition and a blanket and a change of clothes, fresh water in a glass jar. Wanting to be ready to make a run for it when he saw a chance. He cut a new bailer to replace the one he'd used to clean the magnificent cod in the fall.

He listened to the marine forecast morning and evening, but he'd long ago given up lending it any credence. Rain it called for and the sky offered intermittent flurries. It predicted winds out of the north at fifteen knots and the house shook in a gale blowing southeasterly. Sweetland watched the sky at sunrise and sunset and the clouds on the horizon and at night he watched the moon for any sign he might glean there about approaching weather.

On the third night of his vigil he saw the boat riding tight up against the government wharf. The moon almost full, the sea beyond the breakwater's ruins lying flat calm, a shimmering ladder of moonlight across the surface. It was four in the morning and two full hours to the first glimpse of sunrise. Not a breath of wind.

He chanced turning on a flashlight to find his pack and a jigger he'd tied to twenty foot of line. He shoved the flashlight into his pocket, removed the nails from the table tipped across the door frame, levering his weight on the hammer so they slid silently from the wood. Eased the doors open and snuck out with his packsack.

He collected his rifle where he'd left it on the landwash and then carried on to the wharf where he could hear the hollow thunk of the dory butting concrete. He dropped the jigger from the dock to hook it at the bow, hauling the dory along to the metal rungs of the ladder. He climbed down far enough to hold the boat in place with a foot on the bow, reached up to grab his pack and rifle. Water had been seeping into the dory for days, eight or ten inches collected in the bilge, and Sweetland bailed for all he was worth, working himself into a sweat. Took up the oars before he was halfways done and swung the head around for open water, wanting out of the cove.

He could feel the dory lift on the easy swell as he cleared the edge of the breakwater and he turned east for the Fever Rocks. He stayed close enough to shore he could hear the waves shushing the cliffs. The sheer headlands white and black in the moonlight, looking like dented sheets of metal. The night so still it unnerved him. There could only be weather on the other side of a calm so complete. He had a three-hour haul to the Fever Rocks and the better part of the day then on to Little Sweetland. He glanced up at the moon, setting now and edged with frost. The flash of the north-end light a lifetime away over his shoulder.

Before the sun rose the sky was overcast and threatening, a scudding wind kicking a lop on the water high enough to spit over the gunwale. Sweetland leaning forward to bail every few minutes, trying to hold the dory steady with a single oar lodged under his arm. Soaked with ocean spray, his face rimed with salt. He could feel the temperature drop as the wind funnelled out of the coming storm and he didn't think for a moment about turning back. He sculled further off the land to give himself plenty of leeway around the Fever Rocks, thinking if he managed to clear the north-end he would row into the lee of the island, pull up in the alcove below Music House until the weather blew itself out.

The wind shifted easterly and bore down as he cleared the point, a spiralling squall of snow shearing in. The seas rising around him so he lost sight of horizon and sky in the troughs, the island steaming closer every time the boat roller-coastered aloft. The north-end light flashing uselessly through the storm. Sweetland gave up any pretension of strategy or course, rowing all he was worth for open ocean to keep off the cliffs, the Fever Rocks looming black above him through the drift. The boat riding low and heavy, so much water aboard it was all Sweetland could do to hold her face on to the gale. She slewed sideways and slammed and tossed her head like a horse spooked and trying to throw a rider. The wind and the rolling chain of waves driving him onto the island and he could see he had no chance of staying clear.

He was too close to shore now to see the light. Only the edge of the helipad and the square outline of the winchhouse above him made any impression in the dirty blur of the storm and he gave up fighting the sway of things, rowing only to keep upright and abreast of the waves, trying to angle the boat toward those marks as he was hurled shoreward. The crests rising higher as he approached the island, the boat levered almost to ninety degrees and he lay flat to keep from being pitched across the stern. Just making the peak before slamming into the trough. She flipped arse over kettle finally and landed face down on top of Sweetland as he went under in the surf. Flailing mad in the black and roar and sudden icy choking, the boat smashing against the rocks and coming apart around him. Sweetland scraped across the ragged granite as the wave retreated until he was lifted and thrown bodily against the rocks by the next wave steaming in. Scraped and lifted and thrown with the stern board and the oars and scraps of wood. He tried to find a handhold each time, something to stop the relentless pistoning, came up hard against metal finally, wrapped a forearm around a rung of the Coast Guard ladder riveted to the Fever Rocks.

He was buried in each successive wave as he clung there, the weight almost enough to rip him loose. He crawled up one rung at a time between the battering avalanches of water that fell over him with a pendulum's steady rhythm, until he was out of the ocean's reach. Stopped to catch his breath then, to make the world slow down. His head had struck the cliffs each time he was thrown and he couldn't see out of his right eye. A knife working at the same shoulder. He'd lost one boot in the undertow's suck and the other was filled to the lip with seawater.

He glanced up the height of stairs above him and then rested his forehead against a metal rung. His winter coat sopping, the drag on him like an animal tied across his shoulders, but he wouldn't chance removing it for fear of falling. He started up the ladder with his useless arm and blinded eye, his legs quivering helplessly. His one good arm going numb as he went and he held a rung between his teeth to rest it, to shake the blood back into his fingers. The taste of metal and rust in his mouth.

He refused to look up or down once he started, refused to think in terms of progress. There was a rung to climb and a rung that came after it, he ticked the purgatorial steps off without counting or measuring, and he didn't know quite what to make of it when his head crested the rock face at the top of the ladder. He touched a hand to the winchhouse to satisfy himself he was where he appeared to be on the headland, then crawled along the path to the flat surface of the helipad, and across that toward the lighthouse, not trusting himself to stand, the wind blowing wild in the open air.

He stopped in the lee of the keeper's house, sitting back against the skirt around the foundation. He kicked off his one remaining boot, tipped out the water and worked it back over the dripping sock. He touched his face gingerly, the right eye swollen shut. Thick strands of ice in his wet hair.

There was the sway of things, Sweetland knew. There was fighting the sway of things or improvising some fashion of riding it out. And then there was the sway of things beyond fighting and improvisation. It was almost impossible to know the difference between one and the other, but he felt close to making a call on the line. He was soaked and hypothermic and the cold was likely going to kill him. Even if he survived, Loveless's boat was gone and he had no way off the island now.

The snow was falling thick in the wind. Sweetland stood and

hobbled around the keeper's house and at each window he tried to pry off the board fastened over the glass, without so much as loosening a nail. He sat back in the lee, tucked his hands inside his jacket to try and warm them under his armpits. Fumbled at something unexpected in the inside pocket and drew it out. A plastic baggie containing two Bic lighters, the joint and rolling papers he'd taken from the Priddles' cabin in the fall. The bag intact and everything inside, miraculously, still dry. He shook the contents onto the ground between his legs, wet the joint in his mouth. Hid his head in his coat out of the wind to light up. The smoke as foul as he remembered and it tipped him into a coughing fit, his chest seizing up with a crushed-glass agony that told him he must have cracked ribs against the cliff face as well.

He choked down the rest of the joint and then waited for the stone to take the edge off of something, the pain or the cold or the miserable caul of dread that threatened to suffocate him. He managed to drop off eventually, waking every few minutes and drifting away again into a mangled facsimile of sleep. Stayed there in that fitful state until the wind dropped off, snow falling steady and soft.

Sweetland scavenged awhile for firewood, but there was hardly a stick about to burn. Most of the decking at the front of the house had been hauled away by the Priddles after easy firewood, and he'd used most of the remainder himself to boil tea on his Sunday visits. He kicked the last few boards free and added them to his meagre pile. Not nearly enough to dry his clothes or touch the chill at the core. A fire to make him feel the cold all the worse when it was done. He looked up at the barred windows of the keeper's house, thinking of the remaining chairs and the desk and table, the bed frames and bureaus inside. And no way to get at any of it.

He had nothing in the way of kindling or tinder and he crumpled the last half-dozen rolling papers into a ball, cracked one of the lighters with a rock to soak the paper with fluid. Pushed it among the scraps of wood and set it alight. The flame immediate and fragile and Sweetland cozied near with his jacket held wide to protect it from the wind and snow, adding bits of moss to coax the fire along, waiting for something solid to take. Blowing on the embered heart awhile before it all went black and dead.

He sat back from the failure, slapping a hand against his thigh. Not conscious of thinking a thing, as if the little light of his mind had guttered out as well. He reached to pull the longest piece of wood off the pile, pushed himself from the ground and started up the rise, leaning on the three-foot stick for a cane. He walked past the cairns near the cliffs and the quad where it had been abandoned. He was thirty feet beyond the machine when he stopped and limped back to it. Opened the gas cap and moved his head left and right to peer inside. Caught sight of his own reflection in the last skim of gasoline at the bottom.

He worked off his jacket and sweater, but couldn't get his shirt over his injured shoulder. He tore it along the seams, dressed himself again in the soaking gansey and coat before wringing as much water as he could from the torn fabric. It was still too wet to soak up the little gasoline in the tank and Sweetland tipped the machine onto its side. Rested against it as the waves of pain pulsed through him. Removed the gas cap and hauled the machine all the way over onto its back, holding the shirt underneath to catch whatever might leak out. Shaking the quad back and forth to get every drop. He could smell gas on the cloth when he was done, but couldn't even say if it was enough to burn.

He walked back over the rise and down toward the light and he stood considering the pathetic pyre of scrap wood. Glanced across at the keeper's house, took in the wasted length of the place that was slowly rotting into the ground. He moved what he'd gathered against the house's foundation with the shirt balled underneath it. Flicked the lighter. The material so wet that the flame burned blue a few seconds, before the wood caught hold. Sweetland stepped away when the fire got going, but only far enough to stop himself scorching his skin. The heat so feral and delicious he almost wept.

The building's skirt scorched black behind the fire, but for a while it looked like the house would survive his attempt at arson with the smallest of scars to show. He wandered further afield looking for fuel, piled every knuckle of driftwood, every twisted branch of tuckamore he could find against the foundation. Within an hour the place was alight, the boarded windows belching smoke. Sweetland kept moving back as the inferno grew, as it threw wider bands of heat where the flames ate through to open air. He took off his coat and laid it flat on the ground, turning it regularly, like a cut of meat he was cooking over coals. He took off his gansey sweater and pants and socks and did the same with them. It was still snowing outside the fire's fierce circle but not a flake touched him. When his clothes had dried, he dressed and lay down to sleep in one of the outer rings. Waking now and then to shift closer as the fire collapsed and settled.

By late afternoon the walls and ceiling were down and the open flames burned off. The blackened stump of the building was still radiating enough warmth to keep him comfortable, but he expected it wouldn't last through the night and he couldn't risk staying out in the open. The snow coming at him in waves over the remains of the fire. The Priddles' cabin was the closest bit of shelter but he'd cleaned out every scrap of food and firewood in the fall. And he knew he would never manage the climb out of the valley once he got down there.

He pulled his jacket slowly over his injured shoulder, pushed on the one boot left to him. His head was throbbing with a concussion or a weed hangover or a fever, or some combination of all three. He had no idea how much daylight was left to him. He started up the rise toward the mash, the charcoaled ruins of the keeper's house smoking behind him. By the time he made the crest, the snow was steady and drifting and he could just make out the path along the headland, the intermittent cairns marking the way. The ocean in a lather against the base of the cliffs.

The back end of the storm came around as he scuffled along, the wind freshening and blowing northwest, and he walked into the blizzard, the ground drifting over so the path was almost impossible to distinguish. He turned back on to the wind now and then to clear the ice frozen to his eyelashes, trying to guess his location from what he could see nearby. The whiteout so complete that Sweetland lost sight of the ocean and light tower and the smoulder of the keeper's house behind him.

It was coming on to evening before he admitted to himself he was well off the path. He considered turning back to try for the Priddles' cabin, but guessed he was closer to the cove than the lighthouse now, and an hour of daylight at best to travel in. The drifts were knee-deep and Sweetland walked with a curiously mechanical gait through the snow, all the feeling gone out of his legs, his injured arm cradling his injured ribs. Talking himself past the urge to lie down.

It was nearly dark when he walked into the fence around Vatcher's Meadow and it took him a few moments to recognize it for what it was, standing still in the storm, turning the thing over in his head. "Now, Mr. Fox," he said when it finally came clear to him. He was in no shape to climb the fence and he followed the line south, looking for the gate. From there he angled across the meadow until he reached the fence on the far side, using the poles as markers. At the gate he struck as straight as he could manage from the corner post. Stumbled on the King's Seat at the top of the hill above the cove, crouching out of the wind in its shelter awhile. Startled from a snug well of sleep that was almost too narrow to climb out of. He got to his knees, lifted himself into the wind's crosscut.

It was steeply downhill into the cove from there, and he stumbled all the way to the back of his property, his body alight with rivets and hinges and underground cables of pain as he lurched and righted himself and lurched opposite. He leaned against the shed when he reached it, catching his breath. The door of his house invisible in the dark and the blowing snow, though he knew it was only twenty steps distant. Sweetland not quite relieved to have made it back alive.

———

He woke on the daybed, though he had no memory of coming into the house or lying down. He was still wearing his coat and his single boot. His hands felt miles away and they seemed to expand and shrink with his pulse. He was dying for a drink of water but the sink was too far off to get to and he stared helplessly across the room. He couldn't guess what time of day it was, or what day of the week. It was bright outside and the sunlight made his head ache.

Someone walked by the kitchen window as he lay there and he was too feverish to be startled or to wonder who it might be. There was a knock at the door and he took his time trying to fashion a response to it. "Come in," he said finally. The knock came again and Sweetland worked himself onto an elbow, to give some heft to his voice. "Door's open," he called.

The knocking continued and he got to his feet, reaching with his good arm for chairs and door jambs to stay upright as he crossed the kitchen to the porch. He paused in front of Uncle Clar, out of breath, sipping at the air against the welling ache in his chest. Saw the outline of himself superimposed on the ancient picture there, a ghostly image hovering in the background, as if he was a second exposure on the same strip of film. A figure bled of detail and substance, so that all the world showed through him. Moses Sweetland. *This is he.*

The knock startled him and he turned to the door, swung it wide and lifted the latch on the storm door. His visitor standing there in a tweed jacket and tie, tan pants. Hands folded at the waist holding the inevitable briefcase. Sweetland couldn't make out the man's face through his one good eye, the features lost in a glare of sunlight.

"Mr. Sweetland," a voice said from the place where the mouth should have been.

He paused a moment, waiting for the face to resolve out of the shine. He lifted a hand to shade his eyes.

"Do you mind if I come in," the government man said.

Sweetland stood back to let the man go by, followed him into the kitchen. There was something he was meant to do for visitors and he groped through the murk, trying to think of it. The government man took a seat beside the window and placed the briefcase flat on the table in front of him, his hands folded on top. Sweetland went toward the stove and turned back slowly. "I could boil the kettle," he said and stopped short, staring at the man.

"No tea for me," the government man said, his face still missing behind a sourceless swarm of light, the voice rising out of that mouthless glitter.

"All right."

"Maybe you should sit down, Mr. Sweetland."

"All right."

"Before I start," he said, "I wanted to offer my condolences. For the loss of Jesse."

Sweetland eased himself into a chair without looking directly at the figure across the table, stung by the sound of the boy's name.

"And the awful business with the dog," the government man said, "I'm very sorry about that."

"This is a sympathy call, is it?"

The government man opened the briefcase and took out a sheaf of papers. "No," he said. "Strictly professional. Some paperwork to get through."

Sweetland swung the enormous weight of his head around to stare directly at the government man. Squinting to try and push past the blur for some hint of the man's eyes or nose or mouth. Anything human at all. "Can you get me out of here?" he said. "Is that what you come for?"

The government man lifted his arms. "I'm afraid that ship has sailed," he said. "This is simply a routine follow-up. I'll be out of your hair in no time."

Sweetland nodded dumbly.

"On a scale of one to five," he said, holding a pen over a virgin form, "with one being completely satisfied and five being completely dissatisfied, how would you rate your living circumstances at the moment?"

Sweetland didn't answer. There was something in the whole set-up that was wrong and he could almost lay his finger on it.

"Would I be right in thinking a five for this, Mr. Sweetland?" He made a mark on the sheet in front of him. "We'll say five. On a scale of one to five, one being satisfactory and five being certifiable, how would you rate your current mental status?"

Sweetland shook his head, still trying to get his hands around it, the something he knew was wrong and could almost name.

"A five, then," the government man said, and he made another mark on the paper.

Sweetland looked out toward the porch. "You come in the wrong door," he said.

"I'm sorry?"

"Last time you was here, you come to the front."

"We're splitting hairs now, Mr. Sweetland."

"How'd you know about the dog?"

"On a scale of one to five," the faceless voice said, the pen poised again.

"Who was it told you what happened to the dog?"

The government man set his hands on the folder in front of him. "No one told me," he said.

"No one told you," Sweetland whispered. He glanced one more time at the suit across the table, at the face missing behind a shapeless welter of light. He pushed himself out of his chair to reach for the man, but the dark folded in on him like a black comber rolling over and it swallowed the room whole.

The world was askew when he came to himself. He recognized the room, the kitchen of the old house, but couldn't place the pieces where they belonged. All the angles wrong.

He shifted slightly and everything complained against the motion, shoulder and ribs, hips and knees, his back. He was flat out on the floor, his face against the bare wood. He tried to lift his head, but had to settle for flicking his eyes around the room. Daybed, stove. Silver legs of the chairs. Black boots facing him under the table. Someone sitting beside the window. Rough woollen trousers dripping wet. A pool gathering on the floor beneath the feet, the raw smell of salt water in the room.

Sweetland closed his eyes again. "Is Jesse with you?" he said and he waited a long time for a reply before he glanced around again. Still just the one pair of boots under the table. He felt too vulnerable suddenly to stay where he was and he forced himself to his knees, hefted his fractured weight into the chair he'd been sitting in before he passed out. Looked across at his brother in the chair opposite. The young face so pale it glowed like the underside of sea ice. The kelpy hair streaming, his dead eyes glassy and expressionless.

Sweetland was shaking helplessly again, the tremors stirring the scattered territories of his body that were occupied by pain. "I thought Jesse might be with you," he said, clenching to stop his teeth chattering long enough to speak. "Being as you two was friends."

He waited then, expecting something from the figure across the table. "Hollis," he said, to see if the name might wake the thing. But it sat there in the same silence, without so much as glancing his way. He had never felt so cold, not in all his life, not when he was being drowned in the ocean's arctic currents, not when he was soaked to the bone and climbing the lighthouse ladder in the knifing wind. Sweetland bent double over his legs, holding his chest against the fever's palsy as it shook through him. It was a cold he thought would never end. He looked over at his brother again. "You must be some sick of this fucken place by now," he said.

Hollis turned his head then and nodded in a distracted fashion that might have been a response to those words. Sweetland saw his living brother in that expression, the look that came over him when he was buried in some story in the old school reader or hauling at the oars beside him on their way to check the traps in their father's coat. Blank but animate. Hollis absent even as he sat in the company of others, seeming to live elsewhere half the time.

Sweetland thought he might offer some sort of apology then, but even in his addled state he could tell they were beyond apologies. He clenched his teeth against the chattering. "It's good to see you," he said.

And the figure nodded again in the same distracted fashion.

"Say me to Jesse if you sees him," Sweetland said. "And Ruthie."

He had a longer list of names in his head that he wanted to offer his hellos to, but his throat closed over and he got no further.

He woke on the daybed, lay with his eyes closed, listening to a fly buzzing at the kitchen window. Trapped and mad for the light outside.

But it wouldn't be a fly, of course. Months too early in the spring. An outboard engine he was hearing, approaching from a long ways off. The motor geared back as it passed by the breakwater into the cove, 150 horsepower or better, he thought, Evinrude or Honda or Yamaha. All makes sounded more or less the same these days. When he was a youngster you could name a boat's owner by the particular racket of its engine alone. The Coffins drove an old Mianus that spit and complained exactly as its name suggested it might. The Vatchers ran a six-horse-power Acadia, a newfangled jump-start that didn't sit well in wet weather, you could hear them cranking and priming and cranking after everyone else was away and gone in the morning. Ned Priddle's father drove a little Perfection that sent the boat along without a wake or even much of a bow wave, as if it was a magic carpet the man was riding over the surface. He stood aft with the tiller between his knees, smoking a pipe as he made for open water.

Sweetland thumbed through the catalogue of families and engines in his head as he lay there, and he forgot about the boat just arrived in the cove until the motor shut down and the quiet startled him. Voices ballooning in that stillness, two men it sounded like, expecting to find themselves alone in the cove. He ought to be interested in whoever was out there, he figured, but he couldn't summon even that. He felt licked out, as brittle and clear as a pane of glass.

The voices were making the walk up from the government wharf, pausing along the way to bicker back and forth, a note of disbelief or uncertainty creeping into the talk though Sweetland couldn't pick out a single word of what they said. They skirted wide of his house, taking the path up toward the mash. Sweetland eased himself to his feet, looked down toward the water from the kitchen window. A new rig tied to the wharf, a fibreglass forty-footer. Someone with money to burn by the look of it. Those phantom cabin owners from Little Sweetland, maybe, checking the abandoned cove on behalf of friends interested in purchasing their own corner of the strange and far-flung.

He heard the visitors stop at the new cemetery, their voices echoing off the hills like they were shouting to one another from opposite sides of the cove. Something had unsettled them and Sweetland wondered if that fresh grave over Jesse's plot was showing through the snow up there. They started back down toward the water and Sweetland took a seat at the kitchen table. Expecting they'd find him there eventually and happy enough to wait.

It occurred to him they might have food with them. Something store-bought and fresh. He hadn't eaten since the morning he left the cove in Loveless's dory and he had no notion of how long ago that was. Days now. He felt the hunger from a ways off, it almost seemed to be afflicting someone else altogether. A mild curiosity that he was of two minds about satisfying.

The voices made their way to the back of the house. The side door of the shed creaked, the conversation disappearing as they went inside. Moments later they came out into the open and Sweetland heard a voice say, "That's almost a winter's worth of wood gone through."

The latch on the storm door clattered and from his chair Sweetland saw daylight flood the porch.

"Hello, the house," someone called from the doorway.

"Go on in, for fuck sakes," the second voice said.

"You go in, you're so goddamn keen."

"You're such a fucken woman, you know that?"

Sweetland smiling to hear them at each other, even if he was only dreaming the brothers on the island with him. The Priddles came through the porch together, tentative, backlit by sunlight. Stared at him from the doorway.

"B'ys," Sweetland said.

"Lord fuck," Keith said.

Barry pushed his brother so hard that Keith almost fell on his ass in the porch. "I fucken told you!" Barry shouted. "What did I fucken tell you?" He jumped across the kitchen so that all the joists in the floor bowed under him, the teacups swinging on their hooks, tinkling like wind chimes. "Motherfucking Sweetland!" he shouted. "I fucken told you, Keith," he said, shaking his truncated finger at his brother.

Keith was still standing in the doorway, all the blood gone from his face. Sweetland nodded across to him in a way he hoped was reassuring.

"Jesus, Mose," Keith said. "You looks like shit."

Keith came back up from the boat where he'd gone to radio the Coast Guard on the VHF. He'd requested assistance with a medical emergency and was shunted from a call centre in Halifax to a contract outfit in Italy. Keith explaining the circumstances to a doctor speaking broken English, a severely injured man on an abandoned island off the south coast of Newfoundland, he said. Where? the doctor asked. Where is this?

The doctor's grasp of English seemed marginal at best and Keith's accent completely dismantled the language for him. He needed every sentence repeated three or four times and the two men shouted back and forth at one another for fifteen minutes before the situation finally began to come clear. What do you want me to do? the doctor demanded. I am in Rome.

"What is it, the Coast Guard got everything shut down for the Easter holidays?" Barry asked.

"It's got nothing to do with the holidays," Keith said. "That's saving taxpayers' money, that is."

"It's Easter?" Sweetland said.

The brothers stared at him and then looked at one another. They talked about loading Sweetland into the boat, driving the four or five hours to Burgeo. But it was already getting on to dark with a westerly wind rising and they decided to wait the night.

They set Sweetland up against a raft of pillows on the daybed, put a fire in the stove, lit lamps against the evening coming on. They argued the merits of the various pills Keith produced from an inside pocket, ecstasy and Percocet and half a dozen others in a single plastic bottle. Settled on OxyContin and Sweetland swallowed them down.

Barry sat beside him on the daybed, spooning soup into his mouth. It was Keith who made the cross for him while Sweetland was hiding out in the valley, Barry said. Dug the hole and mixed the cement in a beef bucket and set the marker in place. Hand-lettered the name and dates. Wouldn't even let Barry lend a hand.

"You're a miserable prick, you know that?" Keith said. "Making us think you was drowned." He was sitting at the kitchen table with a bottle of rye, watching Sweetland with a skeptical eye. As if he was still unsure Sweetland was the man he claimed to be.

"He spent days out jigging for you before the last ferry," Barry said.

"Who, Keith?" He was adrift on the effects of the pills he'd taken and was feeling no pain, though he was finding it hard to follow the bread crumbs of the conversation.

"Yes, fucken Keith. Out before daylight, going to all the shoal grounds, jigging until after dark. Hoping to strike you as you floated past. He'd of got some fright now, he brought you up with a hook through your eyeball."

"That cunt there wouldn't even get in the boat with me," Keith said.

"I knew you wouldn't down there, that's why. Never believed you was drowned, first nor last. Loveless said you had your pack and some kind of duffle bag aboard when you left the cove that morning and there was nothing on the boat when they found it."

"Fucken Loveless," Sweetland said and he shook his head.

"They had the hardest time getting Loveless to leave," Barry said. "That little dog of his took off the night before the ferry come. He had half the crew up on the mash calling for the goddamn thing. Delayed the ferry six hours. There was a constable out from the RCMP, he had to threaten to arrest him to get Loveless aboard."

"You didn't see the dog, did you?" Keith asked.

Sweetland shook his head. "No," he said. "I don't think so."

The brothers were home in Newfoundland after a six-week stint in Fort Mac. They'd purchased the new rig with their government relocation money, Barry told him, and decided to take it for a spin, look over the cove, maybe spend a night or two at the cabin in the valley.

"I burnt the ladder to the loft out there," Sweetland said.

"Out where?"

"The cabin," he said. "I went along for a visit the winter. You never had enough wood put up to last a night. Had to burn something."

"Fair enough," Barry said.

"And I took the bit of gas you had out there for the generator. And drunk the vodka. And you had some dope tucked away that I got into."

Barry turned to look at his brother. "This fucker belongs in Her Majesty's Penitentiary," he said.

"Anything else?" Keith called.

"No," Sweetland said, and then he corrected himself. "Yes. That map you had on the wall out there."

"What map?"

"The Come Home Year thing," Sweetland said. "It's around here somewhere." He waved vaguely and then he said, "I burnt the keeper's house to the ground a few days ago."

The brothers exchanged a look and he could see them silently dismiss the claim as the drugs talking. "It's a fucken wonder you're alive at all," Barry said. He offered another spoonful of soup and Sweetland raised a hand to hold it off.

"Come on, old man," Barry said. "You're nothing but skin and grief."

He shook his head. "I'm all right," he said. He had no appetite for anything but company and he spent a while asking after the people he'd known his years in the cove, where they'd wound up and how they were doing off the island. Occasionally bringing up names of people who had died decades before Barry and Keith were born. Dozing at times as the brothers offered what they knew, so the news came to him in fragments, as though it was washing up on the beach like flotsam from a wreck.

"We should let you sleep," Barry said finally. "We'll bunk upstairs."

Sweetland shook his head. "Don't leave me down here alone."

"I'll stay with him," Keith said.

"How's them pills holding out? You need another hit?"

"I'm the best kind," Sweetland said.

Barry stood up and set the bowl on the counter. Leaned over him with an arm on either side of his shoulders, his face almost close enough to kiss. Sweetland said something to him then, his voice so weak it was inaudible.

"What is it?"

He worked his mouth a few seconds. "You crowd is real, is you?" he said.

Barry put his hand to the old man's chest. "Real as you are."

Sweetland nodded. "The Golden Priddles," he said.

"Moses fucken Sweetland," Barry said. "I swear to Christ."

Sweetland flickered out then and didn't come to himself until the pain needled through the narcotic, pricking him awake. He glanced across to the table where Keith was sitting up with a kerosene lamp.

"Keith," he said.

The younger man looked up, startled. "What were you on when you did this?" Keith asked. He tapped at the tabletop with a knuckle.

"What is it?"

"The map from the cabin," he said. "You must have been stoned out of your mind."

"You got any more of them pills on you?" Sweetland said.

"Yes, b'y." He came across the room, shaking the contents of the bottle into his palm. Sat beside Sweetland while he picked through the lot. Even in the gloom Sweetland could see the crude letters tattooed on the man's knuckles, F*E*A*R and H*O*P*E. "These'll see you through the rest of the night," Keith said, and he reached to place them on Sweetland's tongue.

Sweetland shook his head. "Other hand," he said.

Keith looked at him. "What's that now?"

"Use the other hand for me."

Keith looked down a second, shifted the pills as he was told. And Sweetland opened his mouth.

"You're some Jesus sook," Keith said.

Sweetland looked up at his face and Keith stared back, unselfconscious in the night's quiet, in the dim light. Barry's snoring overhead almost a peaceful sound through the ceiling. Sweetland reached for the hand that he'd requested, and the two men sat like that for what felt to him a long time.

Keith shook his head. "You got some mess made of yourself, Mose."

"If you scalds your arse," Sweetland said and he smiled weakly. "I got what I was after and then some." He squeezed the hand he was holding. "I wanted to say thanks," he said. "For the cross you put up."

Keith shrugged. "Owed you that much. After all the beer and skin mags you give us."

Sweetland almost asked then about the mutilated rabbits, about the fire that burned his stage, whether the brothers had anything to do with that business. But it seemed too far off. A gauzy, edgeless dream that was bleeding coherence and meaning as he lay there. "I think I'm ready to sleep now," he said. "You go on upstairs, get some rest."

"You sure you're all right?"

"Best kind," Sweetland said. He squeezed Keith's hand once more and let it loose of his own. And before he knew it, he was gone.

It was still dark when he woke, feeling rested and ready to start the day. He sat up carefully, lifting his legs to the floor, surprised how little discomfort the movement caused him. Blessed the wonders of the Golden Priddles' magic pills. Keith had left the kerosene lamp burning on the kitchen table, the light twinned in the windowpane. Even from across the room he could see the soot clouding the glass and he went over to turn back the wick. Noticed the map there, spread across the table's surface, the paper kinked along the rough creases where it had been folded in his knapsack. *Stay Home Year* scrawled across the top. Sweetland shook his head at that now, at the long list of fanciful harbours and coves and islands and straits he'd pencilled around the coast. Along the entire length of Newfoundland's south coast were the words *Here Be Monsters* with a shaky emoticon happy face drawn beside it. His handwriting, though he couldn't for the life of him remember setting them there. Stoned out of his mind, like Keith said.

Sweetland traced his finger down the Avalon Peninsula where he'd crossed out St. John's and renamed the capital city *Loveless Town*, then along the southern shore, across Placentia Bay to the boot of the Burin. Keith had drawn in the leg and high-heeled shoe of Italy there, a dot handy about Italy's knee with *Rome* written beside it. He smiled over that as he glanced past St. Pierre and Miquelon toward Sweetland. And he stood away from the table then, a hand raised to his mouth.

He had to work up the nerve to look closer, bringing the lamp down across the map for the light. Where he expected to see Sweetland there was nothing but blue water. And Little Sweetland beside it the same. The names he'd written across the islands were gone. He thought Keith might have erased them, but even the ink outlines the names had been printed over were missing from the map. As if he'd only imagined seeing them there.

He looked up at the window and his one-eyed reflection stared back at him from that black well. He turned for the door and started along the hall, wanting to wake the Priddles, to make them sit up with him until daylight, but he stopped at the foot of the stairs. Listening for the rattle of Barry snoring or the sound of bedsprings, of the brothers turning in their sleep. But there was only a breathless stillness. And he knew he was alone in the house.

He went back to the kitchen and set a hand to the stove. The fire was out and the metal was cold, like it had been sitting idle a long time. There was no wind in the flue, no habitual creak or settle in the walls of the house. Sweetland crossed the floor to the table and turned the map in quarters as he considered the absence there. So insignificant it would go unnoticed by anyone not looking for it.

He folded the map along the creases and set it in the cold firebox of the stove. He struck a match and dropped it in, watched as the paper curled in the heat, the edges charring black and disappearing in the travelling flame. He set the damper back and took the lamp into the porch to find his coat. Caught sight of Uncle Clar as he slipped into the sleeves and Sweetland nodded goodbye to the young face before he blew out the lamp beside the storm door. Stepped into the still air, into the cavernous silence of the cove. He walked along the back of his property and up beyond the new cemetery, away from all he'd ever known or wanted or wished for. At the King's Seat he turned to look down on the water and there was nothing below but a featureless black, as if the ocean was rising behind him and had already swallowed the cove and everything in it.

"Now, Mr. Fox," he said.

He carried on across Vatcher's Meadow and over the mash toward the light at Burnt Head, following the cairns along the headlands. He was watching for the outline of figures on the rise above the keeper's house and saw them moving toward the light, all travelling at the same methodical pace, with the same lack of urgency. Sweetland fell in with them as he crested the rise, the walkers so close he could feel the cold rising off their coats, a scoured smell in the air around them, linseed and raw salt and spruce. They didn't acknowledge Sweetland or show the slightest concern that he was there. A squat form in rubber boots just ahead of him, a shapeless gansey sweater swaying almost to the woman's knees. He could have reached a hand and traced the pattern in the wool, she was that close to him.

His companions looked to be numberless in the dark and strangers every one of them. But he was grateful for their presence just the same. He followed the procession down to the ruins of the keeper's house and they filed past it without taking any notice, calm and all in silence. He stopped there, not certain he was meant to go on to the cliffs. A boy brushed past him as he hesitated and Sweetland almost called out, thinking he recognized the child by the seashell whorls of a double crown, a rogue lick of hair. But the feeling passed before he made a sound.

The boy disappeared in the crowd and Sweetland carried on in his wake, past the light tower to the cliffs of the Fever Rocks where he lined along the headland beside the others. A press of silent figures with their faces turned to the open sea. They seemed resigned and expectant standing there, their eyes on the fathomless black of the ocean. Sweetland anonymous among that congregation.

He felt of a sudden like singing.

ACKNOWLEDGEMENTS

AS ALWAYS, I'm grateful for the company of Martha Kanya-Forstner.

Thanks to MKF and to Katie Adams for the conversations that helped shape the novel. And to Holly Hogan, Stan Dragland, Martha Webb and Shawn Oakey for commenting at various stages.

For stories and details that I've worked to my own purposes, I'm indebted to Art Crummey, Mazie Crummey, John and Mary Fitzgerald, Paul Dean, Dave Paddon, Helen Crummey, Mark Ferguson, Mrs. Abbie Whiffen (née Ellis), Justin Simms, Beth Follett, Gerry Squires, Sean McCann and Annette Clarke. A number of settings and incidents were suggested by Carl Sharpe's *Memories in the Life of a Twillingate Man*, Harold Paddon's *Green Woods and Blue Waters*, and David McFarlane's *The Danger Tree*.

Thanks to Holly Hogan for letting me borrow Baccalieu Island, and for wildlife intel; the Family Swan and unrelated staff at Adventure Canada; the communities of Francois, Ramea, and Western Bay.

Sara Loveless's cow arrived via Miguel Invierno. Paul Dean quaffed the kerosene. HH delivered the tuxedo dog. Jeff Anderson loaned the oversized coat. The buffalo are compliments of JR Smallwood and a Martin Connelly article in the Spring 2012 issue of *The Newfoundland Quarterly*. The community of boat engines was lifted (along with countless other details) from *Arctic Twilight* by Leonard Budgell.

❧

Thanks to Martha Webb, Anne McDermid et al @ McDermid & Associates. To Julie Barer @ Barer Literary. To Katie Adams, Cordelia Calvert, and company @ Liveright.

I'm grateful for the Canada Council for the Arts in general. And in particular for a Council grant that came at a crucial point in the writing of this novel.

❧

Thanks to Arielle, Robin and Ben for bearing with me.

And to Holly Ann, for everything else.

A NOTE ABOUT THE TYPE

Pierre Simon Fournier le jeune, who designed the type used in this book, was both an originator and a collector of types. His services to the art of print communication were his design of individual characters, his creation of ornaments and initials and his standardization of type sizes. Fournier types are old style in character and sharply cut. In 1764 and 1766 he published his *Manuel Typographique*, a treatise on the history of French types and printing, on typefounding in all its details, and on what many consider his most important contribution to the printed word—the measurement of type by the point system.